· THE ·
WICKEDEST
SHOW ON EARTH

· THE ·
WICKEDEST
SHOW ON EARTH

A Carnival of Circus Suspense

Edited by
MARCIA MULLER and BILL PRONZINI

WILLIAM MORROW and COMPANY, INC.
NEW YORK

Library of Congress Cataloging in Publication Data
Main entry under title:

The wickedest show on earth.

1. Circus—Fiction.   2. Detective and mystery
stories, American.   I. Muller, Marcia.   II. Pronzini,
Bill.
PS648.C48W53   1985   813'.01'08355   85-15229

ISBN 0-688-05355-6

Printed in the United States of America

First Edition

1 2 3 4 5 6 7 8 9 10

BOOK DESIGN BY PATRICE FODERO

CONTENTS

INTRODUCTION

Hurry, hurry, hurry! Step right up, ladies and gentlemen! *The Wickedest Show on Earth* is about to open, featuring an amazing, a stupendous collection of circus, carnival, and amusement park productions. Gathered here for your pleasure are a variety of stirring circus tales, all performed inside the Big Top. Gathered here are electrifying stories of carnival midways and amusement arcades alight and awhirl with Ferris wheels and other thrill rides, with games of chance, with sideshows full of strange and wonderful sights. Listen closely, now. Can you hear the faint roll of drums, the music of calliope and carousel? Take a deep breath. Can you smell the pungent aromas of popcorn and cotton candy, of animals and straw and summer dust?

Yes, these are the things you'll find in *The Wickedest Show on Earth*—and more, much more. For we offer not one but two extra added attractions to thrill and chill and delight you. The first is a special, one-time-only visit behind the scenes—a series of startling glimpses into the lives of the performers, the pitchmen and shills, the owners and handlers and roustabouts, and all the other colorful circus and carny folk.

The second added attraction is Mystery and Murder.

For this *is*, ladies and gentlemen, *The Wickedest Show on Earth*. You've seen nothing like it anywhere; you'll see nothing quite like it again. Don't miss this once-in-a-lifetime opportunity. Hurry, hurry, hurry! Step right up! It won't be long now until the first spellbinding tale begins.

Ah, now that you've come this far inside, we'll pause before the show starts to present for your amusement and edification a few important historical facts. Wait—don't be impatient. You will find this information highly interesting, for once *The Wickedest Show on Earth* closes, your appetite for others of a similar nature will surely be whetted. Mystery and mayhem, after all, are no strangers to the circuses, carnivals, and amusement parks of fiction and film.

The circus, for instance, is the subject of several suspense/adventure and detective novels. To begin with, we have a trio of whodunits featuring intrepid series sleuths: Anthony Abbot's *About the Murder of a Circus Queen* (1932), in which New York City policeman Thatcher Colt solves a Big Top puzzle; Clifford Knight's *The Affair of the Circus Queen* (1940), in which Huntoon Rogers unravels a similarly baffling case in Manila; and Clayton Rawson's *The Headless Lady* (1940), in which the Great Merlini, magician extraordinaire, stalks the murderer of a circus owner and runs afoul of the likes of Hoodoo, the headhunter, and the Mummy of John Wilkes Booth. Bill S. Ballinger's *The Chinese Mask* (1965) provides copious thrills behind the Bamboo Curtain; its featured performer is CIA agent Joaquin Hawks, who disguises himself as a member of a Russian circus troupe in order to rescue three Western scientists held captive by the Red Chinese. *Murder Under the Big Top* (1966), a reprint of a 1940's "Phantom Detective" pulp novel by Robert Wallace, offers a crime spectacular in which—beware!—members of the *audience* are also victims. And for continuous spine-tingling adventure, with the spotlight on the high wire where the hero performs terrifying and death-defying tricks, Alistair MacLean's *Circus* (1975) can't be beat.

For those of you who also enjoy the cinema, there is of course Cecil B. De Mille's 1953 epic, *The Greatest Show on Earth*, starring James Stewart, Charlton Heston, Betty Hutton, Cornel Wilde, and Dorothy Lamour. Stewart portrays a doctor wanted for murder and hiding out in disguise as a circus clown; among other electrifying incidents, the film contains a spectacular circus-train accident. Did you know that Rock Hudson's first film role was in a circus mystery? Yes: *The Fat Man* (1951), based on the radio serial of the same name, starring J. Scott Smart in the title role and featuring that master clown Emmett Kelley in a rare dramatic appearance. Other famous circus performers also portrayed themselves on film, among them animal tamer Clyde Beatty in the 1955 picture, *Ring of Fear*. A most interesting film, this, for another nonactor who is well known in the suspense field (and on television commercials for Lite Beer), Mickey Spillane, also had a featured role, playing himself; and one of its screenwriters was mystery novelist Philip MacDonald. No less a detective than Charlie Chan also spent time under the cinematic Big Top in the 1936 film *Charlie Chan at the Circus*. With Warner Oland (the best of the screen Chans) and Keye Luke, this is one of the best films about the Honolulu detective; Charlie shares the center ring with the entire Chan family, not to mention a most unusual gorilla. A different type of thrill show, for those of you not averse to visual carnage, is *Circus of Fear* (1967), with Christopher Lee and Suzy Kendall— a British extravaganza in the grand Hammer Films tradition.

Perhaps your interest lies instead with the less glamorous, more earthy traveling carnival—or carny, as it is known to insiders. Then you certainly won't want to miss William Lindsey Gresham's *Nightmare Alley* (1946), the best and most famous of all carny novels, in which a young grifter's rise to fame is predicted by a tarot card reader. The film version, produced in 1947 and starring Tyrone Power and Joan Blondell, offers equal excitement. (Gresham also wrote a superb nonfiction look at the world of the carny, *Monster Midway*, published in 1948.) You will also not want to miss three fine novels by the talented Fredric Brown: two whodunits featuring the Chicago detective team of Ed Hunter and his uncle Am, a retired circus performer—*The Fabulous Clipjoint* (1947) and *Dead Ringer* (1948); and the suspenseful tale of a carny crystal gazer named Doc Magus, *Madball* (1953), based on a period in Brown's own life in which he shared a tent with a carny mentalist. Murder claims The Fattest Woman in the World in the 1933 British mystery by Nicholas Brady, *The Carnival Murder*. A carny traveling throughout the west provides a front for a dope ring in Robert Patrick Wilmot's private eye novel, *Death Rides a Painted Horse* (1954). In John Haase's *Road Show* (1960), a carnival community is ravaged by fraud, lynching, and rape; the gentleman who saves the day is one whose "father's sole profession was sawing a woman (his mother) in half."

The carny is also well-represented on the silver screen, beginning with a pair of horror classics by Tod Browning: *The Unholy Three*, a 1925 silent, and the magnificent *Freaks* (1931). That great showman and screen tough guy, Humphrey Bogart, has the lead role in *The Wagons Roll at Night* (1941), a brooding film that also features Anthony Quinn and Eddie Albert. A rousing murder mystery is the central ingredient of the 1954 carny melodrama, *Gorilla at Large*, with Anne Bancroft and Lee J. Cobb. For a touch of cauld grue, try *Berserk!* (1968), a chiller featuring the legendary Joan Crawford (who, according to one film critic, has "better legs than any other 60-year-old ringmaster.") A more recent crime and carnival spectacular is 1980's *Carny*, in which Jodie Foster and Gary Busey display their respective talents.

Amusement parks have had minor roles in numerous novels and films, but relatively few featured shows of their own. Two fictional exceptions of note are James O'Hanlon's *Murder at Coney Island* (1939), a farcical whodunit set at the world's most famous amusement park; and Richard Stark's (Donald E. Westlake) *Slayground* (1971), in which the amoral thief known only as Parker wages a one-man guerrilla war against a bunch of mobsters in a winter-abandoned New Jersey park. On the cinematic side, we have Alfred Hitchcock's adaptation of Patricia Highsmith's *Strangers on a Train* (1951), with Robert Walker and Farley Granger and a script coauthored by Raymond Chandler, which contains the best and most suspenseful amusement park scenes ever filmed.

And that, ladies and gentlemen, concludes our brief historical lecture and encomium. Thank you for your kind attention. Thank you very much.

And now, if you'll come right this way, the show is about to begin. In the astonishing performances to follow, you'll meet acrobats, trapeze artists, ringmasters, animal tamers, elephants, fun house operators, grifters, barkers, shills, and such sideshow attractions as fortune-tellers, nautch girls, Siamese twins, geeks, and the one and only Mad Ghoul. You'll even meet the tiniest circus performers of all in a sumptuous little tale entitled "Beidenbauer's Flea."

Ah, yes, that's it: settle back and relax. We're ready now—and so are you.

Ladies and gentlemen, *The Wickedest Show on Earth* presents Mystery, Murder, and the thrills of a lifetime. . . .

—Marcia Muller and Bill Pronzini
San Francisco, California
January 1985

HOP-FROG

Edgar Allan Poe

This frightening tale of recrimination and vengeance at one of the earliest forms of carnival, the performance of jesters at a king's court, is little known among the macabre tales of Edgar Allan Poe (1809–1849), and yet ranks with his finest stories of this type. Poe, who also wrote brilliant verse and epic poetry, essays, sketches, and literary criticism, was among the first to develop the short story as a distinct literary form. His handful of detective tales foretold the entire evolution of the modern detective story; deduction, ratiocination, suspense, mystery—all these elements were pioneered by this tortured genius of American letters.

15

I never knew any one so keenly alive to a joke as the king was. He seemed to live only for joking. To tell a good story of the joke kind, and to tell it well, was the surest road to his favor. Thus it happened that his seven ministers were all noted for their accomplishments as jokers. They all took after the king, too, in being large, corpulent, oily men, as well as inimitable jokers. Whether people grow fat by joking, or whether there is something in fat itself which predisposes to a joke, I have never been quite able to determine; but certain it is that a lean joker is a *rara avis in terris.*

About the refinements, or, as he called them, the "ghosts" of wit, the king troubled himself very little. He had an especial admiration for *breadth* in a jest, and would often put up with *length,* for the sake of it. Overniceties wearied him. He would have preferred Rabelais' "Gargantua" to the "Zadig" of Voltaire: and, upon the whole, practical jokes suited his taste far better than verbal ones.

At the date of my narrative, professing jesters had not altogether gone out of fashion at court. Several of the great continental "powers" still retained their "fools," who wore motley, with caps and bells, and who were expected to be always ready with sharp witticisms, at a moment's notice, in consideration of the crumbs that fell from the royal table.

Our king, as a matter of course, retained his "fool." The fact is, he *required* something in the way of folly—if only to counterbalance the heavy wisdom of the seven wise men who were his ministers—not to mention himself.

His fool, or professional jester, was not *only* a fool, however. His value was trebled in the eyes of the king, by the fact of his being also a dwarf and a cripple. Dwarfs were as common at court, in those days, as fools; and many monarchs would have found it difficult to get through their days

(days are rather longer at court than elsewhere) without both a jester to laugh *with*, and a dwarf to laugh *at*. But, as I have already observed, your jesters, in ninety-nine cases out of a hundred, are fat, round, and unwieldy—so that it was no small source of self-gratulation with our king that, in Hop-Frog (this was the fool's name), he possessed a triplicate treasure in one person.

I believe the name "Hop-Frog" was *not* that given to the dwarf by his sponsors at baptism, but it was conferred upon him, by general consent of the seven ministers, on account of his inability to walk as other men do. In fact, Hop-Frog could only get along by a sort of interjectional gait—something between a leap and a wriggle—a movement that afforded illimitable amusement, and of course consolation, to the king, for (notwithstanding the protuberance of his stomach and a constitutional swelling of the head) the king, by his whole court, was accounted a capital figure.

But although Hop-Frog, through the distortion of his legs, could move only with great pain and difficulty along a road or floor, the prodigious muscular power which nature seemed to have bestowed upon his arms, by way of compensation for deficiency in the lower limbs, enabled him to perform many feats of wonderful dexterity, where trees or ropes were in question, or anything else to climb. At such exercises he certainly much more resembled a squirrel, or a small monkey, than a frog.

I am not able to say, with precision, from what country Hop-Frog originally came. It was from some barbarous region, however, that no person ever heard of—a vast distance from the court of our king. Hop-Frog, and a young girl very little less dwarfish than himself (although of exquisite proportions, and a marvellous dancer), had been forcibly carried off from their respective homes in adjoining provinces, and sent as presents to the king, by one of his ever-victorious generals.

Under these circumstances, it is not to be wondered

at that a close intimacy arose between the two little captives. Indeed, they soon became sworn friends. Hop-Frog, who, although he made a great deal of sport, was by no means popular, had it not in his power to render Trippetta many services; but *she,* on account of her grace and exquisite beauty (although a dwarf), was universally admired and petted; so she possessed much influence; and never failed to use it, whenever she could, for the benefit of Hop-Frog.

On some grand state occasion—I forget what—the king determined to have a masquerade; and whenever a masquerade, or any thing of that kind, occurred at our court, then the talents both of Hop-Frog and Trippetta were sure to be called into play. Hop-Frog, in especial, was so inventive in the way of getting up pageants, suggesting novel characters, and arranging costume, for masked balls, that nothing could be done, it seems, without his assistance.

The night appointed for the *fête* had arrived. A gorgeous hall had been fitted up, under Trippetta's eye, with every kind of device which could possibly give *éclat* to a masquerade. The whole court was in a fever of expectation. As for costumes and characters, it might well be supposed that everybody had come to a decision on such points. Many had made up their minds (as to what *rôles* they should assume) a week, or even a month, in advance; and, in fact, there was not a particle of indecision anywhere—except in the case of the king and his seven ministers. Why *they* hesitated I never could tell, unless they did it by way of a joke. More probably, they found it difficult, on account of being so fat, to make up their minds. At all events, time flew; and, as a last resort, they sent for Trippetta and Hop-Frog.

When the two little friends obeyed the summons of the king, they found him sitting at his wine with the seven members of his cabinet council; but the monarch appeared to be in a very ill humor. He knew that Hop-Frog was not fond of wine; for it excited the poor cripple almost to madness; and madness is no comfortable feeling. But the king loved his practical jokes, and took pleasure in forcing Hop-Frog to drink and (as the king called it) "to be merry."

"Come here, Hop-Frog," said he, as the jester and his friend entered the room; "swallow this bumper to the health of your absent friends [here Hop-Frog sighed] and then let us have the benefit of your invention. We want characters—*characters*, man—something novel—out of the way. We are wearied with this everlasting sameness. Come, drink! the wine will brighten your wits."

Hop-Frog endeavored, as usual, to get up a jest in reply to these advances from the king; but the effort was too much. It happened to be the poor dwarf's birthday, and the command to drink to his "absent friends" forced the tears to his eyes. Many large, bitter drops fell into the goblet as he took it, humbly, from the hand of the tyrant.

"Ah! ha! ha! ha!" roared the latter, as the dwarf reluctantly drained the beaker. "See what a glass of good wine can do! Why, your eyes are shining already!"

Poor fellow! his large eyes *gleamed*, rather than shone; for the effect of wine on his excitable brain was not more powerful than instantaneous. He placed the goblet nervously on the table, and looked round upon the company with a half-insane stare. They all seemed highly amused at the success of the king's "*joke.*"

"And now to business," said the prime minister, a *very* fat man.

'Yes," said the king. "Come, Hop-Frog, lend us your assistance. Characters, my fine fellow; we stand in need of characters—all of us—ha! ha! ha!" and as this was seriously meant for a joke, his laugh was chorused by the seven.

Hop-Frog also laughed, although feebly and somewhat vacantly.

"Come, come," said the king, impatiently, "have you nothing to suggest?"

"I am endeavoring to think of something *novel*," replied the dwarf, abstractedly, for he was quite bewildered by the wine.

"Endeavoring!" cried the tyrant, fiercely; "what do you mean by *that*? Ah, I perceive. You are sulky, and want more wine. Here, drink this!" and he poured out another goblet full and offered it to the cripple, who merely gazed at it, gasping for breath.

"Drink, I say!" shouted the monster, "or by the fiends—"

The dwarf hesitated. The king grew purple with rage. The courtiers smirked. Trippetta, pale as a corpse, advanced to the monarch's seat, and, falling on her knees before him, implored him to spare her friend.

The tyrant regarded her, for some moments, in evident wonder at her audacity. He seemed quite at a loss what to do or say—how most becomingly to express his indignation. At last, without uttering a syllable, he pushed her violently from him, and threw the contents of the brimming goblet in her face.

The poor girl got up as best she could, and, not daring even to sigh, resumed her position at the foot of the table.

There was a dead silence for about half a minute, during which the falling of a leaf, or of a feather, might have been heard. It was interrupted by a low, but harsh and protracted *grating* sound which seemed to come at once from every corner of the room.

"What—what—*what* are you making that noise for?" demanded the king, turning furiously to the dwarf.

The latter seemed to have recovered, in great measure, from his intoxication, and looking fixedly but quietly into the tyrant's face, merely ejaculated:

"I—I? How could it have been me?"

"The sound appeared to come from without," observed one of the courtiers. "I fancy it was the parrot at the window, whetting his bill upon his cage-wires."

"True," replied the monarch, as if much relieved by the suggestion; "but, on the honor of a knight, I could have sworn that it was the gritting of this vagabond's teeth."

Hereupon the dwarf laughed (the king was too con-

firmed a joker to object to any one's laughing), and displayed
a set of large, powerful, and very repulsive teeth. Moreover,
he avowed his perfect willingness to swallow as much wine
as desired. The monarch was pacified; and having drained
another bumper with no very perceptible ill effect, Hop-
Frog entered at once, and with spirit, into the plans for
the masquerade.

"I cannot tell what was the association of idea," observed he, very tranquilly, and as if he had never tasted
wine in his life, "but *just after* your majesty had struck
the girl and thrown the wine in her face—*just after* your
majesty had done this, and while the parrot was making
that odd noise outside the window, there came into my
mind a capital diversion—one of my own country frolics—
often enacted among us, at our masquerades: but here it
will be new altogether. Unfortunately, however, it requires
a company of eight persons, and—"

"Here we *are!*" cried the king, laughing at his acute
discovery of the coincidence; "eight to a fraction—I and
my seven ministers. Come! what is the diversion?"

"We call it," replied the cripple, "the Eight Chained
Ourang-Outangs, and it really is excellent sport if well enacted."

"*We* will enact it," remarked the king, drawing himself
up, and lowering his eyelids.

"The beauty of the game," continued Hop-Frog, "lies
in the fright it occasions among the women."

"Capital!" roared in chorus the monarch and his min-
istry.

"I will equip you as ourang-outangs," proceeded the
dwarf; "leave all that to me. The resemblance shall be so
striking, that the company of masqueraders will take you
for real beasts—and of course, they will be as much terrified
as astonished."

"Oh, this is exquisite!" exclaimed the king. "Hop-Frog!
I will make a man of you."

"The chains are for the purpose of increasing the confusion by their jangling. You are supposed to have escaped, *en masse*, from your keepers. Your majesty cannot conceive the *effect* produced, at a masquerade, by eight chained ourang-outangs, imagined to be real ones by most of the company; and rushing in with savage cries, among the crowd of delicately and gorgeously habited men and women. The *contrast* is inimitable."

"It *must* be," said the king: and the council arose hurriedly (as it was growing late), to put in execution the scheme of Hop-Frog.

His mode of equipping the party as ourang-outangs was very simple, but effective enough for his purposes. The animals in question had, at the epoch of my story, very rarely been seen in any part of the civilized world; and as the imitations made by the dwarf were sufficiently beast-like and more than sufficiently hideous, their truthfulness to nature was thus thought to be secured.

The king and his ministers were first encased in tight-fitting stockinet shirts and drawers. They were then saturated with tar. At this stage of the process, some one of the party suggested feathers; but the suggestion was at once overruled by the dwarf, who soon convinced the eight, by ocular demonstration, that the hair of such a brute as the ourang-outang was much more efficiently represented by *flax*. A thick coating of the latter was accordingly plastered upon the coating of tar. A long chain was now procured. First, it was passed about the waist of the king, *and tied;* then about another of the party, and also tied; then about all successively, in the same manner. When this chaining arrangement was complete, and the party stood as far apart from each other as possible, they formed a circle; and to make all things appear natural, Hop-Frog passed the residue of the chain, in two diameters, at right angles, across the circle, after the fashion adopted, at the present day, by those who capture chimpanzees, or other large apes, in Borneo.

The grand saloon in which the masquerade was to take

place, was a circular room, very lofty, and receiving the light of the sun only through a single window at top. At night (the season for which the apartment was especially designed) it was illuminated principally by a large chandelier, depending by a chain from the centre of the sky-light, and lowered, or elevated, by means of a counterbalance as usual; but (in order not to look unsightly) this latter passed outside the cupola and over the roof.

The arrangements of the room had been left to Trippetta's superintendence; but, in some particulars, it seems, she had been guided by the calmer judgment of her friend the dwarf. At his suggestion it was that, on this occasion, the chandelier was removed. Its waxen drippings (which, in weather so warm, it was quite impossible to prevent) would have been seriously detrimental to the rich dresses of the guests, who, on account of the crowded state of the saloon, could not *all* be expected to keep from out its centre—that is to say, from under the chandelier. Additional sconces were set in various parts of the hall, out of the way; and a flambeau, emitting sweet odor, was placed in the right hand of each of the Caryatides that stood against the wall—some fifty or sixty all together.

The eight ourang-outangs, taking Hop-Frog's advice, waited patiently until midnight (when the room was thoroughly filled with masqueraders) before making their appearance. No sooner had the clock ceased striking, however, than they rushed, or rather rolled in, all together—for the impediments of their chains caused most of the party to fall, and all to stumble as they entered.

The excitement among the masqueraders was prodigious, and filled the heart of the king with glee. As had been anticipated, there were not a few of the guests who supposed the ferocious-looking creatures to be beasts of *some* kind in reality, if not precisely ourang-outangs. Many of the women swooned with affright; and had not the king taken the precaution to exclude all weapons from the saloon, his party might soon have expiated their frolic in their blood.

As it was, a general rush was made for the doors; but the king had ordered them to be locked immediately upon his entrance; and, at the dwarf's suggestion, the keys had been deposited with *him.*

While the tumult was at its height, and each masquerader attentive only to his own safety (for, in fact, there was much *real* danger from the pressure of the excited crowd), the chain by which the chandelier ordinarily hung, and which had been drawn up on its removal, might have been seen very gradually to descend, until its hooked extremity came within three feet of the floor.

Soon after this, the king and his seven friends having reeled about the hall in all directions, found themselves, at length, in its centre, and, of course, in immediate contact with the chain. While they were thus situated, the dwarf, who had followed noiselessly at their heels, inciting them to keep up the commotion, took hold of their own chain at the intersection of the two portions which crossed the circle diametrically and at right angles. Here, with the rapidity of thought, he inserted the hook from which the chandelier had been wont to depend; and, in an instant, by some unseen agency, the chandelier-chain was drawn so far upward as to take the hook out of reach, and, as an inevitable consequence, to drag the ourang-outangs together in close connection, and face to face.

The masqueraders, by this time, had recovered, in some measure, from their alarm; and, beginning to regard the whole matter as a well-contrived pleasantry, set up a loud shout of laughter at the predicament of the apes.

"Leave them to *me!*" now screamed Hop-Frog, his shrill voice making itself easily heard through all the din. "Leave them to *me.* I fancy *I* know them. If I can only get a good look at them, *I* can soon tell who they are."

Here, scrambling over the heads of the crowd, he managed to get to the wall; when, seizing a flambeau from one of the Caryatides, he returned, as he went, to the centre of the room—leaped, with the agility of a monkey, upon the king's head—and thence clambered a few feet up the chain—holding down the torch to examine the group of ourang-outangs, and still screaming: "*I* shall soon find out who they are!"

And now, while the whole assembly (the apes included) were convulsed with laughter, the jester suddenly uttered a shrill whistle; when the chain flew violently up for about thirty feet—dragging with it the dismayed and struggling ourang-outangs, and leaving them suspended in mid-air between the sky-light and the floor. Hop-Frog, clinging to the chain as it rose, still maintained his relative position in respect to the eight maskers, and still (as if nothing were the matter) continued to thrust his torch down toward them, as though endeavoring to discover who they were.

So thoroughly astonished was the whole company at this ascent, that a dead silence, of about a minute's duration, ensued. It was broken by just such a low, harsh, *grating* sound, as had before attracted the attention of the king and his councillors when the former threw the wine in the face of Trippetta. But, on the present occasion, there could be no question as to *whence* the sound issued. It came from the fang-like teeth of the dwarf, who ground them and gnashed them as he foamed at the mouth, and glared, with an expression of maniacal rage, into the upturned countenances of the king and his seven companions.

"Ah, ha!" said at length the infuriated jester. "Ah, ha! I begin to see who these people *are,* now!" Here, pretending to scrutinize the king more closely, he held the flambeau to the flaxen coat which enveloped him, and which instantly burst into a sheet of vivid flame. In less than half a minute the whole eight ourang-outangs were blazing fiercely, amid the shrieks of the multitude who gazed at them from below, horror-stricken, and without the power to render them the slightest assistance.

At length the flames, suddenly increasing in virulence, forced the jester to climb higher up the chain, to be out of their reach; and, as he made this movement, the crowd again sank, for a brief instant, into silence. The dwarf seized his opportunity, and once more spoke:

"I now see *distinctly*," he said, "what manner of people these maskers are. They are a great king and his seven privy-councillors—a king who does not scruple to strike a defenceless girl, and his seven councillors who abet him in the outrage. As for myself, I am simply Hop-Frog, the jester—and *this is my last jest.*"

Owing to the high combustibility of both the flax and the tar to which it adhered, the dwarf had scarcely made an end of his brief speech before the work of vengeance was complete. The eight corpses swung in their chains, a fetid, blackened, hideous, and indistinguishable mass. The cripple hurled his torch at them, clambered leisurely to the ceiling, and disappeared through the sky-light.

It is supposed that Trippetta, stationed on the roof of the saloon, had been the accomplice of her friend in his fiery revenge, and that, together, they effected their escape to their own country; for neither was seen again.

HURRY, HURRY, HURRY!

Paul Gallico

This nostalgic tale of a turn-of-the-century carny in a small Kansas town features Swami Mirza Baba, "a cynical, dissolute scalawag of a fortune-teller," as Ellery Queen once referred to him, who also happens to be a pretty good detective when the need arises. Any story from the pen of Paul Gallico is bound to be first-rate and this one is no exception. Gallico (1897–1976) was a multitalented writer who produced sports fiction and nonfiction, short stories, novels, and film scripts with equal ease and facility. Among his suspense books are the novels Trial by Terror *(1952) and* The Zoo Gang *(1971), and the collection* The Adventures of Hiram Holliday *(1939), which was the basis for a 1950's TV show of the same title starring Wally Cox.*

One late-summer day around the turn of the century, a cheap carnival came to a small town in Kansas for the county fair, in time to relieve some of the tensions built up by the brutal murder of an innocent widow on a lonely farm and the forthcoming hanging of the farmhand who had been found guilty of the crime.

The morning of the day the fair was to open in Thackerville, the carnival boss, Bowers, strode the busy midway where the concessions were being knocked together—the Ferris wheel and giant swing, the freak and girly shows, the hoopla games and wheels of fortune—and bawled, "Hoi! Gather 'round all hands. The Sheriff wants everybody."

At that moment the curtains parted at the booth over which hung a garish poster showing a turbaned Indian gazing into a crystal ball and advertising: SWAMI MIRZA BABA TELLS THE PAST, PRESENT AND FUTURE—25¢, and Nick Jackson strolled out of the booth, spitting a stream of tobacco juice.

He was an unkempt, friendless, lonely man, past sixty but looking older, with a gray, seamed face and small, red-rimmed eyes. Hard-boiled, irreverent, he had the cynicism of a man whose lifetime had been spent in the city slums doing the best he could, and around cheap burlesque shows, traveling circuses, dime museums, and carnivals. He had been shill, barker, shell-game operator, short-change artist, front worker, and con man, but age and drink had made him unreliable in a tight pinch and he had ended up "dukkerin," as the Romany gypsies called fortune-telling.

"All right now, you rats, listen to me," the Sheriff began his address. He was a big man with a good forehead and hard, clear eyes. He wore a snakeskin belt and ten-gallon hat, and his neck rose from his flannel shirt like the column of a cottonwood tree. "This is a hardworking community

of decent God-fearing people. We're a-goin' to let you operate here long as you behave. I know you for what you are,
a pack o' thieves, rascals, and scalawags. But you ain't goin'
to get away with anything here. I got my eye on all of
you and I been around some too."

Nobody in the group of carny men stirred or said anything with the exception of the old fortune-teller who spat
again.

"You wheel-of-fortune men, keep your bellies away
from them brakes and lever boards. You skin anybody and
you'll spend the next six months in jail. That goes for you
hoopla and ring-the-cane fellers too."

The grifters exchanged looks but said nothing. They
were wondering just how much they would have to shave
to stay on the right side. The Sheriff was pleased with the
effect of his speech on everybody except the fortune-teller.
The hot impudence and contempt in the man's eyes irri-
tated him. He said:

"You Swami there, or whatever your name is. I don't
know that I'm a-gonna let you work."

The old man regarded him unblinkingly and said out
of the side of his tobacco-stained mouth, "Why? What's the
matter with me?"

"You're a faker. You can't read no minds and you can't
predict no future. Let's see you predict mine, if you can."

Nick said, "Cough up first, you the same as anybody
else." The Sheriff reached into his jeans and flung a two-
bit piece to the fortune-teller, who pocketed it and snarled,
"You want a prediction, eh? Couple a months from now
you won't be Sheriff any more."

There was a roar of laughter from the assembled carnival men.

The Sheriff's eyes hardened. "Is that right? What makes
you think so?"

With an election coming off in November, it was a good
fifty-fifty chance and maybe better, Nick knew. He had
spent the previous day in Thackerville lounging around the

general store listening to gossip and picking up stray bits of information which might come in handy. Now he replied, "You got a hangin' comin' off next week. How do you know you're stringin' the right feller?"

The Sheriff flushed red and stood silent for a moment on the bandstand. "You watch yourselves," was all he said finally. He climbed down and strode away, shouldering roughly through the carnival men. Nick merely spat again.

The whole town, Nick had found out, was still on edge over the murder a month ago of the widow Booth, discovered in the kitchen of her farm with her head beaten in with a poker, and over the scheduled execution of Erd Wayne, her hired man, who had been found wandering half-dazed about the kitchen with the murder weapon in his hand and blood on his clothes.

Wayne had been tried and found guilty when banker Samuel Chinter had supplied evidence for the motive, testifying that he had refused Wayne the loan of $1,500 to buy the Coulter farm that was up for sale. There had long been rumors that the widow kept that amount, her late husband's insurance, in the house in cash. But, testified banker Chinter, the widow actually kept her money in the bank and so the murderer would have got no more than a few dollars for his crime. Wayne's defense had been lame. He had been about to enter the kitchen for supper, he had said, when he was struck from behind and remembered nothing more.

It was, as the Sheriff had said, an open-and-shut case, and it had been conducted vigorously by the county prosecutor who hoped to reach the state legislature via the conviction, in spite of the fact that a lot of people had liked Erd Wayne. Some said he wanted the farm so that he could ask June Purvey to marry him but was not the kind to stoop to murder to get it. Still, the evidence seemed conclusive and sometimes fellows in love lost their heads. One never knew. . . .

"Hayseeds," muttered Nick Jackson, eyeing the teemıng midway from the entrance to his booth. He wore a soiled wrapper now, with stars and moons sewn onto it, and a turban with shaving-brush bristles and a ten-cent-store diamond stuck in the front of it.

He gave readings automatically. "A dark man is coming into your life. . . . You have been worried lately, but things will get better. . . . Beware of a blonde woman. . . . You are a sensitive type misunderstood by your family."

The curtains to the booth parted admitting the next customer, a young girl in a white cotton frock tied with a blue sash. Her dark hair, worn long, was gathered together in the back by a ribbon of the same color. She was eighteen, shy, nervous, frightened. But what startled the fortune-teller the most as his shrewd eyes analyzed her, missing nothing, was her innocence.

"Are you Mirza Baba?" she asked.

"Yup!"

"Can I have a reading?"

"Two bits."

She opened her purse. He always made them pay first. A glance into pocketbooks yielded valuable clues. He saw the snapshot of the young man in an open-neck shirt. She handed him a quarter.

"You are worried about someone near and dear to you." A safe opening—her nervousness, the snapshot . . .

Her dark eyes opened wide and she stared at him amazed. Tears formed in them. "I'm June Purvey," she said.

"I knew that," the old man lied. He scrutinized her with renewed interest. Hers was a simple, dewy beauty the contemplation of which unaccountably made his heart ache. Unaccustomed to emotion and pain, he suddenly turned savage and said harshly, "They're a-goin' to hang your man. . . ."

The girl gave a low cry of despair, put her head down on the table, and sobbed uncontrollably. Nick was used to clients dissolving into tears when he sometimes prodded them on the raw or guessed their secrets. Yet the grief of this child touched him.

He hedged, ". . . unless something happens to prevent it."

The girl lifted her tear-lined face and clutched miserably at the straw. "Oh please, Mr. Baba, help me. Please. He didn't do it. Look here—you can see he didn't do it." She opened her purse and presented the photograph.

The odd thing was that at that moment, with the snapshot in his grimy fingers, Nick would have bet that Erd Wayne was innocent. His profession had trained him to read faces instantly. Life in a sordid world more black than white had taught him all the telltale marks left by greed, viciousness, hatred, and malice. The face of the man in the picture was frank, open, and honest.

"That's right," he agreed, "he didn't do it. I can see that."

"Then won't you help him, please, Mr. Baba? I'll pay you. I've brought money. . . ." She opened her purse again and produced a roll of bills that made the old man's eyes light up with cupidity.

"It's eighty-five dollars that I've saved. But I would pay you more—anything you wanted. I could send you some every week. I work at Pete's dry goods store."

"You Erd's girl?" Nick asked.

June shook her head. "No . . ." And then added, "He ain't spoken yet."

"What you doin' this for then?"

"Because I love him."

Nick was unable to understand the depth or simplicity of her reply. To him love was desire. He said, "Supposing he was to get off and go sparkin' someone else, hey?"

June regarded him miserably for a moment, then replied fiercely, "I wouldn't care, 'long as he was alive!" She pushed the money toward him. "You could find out the truth," she said. "You can read their minds. Nobody can hide anything from you. If the murderer came here you'd know."

"Yup, I'd know."

"Then take it." She indicated the bills.

Nick said, "Gimme half. You can pay the rest when I find something out." He counted out forty dollars and then added the odd five-dollar bill. He had no compunction at taking her money. This was how he earned his living, separating the gullible from their cash. It surprised him, though, that he had not taken it all. He said, "I'll keep my inner eye peeled. Don't say nothing to nobody. You can come back tomorrow."

She got up to go. Her eyes were filled with trust and relief. "Oh, thank you, Mr. Baba. God bless you!"

He watched her go, suddenly filled with a strange, angry desire to free hired man Wayne.

Nick Jackson was what was known as a cold reader. With no props such as cards or crystal ball, he sat at a table and dissected his clients, probed them for their weakness and hidden troubles. He employed a combination of ready patter, shrewd observation, knowledge of human nature and evil, and the natural desire of his victims to talk.

"Some men cannot resist the impulse to have just one more drink," he would say to some unhappy housewife with bitter lines about her mouth, watching her face for clues. If the lips tightened, the eyes widened with a hint of tears, he had the secret of her visit. If the expression remained blank he continued smoothly, "But that, fortunately, is not the case with your husband." Then he would fish in other waters—blondes, cards, the ponies. . . . Soon they would be spilling everything to him, convinced that he had read their innermost thoughts and secrets.

The afternoon of the next day a young girl came in. But she was not innocent. Nick could tell when they had had experience.

His knowing eyes estimated her. Straw-colored hair, small greedy mouth, high-school senior ring, good clothes. When she opened her purse to pay him he glimpsed a rouge compact and a diamond ring, the stub of a railroad ticket to Kansas City, and a scrap of paper with the address, in masculine handwriting, of one of that city's shadier hotels. It was as though she had presented her immediate history to him written down in a copybook.

He said, "Sit down, dear." He thought of the Sheriff and his hardworking community of decent God-fearing people and laughed inwardly. "You are the affectionate type; your warm generous nature gives you away. I see someone who loves you. But wait. I see another woman at his side. The man is married, is he not?"

The girl's eyes filled with fear. "How do you know?"

"Nothing is veiled from Mirza Baba. Shall I tell you more?" From outside sounded the cries of the barkers, "Hurry, hurry, hurry!" and the groaning of the carousel organ and the snap-snapping of the cheap rifles in the shooting gallery. The girl nodded silently.

"I see a train ride. You are alone and nervous. You are walking along a street in a big city. You come to a hotel. There you meet your lover. The two of you go inside. . . ."

The girl's moan interrupted him and she appeared on the point of collapse. "Oh, God, you've found out. My father will kill me if *he* finds out."

Her story came pouring from her. Her name was Clytie Vroom. A much older married man in the town had fallen in love with her. She had wanted pretty things. He had given her a diamond ring, which she had never dared wear, and other gifts. He had painted a glowing picture of the wonderful time they would have together in the big city, and she couldn't resist his invitation to spend a weekend there with him. She had told her father she was going to visit a girl friend in a neighboring town.

Nick was doing arithmetic. The ring must have cost nearly a thousand dollars, the other gifts several hundred. Where would a man in a small town lay his hands on that kind of money without his wife or someone finding out? He asked, "What was his name, dear?" It was a mistake.

If he had kept quiet or prodded her some more it would have slipped out.

She was on her feet, her little mouth twisted with fear, her eyes wide with terror. "Oh, God! You'll find out if I stay here any more. You'll read it in my mind. . . ." She snatched her purse and fled from the booth.

Nick went to the entrance and watched her panicky passage down the midway. He gazed at the mingling of farmers and villagers out for a holiday. He wondered what other secrets were to be dredged out from behind those bland, smooth faces, what other guilts smoldered beneath denim, seersucker, dimity, or poplin.

He saw June Purvey standing near the frozen custard stand, her dark unhappy eyes trying to catch his. She probably had been waiting there all day, watching.

Nick signaled to June Purvey with a jerk of his head and went back inside. A moment later she came in. She plucked at his soiled wrapper, crying, "Oh, Mr. Baba . . . have you found out who did it?" Her voice shook with strain and anguish.

He replied, "Nope," and then quickly corrected himself, "Mebbe. The psychical aura is kinda confused. I gotta git more impressions. I see a figure but there is a veil in front of it." Then abruptly changing his tone, "You know a girl named Clytie Vroom?"

June nodded, puzzled. "Yes. I went to school with her."

"Know who her feller is?"

June thought . . . "I don't think she has one, a steady I mean." She blushed suddenly. "I think maybe the Sheriff is sweet on her. I've seen him walking her home from the bank several times. Clytie works at the bank, you know." Then June drew in her breath sharply crying, "Oh . . . but . . ."

"The Sheriff's married," concluded Nick. "Never mind; it probably don't mean nothing. You run along. I'll let you know if I hear anything."

The next day was Sunday and unbearably hot. Although

the fairgrounds were crowded, Nick gave only a few desultory readings and mostly sat waiting in the stifling booth rolling Bull Durham cigarettes, thinking of the man in the county jail waiting to be hanged by the neck until dead and wondering if it could really be pinned on the Sheriff. He daydreamed with vicious satisfaction of unmasking the man who had called them all rats and scoundrels, and singled him out for abuse.

Toward late afternoon Nick heard voices outside the curtain closing the entrance and pricked up his ears. Many workable clues could be mined listening to the snatches of talk between two people before one of them came in, from, "Aw, I dare you. I will if you will," to such admissions as, "Jim would be furious if he knew I had gone to a fortune-teller," exposing the timid wife and the domineering husband.

A woman's voice said, "Vulgar fraud. It oughtn't to be allowed."

The man's: "Oh, I suppose it is amusing. I'd like to see just how far these fakers go."

The woman's (with a snort): "Really, Mr. C. If you can't find something better to spend hard-earned money on. . . ."

The man's: "Maybe he'll tell me how to invest and make a fortune."

The woman's: "Samuel Chinter! That I should live to see the day when you patronized a fortune-teller."

And the man's, finally: "My dear Essie. I see that you are still far from plumbing the more tortuous depths of my character. If you are embarrassed, wait for me at the Ladies Aid Booth."

Nick indexed mentally: *Businessman, but his wife holds one end of the purse strings. Would probably enjoy a fling if he could get it.* And he was trying to remember where he had heard the name before. Then it came to him as the curtain parted. Samuel Chinter, president of the Farmer's Bank, came in.

He sat down opposite the seedy-looking little man in the gown and ridiculous turban. His thin mouth parted in an amiable enough smile as he asked, "Can you make money out of this sort of thing, my friend?"

Nick replied. "Yup. Or I wouldn't be doing it." He was studying the tight, too-smooth face. The banker's skin looked as if it were made of elastic and had been stretched over wood. He noted the lines at each corner of the bloodless mouth and the gleam in the small, butternut-shaped eyes.

"Well, then, my friend, Mirza Baba, if that is your name, supposing you tell me something about myself."

Nick said, "Two bits," and waited, watching while the banker took a leather purse from his left hip pocket. This surprised the cold reader since most men kept their wallets on the right. Chinter laid the coin on the table saying, "Always the best course in any business. Trust no one."

Nick decided he wanted to be rid of him quickly. He said perfunctorily, "I see an office of marble and glass. There is a large mahogany desk. A brass sign on it says, 'President.' "

"Excellent, my friend. Of course you know who I am. Everyone in Thackerville does. Go on."

Nick felt pushed off base. His mind was not working as coldly and analytically as it should. "You are worried about investments," he suggested, picking up the clue.

Chinter's lips parted again, but this time the smile was not amiable. "Every banker worries about investments," he said. "But if I wanted financial information I wouldn't come to you. Is that the best you can do?"

The anger he always seemed to feel against these bland, self-satisfied, well-to-do people possessed Nick. "There is an account at the bank that is causing you concern," he fished, but in safe enough waters. Every bank had at least one account like that. "You do not know how to get out of your difficulty at the moment. Also in this affair you are hindered by a woman." It was also true that in most tangled accounts where there was an overdraft there was usually a woman involved.

Chinter's smooth face remained expressionless. But in the hairless space between nostril and lip line Nick saw a bead of sweat which had not been there before. He switched to flattery.

"You are the sophisticated worldly type, too big for a small community. You belong where your talents would be more appreciated. You have a fatal attraction for women—young women. You are held back by people who do not understand you."

He was watching the banker closely through half-closed eyes as he reeled off the rote spiel he had given a half dozen others. Imperceptibly, almost, he saw Chinter's head nodding in agreement with each point. "Your heart rules your mind. You are generous to a fault. You. . ." He paused, suddenly remembering something that June Purvey had said—"Clytie works at the bank, you know"—a hunch! If he could make this sneering man squirm a little . . .

Nick pinioned the banker hypnotically with his red-rimmed eyes and continued, "I see a ring. A diamond ring in the hands of a blonde woman, a young girl . . ." Had there been no reaction to this he would have said, "but this does not concern you."

But there were now three beads of sweat on the mouth and one coursing down the chin. Nick gambled. "The diamond ring is a present. Yet she dare not wear it. I see her again on a railroad train. She is nervous. There is an address in her bag. I cannot read it clearly but it is the name of a hotel in Kansas City."

He stopped. Chinter did not move. "Go on," he said hoarsely, "what else do you know?"

Bull's-eye! Clytie Vroom, then, had gone to her married lover in panic and told him the mind reader had learned her secret. But why had he come there when Clytie had not named him? What further did he fear? With what other guilt was he burdened?

Nick remembered June Purvey saying, "If the murderer came here, you'd know it." But banker Chinter was the one man who could not have committed the murder for which Erd Wayne was to hang, since he knew that the widow Booth kept her money in his bank and not in her house. Therefore . . .

Nick's sordid, cynical mind was now spinning like the drive wheel of a locomotive, weighing, testing, remembering. Figures bashed through his head—the sum of $1,500, the widow's fortune—enough to buy a diamond ring and other gifts. Who would have easier access to it than banker Chinter? He had only to take it. But if the widow had found out . . .

The atmosphere in the booth was suddenly thick and heavy with animal fear as Nick droned, "I see the woman who hindered you with the account that was giving you difficulty. She will hinder you no longer. She is dead."

"Aaaaaah!" A long sigh came from the man on the other side of the table. His right hand dropped casually to his side.

"I see the widow Booth in her kitchen. Outside there lurks a man who must silence her at all costs. The hired man, Wayne, enters, disturbing his plans. But the man outside sees in him the chance to kill and let another hang for it. *And I know why the murderer had to silence the widow. . . .*"

The explosion of the gun burst shockingly over the noises of the midway and filled the narrow booth with black smoke and powder stink. But the bullet passed harmlessly through the roof, for Nick had seen the glint of metal creeping from the hip pocket where a right-handed man's wallet ought to be, and had kicked viciously under the table, spoiling his aim.

Then he kicked him twice more in the same spot, disabling him into a groveling wreck on the floor as men, carnies, and passersby, led by the ubiquitous Sheriff, rushed in.

The latter shouted, "I warned you to keep out of trouble. By God, it's Mr. Chinter. You'll swing for this, Baba. . . ."

The old man stared at him. "You're mighty quick with that rope, Sheriff. He's got the gun, not me."

Bowers, the carnival boss, had arrived. He took in the situation. "Yeah, Sheriff, take it easy. This bozo, whoever he is, tried to murder one of my men."

Nick began to laugh, a horrid, high-pitched cackle. "Rats, are we?" he gasped. "Thieves, rascals, scalawags, eh? You'll keep an eye on us! What about that sweet-smelling hypocrite there? There's your real murderer of the widow Booth. Are you or aren't, banker Chinter?"—and Nick raised his foot again.

The wreck moaned, "Yes. Oh, God, don't kick me again."

The fortune-teller croaked on, "He embezzled the widow's funds to buy his doxy a diamond and other things. Go ask Clytie Vroom to show you the ring. When the widow discovered her money was gone he had to kill her to keep her quiet."

And he added, "You're through, Sheriff. You hang too fast in this county."

He touched the prone man with his foot as though he were filth and said, "Go on. Get that trash out of here."

The crowd withdrew with the Sheriff and his prisoner, following them silently. Nick Jackson began to set his booth to rights again. He bit off a large chew of tobacco, picked up the overturned table and chair, and fixed the curtain. He fingered the hole in the clapboard roof made by the .38 caliber bullet, and then he grinned. Lack of courage was not one of his failings. He readjusted his turban which had fallen awry in the brief melee and sat down looking moodily before him.

The curtain stirred and parted, admitting June Purvey. She was white, but her eyes were shining with joy. She said, "I heard what happened—what you did. They told me they're a-going to set Erd free tomorrow."

Nick nodded. In the excitement of the shooting he had forgotten all about the girl and the man she loved. Then he made a strange admission. "You helped," he said. "Erd owes you a lot. It was you told me Clytie worked in the bank."

She said swiftly, "I'd never let him know."

Nick said, "Mirza Baba reads the future. Erd's your man."

Tears fell from the lovely eyes again. She opened her purse and took out the forty dollars. "It's all I've got," she said, "but I could mail you a dollar a week for as long as you say."

Nick looked at the money and at the girl. "All right," he said, "gimme it." He took it from her. "You don't need to pay any more. We're square."

June cried, "Oh thank you, thank you, dear Mr. Baba!" Then, going to him, she put her arms around him and kissed him on the side of his bitter, tobacco-stained mouth, and quickly ran out.

The old faker remained sitting there, the wad of bills in one hand. With the fingers of the other he touched the spot that she had kissed, rubbing at it as though the imprint of such goodness, purity, and innocence were something searing and unbearable. He felt older and more in need of a drink than he ever had before and, for the first time in his life, strangely desolate and forlorn.

IF THE DEAD
COULD TALK

Cornell Woolrich

*The novels and stories of Cornell Woolrich are filled
with both a high level of tension and a pervasive sense
of doom and despair, best evidenced in his "black" series:*
The Bride Wore Black *(1940),* Black Alibi *(1942), and* Ren-
dezvous in Black *(1948), among others. His large and varied
output—composed primarily within the confining walls of
various Manhattan residential hotels—reflects a personal
philosophy of inevitability and hopelessness; in this haunt-
ing and suspenseful story, Woolrich shows us that even
that great American dream—running away to join the circus—can ultimately be doomed to failure.*

He was in a dim little room off the arena somewhere. He looked so jaunty, in his tunic picked with spangles. He looked so husky, in the tights that encased his muscular thighs. He looked so devil-may-care and debonair, on the side of his face where there was still pink-tan greasepaint. He looked so dead.

There were a pair of clowns there, near the door, with that sad-eyed expression they always have when you're standing too close to them. There was a Roman charioteer there, in a gleaming cuirass and plumed helmet and kilt. There was a bareback rider in a frothy pink skirt. Just for a minute, taking a last look. Then they all turned and drifted silently outside. There was still a performance going on out there. They had to get back. The others stayed.

There was a girl there, a member of his own troupe, a cape around her tights now, looking down at him. Just looking at him. Just standing looking at him, as though she'd never get through. There was a young fellow next to her, a third member of the same troupe, standing holding one arm around her. The other hung stiffly beside him, ending in a mitten of gauze bandaging, as though he'd hurt his hand at some fairly recent performance. He kept looking at her, only at her, not at the still form she was looking at.

No one said anything. What was there to say? It could have happened to anyone.

Last of all, there was a detective there, jotting something in a notebook. He was all through now. He'd done all his questioning, all his looking around and investigating and reconstructing. It was no secret affair. Nearly a thousand people had seen it happen. He'd found out all there was to find out. Found out all anyone could tell him. Anyone living.

This is what he jotted.

Name: Crosby, Joseph.
Age: Twenty-five.
Profession: Trapeze artist.
Cause of death—

I knew I was going to kill him from the night she said, "I'm sorry, Joe, it's him, not you any more." I knew it from then on. I only didn't know when or how. That's how I am. That's what my blood is, what my nature is. I couldn't change that even if I tried.

I tried to stop myself from doing it, in every way I knew how. But it was no good; I knew it was going to happen anyway, I knew it was coming and there was no holding it back. I knew I was going to see him kissing her sometime, or even just looking at her in a certain way that meant she was his and not mine—and that would bring it on whether I wanted to or not.

It's queer how those things are. It's the closer you are to a guy that makes you hate him the worse, when he takes something away from you. And no one was ever as close as him and me. We were brothers in everything but blood.

Here's how it was: we both ran away from our homes the same night. We first met each other on the same night we both ran away. We were both within a year of one another's age—I was fourteen and a little the older. And we were both on our way to join up with the same traveling circus outfit that had passed through those parts only a day or so before, pitching in his town first, then crossing the hill and pitching in mine. You can't be any closer than that, for a starter.

I was sneaking down a line of boxcars, stalled in the freight yards, in the moonlight, keeping an eye open for the watchman and trying to find one of them that was open, when a hand came out to me and a voice whispered: "Try this one in here, where I am." I could tell by the sound it was somebody my own age, so I took his hand through the narrow black opening and floundered in. We closed it up again after us and got acquainted in the dark, like runaway kids do.

"I'm Tommy Sloan," he said. "What's your name?"

"I'm Joe Crosby. Are you on the lam too?"

"I'm heading after that traveling circus, you know the one."

"That's what I'm doing too." It didn't seem strange to us that we should both have the same idea, and meet like that on the same night we'd both carried it out. What would have seemed strange to us was that one of us should some day want to kill the other.

"I heard 'em say their next pitch was going to be over at Gloversville. *This* 'll take us there. I know because I overheard one of the yardmen telling somebody that. All we gotta do is lie low and keep our eyes open for it when it passes through." He hugged his knees in the gloom and shared his last soda cracker with me. "I wanna get in that trapeze act they got. The one with the man and the lady, and the little girl that they pass back and forth to each other. Gee, them high bars," he sighed wistfully.

I'd had my eye on that too. It had to be that or nothing, don't ask me why. That's how trapeze artists come into being, I guess.

"Think they'll take us?" he asked.

"Not right away. You gotta learn how. But maybe they'll let us string along with them and practice up."

We both gave a gusty sigh of mutual yearning in the shadows of the boxcar. "I ain't never going to be anything but one of them trapeze guys," he said in a low, dreamy voice.

"Me neither," I echoed.

A thousand and two kids have said that in their time. We were the two that carried it through.

The line of boxcars jolted, started to crawl slowly forward under us, and the world began.

That's how it was.

When they saw they couldn't shoo us away, and when they found out neither one of us had come from enough of a home to make it worthwhile sending us back to it, they took us with them and trained us. Mom Bissell mothered us. They broke us into the act while we were still pliable and our muscles hadn't stiffened yet. That's the only way you can be broken in—at that age.

We were still in the embryo stage when we lost Mom one night. Not in the ring, in bed, the way she'd always said she never wanted to go. We cried as though she'd been our own mother, him and me both.

Pop took us into full partnership as soon as we went out again after that. He had to, to keep the turn going. We were ready for it by then anyway. It was a proud night for us when we first stood up there on the takeoff platforms, tall already but skinny in our new tights, alongside Pop and *her,* and then went sailing out into space on our own, not just filler-ins any more. They say about the stage that once you've been an actor, it gets into your blood so, that you never want to be anything else. Tommy and me, we both found out that night that once you've gone sailing out between the bars, light and fast and sure, you never *can* be anything else.

We were a quartet for a while. Then Pop went to his rest too. He was getting too stiff and brittle, he had to drop out. He'd taught us all he knew. We used to visit him in the boardinghouse where we'd left him, whenever we got back to town. Then after a couple of seasons, there wasn't any reason to go around there any more. That's the way life goes; death beckons someone out of line, but the line keeps closing up.

Two men and a girl now. We didn't look lanky in our tights any more, we'd grown into them, and we'd come into our prime. We rearranged the turn. We worked on the blindfolded triple somersault ending in an upside-down hand grip, that Pop had showed us, until we had it cinched. Then we took the net away. The net was just a state of mind anyway. Nothing was going to happen, once we had it down pat.

They both learned the spinning dive, she and Tommy, just so there'd always be an alternate handy in case any little thing went wrong some night, and we wouldn't have to leave it out of the turn. We couldn't do that, it was our showpiece. But in our line it's always good to figure on any little thing going wrong some night, and having a substitute ready. One of you might eat some last week's fish and get a folding pain, or have a hand caught in a bus door.

So they doubled in it between them, Tommy and her. I was always the brake, the anchor. I was a little too heavy to be able to turn fast enough in the air, but the heaviness came in handy for coupling onto and steadying the plunger hurtling down. I was also a good half-head taller than him, and still taller when it came to her, and that meant either of them could take the three complete turns going down in less time than it took me. Have more room left to straighten out for the hand grip at the end, not have to crowd their somersaults to get them all in.

But Tommy was the one usually did it. She just kept warmed up at it, she was like what they call an understudy in the theater. She looked prettier tying the blindfold around him and getting him poised on the edge of the platform. It looked better like that, than for a girl to be risking her neck while a man stood looking on up there doing nothing. Just showmanship. You have to take those things into consideration.

We got good bookings on the strength of it too. Before we knew it, no more dinky little tent shows folding up under us in the middle of nowhere. The big time now, our names on three sheets, winter quarters in Florida, the Garden in New York, and all the rest of the trimmings.

And meanwhile she got lovelier every season. Natalie. The three of us went around together everywhere, always the three of us; her in the middle, with her laughing eyes

and dark-gold hair. That was all right while we were still
two boys and a girl. But before we noticed it we weren't
two boys and a girl any more. We were two men and a
woman. Then it wouldn't work any more. She couldn't like
the two of us the same, the way she had till now. We
wouldn't have wanted her to if she could.

It happened fast when it happened—all at once, like
a flash. She came back to the rooming house and knocked
on my door the night she first found out. I think it was in
Toledo. He wasn't with her. He must have stayed out to
count the stars somewhere.

She said, "I'm sorry, Joe, it's him, not you any more.
I found out for sure tonight. You asked me to tell you,
so I am."

I didn't say anything, I just looked at her. "Good night,
Joe," she said softly. I closed my door again.

I didn't know right away how bad it was going to be.
That was because I'd only seen her by herself as yet, without
his being with her. The poison hadn't been added.

We always shared the same room together, wherever
we stopped. It was only when he came in by himself, afterward, and I heard the way he was whistling to himself while
he undressed in the dark, that I knew how bad it was really
going to be. That I knew I was going to kill him, before
I'd let him have her.

I could hold it back tonight yet. And tomorrow night.
But sometime before long it was going to get away from
me; maybe the night-after-tomorrow. I couldn't do anything
against it. It had me.

It came on slow but sure. Awfully sure. Every look
they gave each other across a midnight lunch table, every
walk they took together, every hidden handclasp down low
at their sides that they thought nobody saw, that brought
it a little closer.

It was in St. Louis I bought the gun. I knew a guy
there in a little pawnshop across the river in East St. Louis,
from when we got stranded there with smaller outfits in

the past, and he let me have one without asking too many questions.

Then we moved on, and the next pitch we made I finally got him alone one night, just like I wanted to. I'd been watching and waiting for this. She was supposed to meet him at some amusement park on the outskirts of town. She'd had something to attend to right after the performance, and instead of waiting for her, he left a note for her telling her where he'd be when she got back. That was my chance. I saw him slip it under the door of her room, and as soon as he'd gone on his way I tore it up, so she wouldn't know where to go looking for him when she returned. Then I gave him about ten or fifteen minutes head start, and followed him out there myself. With the gun.

The place was in a big woodland park just outside of town. The lighted-up part of it, where they had the pavilions and things, just occupied a small fraction of it. The rest was pitch-black, natural woods. It was a good place for it. It was a swell place for it. I couldn't have picked a better one myself.

I found him sitting there waiting for her, drinking root beer at a concession. I told him she'd asked me to find him and tell him she wasn't coming, she felt tired and thought she'd go to bed instead. Right away he wanted to go back, but I managed to talk that out of him. I got him to come for a stroll with me, and little by little, without his noticing, I led him off away from the lights, deeper and deeper under the trees, until we were far enough in so there were no people anywhere around to see it happen. Or even to hear the shot go off.

I was going to claim it was an accident. It would have been easy enough. We'd been fooling with it, and it had gone off and hit him, while we were looking it over. Or we'd been taking pot shots at some stray animal we came across, and he stepped out suddenly from behind a tree and got in the line of fire. They could never prove it wasn't that way.

We stopped finally and sprawled out on the ground side by side in a little open grassy patch under the trees. Even now the fool couldn't keep his mouth shut, couldn't keep from talking about her. Telling me all about how wonderful she was—as if I didn't know—and how lucky he was. "You're not so lucky," I thought to myself, fingering the gun in my pocket.

I left my cigarette in my mouth, and took the gun out and snapped the safety down. Then I reared up on one elbow and pointed it at him, sort of lazy, sort of slow. He'd been looking the other way. He turned his head just then, and when he saw it, instead of getting scared, he asked me in a sort of friendly, drawling way where I got it, and what I was doing carrying it around with me like that.

I just kept it like it was.

Then he laughed and brushed his hand out at it, like at a mosquito, and said, "Don't, Joe. It's liable to go off while you've got it sighted at me like that." And when I still didn't move it, I guess he thought I was trying to play with him. He bunched a fist and pretended to swing it and take a poke at my jaw, but just let it land light.

I couldn't do it, with his face grinning into my own so close. Things kept getting in the way. I saw, instead of his face, the face of a kid of fourteen helping me climb up next to him into a boxcar on a siding. I saw the face of my partner, standing next to me on the takeoff platform, sharing our first spotlight together, the night Pop first broke us into the act. Saying to me out of the corner of his mouth, with a half-scared but awfully proud look, "Are you nervous, Joe? Boy, my knees are knocking together like triphammers!" I couldn't do it.

The thing tipped over of its own weight. I jarred to my feet all of a sudden and grunted, "I'm getting out of here, I'm going back!" and I started to walk away from there fast.

He stayed where he was a minute, overcome by surprise. Then he jumped up and tried to come after me like a fool. He didn't realize how lucky he'd already been once tonight, what a chance he was still taking now. He hollered after me, "What's the matter, Joe? What's your rush? Wait a minute and I'll come with you."

I turned on him and warned him back in a tight, choked voice. "Keep back! Don't walk next to me, understand? Don't walk next to me *until I get out of here!*"

He dropped behind and just stood there looking after me, scratching his head like he couldn't figure out what got into me. I walked away fast. Boy, how fast I walked away from him! I threw the gun into a little lake I passed along the way out.

She was standing waiting on the rooming-house stairs in her wrapper when I got back. She was standing there waiting halfway down from the floor her room was on, almost as if she'd sensed something was wrong, as if she'd had a feeling something had nearly happened tonight. Women are funny that way. She must have been standing there like that for a half an hour or more when I came in. Her face was kind of white too.

It got even whiter, when she saw that it was me and not him.

"Joe?" She said his name in a whisper. "He always leaves me a note when he goes off anyplace—"

"I was with him just now," I said. "He's all right."

I passed by her and went on the rest of the way up without saying anything more. And she looked at me, I could feel her looking. All the way up she looked at me from where she was. That's how I think she knew. But maybe I'm wrong.

They got married a week later. Maybe that hurried it up. Maybe not. Maybe she didn't really guess anything. I know he didn't. We were playing a split week in one of the big upstate cities. They were both late for the Saturday matinee. I got made up and ready, and there was still no sign of either one of them. Our turn didn't come until later, but we'd never missed a grand opening march yet. I went out by the runway leading into the arena, and took my place in the lineup without them. I kept turning my head and looking for them. I knew by now what the reason was.

At the very last minute, all of a sudden there was a lot of shoving and shifting aside behind me, and the two of them showed up, working their way through the other performers and all out of breath. The seams of his trunks were all crooked from pulling them on so fast, and he hadn't had time to put any grease on. But he didn't need it. His face was all lit up. I looked down at her hand and I saw the ring on it.

The band blared up and the three of us went on out.

It was coming now for sure. The hate choking in my chest and the liquid fire running through my veins told me that; I knew this was the last performance I could risk. If I went through any more, it would happen right in the act, and I didn't want that.

I beat it away fast after that show, went off by myself away from the two of them. I went into some eating place just out of habit, sat staring at a cup of coffee that I didn't touch. Then at my usual time for starting back, I got up and walked outside again, still just out of habit. But when I got out on the street, I turned and walked the other way, away from the big auditorium we were using.

I knew I had to stay out of the night performance. I knew what would happen if I went back for it. I was afraid of being in it with Tommy. I knew my only safety lay in missing it.

It was easy at first, while there was lots of time. I roamed around for a while. Finally I came to a little park and sat down on a bench. But as the time for getting back started to tighten up on me, it began to get harder and harder, as though an invisible current had set in, trying to pull me back. I could *feel* it, I tell you, feel the pull of it, like when you're in water and an undertow catches you up.

You see, I'd never missed a show yet. It was my food, my drink, my breath.

I tried to hang onto the park bench I was on, I actually

gripped it with both hands along the edges. I kept talking to myself inside, I kept warning myself: "Stay where you are, now. Stay out of the act, now. You know what's going to happen if you don't! Keep the act clean, at least."

It wouldn't work. I tried not to look at my watch, but there was a big clock there facing the park to tell me anyhow. Eight minutes to show time. You can still make it at an easy walk, from out here where you are. Five minutes. You can still make it, but you'll have to hurry a little now. Four minutes. Three. You ought to have your shirt off already

I couldn't hold out. I got to my feet, like I was being dragged by the scruff of the neck. First I still tried to go the other way, away from the auditorium. I couldn't do that either. My feet turned around under me and started me back the right way. They were a performer's feet, a circus man's feet. You couldn't tell them what to do.

First I was walking slow, still trying to hold out, still trying to fight against it. Then faster, faster all the time—until suddenly I was running like a streak, to make up for lost time. And presto, there I was, back in the dressing room again, all winded and floundering into my chair.

It's an awful feeling, to know what you're going to do if you come back to a place, and yet not be able to stay away.

He was sitting there beside me, finishing up. I didn't look at him.

He didn't say a word to me about their getting married that afternoon; I guess they'd decided to keep it to themselves for a while. All he did say was, "Where'd you disappear to? I wanted to blow you to a swell steak dinner tonight. Nat and me, we both looked high and low for you." So that told me, just the same as if he had.

I sat there in my undershirt; that was as far as I was able to get. I hung onto the edge of the dressing table hard, the way I had that bench in the park, to try to fight it down. I hung on until my knuckles showed white. I was afraid to be in there with him alone like this. There were so many sharp things around loose. And he had that happiness still shining all over his face, almost like phosphorus. He got up to make it decent for me. I said, "Leave the door open."

"There's women out there."

"Leave it open, I tell you! I can go over in the corner. I can hardly breathe in here." I caught hold of my own throat.

He was so dumb. God, how dumb a guy is when he trusts you! "Yeah, it is kind of stuffy," he agreed, with easygoing unconcern. Nothing could have needled him tonight. It was his wedding night. It was also his—

I was in my tights now, but I'd stopped again, I couldn't go ahead. I kept pleading to myself, "Wait till after the show, if you've got to get him. *But don't do it in the act.* Don't go out there with him now, or you're going to do it right in the act!"

He was standing looking over at me from the doorway now, from the passageway outside. He saw me sitting there without moving. He said, "What's the matter?"

I said, "I'm not coming out."

He came in again and stood behind my chair and tried to reason it out with me. He put his hand on the back of my chair. Luckily he didn't put it on me, on my shoulder or anything, or I think it would have happened right then.

I didn't hear most of what he said. I was looking at something in the glass. I seemed to see a death's head in the glass, where our two faces were, his and mine. I'm not kidding, I actually saw it there—some trick of the lighting and shadows, I guess. It came on slow, until I could see the deep, greenish holes where the eye sockets were, and the grinning rows of teeth, and the shiny white dome of the skull. I couldn't see whose face it covered most, his or mine. Then it faded away, slow, again.

He couldn't do anything with me, and the time was

getting shorter. He went outside finally and I heard him whispering to someone down the line. I knew what it was; he was putting her up to work on me, to see if she'd have any better luck. I'd been afraid of that. She was the only one that could, and I didn't want her to try.

I got up quick to try and close the door, but she was already standing there before I could make it. She looked so beautiful it hurt. But she had the wrong hand out, against the edge of the door. The one with the ring on it. His ring.

She said, "Is it something to do with the act, Joe?"

I said, "No, it's nothing to do with the act."

She said, "Then if it's something outside the act, keep it outside the act. This is the act, Joe. If there's one thing I've got no use for, it's a guy that'll let the act down."

I had one last plea left in me. Only one, and then no more. I made it. I made it good and strong too. My whole voice shook. I said, "*Don't* ask me to go out there tonight, will you, Nat? You run through it with him. Do what you can. Fake the triple plays. Only, *don't* ask me to go out there tonight."

She reached out and touched the side of my face, kind of soft. I wish she hadn't. Just as his touch would have meant death, hers meant—"We'll be waiting for you over by the entrance," she said. "There goes the fanfare." The doorway was empty.

I grabbed up my brush and gave a last lick at my hair. My hand stabbed down at the little tube of fixative I sometimes used to shine it up a little. It was a petroleum-jelly base, with a little other stuff added. It was pretty well used up, folded over to within an inch or two of the cap. My hand didn't break motion. It swept it up and stuck it inside the waistband of my trunks. Then I swung around and out, and down the dressing-room alley after her, to take my place in the show.

It went off like clockwork, the turn I mean. It always did, it was such second nature to us by now. The precision climb up the ladders to the two little take off platforms, me on one side of the ring, the two of them over on the other. We even had that timed to a split second, so that the two halves of us always got up to the top at the same instant, not unevenly. Then the steadying of the spots on us, the throwing off of the capes, the dramatic flourishes with the hands. And then into the business.

We mixed it up for a while, and though it might have seemed breakneck to them down below, it was just warm-up stuff to us. "Treading air" from bar to bar, exchanging bars simultaneously so that we passed each other on the fly, turning right-about-face on the wing in midair, from one grip to the next. All that. We'd had that kind of stuff down pat when we were sixteen already. Pop had trained it into us. It was so automatic I could even think while I was doing it. I mean about other things. I didn't tonight; I didn't want to.

I did a specialty, and she did one, and Tommy did a lesser one of his own; not the flash finish yet. Then the three of us worked together in one. The applause sounded like it always did, coming up from way down below: like giant feet treading on gravel. And that brought us up to the break.

We always broke the turn in the middle, and took a breather. We could have run right through it to the end without stopping, without getting too winded, but that was showmanship again. It made it seem like harder work to the audience if we knocked off a minute and passed the cloth around, while the announcer built up what was coming next over the amplifier below.

We were up to the show piece at the end now. That was Tommy's. His blindfold dive down to me, waiting up-side-down for him way down below on the middle trapeze. Three complete turns in the air before he reached me. I knew that was when I was going to get him.

We passed the cloth around, lolling on our perches. I got it from him, and I always sent it on over to her after

I was through with it. We never changed that. It doesn't
pay to vary anything in a precision act, not even the trim-
·mings, like that was.

While I was twirling it around in my hands, I stuck a
finger to my waistband and the tube came up hidden behind
the flourishing cloth. I got the cap off with my nail, and
pinched, and a coil of it spurted out across my palm. It
lay there frozen, like a little twinkling snake. It *was* a snake;
a snake whose bite was death. I got the empty tube back
into my waistband. I could get rid of it easy enough afterwards. And then, still under cover of the flirting cloth, I
greased my wrists up good with it. I saturated the tape
on each one, until they were as slippery as a pair of eels.
That was where he was going to hang onto me, by the
wrists.

It left a sort of cool feeling on my hands, like it always
did when I used it on my hair. And that was all. I sent
the cloth on to her, and that finished its rounds.

I wasn't in any danger, it didn't matter about me, I
used my leg-muscles to hang on by. I'd stay up. Tommy
was the one.

The spiel was through now. They lowered my trap into
position, halfway down, far below the others, to give Tommy
room enough for three spins. She traveled the bars over
to his side and grounded on the platform there, to stand
behind him, ready the blindfold, and poise him on the brink.

I turned over lazily on the bar, hung head-down by
the crevices of my legs, flexed my arms full-length below
me a couple of times, and waited.

He got the spotlight and the play. It was his stunt. It
was also his finish.

A big hush fell. This always got them, every time. Well,
it should have, it was no phony.

I don't know if she found out, or if something really
did go wrong up there. I'll never know. Maybe there was
something about the feel of the cloth when she got it back
from me. Or maybe she got a whiff of a scent that it had

left behind, and remembered having noticed it before that on my hair. Or maybe it was just a guess, her instinct. Like that night in St. Louis, on the stairs.

If she did find out, it must have been hell for her. A hell I'd never wished for her. And only seconds in which to know what to do. The spotlight blazing on them both, for a thousand eyes to see. The drums already beginning to roll. She couldn't grab him and hold him back, we'd have been booed out of the ring and finished in circus business.

But when you love a guy, I suppose there's always a way out.

But maybe it had nothing to do with her at all; maybe it really was a mishap. They'd been married today and maybe they were both a little excited. Or maybe it was just his lucky star.

I missed seeing it at the actual instant it occurred. I heard the gasp go up, and the drums falter. My head was upside-down, and by the time I'd bent my neck to look, his body was already dipping lopsidedly into thin air, off the side of the platform, like when you step into a hole over your head that you're not expecting. He had one hand on the guy rope, that was all that saved him. Anything might have caused it; an accidental nudge of her elbow, or maybe too much of his heel had gone offside at the rim of the platform.

A great shuddering moan of terror, like wind through the trees, came soughing up from below. He went spiralling down, in a sickening, dizzy corkscrew, all the way to the bottom. *But he never let go of the rope.* That one-hand hold on it he crushed tight into a life-and-death grip that nothing could have pried open. And the rope came searing steadily up through this, taking all the skin with it, I suppose, but at least breaking the velocity of his fall.

He landed in a huddle at the bottom. But then he picked himself right up, before anyone could get over to him. So he was evidently all right, nothing broken. You could tell by the way he stood there, though, head low, hand held tightly pressed between his thighs, that he was in stiff pain, couldn't go ahead. Probably his hand was raw.

She never came down off the platform. She was a natural-born trouper if there ever was one. Before they'd even finished helping him out of the ring, she must have passed some signal that I missed seeing, both to the announcer below and the electrician's box way up high in the flies. Suddenly the spotlight had blazed out on her again, brighter than ever, the announcer was booming out that the event would continue and she was adjusting the blind to her eyes.

So I guess she didn't know, after all, and it was just a star, not her.

There was a split second in which she signalled me to drop my head and begin the count, with her eyes still clear, then before I could get my own maddened message back—to stop, not to go ahead—the bandage had dropped over her eyes and I was cut off from her.

The drums began their growling thunder. My voice couldn't reach her now.

There was no way to stop those drums. No way but one.

I opened my left leg a little, and I slipped down a notch on that side. I opened my right a little, and I dipped down a little on that side. They couldn't see it yet, nobody but me.

My left leg was starting to slip down by itself now, without my having to open it any more. Now my right was too. The bar was coming free. It was out. I heard the roar from hundreds of throats come shooting up past me, and I knew that was death.

He looked so jaunty, he looked so husky, he looked so dead.

There was a girl there, standing looking at him. Just standing looking at him, as though she'd never get through.

There was a young fellow standing beside her with his arm around her, looking at her instead. There was a detective there, jotting something in a notebook. He was all through now. He'd found out all anyone could tell him. Anyone living.

This is what he jotted:

Name: Crosby, Joseph.
Age: Twenty-five.
Profession: Trapeze artist.
Cause of death: Accidental fall while engaged in giving a performance.

MOTIVE FOR MURDER

Talmage Powell

Talmage Powell has been a professional writer for more than forty years, having made his first sale (of a mystery novelette to a pulp magazine) in 1943. Hundreds of other stories and twenty novels followed; among his score of books are five in an excellent series featuring a Tampa private detective named Ed Rivers, and such nonseries suspense novels as The Smasher *(1959) and* The Girl Who Killed Things *(1960). "Motive for Murder" is Powell at his criminous short-story best—the poignant tale of a strange carny triangle involving Darlene and Gaspard, the Flying Angels of Death, and one half of a set of Siamese twins.*

You might have seen her when she was performing with Great American Carnivals, Inc. If so, you will remember. . . .

Ladies and gentlemen, she was the one and only Darlene, very dainty and beautiful, with blue eyes and hair like a burst of sunlight. She was half of the act billed as Darlene and Gaspard, Flying Angels of Death.

She and Gaspard performed on the high pole. You have seen such acts, a series of handstands and somersaults done on a perch of slender, swaying steel two hundred feet above the midway. The different thing about their act was its climax, when Gaspard fell and Darlene, trying to catch him, was snatched from her tiny platform. The gasp of horror from the multitude of white, upturned faces would give way to nervous titters when the cable about Gaspard's ankle reached its full length and swung them, pendulum-like, he upside-down with his hands locked with Darlene's.

The climax was as dangerous as it looked; for the fall had to occur in the proper moment for the swaying pole to act as a cushion. Else, gravity and inertia would have snatched Darlene from Gaspard's grip.

Five nights a week and twice each night the act worked, the free attraction to bring the marks flocking to the midway.

Gaspard came of old circus stock; by the time he could walk, he knew the proper way to land in a net—a device which he and Darlene disdained the use of. Show business was his world. He knew nothing else, and was satisfied with the knowledge. He was a perfect foil for Darlene, tall and dark, with movements that reminded one of a black leopard.

He loved Darlene as only the temperamental daredevil can love. She was fond of him; but she could not love him. She loved no one until Castor and Pollux joined the show, as the highest paid attraction in the pit show where I was talker and ran the bally.

The chemistry whereby she fell in love with Pollux remains one of the mysteries of Woman. I think she was first touched with deep compassion, Pollux being so completely normal except for the membrane at the base of his back which since birth had joined him to his twin, Castor. Then she discovered Pollux's wit and intelligence. They shared an interest in books, an interest that Gaspard scorned. Late at night, when silence haunted the midway, she would go to the twins' trailer. There, Pollux would read to her while Castor, a pessimistic, stunted, fearful caricature of Pollux, slept or brooded in silence.

Gaspard laughed at the situation at first; later he viewed it with mounting fury. One night as Darlene came from Pollux's trailer, Gaspard stood in the shadows and watched her throw a kiss and start toward her own trailer.

Gaspard had been drinking, a new custom with him, and grabbed her arm roughly.

"Let me go!" Darlene said.

"Not until I have a word with you!"

The commotion brought Pollux to the door of his trailer, Castor following most unwillingly.

"Take your hands off her," Pollux said with enough bravery for any man.

"Come out and I'll do what nature failed to do—tear you apart and make two of you!"

At this, Castor cried aloud in terror. Pollux choked on his anger and would have dragged his twin behind him to do battle, but Castor managed to catch hold of a pole. Castor clung there, moaning piteously, while Gaspard drunkenly cursed and tried to defend himself against the golden wildcat he found suddenly in his possession.

I and the other carnies were awakened by the set-to. We came out of our trailers, armed with bung starters and blackjacks, thinking it a hey rube.

I managed to take Darlene off Gaspard's hands, having long been a sort of father confessor around the show.

"Happy," she wept against my ample shoulder, "I'll despise Gaspard to the longest day I live." Then she told me what Gaspard had said to Pollux. Gaspard was too proud to apologize. Old T.D. came out of the chief wagon and finally got everyone back to bed. Each carny obeyed T.D.'s order, but there was a troubled look in every face. There was tension and silence in the night. We were like a family, and now hatred had come into our midst.

In midseason we swung west out of the Carolinas into Tennessee. We caught a stretch of rainy, cold weather and bogged down in a little town near Nashville, where Darlene came down with a cold. Everybody's nerves got on edge, the weather ruining business and keeping us clammed in the confines of our trailers. Gaspard's new attitude helped in no wise at times like these. He had grown icy, aloof, keeping his humiliation inside of him.

Things can start happening under such circumstances. The fat girl began losing weight. The knife-thrower's partner lost her good luck charm and developed a dread of the flashing steel. One of Madame Vittorio's snakes died, and the best-looking blonde in the kutch ran off to get married.

We played the town of Dinsmore, Darlene pridefully not missing a performance, though she was still miserable with her cold. Nothing had had the slightest curative effect on the cold. She was now taking liberal quantities of vitamin capsules to keep her strength up and fight off the illness.

The cold wasn't her greatest misery. Words would not lighten her heart. I tried them: "Look, honey, why worry so? The act is going, the smesh is coming in, you and Pollux have time together."

"But it isn't the same, Happy. Gaspard destroyed something when he sneered at Pollux as a geek that night. Each time Pollux looks at Gaspard he is reminded of the difference in them. Gaspard is up there against the sky, so free.

And he—my poor Pollux—with Castor a twisted, whining burden growing out of him. . ."

My heart was heavy for them, for the beautiful young girl and the fine young man who must forever carry with him his dour brother. Castor I pitied. Imagine the mental torture that must have been his, helplessly joined to a brother to whom he was in every way inferior. Small wonder that sometimes Castor's brooding became so intense that he partook lightly of a drug to give him relief in sleep.

I didn't see Darlene again that night until it was time for the high act to go on. Drums rolled, spotlights converged on the high pole with its banners fluttering in the muggy breeze, and Darlene, with Gaspard close behind, began the long ascent.

I was out behind the pit show, catching a smoke. Several other performers shared my notion and were sitting on canvas stools or talking together in groups of two or three. We had little to do until Darlene and Gaspard finished and turned loose on us a swarm of people keyed to high excitement by the act and its terrifying climax.

Castor, in his cowering attitude, and Pollux, erect, stood near me. Pollux watched the tiny golden doll high on the swaying steel needle, and Castor made a noise of distaste. "Courtship, love," Castor said, "a fool have I for a brother! The vixen is crazed by too many somersaults at high altitude. I, Castor, made it my business to study people, perceiving the twisted pathways of their minds as they parade past us on the walk-around, feasting on the sight of abnormality. My brother's blindness is not my blindness; I see that she uses a fool who dares dream of normality in order that she can persecute Gaspard. Why? Because she hates Gaspard. Hates and resents his power of life and death over her twice each night . . ."

Pollux was trembling. "Hush!" Castor lapsed into surly silence and Pollux tried to smile the sadness from his white face as he watched the high pole.

Before the act was three minutes underway, a dreadful feeling that something was wrong came to me. Darlene's timing was faulty as she and Gaspard built toward the climax.

Then the drums stopped, bringing a silence that caused a catch of the breath. While Darlene swayed on the tiny platform, Gaspard climbed thirty feet higher, to the very tip of the pole. Back and forth he rocked, as if daring the pole to whip him into space. Then the pole obliged.

His trajectory flashed him past the tiny platform. Darlene reached. His weight swept her into space. There came the muffled scream of the crowd, but this time it did not give way to nervous gasps of relief. People knocked their neighbors down to get away from the spot where her plummeting body would land, while high against the sky, swaying like the pendulum of a clock that's running down, hung Gaspard, with empty hands. . . .

It was impossible to get through the mass of people, who were in the grip of panic and confusion. I helped the twins to their trailer. Pollux was trembling so violently that I said to Castor, "Give me a little of your drug."

"I haven't any," Castor said.

I sent the human skeleton to the chief wagon for a bottle of T.D.'s brandy. Pollux drank enough of that to stop the shivers that chased over him.

I tried to tell Pollux that perhaps the fall hadn't killed her. But I couldn't meet his eyes. I busted the pitch. We knew that her chances to survive such a fall were so slim as to be nonexistent.

When I went out of the trailer there was one angry sentence passing from mouth to mouth: "Gaspard—may he never be called carny again!"

The show was of course held up while Darlene's body was shipped to the small New York town where she came from, and while the police conducted an investigation.

As a rejected suitor, Gaspard had motive to kill her,

and he was held in jail for three days. Many of us who knew the story were called at the inquest to testify. None spoke to Gaspard, whose face reflected a burning inner torment.

Tears spilled on his cheeks as he told the jury: "Drop her? Never—I loved her. She was ill; she'd had a cold for several days. Twice that night on the high pole I begged her to go down. She would not. She was too proud. We went through the fall. We hit the end of the cable and it snatched us hard, as always. Her strength went away and my strength alone was not great enough to hold her against that force. She slipped—and I wish I might tell you that I dropped her; for then I should die too."

The jury returned a verdict of accidental death and Gaspard was released. He came to the lot Friday afternoon. He was miserably drunk. Reeling down the midway with a bottle in his hand, he approached the carnies one by one.

"She was sick. She slipped. I didn't drop her! Do you understand?"

The carnies said not a word to him, continuing their work as if he did not exist. A rube jury might swallow his story; but the carnies had seen performers work in the first stages of pneumonia. A cold sap her strength? To a fatal extent?

Gaspard hired two men from town to take his rigging down. The show moved on. We got grapevine news of him. We learned that, within a week of his leaving us, he had been thrown out of a flophouse, drunk and broke. He tried to join another show. He sank to the point where he pleaded for a chance to do a single. He would join the circuit as a hated pariah.

J. R. Easley of Eagle Shows gave him a second chance. Gaspard had his rigging set up. For the first time since her death, he tried to mount the high pole. His feet, hands, and heart failed him. He came down to get drunk again, to forget the ghost of her on the tiny platform against the sky. Perhaps, somehow, he *had* dropped her. He was sure of nothing any more, he said; he sold his rig and squandered the money on drink.

Pollux existed, and little more can be said for his miserable state of being. Castor, on the other hand, grew in smug, scornful self-assurance. He took pleasure from knowing that she was gone. He began to drink as if to spur his release from tension and often taunted Pollux with a recounting of her fall.

My nerves were shorter than usual the night Castor and Pollux failed to come out of their trailer to get ready for the bally. I sent the India rubber man to see what was keeping them. He returned in a state of alarm so great he could barely speak, trying to tell me something about the twins and slashed wrists.

I ran across the lot to their trailer. They were lying back to back. Castor was snoring, drunk. While Pollux's wrists pumped red.

Enough sanity returned to me after a moment for me to run to the big wagon, where T.D. always had a telephone strung in. While the midway blared its usual din, I made a pitch over the phone for a doctor and ambulance.

Perhaps you read in the papers about the emergency surgery that was done that night to cut the twins apart. Both lived for a short time; then it was apparent that only Pollux would survive. As dawn broke, the quiet group of carnies at the hospital received the news of Castor's death.

The show had to move on, of course. It was not until we were in winter quarters that I heard that Pollux was fully recovered and released from the hospital.

In the spring I saw him, almost bumping into him as I crossed the lot one night.

"Hello, Happy," he said.

I'm afraid I stared for a second. I'd always been so used to seeing two of him.

"You're looking kosher," I said. "What are you doing now?"

"Planning to buy myself a piece of a show one of these days. I saved some change when we topped the ten-in-one. But the first thing on my agenda is to find Gaspard. Heard anything of him?"

"Not since last winter. Somebody was telling me Gaspard had rolled from the gutter into the charity ward of a hospital for awhile."

"Then I must find him very soon. He didn't drop Darlene, Happy. Castor killed her."

The marks surged around us. A pitchman tried to talk a rube into throwing more baseballs at weighted, wooden milk bottles. A girl on the ferris wheel screamed laughter and the calliope wheezed "The Skater's Waltz." And I stood far away from it all, a cold wind blowing down my neck.

"A thousand times I relived it with her, Happy, that last night on the high pole. I saw the first break in her time. I knew she wasn't right; it was as if she were doped.

"Then I remembered her capsules, which she'd left in my trailer. Castor had spilled them. There were only three capsules in the bottle when she came for them that night. Castor knew what time she would go on with the act. He got her water to take the capsules and insisted that she accept his money for another bottle as his apology for spilling them."

I stared at Pollux, unable to speak, doing some remembering myself. Castor had had no sleeping drug when I'd asked for it to ease Pollux the night Darlene died.

"Castor drugged her," I said.

Pollux nodded. "He substituted the drug for the vitamins. A simple thing, really. We were so accustomed to each other that half the time neither was conscious of the other being there. While I read or listened to the radio or did any one of a dozen things he could have made the substitution."

I felt sweat running down the sides of my face. A drugged girl . . . a high pole whipping back and forth . . .

murder. She might have plunged any time during the act. It had been Gaspard's misfortune that she'd fallen at the climax.

"What on earth led him to do it, Pollux?"

"I loved Darlene," Pollux said simply. "I wanted to marry her. I wanted to have us cut apart. The mere thought of the cutting of a tie he'd known since birth terrified Castor. Surgery terrified him no less. Darlene was the threat to his security, his safety."

Pollux watched the excitement—hungry marks milling about the midway. Then he was able to speak again. "After she was gone, after I had it all figured out in my mind, I told Castor. He was drinking and mocked me. The law could not execute him without executing me; neither could a court order surgery that might endanger my life as well as his.

"I had pinned down his motive, his method, his weapon. Was there to be no completion of the natural order of things, of his having to face his guilt? My brother, yes, but a murderer. I could not stay attached to him longer. I did then what I had to do. What else could I have done, Happy?"

It wasn't for me to say. He had risked his own life so that they would have to be cut apart.

"It's for this reason that I must find Gaspard and see that he knows the truth," Pollux said.

Pollux searched three months before he found Gaspard working as a roustabout with a cheap show. He sobered Gaspard up, brought him a solid meal and new clothes. Then he loaned Gaspard the money to buy a new rig. He was there the night Gaspard, in spangled tights, appeared for his first performance.

They faced each other, the two men who'd once been hated rivals, enemies. They shook hands. Then Gaspard did a strange thing. He bowed. "I bow," Gaspard said, "to a courage and honor far greater than mine."

"There is the music, Gaspard."

"Yes, and something of her waits up there."

Pollux looked at the tip of the pole trapped by spotlights against the black heights of the night sky. Some of the suffering and pain faded from his upraised face, and he stood there as if glimpsing something the eyes about him could not see.

THE HOUSE OF DARKNESS

Ellery Queen

The House of Darkness is the fun house at Monsieur Dieudonné Duval's amusement park, but it ceases to be fun on the day Ellery Queen and his young friend Djuna visit it and stumble over a corpse. How could someone shoot a man from a distance in total blackness? And who could that someone be? It is a task fit for Mr. Queen, the ratiocinative sleuth who starred in numerous clever novels and short stories over a period of more than forty years. The fictional Queen's creator(s), as many readers know, was the collaborative team of Frederic Dannay (1905–1982) and Manfred B. Lee (1905–1971). Dannay and Lee—who were cousins— began their career with the publication of The Roman Hat Mystery *in 1929, and went on to make their pseudonym— and their character's name—known to millions for more than fifty years.*

75

"And this," proclaimed Monsieur Dieudonné Duval with a deprecatory twirl of his mustache, "is of an ingenuity incomparable, my friend. It is not I that should say so, perhaps. But examine it. Is it not the—how do you say—the pip?"

Mr. Ellery Queen wiped his neck and sat down on a bench facing the little street of amusements. "It is indeed," he sighed, "the pip, my dear Duval. I quite share your creative enthusiasm. . . . Djuna, for the love of mercy! Sit still." The afternoon sun was tropical and his whites had long since begun to cling.

"Let's go on it," suggested Djuna hopefully.

"Let's not and say we did," groaned Mr. Queen, stretching his weary legs. He had promised Djuna this lark all summer, but he had failed to reckon with the Law of Diminishing Returns. He had already—under the solicitous wing of Monsieur Duval, that tireless demon of the scenic-designing art; one of the variegated hundreds of his amazing acquaintanceship—partaken of the hectic allurements of Joyland Amusement Park for two limb-rending hours, and they had taken severe toll of his energy. Djuna, of course, what with excitement, sheer pleasure, and indefatigable youth, was a law unto himself; he was still as fresh as the breeze blowing in from the sea.

"You will find it of the most amusing," said Monsieur Duval eagerly, showing his white teeth. "It is my *chef-d'oeuvre* in Joyland." Joyland was something new to the county, a model amusement park meticulously landscaped and offering a variety of ingenious entertainments and mechanical divertissements—planned chiefly by Duval—not to be duplicated anywhere along the Atlantic. "A house of darkness . . . That, my friend, was an inspiration!"

"I think it's swell," said Djuna craftily, glancing at Ellery.

"A mild word, Djun'," said Mr. Queen, wiping his neck again. *The House of Darkness* which lay across the thoroughfare did not look too diverting to a gentleman of even catholic tastes. It was a composite of all the haunted houses of fact and fiction. A diabolic imagination had planned its crazy walls and tumbledown roofs. It reminded Ellery—although he was tactful enough not to mention it to Monsieur Duval—of a set out of a German motion picture he had once seen, *The Cabinet of Dr. Caligari.* It wound and leaned and stuck out fantastically and had broken false windows and doors and decrepit balconies. Nothing was normal or decent. Constructed in a huge rectangle, its three wings overlooked a court which had been fashioned into a nightmarish little street with broken cobbles and tired lampposts; and its fourth side was occupied by the ticket booth and a railing. The street in the open court was atmosphere only; the real dirty work, thought Ellery disconsolately, went on behind those grim surrealistic walls.

"*Alors,*" said Monsieur Duval, rising, "if it is permitted that I excuse myself? For a moment only. I shall return. Then we shall visit . . . *Pardon!*" He bowed his trim little figure away and went quickly toward the booth, near which a young man in park uniform was haranguing a small group.

Mr. Queen sighed and closed his eyes. The park was never crowded; but on a hot summer's afternoon it was almost deserted, visitors preferring the adjoining bathhouse and beach. The camouflaged loudspeakers concealed all over the park played dance music to almost empty aisles and walks.

"That's funny," remarked Djuna, crunching powerfully upon a pink, conic section of popcorn.

"Eh?" Ellery opened a bleary eye.

"I wonder where *he's* goin'. 'N awful hurry."

"Who?" Ellery opened the other eye and followed the direction of Djuna's absent nod. A man with a massive body and thick gray hair was striding purposefully along up the walk. He wore a slouch hat pulled down over his eyes and dark clothes, and his heavy face was raw with perspiration. There was something savagely decisive in his bearing.

"Ouch," murmured Ellery with a wince. "I sometimes wonder where people get the energy."

"Funny, all right," mumbled Djuna, munching.

"Most certainly is," said Ellery sleepily, closing his eyes again. "You've put your finger on a nice point, my lad. Never occurred to me before, but it's true that there's something unnatural in a man's hurrying in an amusement park of a hot afternoon. Chap might be the White Rabbit, eh, Djuna? Running about so. But the *genus* Joylander is, like all such orders, a family of inveterate strollers. Well, well! A distressing problem." He yawned.

"He must be crazy," said Djuna.

"No, no, my son, that's the conclusion of a sloppy thinker. The proper deduction begins with the observation that Mr. Rabbit hasn't come to Joyland to dabble in the delights of Joyland *per se,* if you follow me. Joyland is, then, merely a means to an end. In a sense Mr. Rabbit—note the cut of his wrinkled clothes, Djuna; he's a distinguished bunny—is oblivious to Joyland. It doesn't exist for him. He barges past *Dante's Inferno* and the perilous *Dragon-Fly* and the popcorn and frozen custard as if he is blind or they're invisible. . . . The diagnosis? A date, I should say, with a lady. And the gentleman is late. *Quod erat demonstrandum.* . . . Now for heaven's sake, Djuna, eat your petrified shoddy and leave me in peace."

"It's all gone," said Djuna wistfully, looking at the empty bag.

"I am here!" cried a gay Gallic voice, and Ellery suppressed another groan at the vision of Monsieur Duval bouncing toward them. "Shall we go, my friends? I promise you entertainment of the most divine . . . *Ouf!*" Monsieur Duval expelled his breath violently and staggered backward. Ellery sat up in alarm. But it was only the massive man with the slouch hat, who had collided with the dapper little Frenchman, almost upsetting him, muttered something meant to be conciliatory, and hurried on. *"Cochon,"* said Monsieur Duval softly, his black eyes glittering. Then he shrugged his slim shoulders and looked after the man. "Apparently," said Ellery dryly, "our White Rabbit can't resist the lure of your *chef-d'oeuvre,* Duval. I believe he's stopped to listen to the blandishments of your barker!" "White Rabbit?" echoed the Frenchman, puzzled. "But yes, he is a customer. *Voilà!* One does not fight with such, *hein?* Come, my friends!"

The massive man had halted abruptly in his tracks and pushed into the thick of the group listening to the attendant. Ellery sighed, and rose, and they strolled across the walk.

The young man was saying confidentially: "Ladies and gentlemen, you haven't visited Joyland if you haven't visited *The House of Darkness.* There's never been a thrill like it! It's new, different. Nothing like it in any amusement park in the *world!* It's grim. It's shivery. It's terrifying. . . ."

A tall young woman in front of them laughed and said to the old gentleman leaning on her arm: "Oh, daddy, let's try it! It's sure to be loads of fun." Ellery saw the white head under its Leghorn nod with something like amusement, and the young woman edged forward through the crowd, eagerly. The old man did not release her arm. There was a curious stiffness in his carriage, a slow shuffle in his walk, that puzzled Ellery. The young woman purchased two tickets at the booth and led the old man along a fenced lane inside.

"The House of Darkness," the young orator was declaiming in a dramatic whisper, "is . . . just . . . that. There's not a light you can see by in the whole place! You have to feel your way, and if you aren't *feeling* well . . . ha, ha! Pitch-dark. Ab-so-lutely *black* . . . I see the gentleman in the brown tweeds is a little frightened. Don't be afraid. We've taken care of even the faintest-hearted—"

"Ain't no sech thing," boomed an indignant bass voice from somewhere in the van of the crowd. There was a mild titter. The faint-heart addressed by the attendant was a powerful young Negro, attired immaculately in symphonic brown, his straw skimmer dazzling against the sooty carbon of his skin. A pretty colored girl giggled on his arm. "C'mon, honey, we'll show 'em! Heah—two o' them theah tickets, Mistuh!" The pair beamed as they hurried after the tall young woman and her father.

"You could wander around in the dark inside," cried the young man enthusiastically, "for *hours* looking for the way out. But if you can't stand the suspense there's a little green arrow, every so often along the route, that points to an invisible door, and you just go through that door and you'll find yourself in a dark passage that runs *all* around the house in the back and leads to the—uh—ghostly cellar, the assembly-room, downstairs there. Only *don't* go out any of those green-arrow doors unless you want to *stay* out, because they open only one way—into the hall, ha, ha! You can't get back into *The House of Darkness* proper again, you see. But nobody uses that *easy* way out. Everybody follows the little *red* arrows. . . ."

A man with a full, rather untidy black beard, shabby broad-brimmed hat, a soft limp tie, and carrying a flat case which looked like an artist's box, purchased a ticket and hastened down the lane. His cheek bones were flushed with self-consciousness as he ran the gauntlet of curious eyes.

"Now what," demanded Ellery, "is the idea of *that*, Duval?"

"The arrows?" Monsieur Duval smiled apologetically. "A concession to the old, the infirm, and the apprehensive. It is really of the most blood-curdling, my masterpiece, Mr. Queen. So—" He shrugged. "I have planned a passage to permit of exit at any time. Without it one could, as the admirable young man so truly says, wander about for hours. The little green and red arrows are nonluminous; they do not disturb the blackness."

The young man asserted: "But if you follow the red arrows you are bound to come out. Some of them go the right way, others don't. But eventually . . . after exciting adventures on the way . . . Now, ladies and gentlemen, for the price of—"

"Come *on,*" panted Djuna, overwhelmed by this salesmanship. "Boy, I bet that's *fun.*"

"I bet," said Ellery gloomily as the crowd began to shuffle and mill about. Monsieur Duval smiled with delight and with a gallant bow presented two tickets.

"I shall await you, my friends, here," he announced. "I am most curious to hear of your reactions to my little *maison des ténèbres.* Go," he chuckled, "with God."

As Ellery grunted, Djuna led the way in prancing haste down the fenced lane to a door set at an insane angle. An attendant took the tickets and pointed a solemn thumb over his shoulder. The light of day struggled down a flight of tumbledown steps. "Into the crypt, eh?" muttered Ellery. "Ah, the young man's 'ghostly cellar.' Dieudonné, I could cheerfully strangle you!"

They found themselves in a long narrow cellar-like chamber dimly illuminated by bulbs festooned with spurious spider-webs. The chamber had a dank appearance and crumbly walls, and it was presided over by a courteous skeleton who took Ellery's Panama, gave him a brass disc, and deposited the hat in one of the partitions of a long wooden rack. Most of the racks were empty, although Ellery noticed the artist's box in one of the partitions and the white-haired old man's Leghorn in another. The rite was somehow ominous, and Djuna shivered with ecstatic anticipation. An iron grating divided the cellar in two, and Ellery reasoned that visitors to the place emerged after their adventures into the division beyond the grating, redeemed their checked belongings through the window in the grate, and climbed to blessed daylight through another stairway in the right-hand wing.

"Come *on,*" said Djuna again, impatiently. "Gosh, you're slow. Here's the way in." And he ran toward a crazy door on the left which announced *Entrance.* Suddenly he halted and waited for Ellery, who was ambling reluctantly along behind. "I saw him," he whispered.

"Eh? Whom?"

"*Him.* The Rabbit!"

Ellery started. "Where?"

"He just went inside there." Djuna's passionate gamin-eyes narrowed. "Think he's got his date in *here?*"

"Pesky queer place to have one, I'll confess," murmured Ellery, eying the crazy door with misgivings. "And yet logic . . . Now, Djuna, it's no concern of ours. Let's take our punishment like men and get the devil out of here. I'll go first."

"I wanna go first!"

"Over my dead body. I promised Dad Queen I'd bring you back—er—alive. Hold on to my coat—tightly, now! Here we go."

What followed is history. The Queen clan, as Inspector Richard Queen has often pointed out, is made of the stuff of heroes. And yet while Ellery was of the unpolluted and authentic blood, it was not long before he was feeling his way with quivering desperation and wishing himself at least a thousand light-years away.

The place was fiendish. From the moment they stepped through the crazy doorway to fall down a flight of padded stairs and land with a gentle bump on something which squealed hideously and fled from beneath them, they knew the tortures of the damned. There was no conceivable way of orienting themselves; they were in the deepest, thickest, blackest darkness Ellery had ever had the misfortune to encounter. All they could do was grope their way, one shrinking foot at a time, and pray for the best. It was literally impossible to see their hands before their faces.

They collided with walls which retaliated ungratefully with an electric shock. They ran into things which were all rattling bones and squeaks. Once they followed a tiny arrow of red light which had no sheen and found a hole in a wall just large enough to admit a human form if its owner crawled like an animal. They were not quite prepared for what they encountered on the other side: a floor which tipped precariously under their weight and, to Ellery's horror, slid them gently downward toward the other side of the room—if it was a room—and through a gap to a padded floor three feet below. . . . Then there was the incident of the flight of steps which made you mount rapidly and get nowhere, since the steps were on a treadmill going the other way; the wall which fell on your head; the labyrinth where the passage was just wide enough for a broad man's shoulders and just high enough for a gnome walking erect; the grating which blew blasts of frigid air up your legs; the earthquake room; and such abodes of pleasantry. And, to frazzle already frayed nerves, the air was filled with rumbles, gratings, clankings, whistlings, crashes and explosions in a symphony of noises which would have done credit to the inmates of Bedlam.

"Some fun, eh, kid?" croaked Ellery feebly, landing on his tail after an unexpected slide. Then he said some unkind things about Monsieur Dieudonné Duval under his breath. "Where are we now?"

"Boy, is it *dark*," said Djuna with satisfaction, clutching Ellery's arm. "I can't see a thing, can you?"

Ellery grunted and began to grope. "This looks promising." His knuckles had rapped on a glassy surface. He felt it all over; it was a narrow panel, but taller than he. There were cracks along the sides which suggested that the panel was a door or window. But search as he might he could find no knob or latch. He bared a blade of his penknife and began to scratch away at the glass, which reason told him must have been smeared with thick opaque paint. But after several minutes of hot work he had uncovered only a faint and miserable sliver of light.

"That's not it," he said wearily. "Glass door or window here, and that pinline of light suggests it opens onto a balcony or something, probably overlooking the court. We'll have to find—"

"*Ow!*" shrieked Djuna from somewhere behind him. There was a scraping sound, followed by a thud.

Ellery whirled. "For heaven's sake, Djuna, what's the matter?"

The boy's voice wailed from a point close at hand in the darkness. "I was lookin' for how to get out an'—an' I slipped on somethin' an' fell!"

"Oh." Ellery sighed with relief. "From the yell you unloosed I thought a banshee had attacked you. Well, pick yourself up. It's not the first fall you've taken in this confounded hole."

"B-but it's *wet,*" blubbered Djuna.

"Wet?" Ellery groped toward the anguished voice and seized a quivering hand. "Where?"

"On the f-floor. I got some of it on my hand when I slipped. My other hand. It—it's wet an' sticky an'—an' warm."

"Wet and sticky and wa . . ." Ellery released the boy's hand and dug about in his clothes until he found his tiny pencil-flashlight. He pressed the button with the most curious feeling of drama. There was something tangibly unreal, and yet, final, in the darkness. Djuna panted by his side. . . .

It was a moderately sane door with only a suggestion of cubistic outline, a low lintel, and a small knob. The door was shut. Something semi-liquid and dark red in color stained the floor, emanating from the other side of the crack.

"Let me see your hand," said Ellery tonelessly. Djuna, staring, tendered a small thin fist. Ellery turned it over and gazed at the palm. It was scarlet. He raised it to his nostrils and sniffed. Then he took out his handkerchief almost absently and wiped the scarlet away. "Well! That hasn't the smell of paint, eh, Djuna? And I scarcely think Duval would have so far let enthusiasm run away with better sense as to pour anything else on the floor as atmosphere." He spoke soothingly, divided between the stained floor and the dawning horror on Djuna's face. "Now, now, son. Let's open this door."

He shoved. The door stirred a half-inch, stuck. He set his lips and rammed, pushing with all his strength. There was something obstructing the door, something large and heavy. It gave way stubbornly, an inch at a time. . . .

He blocked Djuna's view deliberately, sweeping the flashlight's thin finger about the room disclosed by the opening of the door. It was perfectly octagonal, devoid of fixtures. Just eight walls, a floor, and a ceiling. There were two other doors besides the one in which he stood. Over one there was a red arrow, over the other a green. Both doors were shut. . . . Then the light swept sidewise and down to the door he had pushed open, seeking the obstruction.

The finger of light touched something large and dark and shapeless on the floor, and quite still. It sat doubled up like a jackknife, rump to the door. The finger fixed itself on four blackish holes in the middle of the back, from which a ragged cascade of blood had gushed, soaking the coat on its way to the floor.

Ellery growled something to Djuna and knelt, raising the head of the figure. It was the massive White Rabbit, and he was dead.

When Mr. Queen rose he was pale and abstracted. He swept the flash slowly about the floor. A trail of red led to the dead man from across the room. Diagonally opposite lay a short-barreled revolver. The smell of powder still lay heavily over the room.

"Is he—is he—?" whispered Djuna.

Ellery grabbed the boy's arm and hustled him back into the room they had just left. His flashlight illuminated the glass door on whose surface he had scratched. He kicked high, and the glass shivered as the light of day rushed in. Hacking out an aperture large enough to permit passage of his body, he wriggled past the broken glass and found himself on one of the fantastic little balconies overlooking the open inner court of *The House of Darkness*. A crowd was collecting below, attracted by the crash of falling glass.

He made out the dapper figure of Monsieur Duval by the ticket booth, in agitated conversation with the khaki-clad special officer, one of the regular Joyland police.

"Duval!" he shouted. "Who's come out of the *House*?"

"Eh?" gulped the little Frenchman.

"Since I went in? Quick, man, don't stand there gaping!"

"Who has come out?" Monsieur Duval licked his lips, staring up with scared black eyes. "But no one has come out, Mr. Queen. . . . What is it that is the matter? Have you—your head—the sun—"

"Good!" yelled Ellery. "Then he's still in this confounded labyrinth. Officer, send in an alarm for the regular county police. See that nobody leaves. Arrest 'em as soon as they try to come out. A man has been murdered up here!"

The note, in a woman's spidery scrawl, said: "Darling Anse—I *must* see you. It's important. Meet me at the old place, Joyland, Sunday afternoon, three o'clock, in that House of Darkness. I'll be awfully careful not to be seen. Especially this time. *He suspects.* I don't know what to do. I love you, love you!!!—Madge."

Captain Ziegler of the county detectives cracked his knuckles and barked: "That's the payoff, Mr. Queen. Fished it out of his pocket. Now who's Madge, and who the hell's the guy that 'suspects'? Hubby, d'ye suppose?"

The room was slashed with a dozen beams. Police crisscrossed flashlights in a pattern as bizarre as the shape of the chamber, with the shedding lantern held high by a policeman over the dead man as their focal point. Six people were lined up against one of the eight walls; five of them glared, mesmerized, at the still heap in the center of the rays. The sixth—the white-haired old man, still leaning on the arm of the tall young woman—was looking directly before him.

"Hmm," said Ellery; he scanned the prisoners briefly.

"You're sure there's no one else skulking in the *House,* Captain Ziegler?"

"That's the lot of 'em. Mr. Duval had the machinery shut off. He led us through himself, searched every nook and cranny. And, since nobody left this hellhole, the killer must be one o' these six." The detective eyed them coldly; they all flinched—except the old man.

"Duval," murmured Ellery. Monsieur Duval started; he was deadly pale. "There's no 'secret' method of getting out of here unseen?"

"Ah, no, no, Mr. Queen! Here, I shall at once secure a copy of the plans myself, show you . . ."

"Scarcely necessary."

"The—the assembly-chamber is the sole means of emerging," stammered Duval. "Eh, that this should happen to—"

Ellery said quietly to a dainty woman, somberly gowned, who hugged the wall: "*You're* Madge, aren't you?" He recalled now that she was the only one of the six prisoners he had not seen while listening with Djuna and Monsieur Duval to the oration of the barker outside. She must have preceded them all into the *House.* The five others were here—the tall young woman and her odd father, the bearded man with his artist's tie, and the burly young Negro and his pretty mulatto companion. "Your name, please— your last name?"

"I—I'm not Madge," she whispered, edging, shrinking away. There were half-moons of violet shadow under her tragic eyes. She was perhaps thirty-five, the wreck of a once beautiful woman. Ellery got the curious feeling that it was not age, but fear, which had ravaged her.

"That's Dr. Hardy," said the tall young woman suddenly in a choked voice. She gripped her father's arm as if she were already sorry she had spoken.

"Who?" asked Captain Ziegler quickly.

"The . . . dead man. Dr. Anselm Hardy, the eye specialist. Of New York City."

"That's right," said the small quiet man kneeling by
the corpse. He tossed something over to the detective.
"Here's one of his cards."

"Thanks, Doc. What's *your* name, Miss?"

"Nora Reis." The tall young woman shivered. "This is
my father, Matthew Reis. We don't know anything about
this—this horrible thing. We've just come out to Joyland
today for some fun. If we'd known—"

"Nora, my dear," said her father gently; but neither
his eyes nor his head moved from their fixed position.

"So you know the dead man, hey?" Ziegler's disagreea-
ble face expressed heavy suspicion.

"If I may," said Matthew Reis. There was a soft musical
pitch to his voice. "We knew Dr. Hardy, my daughter and
I, only in his professional capacity. That's a matter of record,
Captain Ziegler. He treated me for over a year. Then he
operated upon my eyes." A spasm of pain flickered over
his waxy features. "Cataracts, he said . . ."

"Hmm," said Ziegler. "Was it—"

"I am totally blind."

There was a shocked silence. Ellery shook his head with
impatience at his own blindness. He should have known.
The old man's helplessness, the queer fixed stare, that vague
smile, the shuffling walk . . . "This Dr. Hardy was responsi-
ble for your blindness, Mr. Reis?" he demanded abruptly.

"I didn't say that," murmured the old man. "It was
no doubt the hand of God. He did what he could. I have
been blind for over two years."

"Did you know Dr. Hardy was here, in this place,
today?"

"No. We haven't seen him for two years."

"Where were you people when the police found you?"

Matthew Reis shrugged. "Somewhere ahead. Near the
exit, I believe."

"And you?" asked Ellery of the colored couple.

"M'name is—is," stuttered the Negro, "Juju Jones, suh.
Ah'm a prizefighter. Light-heavy, suh. Ah don't know
nothin' 'bout this doctuh man. Me an' Jessie we been havin'

a high ol' time down yonduh in a room that bounced 'n' jounced all roun'. We been—"

"Lawd," moaned the pretty mulatto, hanging on to her escort's arm.

"And how about you?" demanded Ellery of the bearded man.

He raised his shoulders in an almost Gallic gesture. "How about me? This is all Classical Greek to *me*. I've been out on the rocks at the Point most of the day doing a couple of sea-pictures and a landscape. I'm an artist—James Oliver Adams, at your service." There was something antagonistic, almost sneering, in his attitude. "You'll find my paint box and sketches in the checkroom downstairs. Don't know this dead creature, and I wish to God I'd never been tempted by this atrocious gargoyle of a place."

"Garg—" gasped Monsieur Duval; he became furious. "Do you know of whom you speak?" he cried, advancing upon the bearded man. "I am Dieudonné Du—"

"There, there, Duval," said Ellery soothingly. "We don't want to become involved in an altercation between clashing artistic temperaments; not now, anyway. Where were you, Mr. Adams, when the machinery stopped?"

"Somewhere ahead." The man had a harsh cracked voice, as if there was something wrong with his vocal cords. "I was looking for a way out of the hellish place. *I'd* had a bellyful. I—"

"That's right," snapped Captain Ziegler. "I found this bird myself. He was swearin' to himself like a trooper, stumblin' around in the dark. He says to me: 'How the hell do you get out of here? That barker said you've got to follow the green lights, but they don't get you anywhere except in another silly hole of a monkeyshine room, or somethin' like that.' Now why'd you want to get out so fast, Mr. Adams? What do you know? Come on, spill it!"

The artist snorted his disgust, disdaining to reply. He shrugged again and set his shoulders against the wall in an attitude of resignation.

"I should think, Captain," murmured Ellery, studying

the faces of the six against the wall, "that you'd be much more concerned with finding the one who 'suspects' in Madge's note. Well, Madge, are you going to talk? It's perfectly silly to hold out. This is the sort of thing that can't be kept secret. Sooner or later—"

The dainty woman moistened her lips; she looked faint. "I suppose you're right. It's bound to come out," she said in a low empty voice. "I'll talk. Yes, my name *is* Madge—Madge Clarke. It's true. I wrote that note to—to Dr. Hardy." Then her voice flamed passionately. "But I didn't write it of my own free will! *He* made me. It was a trap. I knew it. But I couldn't—"

"*Who* made you?" growled Captain Ziegler.

"My husband. Dr. Hardy and I had been friends . . . well, friends, quietly. My husband didn't know at first. Then he—he did come to know. He must have followed us—many times. We—we've met here before. My husband is very jealous. He made me write the note. He threatened to—to kill me if I didn't write it. Now I don't care. Let him! He's a murderer!" And she buried her face in her hands and began to sob.

Captain Ziegler said gruffly: "Mrs. Clarke." She looked up and then down at the snub-nosed revolver in his hand. "Is that your husband's gun?"

She shrank from it, shuddering. "No. He has a revolver, but it's got a long barrel. He's a—a good shot."

"Pawnshop," muttered Ziegler, putting the gun in his pocket; and he nodded gloomily to Ellery.

"You came here, Mrs. Clarke," said Ellery gently, "in the face of your husband's threats?"

"Yes. Yes. I—I couldn't stay away. I thought I'd warn—"

"That was very courageous. Your husband—did you see him in Joyland, in the crowd before this place?"

"No. I didn't. But it must have been Tom. He *told* me he'd kill Anse!"

"Did you meet Dr. Hardy in here, before he was dead?"

She shivered. "No. I couldn't find—"

"Did you meet your husband here?"

"No . . ."

"Then where is he?" asked Ellery dryly. "He couldn't have vanished in a puff of smoke. The age of miracles is past. . . . Do you think you can trace that revolver, Captain Ziegler?"

"Try." Ziegler shrugged. "Manufacturer's number has been filed off. It's an old gun, too. And no prints. Bad for the D.A."

Ellery clucked irritably and stared down at the quiet man by the corpse. Djuna held his breath a little behind him. Suddenly he said: "Duval, isn't there some way of illuminating this room?"

Monsieur Duval started, his pallor deeper than before in the sword-thrusts of light crossing his face. "There is not an electrical wire or fixture in the entire structure. Excepting for the assembly-room, Mr. Queen."

"How about the arrows pointing the way? They're visible."

"A chemical. I am desolated by this—"

"Naturally; murder's rarely an occasion for hilarity. But this Stygian pit of yours complicates matters. What do you think, Captain?"

"Looks open and shut to *me*. I don't know how he got away, but this Clarke's the killer. We'll find him and sweat it out of him. He shot the doctor from the spot where you found the gun layin'—" Ellery frowned—"and then dragged the body to the door of the preceding room and set it up against the door to give him time for his getaway. Blood trail tells that. The shots were lost in the noise of this damn' place. He must have figured on that."

"Hmm. That's all very well, except for the manner of Clarke's disappearance . . . if it *was* Clarke." Ellery sucked his fingernail, revolving Ziegler's analysis in his mind. There was one thing wrong . . . "Ah, the coroner's finished. Well, Doctor?"

The small quiet man rose from his knees in the light of the lantern. The six against the wall were incredibly still. "Simple enough. Four bullets within an area of inches. Two of them pierced the heart from behind. Good shooting, Mr. Queen."

Ellery blinked. "Good shooting," he repeated. "Yes, very good shooting indeed, Doctor. How long has he been dead?"

"About an hour. He died instantly, by the way."

"That means," muttered Ellery, "that he must have been shot only a few minutes before I found him. His body was still warm." He looked intently at the empurpled dead face. "But you're wrong, Captain Ziegler, about the position of the killer when he fired the shots. He couldn't have stood so far away from Dr. Hardy. In fact, as I see it, he must have been very close to Hardy. There are powder marks on the dead man's body, of course, Doctor?"

The county coroner looked puzzled. "Powder marks? Why, no. Of course not. Not a trace of burnt powder. Captain Ziegler's right."

Ellery said in a strangled voice: "No powder marks? Why, that's impossible! You're positive? There *must* be powder marks!"

The coroner and Captain Ziegler exchanged glances. "As something of an expert in these matters, Mr. Queen," said the little man icily, "let me assure you that the victim was shot from a distance of at least twelve feet, probably a foot or two more."

The most remarkable expression came over Ellery's face. He opened his mouth to speak, closed it again, blinked once more, and then took out a cigaret and lit it, puffing slowly. "Twelve feet. No powder marks," he said in a hushed voice. "Well, well. Now, that's downright amazing. That's a lesson in the illogicalities that would interest Professor Dewey himself. I can't believe it. Simply can't."

The coroner eyed him hostilely. "I'm a reasonably intelligent man, Mr. Queen, but you're talking nonsense as far as I'm concerned."

"What's on your mind?" demanded Captain Ziegler.

"Don't *you* know, either?" Then Ellery said abstractedly: "Let's have a peep at the contents of his clothes, please."

The detective jerked his head toward a pile of miscellaneous articles on the floor. Ellery went down on his haunches, indifferent to his staring audience. When he rose he was mumbling to himself almost with petulance. He had not found what he was seeking, what logic told him should be there. There were not even smoking materials of any kind. And there was no watch; he even examined the dead man's wrists for marks.

He strode about the room, nose lowered, searching the floor with an absorption that was oblivious to the puzzled looks directed at him. The flashlight in his hand was a darting, probing finger.

"But we've searched this room!" exploded Captain Ziegler. "What in the name of heaven are you looking for, Mr. Queen?"

"Something," murmured Ellery grimly, "that must be here if there's any sanity in this world. Let's see what your men have scraped together from the floors of all the rooms, Captain."

"But they didn't find anything!"

"I'm not talking of things that would strike a detective as possibly 'important.' I'm referring to trivia: a scrap of paper, a sliver of wood—anything."

A broad-shouldered man said respectfully: "I looked myself, Mr. Queen. There wasn't even dust."

"*S'il vous plaît,*" said Monsieur Duval nervously. "Of that we have taken care with ingenuity. There is here both a ventilation system and another, a vacuum system, which sucks in the dust and keeps *la maison des ténèbres* of a cleanliness immaculate."

"Vacuum!" exclaimed Ellery. "A sucking process . . . It's possible! Is this vacuum machine in operation all the time, Duval?"

"But no, my friend. Only in the night, when *The House*

of Darkness is empty and—how do you say?—inoperative. But that is why your *gendarmes* found nothing, not even the dust."

"Foiled," muttered Ellery whimsically, but his eyes were grave. "The machine doesn't operate in the daytime. So that's out. Captain, forgive my persistence. But *everything's* been searched? The assembly-room downstairs, too? Someone here might have—"

Captain Ziegler's face was stormy. "I can't figure you out. How many times do I have to say it? The man on duty in the cellar says no one even popped in there and went back during the period of the murder. So what?"

"Well, then," sighed Ellery, "I'll have to ask you to search each of these people, Captain." There was a note of desperation in his voice.

Mr. Ellery Queen's frown was a thing of beauty when he put down the last personal possession of the six prisoners. He had picked them apart to the accompaniment of a chorus of protests, chiefly from the artist Adams and Miss Reis. But he had not found what should have been there. He rose from his squatting position on the floor and silently indicated that the articles might be returned to their owners.

"*Parbleu!*" cried Monsieur Duval suddenly. "I do not know what is it for which you seek, my friend; but it is possible that it has been secretly placed upon the person of one of us, *n'est-ce pas?* If it is of a nature damaging, that would be—"

Ellery looked up with a faint interest. "Good for you, Duval. I hadn't thought of that."

"We shall see," said Monsieur Duval excitedly, beginning to turn out his pockets, "if the brain of Dieudonné Duval is not capable . . . *Voici!* Will you please to examine, Mr. Queen?"

Ellery looked over the collection of odds and ends briefly. "No dice. That was generous, Duval." He began to poke about in his own pockets.

Djuna announced proudly: "I've got everything *I* ought to."

"Well, Mr. Queen?" asked Ziegler impatiently.

Ellery waved an absent hand. "I'm through, Captain . . . Wait!" He stood still, eyes lost in space. "Wait here. It's still possible—" Without explanation he plunged through the doorway marked with the green arrow, found himself in a narrow passageway as black as the rooms leading off from it, and flashed his light about. Then he ran back to the extreme end of the corridor and began a worm's progress, scrutinizing each inch of the corridor floor as if his life depended upon his thoroughness. Twice he turned corners, and at last he found himself at a dead end confronted by a door marked *"Exit: Assembly-Room."* He pushed the door in and blinked at the lights of the cellar. A policeman touched his cap to him; the attendant skeleton looked scared.

"Not even a bit of wax, or a few crumbs of broken glass, or a burnt matchstick," he muttered. A thought struck him. "Here, officer, open this door in the grating for me, will you?"

The policeman unlocked a small door in the grating and Ellery stepped through to the larger division of the room. He made at once for the rack on the wall, in the compartments of which were the things the prisoners—and he himself—had checked before plunging into the main body of the *House*. He inspected these minutely. When he came to the artist's box he opened it, glanced at the paints and brushes and palette and three small daubs—a landscape and two seascapes—which were quite orthodox and uninspired, closed it. . . .

He paced up and down under the dusty light of the bulbs, frowning fiercely. Minutes passed. *The House of Darkness* was silent, as if in tribute to its unexpected dead. The policeman gaped.

Suddenly he halted and the frown faded, to be replaced by a grim smile. "Yes, yes, that's it," he muttered. "Why didn't I think of it before? Officer! Take all this truck back to the scene of the crime. I'll carry this small table back with me. We've all the paraphernalia, and in the darkness we should be able to conduct a very thrilling *séance!*"

When he knocked on the door of the octagonal room from the corridor, it was opened by Captain Ziegler himself.

"You back?" growled the detective. "We're just ready to scram. Stiff's crated—"

"Not for a few moments yet, I trust," said Ellery smoothly, motioning the burdened policeman to precede him. "I've a little speech to make."

"Speech!"

"A speech fraught with subtleties and cleverness, my dear Captain. Duval, this will delight your Gallic soul. Ladies and gentlemen, you will please remain in your places. That's right, officer; on the table. Now, gentlemen, if you will kindly focus the rays of your flashes upon me and the table, we can begin our demonstration."

The room was very still. The body of Dr. Anselm Hardy lay in a wickerwork basket, brown-covered, invisible. Ellery presided like a *Swami* in the center of the room, the nucleus of thin beams. Only the glitter of eyes was reflected back to him from the walls.

He rested one hand on the small table, cluttered with the belongings of the prisoners. "*Alors, mesdames et messieurs,* we begin. We begin with the extraordinary fact that the scene of this crime is significant for one thing above all: its darkness. Now, that's a little out of the usual run. It suggests certain disturbing nuances before you think it out. This is literally a house of darkness. A man has been murdered in one of its unholy chambers. In the house itself—excluding, of course, the victim, myself, and my panting young charge—we find six persons presumably devoting themselves to enjoyment of Monsieur Duval's satanic creation. No one during the period of the crime was observed to emerge from the only possible exit, if we are to take the word of the structure's own architect, Monsieur Duval.

It is inevitable, then, that one of these six is the killer of Dr. Hardy."

There was a mass rustle, a rising sigh, which died almost as soon as it was born.

"Now observe," continued Ellery dreamily, "what pranks fate plays. In this tragedy of darkness, the cast includes at least three characters associated with darkness. I refer to Mr. Reis, who is blind; and to Mr. Juju Jones and his escort, who are Negroes. Isn't that significant? Doesn't it mean something to you?"

Juju Jones groaned: "Ah di'n't do it, Mistuh Queen."

Ellery said: "Moreover, Mr. Reis has a possible motive; the victim treated his eyes, and in the course of this treatment Mr. Reis became blind. And Mrs. Clarke offered us a jealous husband. Two motives, then. So far, so good. . . . But all this tells us nothing vital about the crime itself."

"Well," demanded Ziegler harshly, "what does?"

"The darkness, Captain, the darkness," replied Ellery in gentle accents. "I seem to have been the only one who was disturbed by that darkness." A brisk note sprang into his voice. "This room is totally black. There is no electricity, no lamp, no lantern, no gas, no candle, no window in its equipment. Its three doors open onto places as dark as itself. The green and red lights above the doors are nonluminous, radiate no light visible to the human eye beyond the arrows themselves. . . . *And yet, in this blackest of black rooms, someone was able at a distance of at least twelve feet to place four bullets within an area of inches in this invisible victim's back!*"

Someone gasped. Captain Ziegler muttered: "By damn . . ."

"How?" asked Ellery softly. "Those shots were accurate. They couldn't have been accidents—not four of them. I had assumed in the beginning that there must be powder burns on the dead man's coat, that the killer must have stood directly behind Dr. Hardy, touching him, even holding him steady, jamming the muzzle of the revolver into his back and firing. But the coroner said no! It seemed impossible. In a totally dark room? At twelve feet? The killer couldn't have hit Hardy by ear alone, listening to movements, footsteps; the shots were too accurately placed for that theory. Besides, the target must have been moving, however slowly. I couldn't understand it. The only possible answer was that *the murderer had light to see by.* And yet there was no light."

Matthew Reis said musically: "Very clever, sir."

"Elementary, rather, Mr. Reis. There was no light in the room itself. . . . Now, thanks to Monsieur Duval's vacuum-suction system, there is never any débris in this place. That meant that if we found something it might belong to one of the suspects. But the police had searched minutely and found literally nothing. I myself finecombed this room looking for a flashlight, a burnt match, a wax taper—anything that might have indicated the light by which the murderer shot Dr. Hardy. Since I had analyzed the facts, I knew what to look for, as would anyone who had analyzed them. When I found nothing in the nature of a light-giver, I was flabbergasted.

"I examined the contents of the pockets of our six suspects; still no clue to the source of the light. A single matchstick would have helped, although I realized that that would hardly have been the means employed; for this had been a trap laid in advance. The murderer had apparently enticed his victim to *The House of Darkness.* He had planned the murder to take place here. Undoubtedly he had visited it before, seen its complete lack of lighting facilities. He therefore would have planned in advance to provide means of illumination. He scarcely would have relied on matches; certainly he would have preferred a flashlight. But there was nothing, nothing, not even the improbable burnt match. If it was not on his person, had he thrown it away? But where? It has not been found. Nowhere in the rooms or corridor."

Ellery paused over a cigaret. "And so I came to the

conclusion," he drawled, puffing smoke, "that *the light must have emanated from the victim himself.*"

"But no!" gasped Monsieur Duval. "No man would so foolish be—"

"Not consciously, of course. But he might have provided light unconsciously. I looked over the very dead Dr. Hardy. He wore dark clothing. There was no watch which might possess radial hands. He had no smoking implements on his person; a nonsmoker, obviously. No matches or lighter, then. And no flashlight. Nothing of a luminous nature which might explain how the killer saw where to aim. That is," he murmured, "nothing but one last possibility."

"What—"

"Will you gentlemen please put the lantern and your flashes out?"

For a moment there was uncomprehending inaction; and then lights began to snap off, until finally the room was steeped in the same thick palpable darkness that had existed when Ellery had stumbled into it. "Keep your places, please," said Ellery curtly. "Don't move, anyone."

There was no sound at first except the quick breaths of rigid people. The glow of Ellery's cigaret died, snuffed out. Then there was a slight rustling and a sharp click. And before their astonished eyes a roughly rectangular blob of light no larger than a domino, misty and nacreous, began to move across the room. It sailed in a straight line, like a homing pigeon, and then another blob detached itself from the first and touched something, and lo! there was still a third blob of light.

"Demonstrating," came Ellery's cool voice, "the miracle of how Nature provides for her most wayward children. Phosphorus, of course. Phosphorus in the form of paint. If, for example, the murderer had contrived to daub the back of the victim's coat before the victim entered *The House of Darkness*—perhaps in the press of a crowd—he insured himself sufficient light for his crime. In a totally black place he had only to search for the phosphorescent patch. Then four shots in the thick of it from a distance of twelve feet—no great shakes to a good marksman—the bullet holes obliterate most of the light patch, any bit that remains is doused in gushing blood . . . and the murderer's safe all around. . . . Yes, yes, very clever. *No, you don't!*"

The third blob of light jerked into violent motion, lunging forward, disappearing, appearing, making progress toward the green-arrowed door. . . . There was a crash, and a clatter, the sounds of a furious struggle. Lights flicked madly on, whipping across one another. They illuminated an area on the floor in which Ellery lay entwined with a man who fought in desperate silence. Beside them lay the paint box, open.

Captain Ziegler jumped in and rapped the man over the head with his billy. He dropped back with a groan, unconscious. It was the artist, Adams.

"But how did you know it was Adams?" demanded Ziegler a few moments later, when some semblance of order had been restored. Adams lay on the floor, manacled; the others crowded around, relief on some faces, fright on others.

"By a curious fact," panted Ellery, brushing himself off. "Djuna, stop pawing me! I'm quite all right. . . . You yourself told me, Captain, that when you found Adams blundering around in the dark he was complaining that he wanted to get out but couldn't find the exit. (Naturally he would!) He said that he knew he should follow the green lights, but when he did he only got deeper into the labyrinth of rooms. But how could that have been if he *had* followed the green lights? Any one of them would have taken him directly into the straight, monkeyshineless corridor leading to the exit. Then he *hadn't* followed the green lights. Since he could have no reason to lie about it, it must simply have meant, I reasoned, that he *thought* he had been following the green lights but had been following the red lights instead, since he continued to blunder from room to room."

"But how—"

"Very simple. Color-blindness. He's afflicted with the common type of color-blindness in which the subject confuses red and green. Unquestionably he didn't know that he had such an affliction; many color-blind persons don't. He had expected to make his escape quickly, before the body was found, depending on the green light he had previously heard the barker mention to insure his getaway.

"But that's not the important point. The important point is that *he claimed to be an artist.* Now, it's almost impossible for an artist to work in color and still be color-blind. The fact that he had found himself trapped, misled by the red lights, proved that he was not conscious of his red-green affliction. But I examined his landscape and sea-scapes in the paint box and found them quite orthodox. I knew, then, that they weren't his; that he was masquerading, that he was not an artist at all. But if he was masquerading, he became a vital suspect!

"Then, when I put that together with the final deduction about the source of light, I had the whole answer in a flash. Phosphorus paint—paint box. And he had directly preceded Hardy into the *House.* . . . The rest was pure theatre. He felt that he wasn't running any risk with the phosphorus, for whoever would examine the paint box would naturally open it *in the light,* where the luminous quality of the chemical would be invisible. And there you are."

"Then my husband—" began Mrs. Clarke in a strangled voice, staring down at the unconscious murderer.

"But the motive, my friend," protested Monsieur Duval, wiping his forehead. "The motive! A man does not kill for nothing. Why—"

"The motive?" Ellery shrugged. "You already know the motive, Duval. In fact, you know—" He stopped and knelt suddenly by the bearded man. His hand flashed out and came away—with the beard. Mrs. Clarke screamed and staggered back. "He even changed his voice. This, I'm afraid, is your vanishing Mr. Clarke!"

BEIDENBAUER'S FLEA

Stanley Ellin

Stanley Ellin's place in the annals of suspense fiction was secured in 1948 with the publication of his first story, "Specialty of the House" (which was recently voted a "Hall of Fame" story by his peers in the Mystery Writers of America). In the nearly forty years since, he has gone on to produce numerous notable short stories, including the Edgar-winning "The House Party" and "The Blessington Method," and such novels as The Eighth Circle *(1958) and* Mirror, Mirror on the Wall *(1972). In this tale of the former owner of a much different kind of circus—one where the performers are fleas—Ellin reveals to us the multifaceted personalities of these tiny creatures, and how they can make a man just a* little *crazy.*

I was seated on a bench in Central Park, half drowsing in the autumn sunlight, when a strange figure approached—the cadaverous figure of a man who bore himself with the grandeur of an ancient matinée idol. As he walked, he swung a malacca stick with practised ease. His hair was snowy-white and swept back almost to his collar, and on it was cocked with indescribable panache a battered homburg. His tight-waisted, velveteen-collared overcoat was long out of fashion and badly frayed at the cuffs. His narrow-toed, patent-leather shoes were scuffed and down at the heels. Yet, so noble was his demeanour and so profound the sorrow written on his lined face that I found myself pitying his curious garb, rather than being moved to scorn by it.

He sat down beside me, propped his stick between his legs, and said, "It is a beautiful day, is it not?"

"Yes," I said, "it is." Then I felt a sudden apprehension. I am too easy a mark for the wayfarer's sad story, his melting eyes, his extended palm. I have never learned to say no to the humble derelict who stops me with hat in hand and asks for carfare to places he never intends to visit. Now I had the feeling that I knew what was coming, and I drew a tight rein on my susceptibilities. This time, I silently resolved, I would escape before it was too late.

But there was no escape. As I started to rise, my companion placed a hand on my shoulder and gently pressed me back into my seat. "It is a beautiful day," he said, "but what does that matter to one who is doomed to suffer and search, search and suffer through every day of his life, fair or foul?"

I was resigned to my fate, but in a bitter mood. He might tell his story to the end, but when he held out his hand for the expected offering he would get nothing more than a handshake. That much I took my oath on.

"Evidently," I said, concealing my true emotions with an effort, "you are spending your life in a search for something. What is that something?"

"A flea."

"A flea?"

The aged curio nodded sombrely. "Yes, strange as it seems, that is the object of my search. But perhaps you will understand more readily if I reveal my name to you. It is Beidenbauer. Thaddeus Beidenbauer. There, does that enlighten you?"

He looked at me eagerly, but the light in his eyes faded when I shook my head. "No," I said. "I'm sorry to say it doesn't."

"It doesn't?"

"I'm afraid not."

Beidenbauer sighed. "Well, such is fame. A bubble— a glittering, weightless thing that one holds briefly in hand, and then—but let me tell you my story. There is pain and heartbreak in it, true, but I am inured to that now. I have lived my tragedy over and over so many times in my waking dreams that I can bear to talk about it freely when the occasion arises. I will tell it all to you just as it happened."

"I am sure you will," I said.

There was a time [Beidenbauer said] when my name was known in every mighty city of the world, when I was petted and sought after by the great, when I was drunk each day with my youth and wealth and the joy of my lot. Ah, I should have thought then how the gods destroy those who are too proud, but I did not. I lived only with the happy realization that I was the proprietor of Beidenbauer's Mighty Mites, the greatest flea circus on earth, the one that did more to honour the vast and unsung talents of the flea than any other before or since.

There have been flea circuses before mine and after mine, but always shabby affairs, dismal two-penny entertainments with none of the true glamour of the stage invested in them. But mine was different. It was superlative theatre.

Whether performed before the bumpkins who attend touring carnivals or before a soirée of society's bluest blue bloods, it never failed to stir the audience to its depths, to bring it to its feet shouting for endless encores. And all because as a mere child I had learned the secret of the relationship between the flea and its trainer, and with infinite patience had put the secret to work.

I can see you are wondering what the secret is; you will be astonished to learn of its simplicity. There is a strange and wonderful symbiosis between flea and man. The flea feeds from its trainer's arm and thus strengthened goes into the arena to perform. The money earned this way is then used by the trainer to buy him his dinner, to enrich his blood, that the performer may feed and return to his performance. So we have a perfect cycle, flea and man feeding off each other, each contributing to their mutual existence.

That is all there is to it, but I was the one to discover that there must be more than mere food involved in this relationship. There must be a symbiosis of emotions as well. Respect, sympathy, understanding, and love—yes, love—must be there, for the flea, a quivering mass of sensitivity, needs them desperately. And unlike all other trainers, I provided them. Cruelty was the rule elsewhere. The harsh word, the heavy hand—these were all my confrères knew in trying to master and instruct the flea. But kindness was my rule, and for that reason I soared to success while all others remained mired in failure.

But enough of myself; after all, it was not I who entered the spotlighted ring every day to perform, to act the clown so that the crowd roared with laughter, to risk my neck in acrobatics so that it gasped, to woo it with grace so that it sighed in rapture. All this was done by the fleas, and it is they who must get the lion's share of admiration.

There were twenty-four members of the troupe, handpicked, trained for weary hours on end, and it is impossible to imagine the range of their talents. But the unchallenged star of the show, and, sorrow of sorrows, the star of the tragedy I am unfolding, was a flea named Sebastian. Small, volatile, full of riotous wit and invention, he was our featured clown. And he was a true star in every respect. Tense and withdrawn before a performance, he was at ease the instant the spotlights fell on him and in absolute command of the audience.

I can see him now, waiting behind the scenes as the white silk handkerchief was laid on the table and tacks driven into each of its four corners to moor it securely. Then, as the darning hoop which was our main ring was set on it, Sebastian would fretfully start to pace up and down, his mouth drawn tight, his eyes faraway, fighting the fears reborn in him at every performance. I knew those signs, and I would give him a little nod—just one small nod—to make clear my confidence in him. And he would respond with a little nod of his own to show that he understood. It was our private ritual, those two almost imperceptible gestures, and it was all that was ever needed to assure another sterling performance from him. That, and the knowledge that the prima ballerina of our company, an enchanting, doe-eyed little flea named Selina, had eyes only for him and would stand worshipping from afar while he held the spotlight. For Selina, I think, was the only one on earth other than myself to whom he gave his unquestioning devotion.

But, alas, what he did not know at the time, and what I did not know—such is the cruel deviousness of the female heart—was that Selina worshipped only at the altar of success. She loved him not for himself, but for the glory that was his; the laughter and applause of the crowd, the featured billing given him, and the favoured place on my forearm at feeding time. She was a great dancer, but like so many of her kind she had no true warmth in her heart. Only a fanatic adoration of success.

Had I known that at the time I would have made a different turning somewhere along the road to disaster which lay ahead. But how could I know, how could anyone know, when Selina dissembled so brilliantly? When she looked at Sebastian with melting eyes she almost turned my head as well as his. She clung to him, comforted him in his times of doubt, let him know in a hundred different ways that he was her hero. And he, befuddled by her airs and graces, was completely her slave.

It was an apparently meaningless episode—meaningless at the time it occurred—that brought on the inexorable crisis. Hercules, our flea who performed feats of strength, had become old and stiff-legged, and one night while lifting a grape seed over his head before a hushed and awestruck audience, he suddenly fell to the floor in a writhing agony. The veterinarian who diagnosed the case did not mince words. It was a serious rupture, he said grimly, and Hercules would perform no more.

It was shocking beyond measure to me, that news. Not only because of my warm regard for Hercules, but because it left me without one of my featured acts. I instantly gave orders to agents to scour the world, look high and low, pay any price for a flea who could duplicate Hercules' feats, but I did so with a heavy heart. I had already garnered the best there was in the entire world. What chance was there to find a replacement I had not previously considered and found unworthy?

But miracles can and do happen. I had rejected scores of applicants in despair when suddenly a cable arrived from an agent in Bulgaria. The length of the cable alone suggested his state of emotions, and what it said made them even more vivid. By pure chance he had entered a broken-down café in Sofia where the guests were being entertained by a flea circus. Not even a circus. A few acts badly performed by sullen, half-starved fleas. But one flea there—! Nothing would do, save that I come at once and see for myself.

I did not believe him, because I knew he was inordinately proud of his native fleas who are, at best, temperamental performers; but I went. When a man is desperate he will do anything, even to putting his faith in the potentialities of a Bulgarian flea. So I went. And to paraphrase the saying: I came, I saw, I was conquered.

The flea was named Casimir, and even the unspeakable surroundings in which he performed could not dim his lustre. Barrel-chested, bull-necked, glowing with health, and with a frank, open face that gave clear evidence of an honest nature and willing heart, he dwarfed the fleas around him to insignificance. I saw at a glance that I might be looking at a born star. I waited for his performance in a fever of impatience.

At last the motley acts that preceded his were finished, and the café loungers crowded close around the table, I in their forefront. The trainer, a wizened wretch, placed two small wooden blocks on the table, one of which had a series of steps carved into it. Between the blocks I could see a single strand of dark hair—evidently from the trainer's head since it shone greasily in the dim light around me—which was stretched taut from block to block. The trainer then placed Casimir on the table, and before the flea he placed a gleaming pin two inches long which he drew from his lapel.

I could not believe my eyes. To a flea that pin was as a length of railroad track would be to me, yet Casimir stooped low, got a grip on it, and with bulging muscles suddenly lifted it overhead. I gasped, but I had not yet seen the full capabilities of this magnificent creature. Holding the pin overhead he made his way to the steps of the block, climbed them, and then slowly, cautiously, he stepped on to the hair itself. The hair sagged under the weight on it, and Casimir balanced himself with an effort. Then with precise steps, secure as if he were affixed to that hair, he walked its full length, the pin held high overhead throughout and never wavering in his grip. Only when the other block had been reached and the pin laid down could you detect in the convulsive tremors of his body and the heaving of his chest what the strain must have been.

I knew even before the applause started that my search

was over. Six hours later, after passionate bargaining and endless rounds of slivovitz, I paid for Casimir's contract more money than anyone on earth would ever have dreamed of paying for a flea. And at that I felt I was fortunate.

I took my prize home with me. I allowed time for him to become accustomed to our American ways; I filled his starved soul with my affection and trust; and only when I was sure that he was accepted by the rest of the company and felt at ease with them did I put him on the stage. That night was his night. When the final curtain fell he was the unchallenged star of the show. Simple, honest, unassuming, it was clear that he would not permit this honour to inflate him; but there was no question about it, he was the star. And Sebastian, the great Punchinello, the unparalleled clown, was in second place.

What were Sebastian's feelings then? What could they have been but anguish at having to yield his place to another. But whatever the torments he suffered, he was a trouper through and through. To him the show was the thing, and if he were asked to sacrifice himself to it, he would do so like a stoic. The quality of his performances remained superb. If anything, they were better than ever. Each time he entered the spotlight he flung himself into his role with an abandon, a virtuosity, far beyond the powers of most fleas.

No, it was not the loss of his commanding place in the company that finally shattered him; it was the loss of his beloved. Selina had seen his glory transferred to Casimir. She watched with narrowed eyes as a new star rose on the horizon. And with cold-blooded deliberation, never heeding the consequences, she turned from the old to worship the new. She had eyes only for Casimir now, comfort only for him, flattery only for him, and he, poor, simple-minded male, accepted this at first incredulously, then eagerly, then with rapture.

That was what destroyed Sebastian. The sight of the

couple together transfixed him like a needle. And there was no escaping the sight, no turning away from it. Selina was unabashed in her pursuit, and Casimir nakedly revelled in it. The outsider might have seen this as a stirring romance; to Sebastian it would be an obscenity. Selina was his; what right did some burly stranger have to fondle her before his very eyes? He must have brooded himself into a state of madness over this.

The end came with shocking suddenness. It was during an evening performance, and the show had gone well until Casimir undertook his master feat. The audience leaned forward with bated breath as he lifted the pin over his head. It hummed with excitement as he climbed the block and set forth on his journey across the taut hair which stretched no less than a foot above the table. And it cried out in alarm when, as he reached the middle of the hair, it suddenly parted, and he plummeted to the table, the pin following him and crushing his chest.

I had leaped forward wildly when I saw the hair part, but I was too late. All I could do was remove the oppressive weight of the pin and turn my head away to conceal my tears from the expiring Casimir. He had his own pains to bear; I would spare him mine. But when my misted eyes fell on the broken strand of hair my grief turned to blazing rage. The hair had not worn through; it had been deliberately cut part of the way. I was looking, not at an accident, but at a murder!

I knew at once who the murderer was. And I could tell from the shock on Selina's face and the growing comprehension on the face of every flea huddled there that the story was clear to all of them. But before I could wreak vengeance on the criminal my glance fell on Casimir, lying there, breathing his last. He looked at me with lustrous eyes full of pain; he tried to smile—oh, pitiful sight—and with a great effort he shook his head at me. He understood, too, noble soul, and he was telling me that vengeance was not for him. Only pity for the malefactor, and forgiveness.

It was his last gesture on earth, and the lesson struck me to my heart. It wiped the thirst for vengeance out of me on the spot. I felt only a great need to find Sebastian, to tell him that I alone was the cause of the sorrows that had befallen us. Obsessed by pride in the show, I had put another in his place, had deprived him of his beloved, had driven him at last to insanity and crime.

But when I looked for him I could not find him. Filled with horror at his deed he had fled into the night. And with his disappearance, with Casimir's death, with the company's morale destroyed, there was nothing left. I cancelled my bookings, broke up the company, and set forth with only one thought in mind—to find Sebastian, to face him as a penitent, and to win forgiveness from him.

It has been a weary search. I have walked the lonely streets day and night, combed dog shows and zoological parks, looked every place where a wanderer like Sebastian might take refuge. But all to no avail. I am old and poor now. I must rely on alms from strangers to help me on my way, but I will never give up my search until I am successful in it. There is no other way for me. I am doomed to suffer and search, search and suffer until then.

Beidenbauer's voice ceased and his narrative ended on this plaintive note. We sat together in silence for a long while, contemplating the pigeons burbling on the grass beyond, and then I said, "I have heard tell that the life span of the flea is extremely brief. Is it not likely that by now, in some unmarked grave—?"

"I do not allow myself to think of that," said Beidenbauer with deep feeling. "It would be the final blow."

"Yes," I said, "I can see that it would be."

We sat in silence again, and then with resignation I took a coin from my pocket and offered it to him. He only looked at it reproachfully. I sighed, put the coin away, and offered him a dollar bill. This he took.

"You are kind," he said, getting to his feet. "I am only

sorry that you never saw my circus in its glory. You would better understand then how far I have fallen."

"Well," I said, "that's life."

"No, my friend," said Beidenbauer gravely, "that's show business."

CARNIVAL DAY

Nedra Tyre

The arrival of a carnival in a small town is cause for excitement in both children and adults, and it is against this nostalgic background that Nedra Tyre has woven a powerful story of steadily mounting suspense. Tyre was born in Georgia in 1921, and many of her works are set in small southern towns. Her job experience in the social services has provided fertile material for such excellent novels as Mouse in Eternity *(1952), whose protagonist is an Atlanta social worker, and* Hall of Death *(1960), which takes place in a southern girls' reformatory.*

115

Betty wanted to lie in bed a little longer and look at the lowered shade that held out the sunlight except for a bright streak of it nosing through at the bottom. Then she could think about the nice things that might happen. Except that they might not.

Her mother was in the hall cleaning, doing the brisk morning work of Saturday. Betty listened to the rub of the mop, the whispering of the dust cloth. She pulled the teddy bear from his crumpled position on the floor and placed him on the pillow beside her. His hanging button of a left eye seemed to leer; his fur was worn and in spots was missing, as if he had mange. She took his right paw, that was jerked toward his forehead in a kind of salute, and rubbed it against her face so that he caressed her.

Outside the mop made its way down the hall—the only sound in the house. Then the ringing of the telephone tore open the silence—first the ringing downstairs, then the echoing ring of the extension upstairs. Her mother would answer it, just outside Betty's door.

Betty knocked the teddy bear so that he made a somersault and landed face down on the floor. She knew the telephone call would be the sign she had been waiting for to tell her what kind of day it would be, and she was not quite ready to learn. She grabbed her pillow and burrowed beneath it, pressing the sides tight against her ears. The feathers, the ticking, the pillow case, nothing kept the noise out. She had heard the words before they were spoken, she had dreamed them all through the night.

Her father had said weeks ago—when the first signs were pasted on the billboards, the placards set up in the drug store windows, the shoe shop, the beauty parlors— that of course they must go to the carnival together. Hadn't they gone for years? But she couldn't really believe him because everything had been so different these last months. He understood her fear, her uncertainty, and weeks ago had given her five crisp dollar bills to hide away in her desk. The money was there for her to spend at the carnival, even if he didn't get to go with her.

Betty heard her mother's voice; if her mother had been at the North Pole her voice couldn't have been colder, and yet it was so nice, so distinct, every syllable of every word sounded.

"I tried to tell Betty not to count on you. She'll be hurt. But then you seem to take pleasure in hurting us."

It wasn't fair of her mother to talk to him like that; he'd left the money; he'd made his apologies, he'd said something might come up so that he couldn't take her; and now her mother talked to him as if he had broken a solemn promise.

Her mother didn't say goodbye but Betty heard the little latching click the telephone made as it slid back into place.

The autumn wind puffed the shade so that it slapped the sill. Betty reached down for the teddy bear and threw him across the room.

Outside there were the sounds of her mother putting away the mop in the utility cabinet, then a knock on the door.

"Good morning," her mother said, and filled the room with her briskness. "It's time you were up."

Betty kicked the sheet and made a wad of it at the foot of the bed.

"Your father telephoned to say he can't go to the carnival after all. I know how disappointed you are. But you can go with some of the other children on the street." She stooped over the teddy bear and picked him up, regimenting him so that his legs were straight and his arms were close to his sides. "It's silly the way you hang on to this old thing. You're nearly twelve—much too old for teddy bears. He ought to be thrown in the trash."

She was picking up clothes, straightening shoes—her mother was always, always picking up, straightening up now; she didn't used to be that way.

"Here's your robe. Go on downstairs and eat your breakfast. You'll find a glass of orange juice in the refrigerator. Take your milk from the bottle nearest the freezing unit. I'll be down in a minute to cook your egg."

"I don't want an egg," Betty said.

Betty tried to stamp as she walked down the stairs; she wanted to have the house filled with the jolting sounds of heavy footsteps and to have her mother tell her to stop, but the soft soles of her bedroom shoes sounded quieter than tiptoes.

She stood in the kitchen door looking at the neat rows of cabinets with everything stacked precisely in them, the white sink scrubbed spotless, the chairs lined up tight against the walls like shy children at a party. On the second shelf of the refrigerator she found the glass of orange juice. She held it in both hands and rubbed her nose against the film outside until she made a wobbly circle; then she started to drink the juice—but it wouldn't go down; it held back because this was the day of the carnival and her father wasn't going with her.

Her mother was coming downstairs. Betty heard her precise heels strike the steps. She wanted to gulp the orange juice but the first taste of it made her sick. Betty looked at the full glass in her hands; she couldn't listen to a lecture, not today, on the way thousands of children in foreign countries would give anything for this delicious orange juice. There just might be time to get rid of it. She ran to the sink and poured the juice down the drain.

"You must drink some milk now," her mother said, as she entered the kitchen and saw the empty glass in Betty's hand.

"I don't want any milk," Betty said, waiting for the threat to come, waiting for her mother to say she couldn't leave the house until she had drunk some milk.

"I suppose it won't hurt you to go without it this once. Anyway, you'll eat enough junk at the carnival to fill you up. Run on upstairs and bathe."

Her mother said the words but she wasn't paying attention even to herself; her mother's mind seemed to be deep inside her, digging away at other thoughts.

In the bedroom Betty played the lovely forbidden game. If her mother downstairs buzzing with the vacuum cleaner on the dining room rug knew, she'd be mad. Betty brushed her teeth and punched the brush hard on the back of her tongue so that she gagged and the little bit of orange juice that she had swallowed came up. Next she stood in the middle of the floor, holding a glass of water in her hand, and spat water into the basin, spitting like old man Robinson who could stand in a store door and hit the middle of the street, making a cascade over the sidewalk. She filled the tub half full, then stuck only her toes in the water and rubbed herself hard with the towel as if she had taken a bath all over.

She dressed and was trying to sneak out of the house without last minute admonitions from her mother. But there was no need to try to sneak out. While Betty had dawdled over dressing, her father had left his office and come home. He and her mother were talking now, then shouting; the deadly barrage of their voices was wounding them all. Betty did not matter at such a time, not even on carnival day. She didn't belong to them when they were like that. She was alone. She wasn't even born.

She darted down the hall onto the porch and jumped across the front steps.

At the corner she heard a high scream and then a noise that she had never heard before, but she did not dare stop to listen to it.

Long before she got to the huge vacant lot across the railroad tracks, the sounds of the carnival came to her, the voices jabbering, pleading, cajoling, then the music all scrambled up so there was no tune, like children yelling at each other, nothing making sense. And then she was there. It felt good to walk in the sawdust, to have it slow her down like walking in water, to have it creep inside her shoes. She made the rounds to see what she wanted to do; she might do everything; first, though, she must look things over, be cautious, the way you were careful about a new child or a new teacher or a new book before you accepted them.

Betty thought she had remembered it all, yet she hadn't; her memory had changed the carnival, but now it all came back, like a movie she was seeing for the second time—all the small booths with shelves, almost like the vegetable stalls at the Farmers' Market, but instead of vegetables they were strewn with dolls and animals and blankets and lamps and clocks.

The shooting gallery was just ahead. She stopped, remembering last year her father had stood right there, shooting as hard as he could, yet all the ducks marched past ignoring him and his shots until he had popped off a tail. This was the first place they had gone; she closed her eyes trying to make her memory bring it all back, trying to recall what her father had worn, what she had worn; but nothing came—nothing except the emptiness of her father's absence. A man picked up a rifle and squinted, then shot, and Betty walked past him.

Above all the invitations to step this way folks, try your skill for valuable prizes, she heard someone say, "You, young lady with the pigtails, you look like someone who could win. Toss the ring on the numbered pegs and if they add up to an odd number you can pick out what you want." His smile slashed his face and he waggled his hand at her. Betty pulled the envelope her father had given her out of her skirt pocket. The five new dollars made crackling sounds as she fingered them to be sure she gave the man only one.

The man's fingers reached greedily for the dollar; they lingered in his change box. "Naturally you want more than one chance," he said. "One for a quarter or three for fifty cents."

"One," Betty said firmly.

She bumped hard against the counter as she made her first throw. The twine ring fell to the ground before it reached the target. The next one flew past the target and thumped against the thin wall of the booth; the third one looped a peg from which dangled a little placard with 16 painted on it.

"Too bad," the man said. "Sixteen is not a lucky number. But you made a good try. I'm sure you could win the next time."

"No, thank you," Betty said.

The man's smile dwindled; he erased her from his consciousness the way Miss Collins erased the arithmetic lesson in one swoop from the blackboard so that nothing was left, and was calling out, "You, young man in the corduroy jacket, come this way and try your luck at this interesting game of chance and skill."

"One, please," Betty said and tiptoed to shove her money through the mouse trap of an opening in a ticket booth before a tent splashed with signs reading *Thrill to the Death Defying Riders. Crashes. Spills.*

The roar of the motorcycles frightened her; she leaned down and watched them making rushing-spluttering circles; a man fell off, she screamed, wanting to grab her father, to dig her hands into his arms, the way she had when they had watched the riders in the years before. The helmeted men roared past, goggled men stooping, spread over the motorcycles like frogs.

Nothing was the same without her father; she had done all the things they did together. He wasn't there and it would serve him right if she saw things they hadn't seen together. He hadn't exactly steered her away from them; he had mentioned shows and rides he thought they might enjoy more. Now she walked up to the platform where the girls stood in their costumes, wearing robes, then one girl unloosened her robe and showed her costume. The men near Betty grinned; two whistled. The man on the platform winked and said, "Plenty more of the same on the inside."

Betty bought a ticket and sat down in a chair on the outer circle. The ground was uneven and her chair rocked back and forth. The lights went off; six girls came out on the stage and threw kisses at the audience; then a man came out and said something; hoots followed what the man said. Next to Betty a man placed his hand on the knee of a woman sitting on his right and the man and woman smiled at each other. Hoots came again from the audience—hoots full of a special and secret knowledge, shutting out everyone who didn't understand and share the knowledge; Betty looked at the upturned faces of the men sitting near her, their eyes catching strange lights from the stage; and all around, the sun sprinkled through holes in the tent and sifted through in bright dots to the ground. A woman sang a song while some girls in back of her danced, none of them doing the steps quite like any other or at the same time; then the curtain slapped to in gigantic relief that the show was over. The men around Betty got up and reached for cigarettes and they all walked out into the sunlight.

After that Betty went to the Jungle of Snakes; she looked over the canvas sides of an enclosure down to the waving bodies, the snakes writhing-twisting-squirming like all the nightmares of her life, and in the middle of their weaving a woman sat caressing them, letting them climb around her body, small ones making bracelets around her arms and anklets around her ankles; one large one twisted three times around her waist; heads darted back and forth, back and forth, their tongues licking like flames in and out of their flattened heads; then the woman picked up one from the canvas floor and held it to her, fondling it as if it were a baby, kissing it as if it were sweet. To escape her the snake wiggled down, moving in the shape of an s, then lost himself among the other twists and whorls. Fear like fire swept over Betty and she rushed out of the tent.

She stood shivering and her teeth were clamped hard together as if she were playing in snow on the coldest morning in the year, though the midday sun felt like hot August heat on her shoulders. Twice she made the circuit of the booths and shows, trying to decide which one to see next. A sign beckoned to her. *Consult Dr. Vision the Visionary, the Mystic, the Clairvoyant. He Sees All. He Knows All. Come in and Discuss Your Problems.*

Her father didn't approve of fortune-tellers; he said it was much nicer to wait and see what the future brought. But her father wasn't there. Betty stood half in and half out of the tent opening, the way she did in the dentist's reception room, waiting to push the buzzer to let the dentist's assistant know she had come. There was movement within a tent and a man said, "Do you wish to seek the advice of Dr. Vision?" He wore a green satin suit, with a gold sash, and his head held up the huge burden of a turban from which a limp feather dropped like a coxcomb. His mustache was drawn on in a thin black line and his eyebrows almost filled his forehead.

She nodded. It was still like being at the dentist's, not able to deny having an appointment.

"You are speaking to Dr. Vision," the man said, pointing to a chair. She sat at a table across from him; his turbaned head seemed to sit on the crystal ball that separated them.

"The fee is one dollar," he said. Betty's hand rummaged in her pocket for money. Fifty cents bounced to the ground. Dr. Vision sat still with his hands pressed against his forehead and Betty fell to the ground hunting for the money, beating against a small rug that seemed to float on the grass and rubble beneath it. She found the money near Dr. Vision's feet and was surprised to see that he wore unlaced tennis shoes and no socks. She scrambled back to her chair and gave him an apologetic look, as if she had had to excuse herself from the table to be sick. He paid no attention and said in a voice that was a strange kind of whisper, "Do you have some special problem?"

She answered him in the same kind of whisper. "Yes,

my mother—" And then she could go no further. What she was about to say had been betrayal, spreading the dark misery in her house before him, undressing her mother's hurt and her father's hurt before a stranger.

Dr. Vision looked into the crystal.

"I see," he said. "Your mother. Yes. She's been ill. She'll be all right. Don't worry about her. Is there anything else?"

Betty looked at her fingernails. There was one, just one that wasn't chewed; she had tried to leave at least one; one whole nail showed that she had some control; she held her hand tightly but the finger sprang to her mouth and she started biting the nail.

"Maybe your schoolwork is bothering you. Is that it?"

School. Miss Smith saying, until this year you did good work. What's the matter now? It's not that you aren't capable. Don't you like your teachers? Are you getting lazy? What is it?

She couldn't answer Dr. Vision any more than she could answer Miss Smith; the words stopped in her throat.

He smiled, his mustache curling around in his smile like a cat's whiskers. "It's a little early but maybe you want advice about love."

"No," she shouted. Her voice startled them both, so that she dropped it back to the whisper they were using and said, "No, no."

"Then there's just one thing left. A career. You want advice about your career. Well, finish school first, then decide what you want to do. I predict a successful career for you."

Betty stood up and the chair fell behind her. She expected a banging, jolting noise but the grass caught the chair like a net and hushed the sound of its fall. She started to run.

"Just a minute," Dr. Vision said. "You are permitted to communicate with the Secret Powers of the Universe and ask a secret question or make a secret request. They will send you an answer, and only you will know their answer. Look closely into the crystal and repeat your request or your question to yourself three times." Betty walked toward the crystal and bent over it. She made her request silently, as reverently as she said her prayers, her hands folded and her eyes closed: *Let everything be like it was, let everything be like it was, let everything be like it was.*

There was no noise—the whole carnival seemed quiet and still. Then Dr. Vision said words that she didn't understand and all the time he made huge gestures in the air. His hand moved under the table and his thumb reached around his little finger and he held a paper there. "This is your answer. The Powers have spoken," he said and made a bow as if he were waiting for applause. Betty snatched the paper from him and ran, grabbing at the slit in the tent, feeling herself almost smothered by the curtain as she rushed out. She couldn't look at the paper—she didn't dare look; she had the feeling she had had one Christmas when she had been sure that she wouldn't get anything, when she hadn't dared go to the Christmas tree in the living room. Only this wasn't quite like that; this was more—this wasn't being frightened over not getting presents, this was asking for what had to be. The small piece of paper was her destiny and she wadded it in the desperate knot of her fist.

Ahead of her was the largest cluster of people she'd seen all day. Above them on a platform a man took off his coat and swept his brow; as he raised his hand a huge circle of sweat showed underneath his arm on the yellow silk of his shirt. He had the voice of all the men standing on platforms, a chant that came from the back of his nose. "Ladies and gentlemen, you have seen many remarkable things today but you have seen nothing to equal the phenomenon we are presenting. The half man, half woman. This phenomenon can be legally married in any state of our great and beloved America to either a man or woman. You will hear a scientific lecture, absolutely clean, explaining this sexual phenomenon. I urge you to buy your ticket at once. For this performance only the cost is thirty-five cents, the usual price of admission is seventy-five cents, you will be paying less than half the usual charge. Only adults allowed. No one under sixteen admitted."

People moved against Betty, crushing her, pushing her toward the tall box where a man sold tickets. She tried to move away from them, but the man kept looking down at her and saying thirty-five cents please, thirty-five cents, and the ones behind her were saying go on, what's holding us up, and she was trying to tell the man she was only eleven.

The crowd pushed Betty, shoved her, thrust her closer to the man. She felt that she was being suffocated.

"No," she cried out. "No. I don't want to see." She threw back the rocks of their bodies and squirmed through.

She sobbed and plunged through the sawdust, her feet kicked up little storms of it; then her sorrow told her what she was searching for, longing for, what she loved most of all about the carnival. The merry-go-round. That was all she wanted now. She ran toward it and its piping tune embraced her and she saw the stiff ponies with their arched tails and prancing legs making their rounds far away. She dashed toward the merry-go-round, remembering how her father used to let her ride it for hours; how he rode a pony alongside her, and his long legs dangled, striking the floor when his pony descended; how sometimes he doubled up his legs in the stirrup so that he looked like a jockey; how sometimes they got off their ponies and sat together in a chariot. Her father would get tired at last and stand outside the merry-go-round's circle waving to her as she rode by; their waving lasted so long that one wave was not over before she was back again, passing him, waving to him again.

She reached for money to buy tickets and the paper with her destiny on it dropped to the ground. She did not even notice.

"Five," she shouted above the magic piping. "I want five tickets for the merry-go-round."

She folded the tickets and waited on the outside for the merry-go-round to slow down. Some boys leaped off before it stopped, and the younger children squatted down to jump flatfooted to the ground.

Betty found a red pony and climbed on it.

The music started, the merry-go-round began to revolve, while all the booths and shows were lined up outside, not able to touch the enchanted circle of the merry-go-round; voices were saying what they had been saying all day, but now the music blotted them out so that Betty had to strain to hear—hot dogs ten cents, hamburgers made of the finest beef twenty cents, souvenirs you'll value the rest of your life, canary birds two dollars, pennants of your favorite college fifty cents, see the half man half woman, take a chance at this interesting game of skill . . . hurry, hurry, hurry.

And then she did not hear them at all; she would not let her ears hear and she closed her eyes; she was holding on to her pony and listening only to the music, safe from everything, safe from her mother's eternal cleaning and the sad things that went on at home, the harsh voices and the harsher silences.

The merry-go-round slowed and Betty opened her eyes.

He was there.

Her father was just outside the circle of parents waiting for their children. And Betty's day was saved. She should have known her father would not disappoint her.

He waved at her and she saw that he was not alone. It was funny. She knew the man he was with. It was Mr. Williams the policeman—everybody in town knew Mr. Williams. They must have met each other accidentally at the carnival. Maybe Mr. Williams was waiting for someone he knew to get off the merry-go-round. Her father seemed to be pleading with him, as if he were asking permission, and Mr. Williams nodded.

The music was beginning again, the merry-go-round started its slow turning, the children scrambled on and her father leaped on and came toward her. His arms grabbed for her and his mouth seemed to have words that could not be spoken. Then the man taking the tickets came round and Betty handed him two, one for herself and one for her father. The merry-go-round was going faster and her pony started to rise; the lifting took her from her father's embrace, but his hand reached wildly for her hand and their grip was as strong as their love. The carnival around them was not yet the blur it would be when they went at full speed and Betty could still see Mr. Williams watching them, watching most of all her father, and the policeman's face was very sad.

THE FOUR BLIND MEN

Fredric Brown

Like so many of us, Fredric Brown (1906–1972) had a fascination for carnivals and circuses. He used them as backgrounds for three of his twenty-two criminous novels— The Fabulous Clipjoint *(1947),* Dead Ringer *(1948), and* Madball *(1953)—and for several short stories. "The Four Blind Men" is one of the best of those shorter works, an ironically amusing little tale of murder at a small traveling circus and how it relates to the parable of the blind men and the elephant. Brown was a master of the offbeat plot and one of the most innovative writers in both the mystery/ suspense and science fiction/fantasy fields of his (or any other) generation.*

I was sitting with Cap Gurney in his office and we were batting the breeze about nothing in particular and homicide in general. That's Gurney's department—Homicide. Not committing it, but getting the guys who do. He's good at it, too, damn good.

"A clue," Gurney said, "is the most meaningless thing there is. Nine times out of ten it points the wrong way. It helps fill in a picture, though. See what I mean?"

I said, "Like the blind men and the elephant. Know that old one?"

"No. Should I?"

I said, "You might as well. Four blind men went up to touch an elephant to see what one was like. One touched his trunk and thought an elephant was like a snake; one touched his tail and figured an elephant was like a rope; one got his hands against the elephant's side and thought it was like a wall, and the fourth one got his hands around one of the elephant's legs and thought an elephant was like a tree. They argued about it the rest of their lives."

"Uh-huh," said Gurney. "Now that you tell it, I had heard it. But it's good. It holds water."

"A lot of water," I said. "I carried water for one once when I was a kid, to get tickets to the circus. Fifty buckets, unless they changed elephants on me."

Gurney didn't even grin. "It points up what I meant. A clue doesn't mean anything; it's like what *one* of those blind men got hold of and—"

The phone rang and Gurney picked it up. He said, "Yeah" about ten times at intervals and then for a change he said, "Okay," and put the receiver back.

He said, "Talking about circuses, there's a guy dead over at the winter quarters of Harbin-Wilson Shows. Shot. Ringmaster. Some funny angles. Mutt and Jeff are handling it, and that was Mutt on the phone. He wants me to come over."

He was closing up his desk and putting on his coat while he talked, and I put on mine. He said, "Want to come along?" and I said, "Sure," and we went down and got in his car.

Mutt, I might explain, is Walter Andrews and he's called that because his partner is Jeff Kranich and Jeff's a little guy and Andrews is tall, so naturally they call them Mutt and Jeff.

In the car Gurney said, "He was killed with a blank cartridge. A thirty-two caliber blank cartridge out of the pistol he used in the ring. There are some funny angles."

I said, "That one's funny enough."

"Muzzle of the gun was held to his temple," Cap said. "Even a blank shoots a wad and even if it didn't, with the muzzle jammed tight against a man's temple, the blast alone would kill him."

"Could it be suicide, Cap?"

"Could be," Gurney said. "Gun was in his hand, but it could have been put there. Paraffin test to see if there were powder marks on his hand won't mean anything because there will be anyway. It was a new gun, bought this afternoon, and he'd fired a round of blanks just to try it out, Mutt says. Then he reloaded it."

"But Mutt doesn't think it's suicide," I said, "or he wouldn't have called you. Why isn't it?"

"Some funny angles. Three shots were fired out of the gun. All at the time of the murder. It's hard to picture a man shooting off two blanks in the air and then the third into his temple. It doesn't make sense."

I said, "It doesn't make any more sense for a murderer to have done it. How do they know the three shots were all fired at the time of the murder, if it was a murder."

"Two people heard 'em," Gurney said. "The three shots were within a space of ten seconds. Guy named Ambers heard 'em from about fifty feet away, out in the arena.

He's an animal man. A keeper I mean, not a trainer. He was dozing and they woke him up. A watchman heard 'em from the floor above—he says. One other guy was in the building—a bookkeeper, working late in the office. Says he didn't hear any shots, and that could be because the office was fairly far away."

Gurney braked to a stop for a red light. He could have turned on his flasher and gone on through, but he never did that unless there was a real hurry. I guess he figured the dead ringmaster would wait till we got there.

I said, "I still say it doesn't make any more sense for a murderer to fire two extra shots—with blanks—than for a suicide. You didn't answer that."

"No, I didn't," Gurney said. "Because I don't know. But Mutt says suicide's practically out of the question, and that's why he wanted me over there. He didn't tell me how he figured suicide is out."

He stopped the car and started jockeying it into a parking space. He said, "The ringmaster's name was Sopronowicz. Everybody under him hated his guts because he was an all-around louse. A sadist. The kind of guy anybody might want to kill, even with a blank cartridge.

"Any one of the three men in the building at the time might have done it, far as reason is concerned. Especially Ambers, the animal keeper. Sopronowicz was cruel to animals, and Ambers loves 'em. Ambers admits he'd like to have killed him, but says he didn't. And there aren't any powder marks on his hands."

"How about the others?"

"Watchman is named Carle. He's Sopronowicz's father-in-law. There could be a motive there, even though Sopronowicz got him the job. The bookkeeper's name is Gold. Sopronowicz—"

"Let's just call him Soppy from now on," I suggested.

"The ringmaster had arguments with Gold over bookkeeping. He had a slight percentage interest in the circus, and thought he was being cheated on his statements."

"Nice guy," I said.

Gurney said, "Everybody loved him." We got out of the car and started for the entrance of the building.

"Used to be a skating rink," Gurney told me. "Harbin-Wilson has used it for winter quarters for years now. You've heard of 'em?"

"Small circus, isn't it? A one-ring outfit that plays the smaller towns and some fairs, the way I've heard it. But getting back to friend Soppy, Cap—"

"You know everything I do," Gurney interrupted me. "All I know's what Mutt told me, and you know that now."

The door was locked and he hammered on it until Jeff opened it. Jeff said, "Hi, Cap. Hi, Fred. Come on, this way. It's in a room off the arena."

We followed him down the hall and through a door that led to a high-ceilinged room almost big enough for a football field. You could see that it had been planned, originally, for an ice rink, although it looked more like the inside of a circus tent now. There was a clear space in the middle, with a ring laid out below, and trapezes and other aerial apparatus above. The animals were at the far end, and the place smelled like a circus, too—a very stale circus. There were a dozen horses in stalls, a somewhat frowzy elephant, and a couple of mangy big cats in cages.

The elephant started across the concrete floor to meet us and a wizened little gray-haired man pulled her back gently with a bull-hook.

"That's Ambers," Jeff said. "The little one. The big one is an elephant."

"Thanks," I said. "That all the menagerie they got?"

"All the performing ones. A few more that go along for show don't join up till they hit the road. Couple of weeks from now. There's where the stiff is."

Jeff Kranich was pointing to a double doorway that led off the main arena. Both doors were wide open, hooked back against the wall. Through them we could see the body lying on the floor, back against a door on the far side of the room past the double doorway.

Mutt was leaning gloomily against the wall, staring

down at what had been the ringmaster. He didn't greet us; he just started talking. He said, "It makes nuts. I haven't moved a thing, Cap, except to lift his hand and put it down again in the same position. Three shells fired, all right. And we've questioned the only three men we know to have been in the building and their stories sound O.K., except that they were far apart and none of 'em can alibi the others."

Gurney said, "You said it wouldn't be suicide. Got a good reason?"

"Plenty good," Mutt said. "The guy was happy. He just picked a four-leaf clover. Gold—that bookkeeper—tells me he was getting a full partnership in the show when the season started. Wilson died last year, and Harbin made Sopronowicz the offer. The show's in the black. He'd have cleared thirty–forty thousand or more this coming season, more money than he ever had before. He was in good shape physically; just passed an insurance exam yesterday. And everybody I've talked to says he was so cheerful the last few days he was twice as mean as usual. Ambers says the bull's got hook marks to prove it; he was working the bull early this evening along with the trainer, a guy named Standish.

"He wasn't broke; he's got over two hundred bucks in his wallet. And suddenly he kills himself for no reason at all? Nuts."

Gurney was looking around the room. There wasn't much in it. A big wardrobe cabinet on one side, closed and padlocked. Two closed trunks and two folding chairs, both lying on their sides.

"Chairs were knocked over that way?" Gurney asked.

Mutt nodded. "I didn't move anything that I didn't move back. I been questioning people and getting nowhere. It makes nuts."

"Who found him?" Gurney wanted to know.

"Ambers. But not right away. He was off the arena in a room that has a bunk in it down near the other end.

He was taking a nap; says it's O.K. for him to do that because he's on damn near twenty-four hour duty here. He heard three shots, but figured Sopronowicz was just trying the gun again; didn't think much of it. But he couldn't go back to sleep again and twenty minutes or so later—that's his guess—he came back out into the arena and wandered down to this end of it to get something. He saw the body lying there when he passed that double doorway."

Gurney asked, "How about Carle, the watchman?"

"Heard the shots from the floor above where he was making the rounds. Didn't think anything of it for the same reason Ambers didn't. Says about half an hour after he heard 'em Ambers came hunting him and told him to phone the police. That would fit, for time. And Gold still didn't know about it till we got here. Neither Ambers nor Carle thought to go back to the office to tell him."

"How do they figure it, or do they?"

"They don't, except they're sure it isn't suicide. Carle especially. Says Sopronowicz had a yellow streak a foot wide down his back, and that the only person on earth who wouldn't want to shoot Sopronowicz was Sopronowicz. Besides, they both knew about the partnership and the big luck it was for him to get it."

Gurney jerked his thumb at the door—the only door in the room aside from the open double doorway. "Was that bolted like it is now?"

"Yeah," Mutt said. "Bolted from this side. And it's a tight bolt. I could just barely get it open to see what was through there. It's a hallway. I bolted it again."

I looked around again and then walked back to the arena. I walked down to where Ambers and the animals were. The wizened little man was using a currycomb on a beautiful palomino gelding.

He looked around at me. "Got it doped out yet?" he wanted to know.

"They haven't," I said.

"Good. Hope they don't. Ever."

"You got it doped out?" I asked him.

"Me? Hell no. But if I did I sure wouldn't tell anybody."

"The law says you should."

He chuckled. "Don't tell me the law, son. I read Black-stone once when I was young. It didn't take, but I remember one thing. You got to tell what you know, but you don't got to tell what you think or guess. Now run along and peddle your marbles."

I didn't run along and peddle my marbles, but I did wander back toward the others. I passed Mutt coming out of the doorway of the death room. I went in and Gurney was leaning against the wall at the same spot where Mutt had been leaning, staring thoughtfully down at the body.

I asked him, "Mind if I straighten one of these chairs?"

Gurney said, "Go ahead." I put one of the chairs right side up and sat down on it. I asked him, "Got an idea?" and he said, "Yeah."

I asked, "What?" and he didn't answer. So I tried to get an idea myself and I didn't.

Then Mutt came in, with a kind of funny look on his face, and he nodded at Gurney.

Gurney said, "Good. You can wind it up then, you and Jeff." He turned to me and said, "Come on, Fred. Let's go."

"You got it?" I asked him.

"Yeah. Come on; let's have a beer and I'll tell you about it."

But he didn't, right away, even after we had the beers in front of us.

He said, "To crime," and we took a drink. Then he said, "You solved it, you know. That story about the four blind men."

"All right," I said, "so you want to be coy for a while. So I'll help you by floundering around myself. Here's what I've got—or haven't got.

"I don't think it was suicide because there wasn't any reason for suicide and plenty of reasons against it. So there was a killer and he came in through the open doorway because the door to the hall was tightly bolted on the inside. Want me to play all of the four blind men for you?"

"Go ahead."

I said, "The chairs were both knocked over, so there was a struggle. But I saw, as well as you did, that his hair wasn't mussed, except right over the right temple from the blast. And his shirt wasn't rumpled and his waxed mustache wasn't mussed. So, said the second blind man, there wasn't a struggle."

I took another sip of beer. I said, "The killer was pretty clever, since there wasn't a struggle, to get hold of the gun and trick Soppy into letting him hold the muzzle to his temple. It would have to be by trickery unless Soppy was asleep. But the killer wasn't very clever or he wouldn't have gummed up things by firing two extra shots. They gummed the suicide hypothesis, even if lack of motive for suicide didn't. And yet, said the fourth blind man, the killer tried to make it look like suicide by putting the gun in Soppy's hand. As the fifth blind man, the one named Mutt, said, it makes nuts."

Gurney said, "Your trouble is with the blind men. You took the story from the wrong end. You missed the whole point of the story you told me."

"Yeah?" I said. "And what was the point?"

"The point of the story was that it was an elephant," Gurney said.

He took a long draught of his beer and put the glass down empty. He signaled the bartender, and then he said, "What happened is simple. The elephant wasn't staked out; you saw that. It happened to wander down to the door of the room where Sopronowicz was doing something or other. It saw him, and neither Ambers nor the trainer was around and it recalled whatever cruel treatment it had ever had at Sopronowicz's hands. And Sopronowicz didn't have a bull-hook.

"It started through the double doorway to get him, and what happened from there on in took about ten seconds. The ringmaster saw death lumbering through the double doorway from the arena and he did the best he could. He fired a blank in the bull's face to scare it and the bull kept coming. One or the other of them knocked over the chairs; probably the elephant, because the chairs were right there inside the double door.

"Sopronowicz fired another shot, probably as he reached the single doorway that he could have got through and the elephant couldn't. But it was bolted and the bolt stuck and anyway it opened toward him and he couldn't have made it before the elephant got him.

"And—well, it isn't pleasant, I guess, to be killed by an elephant. You get all your bones broken and maybe a blunt tusk through your guts, and maybe you last thirty seconds and maybe three minutes, but it's a bad thirty seconds or three minutes.

"In the last second, he saved himself that. Probably the elephant's trunk was going around him when he put the muzzle to his temple and pulled the trigger. So he falls down dead and the elephant probably sniffs at him with the end of his trunk and sees—or smells, or knows some-how—that he's dead, and lets it go at that. And goes back about his business."

"It could be," I said. "It makes sense. But—"

"But nothing," Gurney said. "While you were jawing with Ambers I remembered your story about the elephant and got the answer. So I sent Mutt to check with a little paraffin if there were powder marks on the elephant's face and trunk. When he came back and nodded that there were, that was that. So thanks for the story."

I finished my beer and ordered another one apiece for us.

I said, "You still miss the *point* of the story, though. It was the conflicting impressions the blind men got, each from touching a different part of the critter. The fact that it was an elephant wasn't the point of the story at all, damn it."

Gurney said, "But just the same, it *was* an elephant."

"Nuts," I said. And we drank our beer.

THE DOUBLE WHAMMY

Robert Bloch

The "geek" has always been an object of fascination and repulsion on the carnival circuit. Typically he is a man who is down on his luck, often an alcoholic or drug addict, and thus willing to do anything for money—including, as in this story, biting the heads off chickens. Geeks are taken for granted among the carny folk; and when Rod, the protagonist of this tale, finds himself becoming afraid of his show's geek, it is a source of terror. As well it should be. . . . Robert Bloch, who is best known for his excellent novel, Psycho *(1959), is a master storyteller. In both his long and short fiction, he weaves a seemingly effortless web of horror around his all-too-human (or are they?) characters, which neatly obscures the fine dividing line between what is and what seems to be.*

R od pulled the chicken out of the burlap bag and threw it down into the pit.

The chicken squawked and fluttered, and Rod glanced away quickly. The gaping crowd gathered around the canvas walls of the pit ignored him; now all the eyes were focused on what was happening down below. There was a cackling, a scrabbling sound, and then a sudden sharp simultaneous intake of breath from the spectators.

Rod didn't have to look. He knew that the geek had caught the chicken.

Then the crowd began to roar. It was a strange noise, compounded of women's screams, high harsh laughter teetering on the edge of hysteria, and deep hoarse masculine murmurs of shocked dismay.

Rod knew what *that* sound meant, too.

The geek was biting off the chicken's head.

Rod stumbled out of the little tent, not looking back, grateful for the cool night air that fanned his sweating face. His shirt was soaked through under the cheap blazer. He'd have to change again before he went up on the outside platform to make his next pitch.

The pitch itself didn't bother him. Being a talker was his job and he was good at it; he liked conning the marks and turning the tip. Standing up there in front of the bloody banners and spieling about the Strange People always gave him his kicks, even if he was only working for a lousy mudshow that never played anywhere north of Tennessee. For three seasons straight he'd been with it, he was a pro, a real carny.

But now, all of a sudden, something was spooking him. No use kidding himself, he had to face it.

Rod was afraid of the geek.

He crossed behind the ten-in-one tent and moved in

140

the direction of his little trailer, pulling out a handkerchief and wiping his forehead. That helped a little, but he couldn't wipe away what was inside his head. The cold, clammy fear was always there now, night and day.

Hell of it was, it didn't make sense. The Monarch of Mirth Shows had always worked "strong"—out here in the old boondocks you could still get away with murder, particularly if you were only killing chickens. And who gives a damn about chickens, anyway? The butchers chop off a million heads a day. A chicken is just a lousy bird, and a geek is just a lousy wino. A rumdum who hooks up with a carny, puts on a phony wild-man outfit and hops around in the bottom of a canvas enclosure while the talker gives the crowd a line about this ferocious monster, half man and half beast. Then the talker throws in the chicken and the geek does his thing.

Rod shook his head, but what was inside it didn't move. It stayed there, cold and clammy and coiled up in a ball. It had been there almost ever since the beginning of this season, and now Rod was conscious that it was growing. The fear was getting bigger.

But why? He'd worked with half-a-dozen lushes over the past three years. Maybe biting the head off a live chicken wasn't exactly the greatest way to make a living, but if the geeks didn't mind, why should he care? And Rod knew that a geek wasn't really a monster, just a poor old futz who was down on his luck and hooked on the sauce—willing to do anything, as long as he got his daily ration of popskull.

This season the geek they took on was named Mike. A quiet guy who kept out of everybody's way when he wasn't working; under the burnt-cork make-up he had the sad, wrinkled face of a man of fifty. Fifty hard years, perhaps thirty of them years of hard drinking. He never talked, just took his pint and curled up in the canvas on one of the trucks. Looking at him then, Rod was never spooked; if anything, he felt kind of sorry for the poor bastard.

It was only when the geek was in the pit that Rod

felt that ball of fear uncoil. When he saw the woolly wig and the black face, the painted hands that clutched and clawed—yes, and when he saw the grinning mouth open to reveal the rotting yellow teeth, ready to bite—

Oh, it was getting to him all right, he was really uptight now. But nobody else knew. And nobody *would* know. Rod wasn't about to spill his guts to anyone here on the lot, and how would it look if he ran off to some head-shrinker and said, "Hey, Doc, help me—I'm afraid I'm gonna turn into a geek." He knew better than that. No shrinker could help him, and come what may he'd never end up geeking for a living. He'd lick this thing himself; he had to, and he would, just as long as no one else caught on and bugged him about it.

Rod climbed the steps, removing his jacket and unbuttoning his wet shirt as he moved up into the darkness of the trailer.

And then he felt the hands sliding across his bare chest, moving up over his shoulders to embrace him, and he smelt the fragrance, felt the warmth and the pressure even as he heard the whispered words. "Rod—darling—are you surprised?"

Truth to tell, Rod wasn't surprised. But he was pleased that she'd been waiting for him. He took her in his arms and glued his mouth to hers as they sank down on the cot.

"Cora," he murmured. "Cora—"

"Shhhh! No time to talk."

She was right. There wasn't time, because he had to be back on the bally platform in fifteen minutes. And it wasn't a smart idea to talk anyway, not with Madame Sylvia sneaking around and popping up out of nowhere just when you least expected her. Why in hell did a swinging bird like Cora have to have an old buzzard like Madame Sylvia for a grandmother?

But Rod wasn't thinking about grandmothers now, and he wasn't thinking about geeks, either. That was what Cora did to him, that was what Cora did *for* him, dissolving the cold fear in warm, writhing, wanting flesh. At times like these Rod knew why he couldn't cut out, why he stayed with it. Staying with it meant staying with her, and this was enough; this was everything, with ribbons on it.

It was only later, struggling into his shirt, hearing her whisper, "Please, honey, hurry and let's get out of here before she comes looking for me," that he wondered if it was really worth it. All this horsing around for a fast grope in the dark with a teen-age spik who practically creamed her jeans every time the old lady looked cross-eyed at her.

Sure Cora was a beautiful job, custom-made for him. But when you got right down to it she was still a kid and nobody would ever mistake her brain for a computer. Besides, she was a spik—well, maybe not exactly, but she was a gypsy and that added up to the same thing.

Walking back to the bally platform for the last pitch of the evening, Rod decided it was time to cool it. From now on the chill was in.

That night the show folded and trucked to Mazoo County Fair Grounds for a ten-day stand. They were all day setting up and then the crowds surged in, rednecks from the toolies up in the hills; must have been a couple thousand coming in night after night, and all craving action.

For almost a week Rod managed to keep out of Cora's way without making it too obvious. Her grandmother was running the mitt camp concession on the other end of the midway, and Cora was supposed to shill for her; usually she was too busy to sneak off. A couple of times Rod caught sight of her signaling to him from down in the crowd around the bally platform, but he always looked the other way, pretending he didn't see her. And once he heard her scratching on the trailer door in the middle of the night, only he made out that he was asleep, even when she called out to him, and after about ten minutes she went away.

The trouble was, Rod didn't sleep anywhere near that good; seemed like every time he closed his eyes now he could see the pit, see the black geek and the white chicken.

So the next time Cora came scratching on the door

he let her in, and for a little while he was out of the pit, safe in her arms. And instead of the geek growling and the chicken cackling he heard her voice in the darkness, her warm, soft voice, murmuring, "You do love me, don't you, Rod?"

The answer came easy, the way it always did. "Course I do. You know that."

Her fingers tightened on his arms. "Then it's all right. We can get married and I'll have the baby—"

"Baby?"

He sat up fast.

"I wasn't going to tell you, honey, not until I was sure, but I am now." Her voice was vibrant. "Just think, darling—"

He *was* thinking. And when he spoke, his voice was hoarse.

"Your grandmother—Madame Sylvia—does she know?"

"Not yet. I wanted you to come with me when I tell her—"

"Tell her nothing."

"Rod?"

"Tell her nothing. Get rid of it."

"Honey—"

"You heard me."

She tried to hold him then but he wrenched himself free, stood up, reached for his shirt. She was crying now, but the louder she sobbed, the more he hurried dressing, just as if she wasn't there. Just as if she wasn't stuttering and stammering all that jazz about what did he mean, he couldn't do this, he had to listen, and if the old lady found out she'd kill her.

Rod wanted to yell at her to shut up, he wanted to crack her one across the mouth and *make* her shut up, but he managed to control himself. And when he did speak his voice was soft.

"Take it easy, sweetheart," he said. "Let's not get ourselves all excited here. There's no problem."

"But I told you—"

He patted her arm in the darkness. "Relax, will you? You got nothing to worry about. You told me yourself the old lady doesn't know. Get rid of it and she never will."

Christ, it was so simple you'd think even a lame-brain like Cora would understand. But instead she was crying again, louder than ever, and beating on him with her fists.

"No, no, you can't make me! We've got to get married, the first time I let you, you promised we would, just as soon as the season was over—"

"As far as I'm concerned, the season's over right now." Rod tried to keep his voice down, but when she came at him again, clinging, somehow it was worse than feeling her fists. He couldn't stand this any more; not the clinging, not the wet whimpering.

"Listen to me, Cora. I'm sorry about what happened, you know that. But you can scrub the marriage bit."

The way she blew up then you'd have thought the world was coming to an end, and he had to slap her to keep the whole damn lot from hearing her screech. He felt kind of lousy, belting her one like that, but it quieted her down enough so's he could hustle her out. She went away still crying, but very quietly. And at least she got the message.

Rod didn't see her around the next day, or the one after. But in order to keep her from bugging him again, he spent both nights over at Boots Donahue's wagon, playing a little stud with the boys. He figured that if there was any trouble and he had to peel off fast, maybe he could turn a few extra bucks for the old grouch-bag.

Only it didn't exactly work out that way. Usually he was pretty lucky with the pasteboards, but he had a bad run both evenings and ended up in hock for his next three paychecks. That was bad enough, but the next day was worse.

Basket Case gave him the word.

Rod was just heading for the cook tent for breakfast when Basket Case called him over. He was lying on an old army cot outside his trailer with a cigarette in his mouth. "How's for a light?" he asked.

Rod cupped a match for him, then stuck around, knowing he'd have to flick the ashes while Basket Case had his smoke. And a guy born without arms or legs has a little trouble getting rid of a butt, too.

Funny thing, the Strange People never got to Rod, no matter how peculiar they looked. Even Basket Case, who was just a living head attached to a shapeless bundle of torso, didn't give him the creeps. Maybe it was because old Basket Case himself didn't seem to mind; he just took it for granted that he was a freak. And he always acted and sounded normal, not like that rumdum geek who put on a fright wig and blacked up and made noises like a crazy animal when he went after a chicken—

Rod tried to push away the thought and pulled out a cigarette for himself. He was just getting a match when Basket Case looked up at him.

"Heard the news?" he asked.

"What news?"

"Cora's dead."

Rod burned his fingers and the match dropped away. "Dead?"

Basket Case nodded. "Last night. Madame Sylvia found her in the trailer after the last show—"

"What happened?"

Basket Case just looked at him. "Thought maybe you could tell me that."

Rod had to choke out the words. "What's that crack supposed to mean?"

"Nothing." Basket Case shrugged. "Madame Sylvia told Donahue the kid died of a ruptured appendix."

Rod took a deep breath. He forced himself to look sorry, but all at once he felt good, very good. Until he heard Basket Case saying, "Only thing is, I never heard of anyone rupturing their appendix with a knitting needle."

Rod reached out and took the cigarette from Basket Case to dump his ashes. The way his hand was trembling, he didn't have to do anything but let them fall.

"The appendix story is just a cover—Madame Sylvia doesn't want the fuzz nosing around." Basket Case nodded as Rod stuck the cigarette back between his lips. "But if you ask me, she knows."

"Now look, if you're saying what I think you're saying, you'd better forget it—"

"Sure, I'll forget it. But *she* won't." Basket Case lowered his voice. "Funeral's this afternoon, over at the county cemetery. You better show your face along with the rest of us, just so it doesn't look funny. After that, my advice to you is cut and run."

"Now wait a minute—" Rod was all set to go on, but what was the use? Basket Case *knew*, and there was no sense putting on an act with him. "I can't run," he said. "I'm into Boots Donahue for three weeks' advance. If I cop out, he'll spread the word around and I won't work carny again, not in these parts."

Basket Case spat the cigarette out. It landed on the ground beside the cot and Rod stamped it out. Basket Case shook his head. "Never mind the money," he said. "If you don't run, you won't be working anywhere." He glanced around cautiously and when he spoke again his voice was just a whisper. "Don't you understand? This is the crunch— I tell you, Madame Sylvia knows what happened."

Rod wasn't about to whisper. "That old bat? You said yourself she doesn't want any truck with the fuzz, and even if she did, she couldn't prove anything. So what's to be afraid of?"

"The double whammy," said Basket Case.

Rod blinked at him.

"Want me to spell it out for you? Three seasons ago, just before you came with the show, fella name of Richey was boss canvasman. Mighty nice guy, but he had a problem—he was scared of snakes. Babe Flynn was working them, had a bunch of constrictors, all standards for her act and harmless as they come. But Richey had such a thing about snakes he wouldn't even go near her wagon.

"Where he went wrong was, he went near Madame Sylvia's wagon. Cora was pretty young then, just budding out you might say, but that didn't stop Richey from making his move. Nothing serious, only conversation. How the old lady found out about it I don't know and how she found out he was spooked on snakes I don't know either, because he always tried to hide it, of course.

"But one afternoon, last day of our stand in Red Clay it was, Madame Sylvia took a little walk over to Richey's trailer. He was standing outside, shaving, with a mirror hung up on the door.

"She didn't say anything to him, didn't even look at him—just stared at his reflection in the mirror. Then she made a couple of passes and mumbled something under her breath and walked away. That's all there was to it.

"Next morning, Richey didn't show up. They found him lying on the floor inside his trailer, deader'n a mackerel. Half his bones were broken and the way the body was crushed you'd swear a dozen constrictors had been squeezing his guts. I saw his face and believe me it wasn't pretty."

Rod's voice was husky. "You mean the old lady set those snakes on him?"

Basket Case shook his head. "Babe Flynn kept her snakes locked up tight as a drum in her own trailer. She swore up and down nobody'd even come near them the night before, let alone turned 'em loose. But Richey was dead. And that's what I mean about the double whammy."

"Look." Rod was talking to Basket Case, but he wanted to hear it himself, too. "Madame Sylvia's just another mitt reader, peddling phony fortunes to the suckers. All this malarkey about gypsy curses—"

"Okay, okay." Basket Case shrugged. "But if I were you I'd cut out of here, fast. And until I did, I wouldn't let that old lady catch me standing in front of a mirror."

"Thanks for the tip," Rod said.

As he walked away, Basket Case called after him. "See you at the funeral."

But Rod didn't go to the funeral.

It wasn't as if he was afraid or anything; he just didn't like the idea of standing at Cora's grave with everybody looking at him as if they knew. And they damned well did by now, all of them. Maybe it would be smart to ease out of here like Basket Case said, but not now. Not until he could pay off what he owed to Donahue. For the next three weeks he'd just sweat it out.

Meanwhile, he'd watch his step. Not that he believed that crazy story about the double whammy—Basket Case was just putting him on, it had to be a gag. But it never hurt to be careful.

Which is why Rod shaved for the evening performance that afternoon. He knew the old lady was at the funeral like everybody else; she wouldn't be creeping up behind him to capture his soul from his reflection in the mirror—

Damned right she wouldn't!

Rod made a face at himself in the glass. What the hell was the matter with him, anyway? He didn't buy that bit about the curse.

But there *was* something wrong. Because for a moment when Rod looked into the mirror he didn't see himself. Instead he was staring into a black, grinning face, with bloodshot, red-rimmed eyes and a twisted mouth opening to show the yellow fangs—

Rod blinked and the face went away; it was his own reflection peering back at him. But his hand was shaking so that he had to put the razor down.

His hand was still shaking when he reached for the bottle on the top shelf, and he must have spilled more of the whiskey than he managed to get into the glass. So he took a slug straight from the bottle instead. And then another, until his hands were steady again. Good for the nerves, a little snort now and then. Only you had to watch that stuff, not let it run away with you. Because if you didn't, pretty soon you got hooked and some day before you knew what was happening, you wound up in the woolly wig and the blackface, down there in the pit waiting for the white chicken—

The hell with that noise. It wasn't going to happen. Just a couple of weeks and he'd be out of here, no more carny, nothing to bug him ever again. All he had to do now was keep his cool and watch his step.

Rod watched his step very carefully that evening when he walked up to the bally platform and adjusted his mike for the pitch. Standing before the bloody banners he felt good, very good indeed, and the couple of extra belts he'd taken from the bottle just for luck seemed to have unwound that ball of fear inside his head. It was easy to make his pitch about the Strange People—"All there on the inside, folks, on the *in* side"—and watch the marks flocking around down below. The marks—*they* were the real freaks, only they didn't know it. Shelling out their dough to gawk at poor devils like Basket Case, then paying extra for the SPE-CIAL ADDED ATTRACTION, ADULTS ONLY, in the canvas pit behind the ten-in-one tent. What kind of a pervert would pay money to see a geek? What was the matter with people like that?

And what was the matter with him? Standing there beside the pit, holding the burlap bag and feeling the chicken fluttering helplessly inside, Rod felt the fear return-ing to flutter within himself. He didn't want to look down into the pit and see the geek crouching there, growling and grimacing like a real wild man. So he looked at the crowd instead, and that was better. The crowd didn't know he was afraid. Nobody knew he was spooked, let alone what scared him.

Rod talked to the crowd, building his pitch, and his hands started to fumble with the cord around the neck of the burlap bag, getting ready to open it and dump the chicken into the pit.

And that's when he saw *her*.

She was standing over to one side, right up against

the edge of the canvas; just a little old woman dressed in black, with a black shawl draped over her head. Her face was pinched, her skin was brown and leathery, wrinkled into a permanent scowl. An old lady, nobody gave her a second glance, but Rod saw her.

And she saw *him*.

Funny, he'd never noticed Madame Sylvia's eyes before. They were big and brown and staring—they stared right at him now, stared right *through* him.

Rod wrenched his gaze away, forced his fingers to open the sack. All the while, mechanically, he was talking, finishing the buildup as he reached for the chicken, pulled it out, flung the clucking creature down to that other creature in the pit—the creature that growled and grabbed and oh my God it was biting now—

He couldn't watch and he had to turn his head away, seeing the crowd again as they shrieked and shuddered, getting their kicks. And *she* was still standing there, still staring at him.

But now her clawlike hand moved, moved over the rim of the canvas to extend a pointing forefinger. Rod knew what she was pointing at; she was pointing at the geek pit. And that wrinkled face *could* change its expression, because she was smiling now.

Rod turned and groped his way out into the night.

She knew.

Not just about him and Cora, but about everything. Those eyes that stared at him and through him had also stared *inside* him—stared inside and found his fear. That's why she'd pointed and smiled; she knew what he was afraid of.

The midway lights were bright, but it was darker behind the canvas sidewalls except where a patch of moonlight shone on the big water barrel setting next to the cook tent.

Rod's face was damp with sweat; he headed for the barrel and soaked his handkerchief in the water to wipe his forehead. Time for another pitch pretty soon, and the next show. He had to pull himself together.

The cool water helped to clear his head, and he dipped his handkerchief again. That was better. No sense flipping just because a nutty old dame gave him a dirty look. This business about gypsies and the evil eye and the double whammy was all a crock. And even if there *was* something to it, he wouldn't let her get to him. He wasn't about to stand in front of any mirrors—

Then he glanced down at the water in the barrel, saw his features reflected in the moonlight shining there. And he saw her face, standing right behind him. Her eyes were staring and her mouth was mumbling, and now her hands were coming up, making passes in the air. Making passes like an old witch, she was going to turn him into a geek with the double whammy—

Rod turned, and that's the last thing he remembered. He must have passed out, fallen, because when he came to he was still on the ground.

But the ground was somehow different than the earth outside the tent; it was covered with sawdust. And the light was stronger, it was shining straight down between the canvas walls of the pit.

He was in the pit.

The realization came, and Rod looked up, knowing it was too late, she'd caught him, he was in the geek's body now.

But something else was wrong, too; the pit was deeper, the canvas walls much higher. Everything seemed bigger, even the blur of faces crowded around the sides of the pit way up above. *Way up above*—why was he so small?

Then his eyes shifted as he heard the growling. Rod turned and looked up again, just in time to see the black grinning face looming over him, the giant mouth opening to reveal the rotting yellow teeth. It was only then that Rod knew what she had really done to him, as the huge hands grabbed out, pulling him close. For a moment he squawked and fluttered his wings.

Then the geek bit off his head.

ANOTHER BURNT-OUT CASE

Bill Pronzini and Barry N. Malzberg

The happenings in a traveling carnival show are farcical at best—so what better setting for a story that is pure farce? Writing in tandem, Bill Pronzini and Barry N. Malzberg have produced numerous short stories, as well as such novels as The Running of Beasts *(1976),* Night Screams *(1979), and* Prose Bowl *(1980). At times they have a truly comic touch, as in this tale of a down-at-the-heels carny troupe. But in spite of the farcical elements, you'll probably find that the Sicilian Snare Drum, the Human Pyromaniac, Big Tiny, and Little Tiny are reflective of the larger farce of whose climax their somewhat addled boss is fond of speaking—namely, the imminent collapse of Western Civilization.—M. M.*

I was sitting in my trailer, thinking once more about the imminent collapse of Western Civilization, when the Sicilian Snare Drum and the Human Pyromaniac came in and the Snare Drum said, "Boss, we have figured a way out of all this."

"There is no way out," I said. "To die in Boca Gables, Florida, is redundant."

"Seriously," the Human Pyromaniac said. That is, I am pretty sure it was he who made that comment and the Snare Drum the first to speak. It is not easy for me at the age of sixty-one to completely individuate my employees, but then again, they sort themselves out in the long run. "Seriously," he said again, "we have figured out how to shuck the carnival racket."

I ran a small traveling carnival, called Webb Carter's Wonderama, and I should point out that it was located at this time in the very Boca Gables of which I slurringly spoke. "Indeed," I said.

The Human Pyromaniac nodded; his stage name is Giraldo and he has a certain integrity, which is to say that he has never set fire to any person other than himself. "The answer," he said, "is insurance."

"Insurance?"

"Insurance," the Sicilian Snare Drum said.

"What are you talking about? Insure who or what?"

"Ourselves," one of them said.

"Out of the basic assumption," the other one said, "that in death there is life."

I have always resisted the imitative fallacy in art coined by Yvor Winters, holding to the proposition that the employees of Webb Carter's Wonderama are as unique in their spirit as they are in their function; but I must admit that on the instinctual level I cannot accept this. Human Pyro-

154

maniac is, after all, a rather out-of-the-mainstream-of-Western-Civilization occupation, to say nothing of the Snare Drum, who flays himself nightly in place of an orchestra we cannot afford.

I said, "We already have insurance. I have always complied with all of the federal laws on the matter. We carry a large general floater with the Firehouse Fund."

Giraldo's eyes glowed reverently. "Ah," he said, "fire."

The Snare Drum said, "This general floater carries a triple-indemnity clause for loss of life during a public performance. We have checked. The total of such a triple-indemnity death would be two hundred and twenty-five thousand dollars."

I pondered this information for a time, not having previously investigated the policy to any degree. "I am beginning to see the point," I said at length. "In fact the beauty of the conception, to coin a phrase, is now unflowering in all the dense and complicated corridors of my mind."

"We knew it would," one of them said.

"But there arises a question. Who is going to die? Who is elected to perish for the greater good of us all? I cannot say that I detect a suicidal eagerness in either of your faces."

"We did not think it necessary for anyone to actually die," one of them said.

The other one said, "For the purpose of collecting on the triple-indemnity clause, it would seem that the convincing *appearance* of death would be sufficient."

"Kindly elaborate."

"Flame," the Human Pyromaniac said fervently. "We will use the flames for which I am so well known and with which I have constructed my successful if not lucrative career. Someone will appear to perish, leaving not a recognizable *corpus delicti* but little more than wisps and ashes."

I pondered further. "Which someone did you have in mind?"

"Well, it cannot be me," the Snare Drum said, "inasmuch as I must play dramatic accompaniment; otherwise, we will have no musical conviction in the performance."

"This is true," I said. "Therefore, it is obvious who the someone must be."

"We expected you would see it our way."

"I am not that person," I said. "I am not a performer, as you well know. Thus, there is only one person left in our little troupe who qualifies, and that person is Big Tiny." I smiled. "Do you not agree?"

They nodded slowly. "We agree," one of them said. "Have you discussed the plan with him?"

"Not as yet."

"I will attend to that," I said, "and converse further with you after I have done so. I have no doubt that he will see it just as I have."

"Webb," one of them said, "we are glad that you do not consider our proposal as in any way indicative of moral corruption, but merely as a sane and wise means in which to get out of all this on our shared proceeds."

"It is not a moral failure," I said, "it is only symptomatic of the collapse of Western Civilization."

"Surely," the other one said, and both of them withdrew. The closed door of my trailer rattled in the wind.

I considered matters more carefully. After a while I stood, went outside, and walked down the small midway in the rain. Webb Carter's Wonderama takes up no more than half a city block. It is a very small show, although of course it completely lacks exceptional talent. One Human Pyromaniac, one Sicilian Snare Drum, one sixty-one-year-old proprietor, and two people of the small persuasion; our former major attraction, the Mad Ghoul, had long since departed under unfortunate circumstances.

Little drops of water flicked off my craggily distinguished features, or what I like to think of as my craggily distinguished features, as I neared the tent in which Big Tiny and Little Tiny dwelt. I knocked on the flap of the tent, which is not an easy thing to do considering the resiliency of tent flaps. Momentarily Little Tiny appeared. She is in her late twenties, weighs approximately thirty pounds, stands exactly three feet tall, and is quite striking.

"Hello, Emma," I said politely. "Is Big Tiny in?"

"Hello, Webb," she said. "Yes, he is."

When I entered the tent I saw Big Tiny sitting on his little bunk. He weighs approximately thirty-eight pounds and stands three feet two; this makes him the dominant member of the couple. I find it easier to differentiate between Big Tiny and Little Tiny than I do my other employees.

Big Tiny said, "Have you come with the paychecks, Webb?"

"I have come with something much better."

"Nothing could be better than money."

"This is true," I said. I paused. "Perhaps we should talk privately."

"Well, Emma and I are husband and wife."

"I acknowledge the legal sanctions. But it would be better if this discussion were conducted privately for the good of all concerned. Will you accept that, Emma?"

"I will accept that," she said. She is really a beautiful person. I have found her complete miniaturization of the mysteries of femininity to be some objective correlative to my own miniaturization of the world in Webb Carter's Wonderama, or at least this is one of my metaphysical speculations. "I will simply be off. I will drive our van into Boca Gables proper and in a trifle will return with a little bag of groceries." All of us in Webb Carter's Wonderama speak in roughly the same fashion, but then our rhetoric *should* be similar; we have been living together for such a long time.

When Little Tiny had slipped gracefully through the tent flap I gave my attention to Big Tiny. "You come from Bensonhurst, Brooklyn, I believe," I said.

"No, the Bushwick section."

"You would like to return there, would you not?"

"I would."

"You would like to retire in luxury and comfort?"

"Webb," he said, "are you leading up to another ploy to circumvent your financial obligations to us?"

"No," I said, "I am leading up to your death."

"My *what*?"

"Your death—or rather, your apparent death. It is, as you will soon understand, for the good of all of us in Webb Carter's Wonderama."

He stared somewhat sullenly at his feet, which was not a difficult activity under his physical circumstances. "Webb—"

"Allow me to explain," I said, and did so.

The light of knowledge appeared in his eyes. "I see. But are you sure we will be able to get away with it?"

"Certainly," I said. "Do not worry. You must think only of your share of two hundred and twenty-five thousand dollars, for with that share neither you nor Emma will have to worry about purchasing little bags of groceries for the rest of your lives."

"How am I to apparently perish?"

"In flames. You will become, along with Giraldo the Human Pyromaniac, a flaming little person; you will do this in front of a representative of the Firehouse Fund whom we will call in to witness what we will say is a new and interesting act." My mind had been working all of this time, as one may perceive. "Your death will appear to be extremely tragic, not only for the obvious reason, but because it will also bring about the ultimate demise of Webb Carter's Wonderama."

"What of the details of my flaming, ah, demise?"

"It is not up to me to handle details," I said. "You and Giraldo must work them out between you. There will, of course, be a way. There is always a way."

"This is true," Big Tiny said, and for the first time he smiled. Then he paused reflectively. "Even though you did not wish to discuss the matter in front of Emma," he said, "she must nonetheless be told."

"Naturally," I said. "Everyone must be told—except, to be sure, those who would represent the Firehouse Fund. Everyone must work together here in order that we may retire separately."

In the nature of transitions, I should now explain how contact was made with one George Feuer of the Boca Gables office of the Firehouse Fund; and of how it came to pass that Feuer came to the grounds of Webb Carter's Wonderama four mornings subsequent at precisely ten o'clock, so that he would be able to witness the initial practice performance of a new act for which, I said, we hoped to secure additional coverage. At this juncture, however, I wish to point out that I tend to dislike transitional material; I believe life itself, that one great transitional circumstance, provides all of the passage that we need ever know.

Nevertheless, I suppose it is incumbent upon me to explain how the illusion of Big Tiny's death was arranged. Thus:

The platform in the main tent, upon which the Human Pyromaniac sets fire to himself during his thrice-weekly performance, contains a well-hidden trapdoor, should he ever lose control of the fire that he allows to engulf him and therefore need to quickly escape. Below the trapdoor is a tiny cubicle filled with water. It was through this trapdoor and into this cubicle that Big Tiny would be thrust during the dual immolation of himself and Giraldo, under the protective screen of the flames, and it was in this cubicle that he would secrete himself until Feuer could be induced to leave the immediate premises. Then he would emerge and seek a more permanent hiding place somewhere on or near the grounds until the time arrived for his triumphal return to Bushwick with his share of the insurance money. (It is not difficult, naturally, for a little person of three feet two and thirty-eight pounds to locate a hiding place that cannot be detected by individuals of the larger persuasion.) One might well note, of course, that we would need some manner of physical evidence which George Feuer would view as the remains of Big Tiny. The problem, while it may seem to have been a large one, proved quite simply soluble. The Sicilian Snare Drum (or perhaps it was the Human Pyromaniac) recalled that the Mad Ghoul had left with us—as a result of his sudden arrest on an old warrant of such an excruciatingly personal nature that I cannot to this day bear to discuss it—a large trunk that contained, among a variety of other interesting items, a collection of doubtless simulated flesh, bones, and dental remnants. These were to be appropriated and subsequently placed inside pockets in Giraldo's specially constructed asbestos uniform, the same type of uniform, I should add, that Big Tiny himself would wear.

Also in the nature of transition, I should probably discuss George Feuer a bit more. However, I do not think I will. I will say only that he was a large man with a ruddy complexion and strange highlights in his eyes. He did not speak much and seemed somehow bewildered by our proposed new and interesting act, which I had already advised him was to be billed as "The Human Pyromaniac and The Flaming Little Person."

When he arrived on this morning of which I have already spoken, I ushered him to the tent and introduced him to the other members of Webb Carter's Wonderama, who were all grouped near the Human Pyromaniac's platform. There was some dialogue, which I find unnecessary to set down here, and then the Sicilian Snare Drum took his position in our makeshift orchestra pit and commenced to flay himself with palms and knuckles in preparation for the event. Meanwhile, Giraldo and Big Tiny made advance consultations and arranged their necessary props.

Feuer and I, along with Emma, took seats in the nearby grandstand. Staring across at the platform, Feuer said to me, "Damned strange stuff, Carter, that's all I can say. No wonder you people pay such high premiums—setting each other aflame and all."

"People need entertainment," I said perfunctorily.

"Entertainment?"

"It is all a device, all an effect," I said, "and it is merely the illusion of pain which we give them, not pain itself. People are severely disturbed these days; they feel that they have lost essential control of their lives. Perhaps watching a little person consumed by flame along with a Human Pyromaniac will cheer them." I was merely filling in time, as you have no doubt realized; I was at that moment consumed by distraction and nervousness. What if the scheme did not work? What if something went wrong?

"Nothing will go wrong," I said to Feuer. "No one will really be hurt, least of all the little person known as Big Tiny. Rest assured that all is merely and mainly paradigm."

He nodded dubiously.

"Giraldo is inordinately competent in his pursuits, you know," I said. "He first set himself aflame in Sioux Falls at the age of fourteen. His father sent him to an orphanage."

Feuer shuddered. He seemed to be in a strange state of excitation now, I noticed; he was breathing uneasily and he continually rubbed his palms together as if he were rolling a stick between them. "Terrifying stuff," he said. "Terrifying."

"Ad demonstrandum," I said. I had studied some Latin at the Rensselaer Polytechnic Institute before they threw me out during the Great Depression. *"Reductio ad absurdum."*

"That's easy for *you* to say," Feuer said. "I never had the opportunity to learn French. I had to go straight to work when I dropped out of high school. I worked myself up in life and the company."

I said nothing in response to this. I was watching Giraldo as he and Big Tiny finished their preparations and strode to the center of the platform. When they were ready, Giraldo motioned over to me and to the Sicilian Snare Drum, who began to rhythmically thump his chest. On my left, Emma held her breath and clutched her hands together in her tiny lap; on my right, Feuer began to tremble and an odd little crackling sound came from his throat.

Almost casually, Giraldo struck a match and set his hair on fire.

"Fire!" the Human Pyromaniac shouted, in the fashion of one commencing a pursuit that gives him great joy.

"Fire!" Emma shrieked, in the fashion of any frightened person of the female persuasion.

"Fire!" Big Tiny screamed, in the fashion of a little person being immolated.

"Fire!" Feuer flared, in the fashion of a man hypnotized by the sight of flame.

Orange tendrils sprang from Giraldo's hand. The Sicilian Snare Drum struck 6/8, a very difficult double-waltz time restricted normally to Johann Strauss the Elder, the third movement of Ludwig van Beethoven's Eighth Symphony, and certain fire music. Big Tiny, looking suddenly frightened, pressed in close to the Human Pyromaniac. And the flames leaped from Giraldo's right to left hand, and then there was a sheet of fire and I heard Feuer moan, and in that moment the flames engulfed both the figures on the platform.

Big Tiny wailed; then, suddenly, he was gone.

"My God," Feuer rumbled, "he's gone!"

Emma moaned terribly—and skillfully, I thought—and all of us rushed toward the platform where the Human Pyromaniac now stood alone. Just before we got there Giraldo extinguished himself in that mysterious way he has; and when all of the flames were out, there was no sign at all of Big Tiny, or of the simulated remains that had been appropriated from the Mad Ghoul's trunk.

Giraldo looked convincingly horrified; he cried, "I couldn't help it! Something must have happened to his asbestos suit!" Then he flung himself to his knees, found the secret catch on the trapdoor, released it. The opening appeared, and beneath it, the cubicle filled with water.

Only the cubicle was not, at this time, filled with water.

And it did not, at this time, contain the live form of Big Tiny.

What it did contain was the remains of a charred little body—and I knew illusion had become reality after all.

Emma fainted into Feuer's quaking arms. Giraldo wept. The Sicilian Snare Drum thumped his chest softly in 4/4 dirge time. I shook my head and knelt with my shoulders slumped beside Little Tiny as Feuer lowered her to the sawdust.

Someone (I believe it was Feuer) said, "Awful. Awful. I can't believe it. How could he have been burned to nothing more than this, to a lump of smoking charcoal?"

"My clothing is specially treated," the Human Pyromaniac said tearfully, "with a highly flammable substance. When I am on fire the heat is intense—so intense I am myself sometimes burned through the asbestos. Without such an asbestos suit . . ." He spread his arms in a helpless manner.

"I need some air," Feuer said. His eyes had the look of blackened cinders; all the passion within had been extinguished, much as had the flames upon Giraldo's body.

"The authorities should be summoned," I said. "There is a telephone in my trailer."

"Yes," he said. "Telephone. Yes. Authorities and telephone." He used a handkerchief to wipe his forehead and then went away.

I looked at Giraldo and the Sicilian Snare Drum; they looked at me; we all looked away. Big Tiny was dead, truly dead, terribly dead, and we could not believe it. I most of all could not believe it, just as I could not believe that Western Civilization was due for imminent collapse. But it was so.

Yes, oh yes, it was so.

There is more transitional material in order here, but once again I must repeat my dislike for it and my belief that life itself is one great transition: rapid passage from infancy to carnival to grave. Of the grief and shock of the Human Pyromaniac and the Sicilian Snare Drum and of course Emma, of the arrival of the police, and of Feuer's consternation upon coming to terms with the liability of the Firehouse Fund, nothing more need be said. Time passed. A full day passed. Life goes on.

But on the following afternoon, Feuer appeared at the door of my trailer. He no longer appeared dismayed; in fact, he looked rather grim and not a little authoritative.

"We seem to have a small problem here," he said.

"Problem?" I said.

"With your claim. The forensic people in the Boca Gables police department are not entirely satisfied with the remains of Isaac Spritzer, a.k.a. Big Tiny."

I frowned. "Does this mean you are not immediately prepared to pay us our justified triple indemnity?"

"This is what it means," Feuer said. "If forensic is not satisfied, we at the Firehouse Fund are not satisfied."

"Well, you cannot deny that you saw Big Tiny go up in flames, as did we all. Giraldo, the Human Pyromaniac, has been incommunicado ever since the unfortunate accident; he blames himself."

"Nevertheless," Feuer said.

"I do not know what more you can reasonably expect," I said. "After all, *we* cannot be expected to produce a *corpus delicti* on one who has been immolated."

"Let us discuss matters at greater length," Feuer said. "Outside, perhaps? While we stroll about the midway? The rain has stopped, and it really is a pleasant afternoon."

I sighed. "Very well," I said. "And we shall tell sad stories of the death of little people."

He gave me a strange look. "Pardon?"

"Shakespeare," I said. "Henry the Fourth? No. Richard the Three."

We left my trailer and strolled down the deserted midway. We had not had a show since yesterday's tragedy, of course, and would never have one again. But then, judging from past attendance figures, Boca Gables would almost certainly not miss us.

As we neared the main tent, I seemed able to detect little flickers of flame from within. I said, "Giraldo must have come out of his shell and begun reconstituting his act. The old trouper has not abandoned his craft."

"Why don't we go inside?" Feuer said.

We entered the tent. On the platform I saw the Human Pyromaniac and the Sicilian Snare Drum working with the requisite props of Giraldo's act. Feuer and I took seats in the grandstand, as we had the day of Big Tiny's demise. Feuer seemed disinclined to speak, contrary to what he had said in my trailer a few moments earlier; instead we watched Giraldo prepare, heard the Snare Drum begin to thump his tympanic chest. Soon flame blossomed from the Human Pyromaniac's fingertips, passing rapidly from one to the next; he spread his arms in his impressive way and created a rope of fire, then bent and brought blazing tendrils from his shoe tips to his head. Then he disappeared behind a wall of fire, and—

And incredibly, as if from the very center of the conflagration, there appeared Big Tiny: reconstructed amid the flames.

And he was pointing, pointing straight at me.

"You, Webb!" he shouted. "You did this to me!"

I jumped to my feet and hurried to the edge of the platform. "You're dead," I said. "I made sure of that—didn't I?"

"No," Big Tiny said. "Your plot to murder me did not succeed after all, Webb. Giraldo discovered that you—it could only have been you—had exchanged my asbestos suit for a flammable cotton one, and then had emptied the water from the cubicle under the trapdoor. Immediately he effected another exchange of suits."

"But how could you have gotten out of the cubicle during the performance?"

"We created another exit, carefully concealed. Or so

we thought." His voice turned sadly sardonic. "We plotted to carry through the illusion of my death only until we could collect the triple indemnity from Firehouse Fund; then I intended to confront you. Unfortunately, things have not worked out as any of us planned."

I realized Feuer was beside me. I also realized that there were several uniformed policemen nearby, and that Emma was there as well—and that Western Civilization was already, alas, in the throes of collapse.

Feuer's eyes reflected the flames surrounding Giraldo and Big Tiny, and his voice crackled as he spoke. "Extinguish yourselves," he told them.

Giraldo extinguished himself and Big Tiny; they stood smoking in the center of the platform.

Feuer released a shuddering breath. "Now then," he said, "where were we? Ah yes." He fixed me with a cindered eye. "You see, Carter, I discovered the second exit to the cubicle. I also discovered, with the help of the Boca Gables forensic people, the fact that the remains which Big Tiny placed inside the cubicle before departing were those of several different and quite ancient individuals. Thus I confronted Giraldo and the Sicilian Snare Drum, and was able to elicit their confession when I suggested you would all be charged with grave-robbing in addition to attempted extortion of the Firehouse Fund."

"He left us with no choice," the Human Pyromaniac said. (Or perhaps it was the Sicilian Snare Drum.)

"No choice at all," the Snare Drum said. (Or perhaps it was the Human Pyromaniac.) "Which is the reason we have complied with this ploy of his to expose you, Webb, by forcing you into a self-admission of guilt."

Feuer looked at me. "I can understand the extortion scheme, though I do not of course condone it," he said. "What I do not understand is why you contrived to murder your employee, Big Tiny."

"Love," I said.

"Love?"

"Of dear Emma," I said. I turned to face her small, flawless self. "You never suspected how great was my reverence for your beauty, Little Tiny—how beatific and pure was my love."

Curiously, she did not seem particularly surprised by my confession of motive; none of them did.

"I really do love you," I said. "All thirty pounds and three feet of you."

"Thirty pounds and three feet?" Feuer said bewilderedly.

"Oh yes," the Snare Drum said. (Or perhaps it was the Human Pyromaniac.) "We have known all along of Webb's delusion, and have humored him because he was our employer and, we thought, our friend. Now, naturally, the masquerade cannot be continued."

"Delusion?" I said. "Masquerade?"

"Webb," one of them said, "Webb, Big Tiny and Little Tiny each stand approximately six and a half feet tall and weigh in the neighborhood of two hundred and seventy-five pounds. They are and always have been our Strong Man and Strong Lady."

"Really?" I said. "I thought they were midgets."

They took me away.

THE THEFT OF
THE CIRCUS
POSTER

Edward D. Hoch

Edward D. Hoch, one of the few suspense writers whose output is comprised mainly of short stories, has developed a number of series characters during his nearly thirty-year career. Among these are such notable individuals as Police Captain Leopold; Rand, the retired spy; Dr. Sam Hawthorne, a country doctor of the 1920's and 30's; and Simon Ark, who claims to be a two-thousand-year-old Coptic priest. One of Hoch's most popular characters is the unusual thief, Nick Velvet, who will steal anything as long as it has no monetary value. Often Velvet's clients won't tell him the reasons they desire these objects, and in this entertaining story, he is—for a while, anyway—genuinely puzzled as to why anyone would want a tattered old circus poster.

Nick Velvet had been home for weeks, in a state of brooding inactivity, when the summons came. It was from a man in Brooklyn whom Nick had once helped, and his voice was raspingly familiar on the phone.

"It's for a friend of mine in Miami," the man told him. "If you can fly down there tonight he'll meet you at the airport."

Nick hesitated only a moment. "I'll be there. What's his name?"

"He'll be using the name of Mason."

"How will I recognize him?"

"He'll recognize you."

Nick went upstairs to the fancy yellow bedroom and began to pack. After a while Gloria came in with two cans of beer. "You're not going away again, Nicky?"

"I have to look over some new plant sites in Florida. Should be back by the end of the week."

She leaned against the door frame, her long hair tumbling over the softness of her face. "I was hoping we could go sailing now that the weather's warm."

"We'll go as soon as I get back," he promised. "I won't be long, really. I have to make some money for us, don't I?"

"Sure, Nicky. Send me a postcard, will you? Something pretty, with an orange grove on it."

He kissed her lightly on the lips and went downstairs with his suitcase.

The flight down the Atlantic coast was smooth and uneventful, and the skyline of Miami was much as he remembered it from his last visit during the 1972 political conventions. That time he'd stolen something for the staff of an unsuccessful presidential candidate, and he liked to think his action may have altered the course of the convention.

This trip started out in a much more prosaic manner. He was met at the airport by a beefy-cheeked man in a rumpled summer suit who ushered him into a waiting car. "Mr. Mason is sorry he couldn't meet you in person," the man said.

"Are we going to his home?"

"A hotel room. He conducts all his business in hotel rooms."

"I see."

The man, who said his name was Jimmy, spoke little until they reached their destination, a third-rate hotel north of the city and near the Hialeah racetrack. "Room twenty-six," Jimmy said. "I'll wait out here for you."

Nick found the door to Room twenty-six slightly ajar and pushed it open. He was utterly unprepared for the sight that greeted him—a man in garish clown's makeup and wearing an old tuxedo sat in a chair facing the door.

"You're Nick Velvet? Come in, come in!" The voice was obviously disguised.

"Mr. Mason?" Nick asked, stepping forward uncertainly. He could see nothing of the man's face beneath the heavy layers of makeup. The skin was dead-white, with big red lips, red spots on each cheek, and a red rubber ball for a nose.

"Mason is the name I use. You'll forgive the clown makeup, but I find it necessary at times to conceal my appearance and identity. I was told by a friend in Brooklyn that you're an expert thief who specializes in the unusual."

"I steal anything without value—never money or jewels. My fee is $20,000—in cash." Nick's eyes roamed the hotel room, searching for some clue to the man's identity. All he saw was a briefcase pushed half under the bed. He thought the initials on it were JKS.

"Could you steal a circus poster?" the clown asked.

"Certainly."

"It's part of a collection owned by a retired old clown named Herbie Benson. He lives near Miami. I'll give you the address."

"Why is it worth so much to you? Is the poster a collector's item?"

"Be curious on someone else's time, Velvet." The harsh words seemed somehow incongruous with the grinning clown's face. "Here's a down payment, along with Herbie Benson's address and a description of the poster I want. How long will it take you?"

"Seems fairly simple," Nick replied. "This is Monday. Let's say Thursday night, or sooner. I'll come here with the poster."

"Fine."

Nick shook the man's gloved hand and left the room. Jimmy, the driver, was lounging by his car, and Nick gave him the address of a moderately priced hotel on Biscayne Bay. Heading downtown, he opened the envelope and counted ten hundred-dollar bills inside. Then he put Benson's address in his wallet and read over the description of the circus poster he'd been hired to steal:

Great National Circus Poster of the 1916 season, with five acrobats at top, rhinoceros and clowns at bottom.

Nick put it back in the envelope with the money. At the hotel entrance he thanked Jimmy for the ride and checked into a room overlooking the bay. There were hotel postcards in the drawer, and he mailed one to Gloria.

The town of Snake Creek was north of Miami, along a canal that ran inland from North Miami Beach to the edge of the Everglades. It was a rural area, barely touched by the spreading suburbs of the city proper, and as Nick drove his rented car down the main street he might have been in any part of the South, far removed from the luxury hotels of Miami Beach.

Herbie Benson seemed much like the other retired residents of Snake Creek, and at first glance there seemed nothing about his sagging face and dull eyes to suggest a former circus clown. He lived in a small white house with peeling paint and steps worn to the bare wood by the passage of feet. He was a little man, aging like his house, and his weak eyes focused on Nick with difficulty.

"Do I know you?" he asked, standing at the front door behind the protection of the screen, a few strands of thin white hair drifting over his forehead.

"My name is Nicholas. I understand you were once a circus clown."

The old eyes sparkled for an instant behind their thick glasses. "That was long ago. Nobody's interested in old clowns any more."

"I'm interested," Nick said. "May I come in?"

"You're not going to rob me, are you? Person can't be too careful these days."

Nick chuckled. "Do I look like a thief?"

The man studied him. "No, I guess not." He unlatched the screen door. "Come on in."

The little house was surprisingly cool after the warmth of the street. Furnished in a worn drabness that seemed to reflect the years of Herbie Benson's life, it was still a place for pleasant relaxing.

Nick suddenly realized they were not alone in the house. There was a noise from the kitchen and a young tawny-haired woman appeared carrying a glass of fruit juice. "This is my granddaughter, Judy," the old man said, wiping his old-fashioned spectacles with a soiled handkerchief.

Nick nodded and introduced himself. "Nicholas is my name. I have an interest in circus lore, mainly as a hobby. I couldn't pass through town without stopping to see Mr. Benson."

"He lives here alone," she answered bluntly. "He shouldn't be opening his door to strangers." He guessed her age at about twenty-three, and she wore the cool unsmiling expression one saw on so many other young faces these days.

"Now, Judy," the old man started to protest.

"It's true, Grandpa! What do you know about this man?

If I weren't here he could hit you over the head and steal everything in sight!"

"He looks honest, Judy."

"I can assure you—" Nick began, but she waved him into silence. Her long tawny hair swirled as she turned and disappeared into the kitchen.

"Don't mind her," Herbie Benson said. "She just grows tired of all the circus talk sometimes."

Nick sat down, feeling more welcome. "This is a nice little town you have."

"I like it. Close to Miami, and not too far from Winter Haven and Sarasota, where a lot of circus people spend the winter."

"You still see your old circus friends?"

"I see the ones that are left. I joined the circus back during the First World War, when I shoulda been in school." His old eyes clouded for an instant. "Most of the people I knew are dead now."

"You were a clown that long ago?"

"No, no, not at first. Believe it or not, Mr. Nicholas, my first circus job was carrying water for the elephants, just like in all the old stories. But I was a clown before I was twenty, and I stayed a clown for nearly forty years, till my first heart attack. I was there. I saw it all. I started with the Great National Circus in their final years, and then switched to Barnum and Bailey."

Judy Benson came back carrying another glass of fruit juice. "This is for you," she told Nick. Then she sat down, still unsmiling.

"Thank you. Your grandfather was just telling me about his early circus days."

She eyed Nick in silence and Herbie Benson continued, "I think those early days with Great National were the best of all. They had a really big spread, with acrobats and lions and even a Wild West show. Come in here, I'll show you some of their posters."

"Grandpa," Judy cautioned, but the old man was already on his feet, leading Nick into the next room.

It had been a dining room at one time, but when Nick passed through the swinging door he saw that it was now given over completely to the memories and trophies of a lifetime. There were garish circus posters and framed programs dating back more than fifty years, along with dozens of photographs of a sad-faced clown with groups of children or greeting some celebrity or simply alone in a circus ring. A cluster of limp balloons bearing the words *Herbie the Clown* hung over a picture of two clowns inscribed *Herbie and Willie.*

But it was one of the circus posters that interested Nick. Yellowed with age and curling at the edges, there could be no doubt this was the poster he'd been hired to steal. Five stiff-bodied acrobats at the top flew through the air with awkward grace, with the one in the foreground sporting a Teddy Roosevelt mustache that made him seem the twin of the one high on a trapeze in the background. A slim banner beneath them read: *The Flying Fantini Brothers.*

In the lower portion of the poster a faded purple rhinoceros glowered out from a swampy setting of trees and ferns. "I never saw a purple rhino," Nick said, recalling the famous verse by Gelett Burgess about a purple cow.

"These posters are real Americana," the old man told him. "I've been offered a thousand dollars for my whole collection intact, but of course I would never sell."

"How much would an individual poster be worth?"

"Alone? Not much—next to nothing, unless you came across some kind of a crank collector. They reprint these things too much nowadays. Who'd want to pay good money for an original when he could buy a reproduction at the local bookstore for a dollar or two?"

"You've got something there," Nick admitted. He pointed to the 1916 poster. "This must have been early in your career."

"The year before I joined Great National," he answered with a trace of pride.

"You must have known a lot of clowns in your day."

"All the big ones. Willie was a special friend."

"Ever know one named Mason?" If a man wore clown makeup, it seemed logical to Nick that he might be a former clown.

"What circus was he with?"

"I don't know. I could have the name wrong." His eyes strayed back to the purple rhino and the clowns and the five acrobats. "You know, there's something peculiar about that poster, but I don't know what."

"They're funny-looking by today's art standards, I guess, but I love every one of them."

They chatted a while longer and then Nick rose to leave. Stealing the poster seemed so simple that he wondered why the mysterious Mr. Mason hadn't simply hired the first crook he could find and pay him fifty dollars to do the job. Herbie walked him to the porch and they shook hands. "You've brightened my day," the former clown said. "I always like to talk circus. Come back sometime and I'll put on my clown makeup for you."

"I'll do that," Nick said, and waved goodbye.

He was just starting the car when Judy Benson came running out of the house. "Mr. Nicholas, could you give me a ride down to the store? I have to do some shopping for my grandfather."

"Sure. Climb in."

"Nice car you have."

Nick nodded.

"You don't talk like a southerner. Are you from this area?"

He pulled slowly away from the curb, aware that her sudden friendliness was in sharp contrast to her earlier coolness. "No, I'm from up north. Just driving through."

"But this is a rented car, rented here in Florida. You're not just driving through at all." Her voice was suddenly accusing.

"I happen to live in New York and I don't own a car. I flew down here and rented this one."

She didn't reply immediately but stared straight ahead. Finally she said, "My grandfather is a sick old man, Mr. Nicholas. His heart is very bad. If anyone were to swindle or steal his possessions, the shock would kill him."

"Why do you tell me this?"

"Because another man came to see him only a week ago. He wanted to buy one of my grandfather's posters, and then he just tried to steal it. Luckily I arrived in time and threatened to call the police unless the man left. After that I made Grandpa promise never to let anyone in the house unless I was there."

"And you think I'm connected with this other man? What's his name?"

"I don't know. He had fat cheeks and wore a rumpled suit."

Nick recognized the description of Mason's driver, Jimmy. So the man in the clown makeup had made a previous attempt to get the poster. Still, why had he felt it necessary to hire Nick?

"I don't know the man," Nick said.

"All right, Mr. Nicholas. I hope you're telling the truth, because there's an unpleasant surprise waiting for the next person who tries to rob my grandfather."

He ignored the threat in her words and said, "Tell me one thing. Why was this man so anxious to buy or steal the poster, when your grandfather is so sure it's valueless?"

She turned her deep brown eyes toward him. "I haven't the least idea, Mr. Nicholas."

Nick knew he could do nothing further that day, so he returned to his Miami hotel and spent the early evening on the beach, watching the yachts cruising over the blue waters of Biscayne Bay. At sunset he went in for a swim, and when he returned to the damp sand he found Jimmy, the man in the rumpled suit, awaiting him.

"So you been to see old Herbie?"

"Yes," Nick said warily.

Jimmy smiled a lopsided sort of smile. "Mason thought you'd be better than me. He thought you could get the poster after I failed. But he was wrong, wasn't he?"

"I don't know. I haven't tried yet."

The smile broadened. "He said you were pretty good. A unique thief-detective, he called you."

"Anyone could climb through his window and steal that poster."

"Yeah? You think so? You met the granddaughter yet?"

"I've met her."

"She tell you what she does for a living?"

"I didn't ask."

"She's with the circus, same as her grandfather used to be."

"As a clown?" Nick asked, unbelieving.

Jimmy shook his head. "She has a sideshow act with a little circus that tours around Florida. She's a snake charmer."

"A snake—"

"That's right, wise guy. Every night she puts her grandfather to bed and lets loose a sackful of rattlesnakes in that house. Still think you can just climb through the window and steal that poster?"

Nick Velvet drove to the hotel where he'd met Mason the previous evening. There were some things to be straightened out, among them his fee. For wrestling rattlesnakes Nick charged more.

As he went down the hall toward Mason's room he saw a tall graying man with his hand on the knob. The man turned suddenly as Nick approached and asked, "Are you looking for Mr. Mason, too?"

"I am."

"He's not here. I've been knocking and no one answers."

Nick tried the door. It was locked. "You a friend of his?"

"I'm a lawyer." The man flipped a card from his inside pocket and Nick read:

> Haskin Kimbell
> Jeans, Kimbell & Sachs
> Miami, Florida

"Pleased to meet you. My name is Nicholas."

"Are you in Mr. Mason's employ?"

"In a way, yes."

The lawyer pursed his lips, hesitating. "Would you be the man he hired to get the circus poster?"

"Yes," Nick admitted. "But I have to speak to him about our arrangement. A complication has come up."

The tall lawyer glanced around. "Let's go somewhere and talk. The downstairs bar, perhaps."

The bar had a scattering of late-evening drinkers, but Nick and the lawyer easily found a booth where they could not be overheard. When the drinks arrived, Haskin Kimbell dropped the small talk and said, "Let's get down to business, Mr. Nicholas."

"What sort of business?"

"Do you have the poster?"

"I told you, there's a complication."

"It's urgent that we obtain it."

"We?"

Haskin Kimbell sighed. "I represent the sole surviving heir to the Fantini oil fortune."

"Fantini?" Nick remembered the name on the poster— *The Flying Fantini Brothers.*

"They were acrobats in their younger days, traveling with the circus. But after one of them was crippled in a fall they left the circus and went into the oil business, drilling wildcat wells. It was in the early nineteen-twenties, a good time for wildcatters. They struck it rich and over the years built up a considerable fortune. The last of the brothers—

so everyone thought at the time—died a year ago at the age of seventy-three. He left no family, no heirs, and an estate estimated at ten million dollars."

"Is there a will?"

"There is, but it was drawn a decade earlier while his brothers were still alive. It left his entire estate to the brothers or brother who survived him. If none survived, the estate went to various charities."

"And you say no brother survived?"

The lawyer sipped his drink. "So it was believed at the time. Now a man has appeared who claims to be the last surviving brother. His name is Anthony Fantini, and he is my client."

"He must have offered you some proof."

"Proof of events sixty or seventy years ago can be hard to produce. The brothers were born in Italy and came here in the early years of this century. The birth records in their Italian village were destroyed during World War Two, and no one alive today remembers the family. Unfortunately, the records of the Great National circus have also been lost over the years. In simple truth we don't know with certainty just how many Fantini brothers there were. Four can be accounted for, but my client claims he is the fifth brother. If that is true he is entitled to the estate."

"He must have something to support his claim."

"A great deal. He knows everything about the family's early life. The one thing we're lacking is convincing evidence there were five Flying Fantini Brothers instead of four."

"The circus poster!"

"Exactly. The number of Ringling Brothers, for example, can easily be certified as five because a group portrait of them appeared on early Ringling posters. Likewise, that Great National poster can prove there were five Fantini brothers. Shortly after I took the surviving Fantini's case, this man named Mason approached me with an offer. He claimed to know of this old circus poster which would prove there were five Fantinis. He offered to deliver it for what might be called a finder's fee."

"How big a fee?"

"Six figures. Recently he told me he'd hired you to get the poster. I came here tonight to see if he had it yet."

"My agreement is for delivery by Thursday or before."

"Then you can get it? You know where it is?"

"I've seen it," Nick admitted. "But tell me about Mason. What does he look like?"

The lawyer seemed puzzled. "Haven't you met him?"

"Not in the flesh."

"He looks fairly ordinary. Middle-aged, gray hair. Nothing unusual."

Nick decided not to mention the clown makeup. "All right. I'll have the poster by Thursday morning. You can meet me in Mason's hotel room if you wish."

"Fine."

"One last thing. You mentioned a fall that crippled one of the Fantinis. Surely there must be newspaper accounts of it. Even if the circus records are lost, the papers would tell you if there were four or five brothers."

Kimbell shook his head. "I've been over all that—everything. There were some brief newspaper accounts, but none mentioned the number of brothers. I even checked back issues of trade papers like *Variety* and *Billboard,* but they only added to the confusion. It seems when the brothers first started out, there were only three because the others were still too young. I've found mention of three Fantinis and four Fantinis, but nothing about my client—the fifth and youngest of them. He was only with Great National that one season, so that poster is the only proof in existence."

"There were only boys in the family? No surviving sisters?"

"All boys. Born a year or two apart just before the turn of the century. My client was seventeen when he joined the act, and of course he's well into his seventies now."

"So you really need the poster."

"I really need it."

"I'll get it," Nick promised.

He spent most of the next day in his hotel room experimenting with a variety of grease paints and makeup kits. Finally, around dinnertime, he gazed into the mirror and was satisfied. He washed off the makeup and ate a quick dinner alone. Then, as the long evening shadows began to fall across the bay, he put the materials he'd need in a paper bag and carried them down to his rented car. Less than an hour later he was back in Snake Creek.

Herbie Benson's house was dark except for a single light in an upstairs bedroom. Nick parked down the street and worked quickly to apply his makeup. It was more difficult in the car than it had been in his hotel room, but after a half-hour's work he was satisfied. As a final touch he stuck on the round rubber nose and then walked quickly down the street to the house.

He rang the doorbell twice before Herbie appeared at an upstairs window. "I can't come down!" he shouted. "Go away, whoever you are!"

Nick stepped into the glow from a street light. "Herbie! Don't you remember me?"

"Who is it?"

"Herbie, I used to work with you years ago. Don't you remember Willie?"

"Willie? Is that you, Willie?"

Nick had remembered the clown on the photograph with Herbie and had tried to duplicate his makeup. With Herbie's age and poor eyesight in Nick's favor, he thought he could bring it off. "Come down and open the door, Herbie. I have to talk to you."

"I can't come down. She's turned the snakes loose."

"Then I'll come up."

Nick boosted himself onto the porch railing and from there to the drainpipe and the porch roof. In a few moments he was at the old man's window. Herbie squinted, reached for his thick glasses and put them on. "You look different. You sure you're Willie?"

"Who else would come to see you with a clown outfit on?" Nick climbed quickly through the window. "Remember the old days? The good times we had?"

"You're not Willie." The voice was firm. "You're too young."

"I'm Willie's son. He sent me to you. He needs something from you, Herbie, and he needs it pretty bad."

"What's that?"

"One of your circus posters, Herbie."

The old man let out his breath. "I couldn't! That's what the snakes are for! She said that guy tried to steal my collection. She leaves the snakes every night and comes back to pick them up in the morning."

"But you could get through the snakes, couldn't you, Herbie?"

"Oh, sure. But Judy would be awfully upset."

"Even if you did it for an old friend?"

"Well . . ." He hesitated, and Nick saw him eye the clown makeup with something like nostalgia. "You did a nice job of putting that on, but the mouth's too crooked."

"Think you could fix it?"

"Sure. I'll show you how. Us clowns gotta stick together."

He sat Nick down on a straight-backed chair and got out a couple of jars of grease paint. After a few minutes of work he was satisfied. "There now, that's lots better! You look like a real clown now."

"About the poster—"

"Sure, your dad can have it—I got plenty of them. Which one does Willie want?"

"The Great National, from 1916."

"Yeah. That's the one the other fellow wanted, too. Kind of a popular poster, isn't it? Come on down with me."

"But the snakes—"

"They won't hurt you."

Nick followed him gingerly down the stairs, watching and listening. As he crossed the dark living room behind the old man he heard a warning rattle and his hand went for the little pistol under his arm.

"I said not to worry," Herbie insisted. "They're carnival snakes. The poison sacs have been removed. Think she's dumb enough to work with the real thing?"

Nick relaxed, realizing it was true. "They certainly do their job, keeping prowlers away." By the glow of the street light he saw a diamondback rattler slowly uncoil and slither away under a table.

Old Herbie removed the 1916 Great National poster from the wall and started to roll it up. "Say hello to your dad for me."

"Can I pay you for it?"

"It's not worth anything alone. Take it—a gift from a fellow clown. It was your father who helped me put together most of this collection."

"Did you know these fellows—the Fantini brothers?"

"No, they left the circus just about the time I joined."

"But you probably heard some talk about them. Wasn't one of them crippled in a fall?"

"Yeah, I remember."

Staring at the poster, Nick asked Herbie one more question—but he was already sure what the answer would be.

In the morning he dressed quickly and retrieved the poster from its hiding place in the closet. He was just opening the door of his room when Judy Benson stepped off the elevator.

"Not so fast, Mr. Nicholas. Back inside!"

He was about to ignore her command when he saw the .22 automatic come out of her purse. "What is this?"

"Back inside," she repeated.

"How did you find me?"

"I checked the license of your rented car and found it was assigned to the rental agency at this hotel. Then I just asked at the desk for Mr. Nicholas' room."

"What do you want? And what's the gun for?"

"I came for the poster you stole from my grandfather."

"He gave it to me. Didn't he tell you?"

"You tricked him, claiming to be the son of an old circus friend. He's an old man, Mr. Nicholas, and very gullible. Someone came to him in clown makeup, so he believed what he was told. But now you're dealing with me, and I have a gun."

"Are you really a snake charmer?" Nick asked. "You don't look like one."

"I've been around carnivals all my life, and I know a con man when I see one. My snakes may have failed to stop you, but I won't!" She raised the gun in a threatening gesture.

"All right. But you should know what you're getting into."

"Meaning?"

"This poster is part of a swindle to obtain a ten-million-dollar inheritance. Let me show you." He started to unroll the poster.

"No tricks now!"

"No tricks." He held up the poster for her to see. "Notice the illustration of the acrobats. *The Flying Fantini Brothers.* There are five of them, and this poster will be the main item of proof to establish one Anthony Fantini as the rightful claimant to the Fantini oil fortune. But do you notice anything peculiar about these acrobats?"

Before she could answer there was a knock on the door. Judy Benson slipped the gun into her oversized purse as Nick opened the door a crack. The door was shoved back into his face as the beefy-cheeked Jimmy forced his way in. He wore the same rumpled suit, but now he carried a heavy automatic in his hand. The lawyer Haskin Kimbell was right behind him.

"Come in," Nick said, hiding his surprise and rubbing his cheek where the door had hit him. "It's good to see you both again, and especially to see that you've decided to skip the clown makeup this time, Mr. Kimbell."

* * *

"We came for the poster," Kimbell said. "When Jimmy saw the girl come up here, he thought you were double-crossing us."

"Not a chance. The poster is all yours, as soon as I collect the rest of my fee." He was careful not to look at Judy Benson.

"All right," Kimbell agreed, but the gun was steady in Jimmy's beefy hand. Then, almost as an afterthought, the lawyer asked, "How'd you know I was Mason?"

"When I went to his hotel room Tuesday night I caught you as you were leaving. You pretended to be knocking on the door, looking for Mason yourself, but you didn't fool me. Mason had a briefcase in his room with the initials JKS on it. They weren't the initials of a person, but of your law firm—Jeans, Kimbell and Sachs. But your clown makeup did give me the idea of how to steal the poster from Herbie, so I have to thank you for that."

"I'm taking back that poster," Judy Benson said suddenly, her hand reappearing with the gun. "You're all a bunch of crooks!"

Jimmy swung around quickly and hit her arm, sending her pistol flying across the room. The familiar smile was on his face as he pushed her onto the bed. "Stay there or you'll get hurt."

Haskin Kimbell looked distressed. "Give me the poster, Velvet."

"I was about to show Miss Benson something peculiar about it," Nick said. He didn't like to see girls pushed around, and just then he wasn't feeling too kindly toward Kimbell and his goon. "In fact, there's been something peculiar about this whole business."

"What's that?" the lawyer asked.

"Three questions: Why did you go to the trouble of creating a mythical middleman in clown makeup rather than simply hire me yourself to get the poster? Why have it stolen in the first place when you could have asked Herbie

Benson to lend it to you for the court hearing? And finally, why not simply have Herbie testify as to the number of Fantini brothers?"

"All right, why?"

"Because this poster is deceiving. Because there never was a fifth Fantini. Because your claimant to the fortune is an impostor, carefully coached by you, Kimbell. I asked Herbie last night how many brothers there were and he told me four—as I knew he would. The records you found listed three or four brothers—but never five. Only this poster showed five brothers, and that's why you couldn't have Herbie in court where someone could ask him about it. You had to steal the poster, and you created Mason to do it so that if the truth came out you'd be in the clear."

"You mean the poster is a fake?" Judy asked from the bed.

"No, it's real enough. But in the style of many such posters it duplicated performers to give the impression of a great number. Notice the Teddy Roosevelt mustache on this man in the foreground and the man up here. The two men look alike, yet there were no Fantini twins—you told me yourself they were born one or two years apart, Kimbell. These two look alike because they're the same man, shown in two different poses, once alone and once with his brothers."

"Could he prove the existence of a fifth brother merely with this poster as evidence?" Judy asked.

"Maybe, maybe not. But for ten million dollars it was worth a try. Right, Kimbell?"

"It's still worth a try," the lawyer said. "But now we have to get rid of you two. Jimmy—"

"There's another gun in my purse," Judy shouted to Nick.

At first her words baffled him. The oversized purse was on the floor almost at Jimmy's feet. There was no way Nick could reach it first.

"Hold it!" Jimmy said, leveling his gun at Nick. He

kicked over the purse, spilling its contents across the floor, and bent to inspect a drawstring pouch. "It's a snake!" he yelled, his voice close to a high-pitched scream.

That was when Nick moved.

Later, when he was alone with Judy, Nick said, "You really are a snake charmer."

"That was just a little ground snake, but it scared him enough for you to get hold of his gun."

"*And* the rest of my fee from Kimbell." He handed her the poster. "You can take this back to your grandfather now. I think Kimbell's decided to forget all about his scheme."

"What kind of thief does that make you, returning the loot?"

"A good thief," he said. "Don't you think I should get a reward?"

"I think so," she agreed with a grin. "Have you ever been kissed by a snake charmer?"

CAROUSEL

August Derleth

This strange, chilling fantasy about a tragically aban-
doned carnival and a child's obsession with its merry-go-
round is typical of the macabre work of August Derleth
(1910–1972). Derleth wrote scores of stories for the legend-
ary pulp magazine Weird Tales *("Carousel" among them)*
and was considered the world's foremost expert on weird
fiction; in 1939 he founded Arkham House, a publishing
company that continues to specialize in the prose and poetry
of such writers as H. P. Lovecraft. Among Derleth's consid-
erable number of other accomplishments is a series of stories
about detective Solar Pons, perhaps the most successful of
all Sherlock Holmes pastiches.

The abandoned carnival stood behind a high board fence directly across from the Benjin house at the edge of town, and in one corner of it, under a graceful mulberry tree, stood the merry-go-round. Someone had come in before the legal notices appeared, dismantled the ferris wheel, and made away with it. Otherwise it stood just as it had done on that night of carnage when that poor bewildered lonely fellow, goaded beyond endurance by people who hated him for no other reason than that he was a poor, harmless black man, had exploded into long-suppressed passion and killed the owner of the carnival—torn him literally to pieces before he was fallen upon and lynched by the maddened crowd. The creditors had closed the carnival, hoping to sell it; the ferris wheel had been sold before complications had appeared; then the fence went up. For a little while it was a sort of never-never land for the village boys and girls; but even they forgot about it at last, and now it was the sole and exclusive domain of Marcia Benjin.

She spent a large part of each day in the carnival grounds, and haunted the merry-go-round. It was not without reason that she went through the opening the children had made in the fence; she needed the security and escape from her stepmother, for when Marcia's father was away at work, his second wife made no secret of her resentment for the only child of his first.

The child was five, and much alone. Because of her stepmother's malicious hatred, she was far lonelier than she should ever have been. In another year, she would be old enough to go to school, but in that time, too, she would escape her stepmother, and Mrs. Benjin did not know whether she wished that end.

Mrs. Benjin was dark, with a thin mouth and snapping brown eyes. She was jealous of her stepdaughter, who she looked upon as the symbol of John Benjin's first wife. She was jealous of her with a dark, sultry passion, and yet she resented with ill-suppressed fury, the little girl's escape into the carnival grounds.

Unfortunately for the child, she did not always notice the passage of time, and so from time to time came home late to her meals. This only increased her stepmother's rage, but Mrs. Benjin saw in Marcia's laxity a possible way in which the girl could be brought wholly into her power.

"I don't want to speak to Marcia about her habits, John," she said silkily. "You know I hesitate. After all, she is *your* daughter, and I don't want to intrude between you, but I think she ought to learn to come home on time."

"Of course, she should," agreed John Benjin, good-naturedly. He was a large, broad-shouldered man, easy-going and completely unaware of anything in his wife but the aspect she chose for him to see. "I'll talk to her."

Marcia came into the house and brought the evening sunlight with her. She kissed her father, smiled gravely at her stepmother, and sat down.

"I'm sorry I'm late," she said.

"You ought not to be late," said Benjin gently. "It's hard enough to keep supper warm till I get home, and it's twice as hard to keep after that. Your mother works hard all day and she's always glad to get the dishes off the table."

"I just didn't notice," said Marcia.

"Oh, it doesn't really matter about me, I suppose," Mrs. Benjin interjected with a helpless air.

"I didn't notice, really," persisted Marcia earnestly. "We were playing, and before I knew it I heard the six o'clock bell."

"With whom were you playing?" asked John Benjin casually, feeling that now he had done his duty.

"With the black man," said Marcia ingenuously.

Benjin went on buttering his bread unconcernedly, but Mrs. Benjin pricked up her ears. "With whom?" she asked, unable to keep a little sharp excitement out of her voice.

Suddenly there was an unaccountable tension around

the table. A baffling obstinacy came into Marcia's eyes; Benjin looked up, puzzled; across from him his wife held herself in and repeated her question.

"Answer your mother, Marcia."

"I said it."

"Then say it again."

"No." Her answer was barely whispered.

"Of course, perhaps she cannot be expected to trust me," said Mrs. Benjin, looking distressed, clasping her hands at her breast, turning her wedding ring nervously.

"Answer your mother, Marcia," said Benjin in a sharp voice. "With whom were you playing?"

"With the black man."

"But there is no black man in town, surely," said Mrs. Benjin. "Not since—well, since long ago, when you were a little baby."

"When Mum was still here."

"Yes, dear."

They waited for Marcia to say more, but she did not. After she had been put to bed, Mrs. Benjin expressed some concern for her. But not so he; by that time he had more or less figured it out. It was perfectly natural that children should imagine playmates; he had done it himself as a boy. It was especially true of lonely children, and it could not be denied that all the other children of the neighborhood were either in school or were too much under five to serve as adequate companions for Marcia.

"Still, a *black man!*" said Mrs. Benjin with an alarm which she pretended very hard to feel.

"Yes, I admit that *is* a strange coincidence, isn't it?"

"It's three years now," she said musingly. She remembered it very well because it was at the carnival that she had first caught a good look at John Benjin and determined to have him for her own, if something could be made to come between his wife and him. Something had come between them, but it was none of her doing; Mrs. Benjin's death had taken place only a little over a year afterwards, and she had had her way with John a year later.

She thought about what Marcia had said and saw in this too something she could utilize to widen a rift between the child and her father, and once she could turn Marcia towards her, she could mold her as she wished. She did not know quite what she wanted to do with the girl, but in her heart she wished devoutly the girl was not here so that she could be free of that feeling of being watched as if—as if from beyond; yes, that was it; it was as if the eyes of John Benjin's first wife looked at her out of the dark eyes of her daughter.

Two days later Marcia was late again.

"If this doesn't stop," said Benjin in his placid way, though there was no mistaking his determination, "you'll not be permitted to go over to that merry-go-round any more, Marcia."

Of this, plainly, Marcia was afraid. "Oh, no, please!" she cried.

"You *must* learn to come home on time. Anyway, I don't think it's good for you to be over there alone all the time. That machinery is getting old, and may be falling to pieces. You may get hurt."

"But I'm not . . ." She sealed her lips and shot a quick, contemplative glance at her stepmother.

"What, dear?" asked Mrs. Benjin, leaning towards her with a synthetic sweetness on her hard features.

"Nothing."

"Marcia!" said her father.

"Nothing, Mother," she said.

It enraged Mrs. Benjin that the child hesitated to call her "Mother." It had been so from the first, and every attempt to force her to obey her father's wishes in this only made it more obvious.

"I wish she would trust me," she said, biting her lip with such force as to bring tears to her eyes.

"Now, now, Nell—take it easy," he said, putting one hand on her arm, and looking at Marcia with tired indignation.

Once again there was that tension around the table.

What stirred and further angered Mrs. Benjin was this; she was convinced with the deepest conviction that somehow the child knew what her stepmother was about; Marcia could not tell her father, she could not put her feeling into words, but somehow she *knew;* and it was a source of rage and humiliation that this five-year-old girl should so easily see through what was a mystery to Benjin. Perhaps Marcia had even guessed that her stepmother's quick hope had sprung up when Benjin had spoken of physical danger for her if the machinery fell apart.

"Now then," said Benjin, turning to his daughter, "whatever it was you were going to say, say it now; we've got to show your new mother that we trust her, haven't we?"

"Yes." She said this reluctantly.

"Well, then."

No answer.

"Come Marcia—please. Just pretend you're playing a game with us—with me, then."

She shook her head.

"It was the black man again, wasn't it?" Mrs. Benjin could not keep herself from making the guess.

Marcia looked at her blandly, saying nothing.

Overflowing with irritation, Benjin said angrily, "Answer your mother at once, Marcia, or take the consequences."

"Yes," said Marcia in a low voice.

"There, I knew it!" said Mrs. Benjin triumphantly. "And now I wonder, John—is it imagination, or is it just plain lying?"

"I don't tell lies," said Marcia scornfully. She was hurt.

"No, dear—I didn't mean that you meant to tell lies, but that perhaps you just couldn't help it."

The girl gazed at her without expression; what she thought and felt lay hidden behind her eyes, and this wall against her curiosity baffled and further infuriated Mrs. Benjin. It was inevitable, the woman knew, that soon now the child must be broken, and she must be broken to the woman's taste.

After that, Marcia was gone from the house more and more often. Perhaps she sensed the woman's waiting cruelty; perhaps the house in which once her own mother had created her world was too dark with this other woman's hatred and jealousy and angry suspicions; she sought her haven from dawn to sunset, and would have gone back of evenings if she had not been prevented from doing so. Seeing this, Mrs. Benjin set about to circumvent the girl as much as possible.

But Marcia quickly learned to develop a remarkable deviousness; she escaped her stepmother repeatedly; she began to assume a wiliness and shrewdness to match the woman's, and always managed, at times of crisis, to keep her father between them in such a way that there were times when it became impossible for the woman to conceal her exasperation, and Benjin had to remind her to be patient and understanding—"Let Marcia come to you, my dear; don't force yourself upon her."

"Ah, I try so hard!" Mrs. Benjin cried out, making her habitual gesture of twisting her wedding ring in agitation.

It was a touching scene, in which Marcia did not come off at all well. She was ultimately forbidden to go to the carnival grounds.

She disobeyed, and went anyway.

That was the result Mrs. Benjin desired.

She was curiously unable to face her husband that night at supper table, to which for once, knowing she had done wrong, Marcia preceded her father. Mrs. Benjin avoided his eyes in so telling a manner that he could not help noticing that something was wrong. Finally, he asked. She shook her head. He divined that it concerned Marcia, and finally sent the girl to her room.

"Oh, I don't want to say it," she said, distressed. "But Marcia ran away and spent the whole day over there."

"Then I will have to punish her," he said.

Punishment did not prevent her from running away.

"It's humiliating," said Mrs. Benjin on the second occasion. "I mean, it hurts me to know that she must dislike me so much that she wants to risk being punished by you— and she loves you; I can see that—by going over there. To that black man or whoever it is she imagines plays with her there."

"Is she still talking about that?"

"Yes."

He shook his head. "She must learn to obey you, Nell. We can't go on like this. It will disrupt the household."

"I'm afraid it may."

"It can't be. You'll have to take her in hand."

"But I can't—I really can't." But inwardly she exulted; she had waited patiently for this. "How could I punish her?"

"I'm afraid you must; she must learn to respect you."

She played her part to perfection, so that in the end poor deluded John Benjin, who sincerely loved his daughter, actually felt sorrier for his wife than he did for Marcia at the thought of the girl being punished. He was a stern man, but not an unkind one; he was simple, and had no knowledge of complexity; his first wife had been similar to him, unmotivated by complex passions and frustrations, and he would have been honestly horrified if he could have seen into his second wife's mind.

Mrs. Benjin bided her time.

After Marcia had been lulled into a sense of false security, Mrs. Benjin asked about "the black man. Does he still play with you?"

Marcia admitted that he did. "He told me not to worry any more, he would watch over me. Over papa, too."

"Oh, he did, did he?" She could not keep the chilliness from her voice. "Weren't you told not to tell lies, dear?"

She whipped her very thoroughly, and when he came home, Benjin found his wife in tears, which stood in her eyes in contrast to his daughter's white-lipped pain and indignation which could not hide a kind of sullen loathing for her stepmother. Thus victimized, Benjin was more than ordinarily sympathetic with his wife; he simply could not understand what had come over his daughter.

After Marcia had gone to bed, her father went to her room and sat beside her bed and talked to her. He was trying very hard to understand, and when he had softened his daughter sufficiently, she clung to him and sobbed. She was lonesome. Her stepmother hated her; why couldn't he understand? She was like the black man. He was lonesome, too. He had always been lonesome, all his life.

Benjin shook her. "Marcia! What are you talking about?"

She tried to explain, faltered before the look in his eyes, and was silent, retreating behind the wall of childhood into that world of her own, peopled with fantasies and strange beings sprung from her lonely imagination.

He made another attempt, trying to be patient. "How big is he—this black man?" he asked.

"Real big—bigger than you, Daddy. And he's so strong. He makes the merry-go-round go for me. I get a ride every day."

"Is he nice?"

"He's glad to see me whenever I come. He just stays there all the time, by the merry-go-round waiting for me. He's the nicest man I ever knew, except you, Daddy. And he's going to watch over me and you, too."

"Like your guardian angel?"

"Yes, except that he's black, and I guess my guardian angel's white."

It was not a very satisfying or illuminating conversation. He was very puzzled when he sought his own bed, fretting now lest his daughter's loneliness was affecting her mind.

Having made so auspicious a beginning, Mrs. Benjin could hardly contain herself until a second opportunity to punish Marcia was offered. But that initial whipping had betrayed the violence of her hatred to the child, and Marcia walked with care. She came home to supper on time night after night, and the summer deepened towards autumn. As day followed day without overt disobedience upon which Mrs. Benjin could seize as a pretext to work her angry way with her stepdaughter, she grew more irate and frustrated, and at last, one day, when she knew John Benjin would be remaining at his desk longer than usual, and so would not be home on time for supper, she took matters into her own hands to force the issue, and peremptorily forbade Marcia to go again to the carnival grounds.

Marcia ran away. Mrs. Benjin had known she would.

She waited with an almost unholy anticipation for the day to end.

Promptly at a quarter to six Marcia came tripping across the street and into the house, humming a little melody. She stopped short at sight of her stepmother waiting in sultry triumph.

"You disobeyed me," said Mrs. Benjin coldly.

"What are you going to do to me?"

"I'm going to punish you. Your father said I must."

"No, please."

"Please what?"

"Please, Mother. Don't."

"Yes, it's for your own good."

Mrs. Benjin could not keep herself from prolonging the child's torture. She came slowly around the table, bringing the stout whip she had held behind her gradually into sight of the child's horrified eyes.

With a shrill cry of fear, Marcia turned and fled.

Across the street, through the hole in the fence, into the carnival grounds.

But Mrs. Benjin was not to be so easily thwarted. She went after her, crossing the road and working her way into the grounds through that small opening in the fence, being careful to bring the whip with her, and remembering how easily some of that machinery might collapse and fall or be brought to fall on someone, a child who would know no better. . . .

She saw the child readily enough, clinging to one of the weather-beaten horses of the carousel. But Marcia was no longer afraid; she sat there with a curiously dispassionate air, watching her come on with such a sense of security from her that for a moment Mrs. Benjin was nonplussed.

As she came up to the merry-go-round, she heard her stepdaughter's voice come out at her.

"Don't! Don't touch me! Mr. Black Man won't let you. Mr. Black Man is watching over me."

Slowly, slowly, almost imperceptibly, the carousel began to move.

Mrs. Benjin, seeing only that somehow the child seemed to be escaping her, leaped forward. At the same time Marcia slipped from the back of the wooden horse, darted quickly across, and dropped off the other side of the carousel.

As Mrs. Benjin stepped up into the merry-go-round, something took hold of her.

There was one horrible scream, and then a succession of terrible sounds that mounted together with the grinding of the carousel going faster and faster. Into the gathering dusk curious oddments spun and flew from the merry-go-round, most of them spattering red upon the carousel and the earth beyond.

Marcia watched with interest and satisfaction.

When the carousel was still again, she walked around it towards the hole in the fence. There was nothing to be seen of her stepmother save some dark masses here and there. One of them lay between Marcia and her way of egress. She walked around it with almost savage detachment.

It was Mrs. Benjin's left hand, with the wedding ring still on one finger.

TOO LONG AT THE FAIR

R. L. Stevens

An amusement park which is closed for the winter lies blanketed in snow; even the merry-go-round animals wait in suspended animation. To this ghostly place comes Chicago lawyer Sam Clinton, with the intention of keeping an appointment for a dead man. Writing here under his R. L. Stevens pseudonym, Edward D. Hoch employs a non-series character to expose what really goes on while Bayshore Amusement Park slumbers.

Sam Clinton had traveled nearly a thousand miles to stand here before the empty, snow-blanketed parking lot of the Bayshore Amusement Park, and now, seeing it by fragile moonlight, he wondered if the trip had been worth it. There seemed to be no one about, though he noticed that the double gates in the high wire fence had been left ajar. Perhaps he would find somebody inside, lurking beneath the great snow-covered roller coaster.

The place was strange to him, as such places were even in the summertime. There seemed to his mind no way of explaining the logic of amusement parks, with their tinkling gaiety and ten-cent charm, waiting with great open mouths to swallow up the innocents who came hand-in-hand every weekend. Perhaps this was evil—evil as practiced in Twentieth Century New England, where they no longer hanged their witches.

This night, if there were evil, it had been covered by a two-inch fall of sticky snow blowing in off the Atlantic. As Clinton plodded along, leaving his virgin prints in the unmarked white, it seemed to him that even the elements had conspired against him. He passed the shuttered Fun House, the Shooting Gallery, the Airplane Ride, the Dragon Coaster, without seeing evidence of another living soul. But then, as he was about to abandon the fruitless quest, a line of tiny, Friday-like footprints crossed his own path. He followed them with a growing sense of elation, knowing now that all was not yet wrong with the world.

Ahead, in the damp, fog-laden night, he saw the lights that told him he was not alone in this place. They were in the oddly circular building which housed the merry-go-round, and the tiny footprints he followed led directly to its door.

"Hello," he said from the doorway by way of warning. "May I come in?"

From somewhere in the maze of resting animals, a girl in jeans and a paint-stained shirt appeared. "I don't know. Who are you?"

"Merry-go-round inspector," he said, stepping in and closing the door firmly behind him.

"What? Look, mister, the park is closed for the winter." She put down her paint brush and hopped to the floor to meet him on equal terms. He guessed her age to be about twenty-five, and he couldn't help admiring the contour of her legs beneath the tight jeans. When he reached her face, he saw an impish upturned nose and deep blue eyes that sparkled with challenge. She wore no makeup, but just then she didn't need any.

"Sorry," he said. "I am here on business. Is there a manager around the place?"

"In the middle of winter? My father owns the park, and he goes south every December for two months. I just came down to touch up a few of the animals. Want to help me paint the stripes on the zebra?"

She had obviously judged him and found him harmless. Many people did, and he'd almost come to expect it. "I'd be happy to," he told her. "I've always wanted to paint stripes on zebras."

She smiled then, and introduced herself. "I'm Jane Boone. Don't let me scare you in this costume."

"I won't. Sam Clinton—I'm a lawyer."

"Really?" She was back on guard at once. "Then this really is a business visit."

"Afraid so. I'll try to make the next one more pleasant. Is there somewhere we can talk?"

"Right here is the best place. It's warm and private, and I can go on with my work while you talk." She pulled herself back onto the merry-go-round, and he was forced to follow. There, in the inner row of prancing animals, was indeed a paint-peeled zebra badly in need of first aid.

"You're pretty skillful with that brush," he said. "Aren't you ever afraid, working here alone nights? Anybody could walk in here."

"The gate's usually locked. Besides, a friend of mine always stops by for me. He should be coming pretty soon, so don't get any ideas."

He felt himself beginning to blush. "I wasn't thinking of myself, believe me."

She daubed a bit at the wounded zebra. "You said you're a lawyer."

"That's right. I've traveled here all the way from Chicago because a man died there with your name in his pocket."

"*My* name?"

"The name of the amusement park—Bayshore—and the city, and a date."

"A date? What date?"

"Tomorrow's, as a matter of fact. January 14th. What's happening here tomorrow?"

She pursed her lips, and carefully curved a thin black line over the zebra's tired flank. "Same thing that happens every day during the winter. Nothing."

"Nothing?"

"Nothing. Who was the man that died?"

"A client of mine. His name was Felix Waterton."

"I never heard of him. I can't imagine what he would have been doing with our name."

"Might he be a friend of your father?"

"I doubt it. I help out in the office and handle all the correspondence. I never heard the name." She looked up and her eyes were suddenly shaded. "How did this Felix Waterton die?" she asked casually.

"You may have seen it in the papers. He . . ." But the door opened behind him at that moment, and Clinton turned to see a tall young man enter, stamping the clinging snow from his feet.

"Hi, Dick. You're early." She started to put down the paint brush, then changed her mind and went on with it. "This is Sam Clinton, Dick Mallow. Mr. Clinton's a lawyer from Chicago on business."

They shook hands and Clinton felt the firmness of the other's grip. "I finished my business early," he explained to the girl. "Two calls and nobody home." Then, by way of explanation to Clinton, "I sell insurance."

"Pleased to meet you," Clinton said, deciding he looked the type.

"What say you knock off on that zebra, and we hop across the street for a drink," Mallow said to the girl.

"Well . . . I was talking to Mr. Clinton. . . ."

"He can come too. Heck, man, I'll buy you a beer or something!"

"That's very nice of you. I'll admit I could use a beer."

"Then it's settled. Down with the paint brush, woman."

They left the lights burning in the merry-go-round, perhaps as a reminder to the zebra that they'd be back. Dick Mallow blazed a heavy-footed trail through the snow of the parking lot, while Jane Boone and Clinton followed behind. The place across the street proved to be an uncertain little neighborhood bar that seemed to lead a double life. The signs of summertime were still visible almost everywhere—in the exhausted blue balloon hanging from the bar mirror, the dusty college pennants tacked to the walls, the faded Polaroid snapshots of clowning teenagers. But now it was winter, and the bar led its other existence— quiet, dim, waiting, catering to the few who made the neighborhood their home, waiting for another summer.

Dick Mallow ordered three beers, and they clustered around a little cigarette-scarred table in one corner. It was obvious to Clinton that he was being allowed to participate in a nightly ritual, and when he noticed Mallow's hand beneath the table he managed to drop a cigarette on the floor so he could retrieve it and confirm the fact that the hand rested in Jane's.

"So you're a lawyer," Mallow said, skimming the foam from his lips with an experienced tongue. "From Chicago."

"That's right. We don't have any snow there. Not this week, anyway."

"You were telling me what brought you here," Jane Boone reminded him.

"A dead man with a note in his pocket. It said simply, *Bayshore Amusement Park, Rhode Island, January 14th.* So I came to find out what's happening here tomorrow."

Dick Mallow scratched an ear with his free hand. "What's happening, Janie? You giving away free kisses or something?"

"Nothing. I told Mr. Clinton that already. I haven't a clue."

Mallow suddenly snapped his fingers. "You forgot the General! It's the second Friday of the month; the General's coming tomorrow night!"

"Of course. The General . . ."

Sam Clinton tensed with interest. "What General? What's he coming for?"

"Major General Tracy Spindler, U.S. Army, Retired," the girl recited. She took a quick swallow of beer and hurried on. "He rents our bingo hall for his meetings, once a month during the winter. My father figures it's income, but I figure it's just a pain."

"What sort of meetings?"

"You wouldn't believe it. They have some crazy club that believes we all came from Mars or some place. I sat in on one of their meetings a few months back, but after ten minutes I'd had enough."

Clinton frowned over his glass. "It doesn't sound like the sort of thing one finds in the depth of New England. It has more a New York or California sound about it. But I'd like to come out tomorrow night, if it's an open meeting."

"They let me in," she said. "I suppose it would be all right."

Dick Mallow downed the rest of his beer with a few quick gulps. "You think this dead guy might have belonged to the General's club, huh? Any good reason?"

"It's a possibility. Right now it seems to be the only possibility."

"What did you say his name was?" Jane Boone asked.

"Felix Waterton." Clinton watched Mallow's face, but his expression was frozen into a bland sort of nothingness that didn't change at the name. "He was a client of mine."

"And what did you say he died of?"

"I guess I didn't say. He was murdered."

Mallow got unsteadily to his feet. "Let's have another round of beers," he called to the sleepy bartender. Then he disappeared into the men's room, leaving Clinton and Jane alone.

"You're some kind of a detective, aren't you?" she asked.

"I told you I was a lawyer."

"I know. I guess I just don't believe you. Maybe it's because I couldn't ever picture you in court, before a jury."

He smiled at that. "You've been watching too much television. There are lawyers and lawyers."

Dick Mallow came back just as the bartender returned with the second round. He slid into the booth next to Jane and his hand disappeared from view once more. "Beer is the staff of life," he said, licking at the foam. "Pretty soon I'll be ready to go back and help you paint zebras all night."

As the second round gradually disappeared from the glasses, Clinton saw quickly enough that he was no longer to be a part of the ritual. He finished his beer and got to his feet. "I have to be going. I would like to stop by tomorrow though, Miss Boone."

"Sure. Come ahead."

Outside, it was beginning to snow. He stood for a moment looking across the street at the deserted amusement park with its monuments of white. The night was very quiet, and he wondered if the zebra would ever get painted.

Felix Waterton had been a strange man in life. Born in the closing days of the First World War, he'd spent his teen years fighting for survival in the streets of a depression-racked Chicago. His father, a minor figure in the vast complex of bootlegging, had come home one Christmas night bleeding to death from three bullet wounds in the side, and the shock of it all had put his frail mother in an institution from which she never returned.

Even in those early pre-war days when Sam Clinton first met him, Waterton spoke almost incessantly of avenging his father's death. He carried a loaded gun with him at all times, a tiny French automatic he'd procured from somewhere, and Sam Clinton was just enough younger than Waterton to be impressed and a bit terrified. The war years had separated them, and after it was over Clinton had returned to Chicago and studied law. He'd set up practice in a one-room office in the Loop, then sat back and slowly starved, until the day Felix Waterton walked through the door.

After that, things had changed in a somewhat oblique manner. Waterton managed a position for him with a leading law firm, and Clinton found himself on the rise. He began to specialize in tax law, at Waterton's suggestion, and the man threw him a good deal of business. This had gone on for better than ten years, through the economic boom of the Fifties and into the Sixties. Felix Waterton grew with the years, and became wealthy while other men, sometimes better men, had sunk into the mire of failure and futility.

Waterton's large holdings were mainly in Chicago real estate, though Sam Clinton had heard frequent rumors of other, less respectable, activities. The man was a known associate of midwest underworld characters, and if he still carried the little French automatic it was no longer to avenge the death of his father. Oddly enough, Clinton's activities on various tax problems for Waterton enterprises had left him with surprisingly little knowledge of the man's sources of income—little knowledge, that is, until he'd spent an evening with a friendly and talkative secretary who told him how he'd been played for a sucker all those years.

Clinton had been carefully groomed by Felix Waterton to fill a specific need in the organization. As a tax lawyer, he'd been used to throw up a smokescreen, while Waterton and his associates systematically diverted funds from their own real estate holding companies. When Clinton accused Waterton of the protracted swindle, the man had merely laughed. And fired his secretary.

That was where things stood on the night Felix Waterton was murdered.

The brief snow of the previous night had given way to rain, and the parking lot of the Bayshore Amusement Park was a shimmering sea of slush by the time the first cars began to pull in. Sam Clinton watched it all from the shelter of the roller coaster, shorn now of its sticky white coat, and he noted with interest that the arrivals for General Spindler's meeting seemed not at all what he had expected. They were neither beat nor bearded, and for the most part seemed to be just ordinary people, men and women, bundled in raincoats against the wind-blown drizzle.

"Here you are," Jane Boone said suddenly, coming up behind Clinton. "I thought I'd find you."

"Well, I said I'd be back. Finish your paint job?"

She nodded. "Finally." Her hair was covered with a pale blue scarf and the wide collar of her coat was turned up against the weather. He could see that she still wore the paint-stained jeans from the previous night.

"Going to the meeting?" he asked.

"I'll sit in with you for a few minutes, near the back. By the way, I've already spoken to the General and told him you'd be around. He said it's all right."

"Just what did you tell him?" he asked, trying to concentrate on her face in the rain. It was a pretty face, and he guessed that it was not at the height of its beauty.

"About this man who was killed in Chicago, and the note he had on him. Of course the General was interested."

"I'll bet." He tried to light a cigarette but it was hopeless in the rain. "By the way, I wanted to ask you something. About your friend, Dick Mallow, if you don't mind."

"Dick?" She wrinkled up her nose in an expression

that might have been coy. "You want to know if he's my boy friend."

"Not exactly. I want to know if he's been here every night this week."

She seemed puzzled by the question, and stepped a bit further into the darkened shadows of the sheltering roller coaster. "Why? Why do you ask? Do you think he killed that man in Chicago? Is that it?"

"Not really, but Felix Waterton was connected with someone here. Since you mentioned the killing, though, what about it? Last Monday night, specifically."

"I don't remember. Dick has to work late sometimes. He missed one or two nights early in the week."

"Then he could have hopped a plane to Chicago."

"Sure. And he could have flown to the moon. But he didn't. He never heard of your friend Waterton."

"He seemed awfully quiet last night after the name was mentioned."

Even in the near darkness her eyes sparkled with a touch of fury. "He was probably quiet because he was anxious to be alone with me. Or didn't that thought ever cross your mind, romance still exists?"

"All right, all right. Are you going to take me in to meet the General, or not?" He was growing impatient with her defense of Mallow, who didn't really seem worth all the concern.

"Come on," she replied, "while the rain has let up a bit."

June led him through the slush to a long, low building next to the shuttered Fun House. The lights from its glowing windows seemed to cast a bit of unreality across the deserted landscape, which had seemed so natural in the dark. He slid through the partly opened door behind her and found himself in a stark room, filled almost to capacity with people seated at the long makeshift bingo tables. Here and there, on shelves set against the walls, a stuffed animal or packaged blanket remained unclaimed from summer's prizes.

Toward the front of the room, on the little raised platform where the bingo operator usually sat, a tall, slim man with a shock of white hair stood waiting to address his audience. A movie screen was set up behind him, its glass beading catching and reflecting the overhead lights. Clinton knew without being told that he was looking at General Tracy Spindler.

"Ladies and gentlemen," the speaker began, "I'm pleased to see such a good turnout tonight, in view of the nasty weather." Clinton glanced around and figured the audience at nearly a hundred. It was indeed a good turnout, all things considered. He wondered whether Felix Waterton would have been here, had he lived.

"I'm General Spindler, for those few of you who might be new to our little group. Actually, the beliefs of the Noahites are quite simply stated, and we do state them at the beginning of every meeting. We believe that the ark of Noah did not travel the seas of an earthly flood, but rather voyaged here to our planet across a sea of space. We believe that Noah and his family and the creatures that journeyed with them came from a far planet, and brought the first life to this planet earth."

Clinton leaned against the wall and lit a cigarette. He wondered if the General really believed any of what he was saying. The audience, an oddly homogeneous middle-class group, seemed to believe, and they sat in rapt attention through the twenty-minute film that followed. It was a poorly photographed record of archaeological diggings in the region of Mount Ararat, with blurred close-ups of hands holding oddly-shaped pieces of stone and metal, which might have come from another planet, or from the corner junkyard. Clinton, being by nature a disbeliever, was inclined toward the latter.

At the end of the film, General Spindler was joined on the platform by a tall, leggy girl with close-cropped black hair. She was wearing dark leather boots, and they reached almost to her knees. "Thank you, thank you," Spindler said,

responding to the scattering of applause at the conclusion
of the movie. "Now we'll take a little break before our
discussion period, and Zelda will be serving you coffee and
doughnuts."

Clinton followed Jane Boone through the suddenly ac-
tive audience. While the dark-haired Zelda began dispens-
ing refreshments, they cornered General Spindler on the
platform. "This is Sam Clinton," Jane said. "I told you
about him."

"Yes," the General acknowledged, nodding his white
mane. "You're the man from Chicago. I read about that
killing in the papers."

Clinton shook hands with the man, and felt the damp-
ness of his palm. "I hope you can shed some light on it,
General."

The older man's eyes clouded over for a moment. "All
I know is what I read. Do you have any further details?"

Clinton glanced around at the crowd lined up for coffee
and doughnuts. "Can we go some place and talk?"

"I only have five minutes before the discussion begins."

"Let them linger over their coffee. I won't take long."

"Very well," the General agreed, and Jane Boone led
them behind the platform to a little storeroom cluttered
with prizes.

Clinton seated himself gingerly on a carton filled with
dusty bingo boards. "Well, as you probably know from the
papers, Felix Waterton was murdered in Chicago last Monday night. He was shot twice in the head, and his body
was dumped by the side of a country road and set afire
with gasoline. He was a client of mine, a very good client."

General Spindler shrugged. "Outside of the newspa-
pers, the name means nothing to me. Should it?"

"Waterton was involved in certain financial transactions
in Chicago. As near as I've been able to piece together
since his death, large quantities of money were being si-
phoned off and hidden somewhere. I know he often made
mysterious trips east, and I believe he was planning to come
here tonight."

Spindler nodded. "Miss Boone told me about the note. But that's no connection with me, or with the Noahites."

"What else is happening at the Bayshore Amusement Park today?" Clinton asked. He started to light a cigarette but then thought better of it. The place was a firetrap just waiting for a spark to set it off.

General Spindler glanced at Jane. "Perhaps you should ask Miss Boone."

She seemed to resent the implication of it. "You're the only thing happening here today, General Spindler. And, frankly, I don't think my father would have rented you the place if he knew what he was getting into."

The door of the storeroom swung open and the dark-haired Zelda entered. "They're waiting for you," she said quietly, without changing expression.

General Spindler got to his feet. "You must excuse me. My public awaits. Perhaps later we can continue this."

Clinton and Jane drifted back to their places at the rear of the bingo hall and settled down to witnessing a protracted discussion of the film they'd seen earlier. After a somber young man had risen to ask why the Great Powers conspired to keep the truth of human origin such a closely guarded secret, Jane apparently decided she'd had enough. "I have to go," she said, giving his arm a slight and unexpected squeeze. "Dick's probably looking all over for me."

"I'll see you later," Clinton told her. "I have to talk with the General some more."

He stood, leaned, and finally sat through another hour of questions, answers, and general discussion. The mood of the meeting was a gloomy seriousness that pervaded to the end, when the would-be space people began filing slowly out. Only a few remained grouped around the platform, and those seemed as intent upon the girl, Zelda, as upon anything else.

"Can we continue our discussion?" Clinton asked the General.

"Not here. There's a little bar across the street that's usually open."

"I know the place," Clinton replied, wondering if Mallow would be there with his hand in Jane's.

Spindler turned to the girl. "Zelda, pack up the projector and screen. I'll be back shortly."

As they crossed the rapidly emptying parking lot toward the glow of light from the little bar, Clinton said, "That Zelda is a very attractive girl."

Spindler snorted. "Thank you, she's my daughter. Her looks get her into trouble occasionally."

When they were settled for a drink, Clinton continued, "Do you really believe all this bunk about the ark coming from another planet, General?"

"I see that you are a doubting man. Of course I believe it—publicly. And you'll never get me to say anything else."

"What does the government think of your activities?"

"I'm retired, sir. Have been since just after Korea. While I was an army man, I gave it a full measure of devotion and ability. Now I'm something else."

But Clinton wondered if he was. "Did you start the Noahites?"

"I did. They're all mine."

"Your own private army."

General Spindler smiled, but there was no humor in his eyes. "They are believers, every last one of them. They believe with an intensity that would be hard for someone like yourself to imagine. Some of these people drove all the way from Boston to be here tonight."

The bar was empty except for them, and Clinton wondered vaguely where Mallow and Jane might be. Back at the merry-go-round, probably. "There are always people like that, General, waiting to be found and herded together by someone like you."

"I admit it. Perhaps that is the basis of our civilization."

"Would they do anything for you?"

"I think so."

"Would they kill for you? Did they kill Waterton?"

The General closed his eyes. "You are a devious man, Mr. Clinton. What is it you want?"

"The truth, only that. I worked for Felix Waterton all these years, and I want to know what he was up to. I want to find the money he was stealing from a lot of people."

"I know nothing of any money."

Clinton leaned back against the firm leather of the booth. "I'm a tax lawyer, General. My mind works in devious ways. It took me a long time to tumble to what Waterton was up to, but once I did the rest of it wasn't too tough. I gather your Noahites is incorporated? And it's probably a non-profit institution, a quasi-religious group of sorts. As such, it would pay no income tax on donations. Felix Waterton was looking for such an organization. He could have made donations to you through his various corporations, and achieved a double purpose. He would have avoided tax payments on his sizeable profits, and at the same time he would have removed the money to a perfect hiding place, a place where it would be waiting for him. I think you and the Noahites have a good big chunk of Waterton's money, General."

Spindler's frown deepened. "You'd have a difficult time proving all this, just on the basis of that piece of paper. Perhaps Waterton was delivering the money to Miss Boone, or even to that friend of hers who's always around."

But Sam Clinton shook his head. "First of all, an amusement park wouldn't be in a position to hide large profits in their books. And, more important, if Waterton's contact all these years had been the amusement park itself, he'd hardly have needed to write down its name. I'm sure he'd have remembered it. No, he wrote down the name because he *wasn't* familiar with it, because you've only been holding your monthly meetings here since the park closed in the fall. I suppose he usually sent you the money by check at regular intervals, but this time he decided to visit you for some reason, perhaps because he knew I was starting to uncover the truth about his operations."

"I repeat, prove it!"

"You'll have to open the Noahite books to an investigation. And, of course, the whole set-up makes you the logical suspect in Waterton's killing. You can explain that away too, if you'd like."

"I was in New York last Monday. A dozen people saw me."

"Maybe."

The white-haired man's eyes flicked with an icy fury. "What do you want? Money?"

"*The* money."

He let out his breath. "You asked me if they'd kill for me. They will."

"I don't scare," Clinton said, getting to his feet. The beer was half-finished on the table between them. "Think it over."

He walked out of the bar and back across the street to the towering darkness of the amusement park. It was colder now, and the intermittent drizzle gave hints of turning to snow.

Clinton followed the lights and found Jane Boone cleaning up in the bingo hall after the meeting. Spindler's daughter, Zelda, was still in evidence, talking quietly with two younger members of the departed audience.

"Hello," he said. "Where's Dick tonight?"

"He's working. He said maybe he'd drop by later." She was busy picking up paper cups with coffee dregs and damp cigarette butts in their bottoms. "Did you talk to the General?"

Clinton nodded. "I think we understand each other."

She brushed some gray ashes from the tabletop. "You know something? I read mysteries once in a while, and I've got a theory about your murder case."

"Oh?"

"I heard you and the General talking about Waterton's body being burned."

Clinton nodded. "Almost beyond recognition. They weren't sure it was he until Tuesday."

"That's my theory. Maybe it *wasn't* Waterton at all, see!" She faced him with sparkling eyes. "He killed someone else, poured gasoline on the body and set it afire. Now that he's declared dead, he can safely collect this money you say he's hidden."

But Sam Clinton shook his head. "It was Waterton, all right. They got a couple of fingerprints off the body. The Chicago police think it was more an attempt to make the killing look like a gang job, rather than hide the identity."

"Why is it so important to you, all of it?"

He sat on the edge of the table. "I don't know. Maybe just because I was a sucker for so many years. I never tumbled to what he was doing until too late, and now I want to find that money."

Suddenly the dark-haired Zelda had joined them, her booted feet moving silently across the floor. Clinton didn't know if she'd heard their conversation, but she said softly, "I can tell you about my father and Felix Waterton—*all* about them. I'll meet you back here in an hour." Then she was gone, as quickly as she'd come, and they saw her join General Spindler and the two young men outside.

"Well," Jane breathed. "What was all that?"

"The break I'd been hoping for. If she tells me what I think . . ."

"Come on," Jane Boone said. "I'll make you a cup of coffee."

"Thanks. Guess I'll be around for a bit longer tonight."

They sat in the merry-go-round pavilion and drank black coffee, and after a while Jane Boone threw the switch that started it turning. "There's no music," she explained a bit sadly. "The loudspeaker's disconnected. But I left the rest of the power on for when I was working in here."

Clinton watched it turning, slowly at first, but with the inevitable quickening of pace. "That's too bad. It doesn't seem quite real without the music."

"In the winter nothing's quite real around here," she said.

"To me it never seemed real in the summertime, either. I remember going to these places as a boy and, after a few hours of the unreality, crying to go home. I guess I was afraid of staying too long, of losing touch with the real world outside."

She nodded vaguely, her eyes on the prancing, revolving animals. "Sometimes I think I've been here too long. I think of the whole world as a merry-go-round without music, or a fun house boarded up for the winter."

"Maybe it is, these days. Maybe that's the reality of it."

She hopped aboard the slowing carousel and threw a leg over one of the gaily colored horses. "Zelda will be back soon, if she's coming."

"And Dick?"

"You're a strange guy, Clinton."

The merry-go-round was picking up speed again, and he was about to join her on it when the door slid open to admit Zelda Spindler. "I couldn't find you at first," she said quietly.

Clinton walked over to her. She was shorter, close up, than she appeared. The leggy look was somehow a trick of distance, and the black boots. "I'm here," he said. "What have you got to tell me?"

Zelda shot a glance at Jane Boone, still riding the silent carousel horse. "Can I talk in front of her?"

"Of course."

"All right. What you suspected is true. Felix Waterton met my father during the war. He has been giving my father money for years. I have the financial records of the Noahites in the car. They show assets of more than a half-million dollars."

Clinton's heart pounded a bit faster. "Why are you telling me all this?"

"Because once my father was a good man, a highly respected army officer. I've seen him change since he retired, or maybe not change enough. I've seen him form the Noahites into an army to follow his crazy dreams. These old ladies, and lonely middle-aged men, and insecure kids—they follow him without knowing where they're going. And all the time he's using the Noahites as a front for his schemes with Felix Waterton. I took a lot, but I'm not taking murder. I'm telling all about it, to you and anyone else who wants to listen."

And at that moment the angry, unmistakable voice of General Spindler boomed out from the door. "A very nice speech, Zelda. I'm pleased I arrived in time for it."

Clinton saw the two men moving in behind the General, saw them circling to flank him, and knew that the battle was joined.

In the instant of frozen fear that followed, it was Jane Boone who was the first to act. She swung suddenly off the revolving merry-go-round and yanked Zelda away from her father's menacing approach. Clinton used the distraction to stiff-arm one of the men out of the way, and when the other reached for his pocket, the lawyer hit him hard in the stomach. Then he was outside, running, and he saw that Jane was close behind him. "They've got guns!" she gasped out. "We've got to get the police!"

As if in confirmation of her statement, a dull, flat crack sounded behind them. Clinton dived for cover, pulling the girl with him. They were behind the sheltering entrance to the Fun House, with only a few inches of plywood for protection. "Keep down," he warned. "They mean serious business."

"What about Zelda?"

"She'll have to take care of herself. Right now I'm more interested in getting those records from her car."

In a brief burst of moonlight through the patchwork clouds, they saw the two cars parked near the bingo hall. "The foreign one is Zelda's," Jane confirmed.

"Can you get into this place?" he asked, indicating the padlocked door of the Fun House.

"I've got a key."

"Stay there, out of sight. I'll be back for you." Then he was gone, running bent over across the slushy midway.

He reached the shelter of the bingo hall, and was about to make a dash for the car when he saw Spindler suddenly loom up before him, holding Zelda by the arm in a steely grip. "Stay right there," Spindler commanded. "I have a gun."

Sam Clinton froze. "All right," he answered, trying to keep his voice calm. "Can't we talk this over?"

"The time for talking is past," General Spindler said.

"You can't kill me and get away with it."

"No? You could die the way Felix did. These buildings would make a wonderful funeral pyre."

Clinton was trying to determine where the other two men were, but he wasn't sure of their location. Perhaps they were searching for the girl. But then, out on the highway, he saw a car begin to turn into the parking lot. Dick Mallow was arriving for his belated visit with Jane.

As in slow motion, he saw the General turn toward the approaching car, saw the gun waver only for an instant. But that was the instant he needed. His own gun was out before Spindler's weapon could quite get back, and the roar of the two pistols blended simultaneously with Zelda's scream.

Clinton found Jane in the darkened passage of the Fun House, huddled in a corner against some unknown terror. "I heard a shot," she said.

"Two shots. We both fired at once."

"Spindler?"

"I think he's dead. I didn't wait to see. I guess your boy friend's calling the police."

"What's the matter with your voice?"

"His bullet caught me in the side. I'm bleeding a bit." He sat down on the floor next to her.

"We have to get a doctor!" Her hands touched him, but quickly withdrew on contact with the bleeding.

"Stay here! At least till the police come. Those two goons are still prowling around. I'm not hurt badly."

"What about Zelda?"

"She seemed all right. She was screaming when I shot her father."

Somewhere far off, a world away, a siren began its mournful wail. "Where is it all going to end?" Jane Boone asked, her voice almost a sob.

"It's ended."

"Is it?"

In the distance, the sound of the siren was building steadily. She shuddered at the sound. "They're coming," he said simply.

"You wanted the money, didn't you? That's why you came here."

Suddenly he seemed too tired to answer. "What?"

"I have a new theory about Waterton's murder, Sam. Do you want to hear it?"

"No."

But she hurried on anyway, as if the time was growing short. "His body was doused with gasoline and burned almost beyond recognition, and yet you told us about the piece of paper found in his pocket. If there were a paper, Sam, the only one who could have found it was the murderer, before he set the body on fire. I guess you killed him, Sam. I guess you killed him yourself, and then came here after the money." When he didn't answer, she added, "You must really have hated him."

Clinton rolled over, trying to see in the dark, trying to hear beyond the all-powerful siren that filled the night around them. "I hated him," he said, but he didn't really know if she heard.

"They're here now," Jane said as the siren suddenly died to nothing.

"What are you going to do about it?" he asked. "Are you going to tell them?"

For a long time she didn't answer, and it was as if they truly were alone in the world, the only two left in a dark tunnel that led to nowhere. But then there was Mallow's voice outside, calling her name, searching for her.

And she answered. "I don't know what I'm going to do. Does anybody ever know, really?"

THE FALLEN ANGEL

Evan Hunter

Best-selling novelist Evan Hunter, like so many other writers, began his career by producing short fiction for the pulp and digest genre magazines: he published more than one hundred mystery, suspense, science fiction, fantasy, and Western stories during the 1950's. This is one of those early tales—the delightfully whimsical account of a circus owner named Anthony Mullins, "a good name, you will admit," and his star attraction, a very unusual trapeze artist with an amazing act that allows him to be billed as "The Fallen Angel." Some of Hunter's gritty, realistic crime stories from that same period can be found in his collections, The Jungle Kids *(1956) and the recent* The McBain Brief *(1983), the latter title published as by Ed McBain, the pseudonym under which more than forty of his widely acclaimed 87th Precinct police procedurals have appeared.*

He first came in one morning while I was making out the pay-roll for my small circus. We were pulling up stakes, ready to roll on to the next town, and I was bent over the books, writing down what I was paying everybody, and maybe that is why I did not hear the door open. When I looked up, this long, lanky fellow was standing there, and the door was shut tight behind him.

I looked at the door, and then I looked at him. He had a thin face with a narrow moustache, and black hair on his head that was sort of wild and sticking up in spots. He had brown eyes and a funny, twisted sort of mouth, with very white teeth which he was showing me at the moment.

"Mr. Mullins?" he asked.

"Yes," I said, because that is my name. Not Moon Mullins, which a lot of the fellows jokingly call me, but Anthony Mullins. And that's my real name, with no attempt to sound showman-like; a good name, you will admit. "I am busy."

"I won't take much time," he said very softly. He walked over to the desk with a smooth, sideward step, as if he were on greased ball bearings.

"No matter how much time you will take," I said, "I am still busy."

"My name is Sam Angeli," he said.

"Pleased to meet you, Mr. Angeli," I told him. "My name is Anthony Mullins, and I am sorry you must be running along so quickly, but—"

"I'm a trapeze artist," he said.

"We already have three trapeze artists," I informed him, "and they are all excellent performers, and the budget does not call for another of—"

"They are not Sam Angeli," he said, smiling and touching his chest with his thumb.

"That is true," I answered. "They are in alphabetical order: Sue Ellen Bradley, Arthur Farnings and Edward the Great."

"But not Sam Angeli," he repeated softly.

"No," I said. "It would be difficult to call them all Sam Angeli, since they are not even related, and even if they were related, it is unlikely they would all have the same name—even if they were triplets, which they are not."

"*I* am Sam Angeli," he said.

"So I have gathered. But I already have three—"

"I'm better," he said flatly.

"I have never met a trapeze artist who was not better than every other trapeze artist in the world," I said.

"In my case it happens to be true," he said.

I nodded and said nothing. I chewed my cigar awhile and went back to my books, and when I looked up he was still standing there, smiling.

"Look, my friend," I said, "I am earnestly sorry there is no opening for you, but—"

"Why not watch me a little?"

"I am too busy."

"It'll take five minutes. Your big top is still standing. Just watch me up there for a few minutes, that's all."

"My friend, what would be the point? I already have . . ."

"You can take your books with you, Mr. Mullins; you will not be sorry."

I looked at him again, and he stared at me levelly, and he had a deep, almost blazing way of staring that made me believe I would really not be sorry if I watched him perform. Besides, I could take the books with me.

"All right," I said, "but we're only wasting each other's time."

"I've got all the time in the world," he answered.

We went outside, and sure enough the big top was still standing, so I bawled out Warren for being so slow to get a show on the road, and then this Angeli and I went inside, and he looked up at the trapeze, and I very sarcastically said: "Is that high enough for you?"

He shrugged and looked up and said, "I've been higher, my friend. Much higher." He dropped his eyes to the ground then, and I saw that the net had already been taken down.

"This exhibition will have to be postponed," I informed him. "There is no net."

"I don't need a net," he answered.

"No?"

"No."

"Do you plan on breaking your neck under one of my tops? I am warning you that my insurance doesn't cover—"

"I won't break my neck," Angeli said. "Sit down."

I shrugged and sat down, thinking it was his neck and not mine, and hoping Dr. Lipsky was not drunk, as usual. I opened the books on my lap and got to work, and he walked across the top and started climbing up to the trapeze. I got involved with the figures, and finally he yelled:

"O.K., you ready?"

"I'm ready," I said.

I looked up to where he was sitting on one trapeze, holding the bar of the other trapeze in his big hands.

"Here's the idea," he yelled down. He had to yell because he was a good hundred feet in the air. "I'll set the second trapeze swinging, and then I'll put the one I'm on in motion. Then I'll jump from one trapeze to the other one. Understand?"

"I understand," I yelled back. I'm a quiet man by nature, and I have never liked yelling. Besides, he was about to do a very elementary trapeze routine, so there was nothing to get excited and yelling about.

He pushed out the second trapeze, and it swung away out in a nice clean arc, and then it came back and he shoved it out again and it went out farther and higher this time.

He set his own trapeze in motion then, and both trapezes went swinging around up there, back and forth, back and forth, higher and higher. He stood up on the bar and watched the second trapeze, timing himself, and then he shouted down, "I'll do a somersault to make it interesting."

"Go ahead," I said.

"Here I go," he said.

His trapeze came back and started forward, and the second trapeze reached the end of its arc and started back, and I saw him bend a little from the knees, calculating his timing, and then he leaped off, and his head ducked under, and he went into the somersault.

He did a nice clean roll, and then he stretched out his hands for the bar of the second trapeze, but the bar was nowhere near him. His fingers closed on air, and my eyes popped wide open as he sailed past the trapeze and then started a nose dive for the ground.

I jumped to my feet with my mouth open, remembering there was no net under him, and thinking of the mess he was going to make all over my tent. I watched him fall like a stone, and then I closed my eyes as he came closer to the ground. I clenched my fists and waited for the crash, and then the crash came, and there was a deathly silence in the tent afterward. I sighed and opened my eyes.

Sam Angeli got up and casually brushed the sawdust from his clothes. "How'd you like it?" he asked.

I stood stiff as a board and stared at him. "You're— You're—" I stammered.

"How'd you like it?" he repeated.

"Dr. Lipsky!" I shouted. "Doc, come quick!"

"No need for a doctor," Angeli said, smiling and walking over to me. "How'd you like the fall?"

"The—the fall? I—I—You mean—?"

"The fall," Angeli said, smiling. "Looked like the real McCoy, didn't it?"

"Wh-what do you mean?"

"Well, you don't think I missed that bar accidentally, do you? I mean, after all, that's a kid stunt."

"You—you fell on purpose?" I gulped and stared at him, but all his bones seemed to be in the right places, and there was no blood on him anywhere.

"Sure," he said. "My specialty. I figured it all out, Mr. Mullins. Do you know why people like to watch trapeze . acts? Not because there's any skill or art attached. Oh, no." He smiled, and his eyes glowed, and I watched him, still amazed. "They like to watch because they are inherently evil, Mr. Mullins. They watch because they think that fool up there is going to fall and break his neck, and they want to be around when he does it." Angeli nodded. "So I figured it all out."

"You—you did?"

"I did. I figured if the customers wanted to see me fall, then I would fall. So I practised falling."

"You—you did?"

"I did. First I fell out of bed, and then I fell from a first-storey window, and then I fell off the roof. And then I took my biggest fall, the fall that—But I'm boring you. The point is, I can fall from any place now. In fact, that trapeze of yours is rather low."

"Rather low," I repeated softly.

"Yes."

"What's up?" Dr. Lipsky shouted, rushing into the tent, his shirt flaps trailing. "What happened, Moon?"

"Nothing," I said, wagging my head. "Nothing, doc."

"Then why'd you—?"

"I wanted to tell you," I said slowly, "that I've just hired a new trapeze artist."

"Huh?" Dr. Lipsky said, drunk as usual.

We rolled on to the next town, and I introduced Angeli to my other trapeze artists: Sue Ellen, Farnings and Edward the Great. I was a younger man at that time, and I have always had an eye for good legs in tights, and Sue Ellen had them all right. She also had blonde hair and big blue eyes, and when I introduced her to Angeli those eyes went all over him, and I began to wonder if I hadn't made a mistake hiring him. I told them I wanted Angeli to have exclusive use of the tent that afternoon, and all afternoon I sat and watched him while he jumped for trapezes and missed and went flying down on his nose or his head or his back or whatever he landed on. I kept watching him when he landed, but the sawdust always came up around him like a big cloud, and I never could see what he did inside that cloud. All I know is that he got up every time, and he brushed himself off, and each time I went over to him and expected to find a hundred broken bones and maybe a fractured skull, but each time he just stood up with that handsome smile on his face as if he hadn't just fallen from away up there.

"This is amazing," I told him. "This is almost supernatural!"

"I know," he said.

"We'll start you tonight," I said, getting excited about it now. "Can you start tonight?"

"I can start any time," he said.

"Sam Angeli," I announced, spreading my hand across the air as if I were spelling it out in lights. "Sam Angeli, the—" I paused and let my hand drop. "That's terrible," I said.

"I know," Angeli answered. "But I figured that out, too."

"What?"

"A name for me. I figured this all out."

"And what's the name?" I asked.

"The Fallen Angel," he said.

There wasn't much of a crowd that night. Sue Ellen, Farnings and Edward the Great went up there and did their routines, but they were playing to cold fish, and you could have put all the applause they got into a sardine can.

Except mine. Whenever I saw Sue Ellen, I clapped my heart out, and I never cared what the crowd was doing. I went out after Edward the Great wound up his act, and I said, "Ladieeees and Gen-tulmennnn, it gives me great pleasure to introduce at this time, in his American première, for the first time in this country, the Fallen Angel!"

I don't know what I expected, but no one so much as batted an eyelid.

"You will note," I said, "that the nets are now being removed from beneath the trapezes, and that the trapezes are being raised to the uppermost portion of the tent. The Fallen Angel will perform at a height of one hundred and fifty feet above the ground, without benefit of a net, performing his death-defying feats of skill for your satisfaction."

The crowd rumbled a little, but you could see they still weren't very excited about it all.

"And now," I shouted, "the Fallen Angel!"

Angeli came into the ring, long and thin, muscular in his red tights, the sequins shining so that they could almost blind you. He began climbing up to the bars, and everyone watched him, a little bored by now with all these trapeze acts. Angeli hopped aboard and then worked out a little, swinging to and fro, leaping from one trapeze to another, doing a few difficult stunts. He looked down to the band then, and Charlie started a roll on the drums, and I shouted into my megaphone, "And now, a blood-chilling, spine-tingling, double somersault from one moving trapeze to another at one hundred and fifty feet above the ground— *without a net!*"

The crowd leaned forward a little, the way they always will when a snare drum starts rolling, and Angeli set the bars in motion, and then he tensed, with all the spotlights on him. The drum kept going, and then Angeli leaped into space, and he rolled over once, twice, and then his arms came out straight for the bar, and his hands clutched nothing, and he started to fall.

A woman screamed, and then the crowd was on its

feet, a shocked roar leaping from four hundred throats all together. Angeli dropped and dropped and dropped, and women covered their eyes and screamed, and brave men turned away, and then he hit the sawdust, and the cloud rolled up around him, and an "Ohhhhhhh" went up from the crowd. They kept standing, shocked, silent, like a bunch of pall-bearers.

Then suddenly, casually, the Fallen Angel got to his feet and brushed off his red-sequined costume. He turned to the crowd and smiled, a big, happy smile, and then he turned to face the other half of the tent, smiling again, extending his arms and hands to his public, almost as if he were silently saying, "My children! My nice children!"

The crowd cheered and whistled and shouted and stamped, and some men yelled, "*Bravo! Bravolissimo!*" or something like that. Sue Ellen, standing next to me, sighed and said, "Tony, he's wonderful," and I heard her, and I heard the yells of "Encore!" out there, but I didn't bring Angeli out again that night. I tucked him away and then waited for the landslide.

The landslide came the next night. We were playing in a small town, but I think everyone who could walk turned out for the show. They fidgeted through all the acts, crowding the tent, standing in the back, shoving and pushing. They were bored when my aerial artists went on, but the boredom was good because they were all waiting for the Fallen Angel, all waiting to see if the reports about him were true.

When I introduced him, there was no applause. There was only an awful hush. Angeli came out and climbed up to the bars and then began doing his tricks again, and everyone waited, having heard that he took his fall during the double somersault.

But Angeli was a supreme showman, and he realized the value of his trick lay in its surprise element. So he didn't wait for the double somersault this time. He simply swung out one trapeze and then made a leap for it, right in the middle of his other routine stunts, only this time he missed, and down he dropped with the crowd screaming to their feet.

A lot of people missed the fall, and that was the idea, because those same people came back the next night, and Angeli never did it the same way twice. He'd fall in the middle of his act, or at the end, or once he fell the first time he jumped for the trapeze. Another time he didn't fall at all during the act, and then, as he was coming down the ladder, he missed a rung and down he came, and the crowd screamed.

And Angeli would come to me after each performance and his eyes would glow, and he'd say: "Did you hear them, Tony? They want me to fall, they want me to break my neck!"

And maybe they did. Or maybe they were just very happy to see him get up after he fell, safe and sound. Whatever it was, it was wonderful. Business was booming, and I began thinking of getting some new tops, and maybe a wild-animal act. I boosted everybody's salary, and I began taking a larger cut myself, and I was finally ready to ask Sue Ellen something I'd wanted to ask her for a long, long time. And Sam Angeli made it all possible. I spoke to her alone one night, over by the stakes where the elephants were tied.

"Sue Ellen," I said, "there's something that's been on my mind for a long time now."

"What is it, Tony?" she said.

"Well, I'm just a small-time circus man, and I never had much money, you know, and so I never had the right. But things have picked up considerably, and—"

"Don't, Tony," she said.

I opened my eyes wide. "I beg your pardon, Sue Ellen?"

"Don't ask me. Maybe it could have been, and maybe it couldn't. But no more now, Tony. Not since I met Sam. He's everything I want, Tony; can you understand that?"

"I suppose," I said.

"I think I love him, Tony."

I nodded and said nothing.

"I'm awfully sorry," Sue Ellen said.

"If it makes you happy, honey—" I couldn't think of any way to finish it.

I started work in earnest. Maybe I should have fired Angeli on the spot, but you can't fire love, and that's what I was battling. So instead I worked harder, and I tried not to see Sue Ellen around all the time. I began to figure crowd reactions, and I realized the people would not stand still for my other aerial artists once they got wind of the Fallen Angel. So we worked Farnings and Edward (whose "Great" title we dropped) into an act, and we worked Sue Ellen into Angeli's act. Sue Ellen dressed up the act a lot, and it gave Angeli someone to play around with up there, and it made his stunts before the fall more interesting.

Sue Ellen never did any of the fancy stuff. She just caught Angeli, or was caught by him—all stuff leading up to Angeli's spectacular fall. The beautiful part was that Sue Ellen never had to worry about timing. I mean, if she missed Angeli—so he fell. I thought about his fall a lot, and I tried to figure it out, but I never could, and after a while I stopped figuring. I never stopped thinking about Sue Ellen, though, and it hurt me awful to watch her looking at him with those eyes full of worship, but if she was happy, that was all that counted.

And then I began to get bigger ideas. Why fool around with a small-time circus? I wondered. Why not expand? Why not incorporate?

I got off a few letters to the biggest circuses I knew of. I told them what I had, and I told them the boy was under exclusive contract to me, and I told them he would triple attendance, and I told them I was interested in joining circuses, becoming partners sort of, with the understanding that the Fallen Angel would come along with me. I guess

the word had then got around, because all the big-shot letters were very cordial and very nice, and they all asked
me when they could get a look at Angeli because they would
certainly be interested in incorporating my fine little outfit
on a partnership basis if my boy were all I claimed him
to be, sincerely yours.

I got off a few more letters, asking all the big shots to
attend our regular Friday-night performance so that they
could judge the crowd reaction and see the Fallen Angel
under actual working conditions. All my letters were answered with telegrams, and we set the ball rolling.

That Friday afternoon was pure bedlam.

There's always a million things happening around a
circus, anyway; but this Friday everything seemed to pile
up at once. Like Fifi, our bareback rider, storming into
the tent in her white ruffles.

"My horse!" she yelled, her brown eyes flashing. "My
horse!"

"Is something wrong with him?" I asked.

"Is *something* wrong with him?" she ranted. "Is something *wrong* with him?"

"Is?" I asked.

"No, nothing's wrong with him," she screamed. "But
something's wrong with José Esperanza, and I'm going to
wring his scrawny little neck unless—"

"Now easy, honey," I said; "let us take it easy."

"I told him a bucket of *rye*. I did *not* say a bucket of
oats. JuJu does not eat oats; he eats rye. And my safety
and health and life depend on JuJu, and I will not have
him eating some foul-smelling oats when I distinctly told
José—"

"José!" I bellowed. "José Esperanza, come here."

José was a small Puerto Rican we'd picked up only recently. A nice young kid with big brown cow's eyes and a
small, timid smile. He poked his head into the wagon and
smiled, and then he saw Fifi and the smile dropped from
his face.

"Is it true you gave JuJu oats, José, when you were told to give him rye?" I asked.

"*Si, señor,*" José said, "that ees true."

"But why, José? Why on earth—"

"I could not do eet, *señor.*"

"You could not do what?"

José lowered his head. "The horse, *señor;* I like heem. He ees nice horse. He ees always good to me."

"What's that got to do with the bucket of rye?"

"*Señor,*" José said pleadingly, "I did not want to get the horse drunk."

"Drunk? Drunk?"

"Si, *señor,* a bucket of rye. Even for a horse, thees ees a lot of wheesky. I did not theenk—"

"Oh," Fifi wailed, "of all the inexcusably—I'll feed the horse myself. I'll feed him myself. Never mind!"

She stormed out of the wagon, and José smiled sheepishly and said, "I did wrong, *señor?*"

"No," I said. "You did all right, José. Now run along."

I shook my head, and José left, and when I turned around Sam Angeli was standing there. I hadn't heard him come in, and I wondered how long he'd been there, so I said:

"A good kid, José."

"If you like good kids," Angeli answered.

"He'll go to heaven, that one," I said. "Mark my words."

Angeli smiled. "We'll see," he said. "I wanted to talk to you, Tony."

"Oh? What about?"

"About all these people coming tonight. The big shots, the ones coming to see me."

"What about them?"

"Nothing, Tony. But suppose—just suppose, mind you—suppose I didn't fall?"

"What do you mean?" I said.

"Just that. Suppose I don't fall tonight?"

"That's silly," I said. "You have to fall."

"Do I? Where does it say I have to fall?"

"Your contract. You signed a . . ."

"The contract doesn't say anything about my having to fall, Tony. Not a word."

"Well . . . Say, what is this? A hold-up?"

"No. Nothing of the sort. I just got to thinking. If this works out tonight, Tony, you're going to be a big man. But what do I get out of it?"

"Do you want a salary boost? Is that it? O.K. You've got a salary boost. How's that?"

"I don't want a salary boost."

"What, then?"

"Something of very little importance. Something of no value whatever."

"What?" I said. "What is it?"

"Suppose we make a deal, Tony?" Angeli said. "Suppose we shake on it? If I fall tonight, I get this little something that I want."

"What's this little something that you want?"

"Is it a deal?"

"I have to know first."

"Well, let's forget it, then," Angeli said.

"Now wait a minute, wait a minute. Is this 'thing'— Sue Ellen?"

Angeli smiled. "I don't have to make a deal to get her, Tony."

"Well, is it money?"

"No. This thing has no value."

"Then why do you want it?"

"I collect them."

"And I've got one?"

"Yes."

"But it's not worth any money?"

"No, Tony. No money at all."

"Well, what—?"

"Is it a deal, or isn't it?"

"I don't know. I mean, this is a peculiar way to—"

"Believe me, this thing is of no material value to you.

You won't even know it's gone. But if I go through with my fall tonight, all I ask is that you give it to me. A handshake will be binding as far as I'm concerned."

"You sound as nuts as Fifi does," I said.

"A deal? If I fall, I get what I want."

I shrugged. "All right, all right, a deal. Provided you haven't misrepresented this thing, whatever it is. Provided it's not of material value to me."

"I haven't misrepresented it. Shall we shake, Tony?"

He extended his hand, and I took it, and his eyes glowed, but his skin was very cold to the touch. I pulled my hand away.

"Now," I said, "what's this thing you want from me?"

Angeli smiled. "Your soul."

I was suddenly alone in the wagon. I looked around, but Angeli was gone, and then the door opened and Sue Ellen stepped in, and she looked very grave and very upset.

"I heard," she said. "Forgive me. I heard. I was listening outside. Tony, what are you going to do? . . . What are *we* going to do?"

"Can it be?" I said. "Can it be, Sue Ellen? He looks just like you and me. How'd I get into this?"

"We've got to do something," Sue Ellen said. "Tony, we've got to stop him!"

We packed them in that night. They sat, and they stood, and they climbed all over the rafters; they were everywhere. And right down front, I sat with the big shots, and they all watched my small, unimportant show until it was time for the Fallen Angel to go on.

I got up and smiled weakly and said, "If you gentlemen will excuse me, I have to introduce the next act."

They all smiled back knowingly, and nodded their heads, and their gold stickpins and pinky rings winked at me, and they blew out expensive cigar smoke, and I was thinking, MULLINS, YOU CAN BLOW OUT EXPENSIVE CIGAR SMOKE, TOO, BUT YOU WON'T HAVE ANY SOUL LEFT.

I introduced the act, and I was surprised to see all my

aerial artists run out on to the sawdust: Sue Ellen, Farnings, Edward and the Fallen Angel. I watched Angeli as he crossed one of the spotlights, and if I'd had any doubts they all vanished right then. Angeli cast no shadow on to the sawdust.

I watched in amazement, as the entire troupe went up the ladder to the trapezes. There was a smile on Angeli's face, but Sue Ellen and the rest had tight, set mouths.

They did a few stunts, and I watched the big shots, and it was plain they were not impressed at all by these routine aerial acrobatics. I signalled the band, according to schedule, and I shouted, "And now, ladies and gentlemen, the Fallen Angel in a death-defying, spine-tingling, blood-curdling triple somersault at one hundred and fifty feet above the ground, *without a net!*"

Sue Ellen swung her trapeze out, and Angeli swung his, and then Sue Ellen dropped head downward and extended her hands, and Angeli swung back and forth, and the crowd held its breath, waiting for him to take his fall, and the big shots held their breaths, waiting for the same thing. Only I knew what would happen if he did take that fall. Only I knew about our agreement. Only I—and Sue Ellen, waiting up there for Angeli to jump.

Charlie started the roll on his snare, and then the roll stopped abruptly, and Angeli released his grip on the bar and he swung out into space, and over he went, once, twice, three times—and *slap*. Sue Ellen's hands clamped around his wrists, and she held on for dear life. I couldn't see Angeli's face from so far below, but he seemed to be struggling to get away. Sue Ellen held him for just an instant, just long enough for Edward to swing his trapeze into position.

She flipped Angeli out then, and over he went and *wham*. Edward grabbed his ankles. Angeli flapped his arms and kicked his legs, trying to get free, but Edward—Edward the Great!—wouldn't drop him. Instead, he swung his trapeze back, and then gave Angeli a flip and Farnings grabbed Angeli's wrists.

Farnings flipped Angeli up, and Sue Ellen caught him, and then Sue Ellen swung her trapeze all the way back and tossed Angeli to Edward, and I began to get the idea of what was going on up there.

Edward tossed Angeli, and Farnings caught him, and then Farnings tossed him to Sue Ellen, and Sue Ellen tossed him right back again. Then Farnings climbed on to Sue Ellen's trapeze, and they both swung back to the platform.

Edward took a long swing, and then he tossed Angeli head over heels, right back to the platform, where Sue Ellen and Farnings grabbed him with four eager arms.

I was grinning all over by this time, and the crowd was booing at the top of their lungs. But who cared? The big shots were stirring restlessly, but they'd probably heard that Angeli sometimes fell coming down the ladder, and so they didn't leave their seats.

Only tonight, Angeli wasn't doing any falling coming down any ladder. Because Sue Ellen had one of his wrists and Farnings had one of his ankles, and one was behind him, and the other was ahead of him; and even if he pitched himself off into space, he wouldn't have gone far, not with the grips they had on both him and the ladder. I saw the big shots get up and throw away their cigars, and then everybody began booing as if they wanted to tear down the top with their voices. Angeli came over to me, and his face didn't hold a pleasant smile this time. His face was in rage, and it turned red, as if he would explode.

"You tricked me!" he screamed. "You tricked me!"

"Oh, go to hell," I told him, and all at once he wasn't there any more.

Well, I'm not John Ringling North, and I don't run the greatest show on earth. I've just got a small, unimportant circus, and it gives me a regular small income, but it's also a lot of trouble sometimes.

I still have my soul, though; and, what's more, I now have a soul-mate, and she answers to the name of Sue Ellen Mullins, which is in a way most euphonic, you will agree.

THE SHILL

Stephen Marlowe

Stephen Marlowe is another writer who learned his craft through the writing of suspense and science fiction stories for the early 50's genre magazines. His series of paperback originals featuring globe-trotting private investigator Chester Drum, begun during that decade, ran to twenty titles and was highly popular with readers. After the last Drum novel, Drum Beat—Marianne, *was published in 1968, Marlowe turned to the writing of large-scale suspense novels such as* The Summit *(1970) and* The Cawthorn Journals *(1975). About "The Shill," one of his early stories, he has written, "There are shills in carnivals and along midways everywhere—like music they know no national boundaries . . . I've seen shills in Coney Island and in Rockaway Park, and I've seen them in the Prater in Vienna and along the Boulevard St. Michel in Paris's St. Germain, and wherever I've seen them their soft-lure of the paying customers is uncanny."*

Eddie gawked and gawked. The crowd came slowly but steadily. They didn't know they were watching Eddie gawk. That's what made a good shill, a professional shill.

He was, naturally, dressed like all the local thistle chins. He wore an old threadbare several years out of date glen plaid suit, double-breasted and rumpled-looking. He wore a dreary not quite white shirt open at the collar without a tie. And he gawked.

He had big round deep-set eyes set in patches of blue-black on either side of his long narrow bridged nose. His lower lip hung slack with innocent wonder. He had not shaved in twenty-four hours. He looked exactly as if he had just come, stiff and bone weary and in need of entertainment, off the assembly line of the tractor plant down the road at Twin Falls. He stared in big eyed open mouthed wonder at Bart Taylor, the talker for the sideshow, as Bart expostulated and cajoled, declaimed and promised the good-sized scuff of townsfolk who had been drawn consciously by Bart Taylor's talking and unconsciously by Eddie's gawking.

He was a magnificent shill and he knew it and Bart Taylor knew it and not only the people at the Worlds of Wonder sideshow knew it but all the folks from the other carnival tents as well, so that when business was slow they sometimes came over just to watch Eddie gawk and summon the crowd with his gawking and they knew, without having studied psychology, as Eddie knew, that there was something unscientifically magnetic about a splendid shill like Eddie.

They used to call Eddie the Judas Ram (cynically, because the thistle chins were being led to financial slaughter) and the Pied Piper (because the thistle chins followed like naive children the unheard music of his wondering eyes and gaping mouth). But all that was before Eddie fell in love with Alana the houri from Turkestan who did her dance of the veils at the Worlds of Wonder, Alana who was from Baltimore and whose real name was Maggie O'Hara and who, one fine night when she first joined the carnival at a small town outside of Houston, Texas, stole Eddie's heart completely and for all time. After that Eddie was so sad, his eyes so filled with longing, that they didn't call him anything and didn't talk to him much and just let him do his work, which was shilling.

From the beginning, Eddie didn't stand a chance. He was a shill. He was in love with Alana, who was pale, delicate and beautiful, and everyone knew at once he was in love with her. In a week, all the men in the carnival were interested in Alana, whom nobody called Maggie. In a month, they all loved Alana, each in his own way, and each not because Alana had dunned them but because Eddie was a shill. It was as simple as that. Alana, however, for her own reasons remained aloof from all their advances. And the worst smitten of all was Bart Taylor, the talker and owner of Worlds of Wonder.

Now Bart finished his dunning and Eddie stepped up to the stand, shy and uncertain looking, to buy the first ticket. Bart took off his straw hat and wiped the sweat from the sweat band and sold Eddie a ticket. A good part of the scuff of thistle chins formed a line behind Eddie and bought tickets too. They always did.

Inside, Eddie watched the show dutifully, watched Fawzia the Fat Lady parade her mountains of flesh, watched Herko the Strong Man who actually had been a weight lifter, watched the trick mirror Turtle Girl, who came from Brooklyn but had lost her freshness in Coney Island and now was on the road, and the others, the Leopard Man and the Flame Swallower who could also crunch and apparently swallow discarded light bulbs and razor blades, Dame Misteria who was on loan from the Mitt camp down the midway to read fortunes at Worlds of Wonder and Sligo, a sweating red-faced escape artist who used trick handcuffs to do what Houdini had done with real ones.

But there was no Alana. Eddie waited eagerly for her act of the dancing veils, which was the finale of the show, but instead, the evening's organized entertainment concluded with Sligo. After that, the booths and stalls inside the enormous tent would remain in operation although the central stage was dark. The thistle chins, wandering about listlessly under the sagging canvas both because it was hot and because they too sensed something was missing from the show, had left the expected debris, peanut bags and soft drink bottles and crumpled sandwich wrappers, in the narrow aisles among the wooden folding chairs in front of the stage.

Eddie found Bart Taylor outside in his trailer, spilling the contents of his chamois pouch on a table and counting the take. "Two and a half bills," Bart said. "Not bad."

"How come Alana didn't dance?" Eddie wanted to know.

"Maybe she's sick or something."

"Didn't she tell you?"

"I haven't seen her," Bart Taylor said, stacking the bills and change in neat piles on the table in front of him. He was wearing a lightweight loud plaid jacket with high wide peaked lapels of a thinner material. One of the lapels was torn, a small jagged piece missing from it right under the wilted red carnation Bart Taylor wore. The carnation looked as if it had lost half its petals too.

"Well, I'll go over to her trailer," Eddie said.

"I wouldn't."

Eddie looked at him in surprise. "Any reason why not?"

"No," Bart said quickly. "Maybe she's sick and sleeping or something. You wouldn't want to disturb her."

"Well, I'll go and see."

A shovel and a pick-ax were under the table in Bart Taylor's trailer. Eddie hadn't seen them before. "Don't," Bart said, and stood up. His heavy shoe made a loud scraping sound against the shovel. He was a big man, much bigger than Eddie and sometimes when the carnival was on a real bloomer with no money coming in they all would horse around some like in a muscle camp, and Bart could even throw Herko the Strong Man, who had been a weight-lifter.

"O.K.," Eddie said, but didn't mean it. He went outside and the air was very hot and laden with moisture. He looked up but couldn't see any stars. He wondered what was wrong with Bart Taylor, to act like that. He walked along the still crowded midway to the other group of trailers on the far side of the carnival, past the lead joint where the local puddle-jumpers were having a go at the ducks and candle flames and big swinging gong with .22 ammo, past the ball pitching stand where shelves of cheap slum were waiting for the winners, past the chandy who was fixing some of the wiring in the merry-go-round. For some reason, Eddie was frightened. He almost never sweated, no matter how hot it was. A shill looked too obviously enthusiastic if he sweated. But now he could feel the sweat beading his forehead and trickling down his sides from his armpits. He wasn't warm, though. He was very cold.

There was no light coming through the windows of Alana's trailer. The do not disturb sign was hanging from the door-knob. The noise from the midway was muted and far away, except for the explosive staccato from the lead joint. Eddie knocked on the aluminum door and called softly, "Alana? Alana, it's Eddie."

No answer. Eddie lit a cigaret, but it tasted like straw. His wet fingers discolored the paper. He threw the cigaret away and tried the door. It wasn't locked.

Inside, Eddie could see nothing in the darkness. His hand groped for the light switch. The generator was weak: the overhead light flickered pale yellow and made a faint sizzling sound.

Alana was there. Alana was sprawled on the floor, wearing her six filmy veils. In the yellow light, her long limbs were like gold under the veils. Eddie knelt by her side.

He was crying softly before his knees touched the floor. Alana's eyes were opened but unseeing. Her face was bloated, the tongue protruding. From the neck down she was beautiful. From the neck up, it made Eddie sick to look at her.

She had been strangled.

He let his head fall on her breast. There was no heart beat. The body had not yet stiffened.

He stood up and lurched about the interior of the small trailer. He didn't know how long he remained there. He was sick on the floor of the trailer. He went back to the body finally. In her right hand Alana clutched a jagged strip of plaid cloth. Red carnation petals like drops of blood were strewn over the floor of the trailer.

"All right, Eddie," Bart Taylor said softly. "Don't move."

Eddie turned around slowly. He had not heard the door open. He looked at Bart Taylor, who held a gun in his hand, pointing it unwaveringly at Eddie.

"You killed her," Eddie said.

"*You* killed her," Bart Taylor said. "My word against yours. I own this show. Who are you, a nobody. A shill. My word against yours."

"Why did you do it?"

"She wouldn't look at me. I loved her. I said I would marry her, even. She hated me. I couldn't stand her hating me. But I didn't mean to kill her."

"What are you going to do?" Eddie said.

"Jeep's outside. Tools. We'll take her off a ways and bury her."

"Not me," Eddie said.

"I need help. You'll help me. A shill. A nobody. They all know how you were carrying a torch for her. You better help me."

"Your jacket," Eddie said. "The carnation. They'll know it was you."

"Not if we bury her."

"Not me," Eddie said again.

"It's late. There are maybe thirty, forty people left on the midway. We've got to chance it now. It looks like rain. Won't be able to do it in the rain. Let's get her out to the jeep now, Eddie."

"No," Eddie said. He wasn't crying now, but his eyes were red.

Bart came over to him. Eddie thought he was going to bend over the body, but instead he lashed out with the gun in his hand, raking the front sight across Eddie's cheek. Eddie fell down, just missing Alana's body.

"Get up," Bart said. "You'll do it. I swear I'll kill you if you don't."

Eddie sat there. Blood on his cheek. The light, yellow, buzzing. Bart towering over him, gigantic, menacing. Alana, dead. Dead.

"On your feet," Bart said. "Before it starts raining."

When Eddie stood up, Bart hit him again with the gun. Eddie would have fallen down again, but Bart held him under his arms. "You'll do it," Bart said. "I can't do it alone."

"O.K.," Eddie said. "I feel sick. I need some air."

"You'll get it in the jeep."

"No. Please. I couldn't help you. Like this. Air first. Outside. All right?"

Bart studied him, then nodded. "I'll be watching you," he said. "Don't try to run. I'll catch you. I have the gun. I'll kill you if I have to."

"I won't try to run," Eddie promised. He went outside slowly and stood in front of the trailer. He took long deep breaths and waited.

Eddie gawked at the trailer. It was like magic, they always said. It had nothing to do with seeing or smelling or any of the senses, not really. You didn't only gawk with your eyes. Not a professional shill. Not the best. You gawked with every straining minuteness of your body. And they came. The thistle chins. The townsfolk. Like iron filings and a magnet. They came slowly, not knowing why they had come, not knowing what power had summoned them. They came to gawk with you. They came, all right. You've been doing this for years. They always came.

You could sense them coming, Eddie thought. You didn't have to look. In fact, you shouldn't. Just gawk, at the trailer. Shuffling of feet behind you. A stir. Whispering. What am I doing here? Who is this guy?

Presently there were half a dozen of them. Then an even dozen. Drawn by Eddie, the magnificent shill.

There were too many of them for Bart to use his gun. They crowded around the trailer's only entrance. They waited there with Eddie. Unafraid now, but lonely, infinitely lonely, Eddie led them inside.

They found Bart Taylor trying to stuff carnation petals down his throat.

SPOOK HOUSE

Clark Howard

An amusement park is no place to be trapped after everything shuts down for the winter—one of those long, cold midwest winters. But that is what happens to the narrator of this chilling and grimly realistic tale, the operator of a harmless (if not strictly legal) game of chance, when he finds himself menaced by three young hoodlums. The considerable suspense here is typical of the work of Clark Howard; he is one of the two or three best contemporary writers of criminous short stories, as evidenced by his receipt of a Mystery Writers of America Edgar for his 1980 story "Horn Man." Howard is also an accomplished novelist and the author of a number of incisive true-crime studies.

I made it all the way through last season without a nickel's worth of trouble—right up until the last night, almost the last hour of the last night. And then I ran into enough trouble to make up for every minute of that peace and quiet and still last me a couple of lifetimes.

I run a little game of chance on the midway of one of the biggest amusement parks in the midwest. Got myself a nice one-man operation that I work in a seven-foot-long wooden stand with a counter in front for my wheel. Behind me, on the backboard, I've got shelves with all kinds of toasters and radios and shiny stuff like that to attract attention. It's a nice little setup, see, and I keep the place dressed up with colored banners and crepe paper to make it kind of stand out from the rest of the stalls.

My gimmick is simple. I got this wheel with twenty-one numbers on it. It's like a roulette wheel only it stands up straight. You pick a number for two-bits a chance and if your number hits, you get a coupon. Three coupons and you pick out any prize in the house.

I control the wheel, naturally. I ain't in business for my health or anything like that. But I generally give the players a fair shake. I get all the prizes at wholesale, see, and all I want to do is make a dollar or two on everything I hand out; it's just like running a store or something. Most people lay down a buck and after four turns of the wheel they only got one coupon so they quit. So I give 'em a cheap ballpoint pen or a pair of paste earrings for the coupon and I've made eighty-five cents. A few of them, if they're really after one of the big prizes, keep laying the money down as fast as I can pick it up. In that case, I let 'em feed me until I've got my two or three bucks' profit on the prize and then I let the wheel hit for their third coupon. They get their radio or whatever they want for a few bucks less than it would cost them in a store, and I get a coupla bucks more than it cost me in the beginning, so everybody's happy.

Like I said, it's a nice little one-man operation and I usually don't have any trouble. The season is four months long, May to September, and I take it easy the rest of the year with what I make during the summer. My location on the midway is a choice spot, right next to the Spook House. I get the people as they're coming out, see, after they've been scared out of their pants by all those big spiders and weird faces that jump out of the walls in that place. By the time they've been through the Spook House, they're ripe for a nice, quiet little game of chance.

The park closes at midnight. It was a little after ten, the last night of the season, when these three guys came up to my stall. They were young, but all pretty big guys—the motorcycle-boots and leather-jacket types, the kind that tries to push everybody around. They looked mighty mean under the amber lights I had strung across my stall.

I went into my spiel right away and they all three started playing. I let one of them have a coupon the first time around and then passed all three of them for the next two turns. On the fourth turn I let another guy have a coupon and then let 'em all pass again for four more turns. After that, I gave the last guy his first coupon and then they all had one apiece. Each player gets a different color coupon, see, so they can't put 'em together and snag a prize before I make a profit.

They kept laying the dough down and I kept spinning the old wheel. In the next eight runs of the wheel, I gave only one of them a second coupon. The game goes pretty fast. They'd been at the counter only about five minutes and already I'd pulled in twelve bucks.

Two of the guys finally quit and each of them took a ballpoint pen. But the third guy was bound and determined to go away with one of my little pocket radios. He was the biggest and meanest-looking of the three and he got meaner-looking every time he lost. Also, he was the guy with two coupons already and he was hot after that last one.

He started playing a buck at a time, taking four numbers on the board. I kept a mental count on how much he had laid down and he was still about fifteen bucks away from that little portable. But he kept flipping those dollar bills on the counter and I kept spinning, making sure the wheel didn't hit any of his numbers.

Ten bucks later he was real mad. And he was also broke. He scratched around in his pockets looking for more money, but I could tell by his face he knew he didn't have any. While he was dragging everything out of his pockets, though, I saw something he did have. A long, shiny switchblade knife.

Finally, he stepped real close to the counter and pushed out his jaw at me. "I want one of them radios," he said.

I gave him my best carny smile. "Sure, friend," I said. "A few more turns of the wheel ought to do it. Your luck's bound to change."

"I ain't got any more dough," he said accusingly. "You got it all."

"Sorry, friend," I said. "If you want a radio, you gotta keep playing. Get a few bucks from your pals. Number eighteen's about due in four or five more turns." For another fin, I figured, I'd let him have the radio and be glad to get rid of him.

"I ain't borrowing any dough," he told me. "You got all you're gonna get, sharpie. Now gimme one of them little radios before I come behind there and get it!"

I stood my ground, dropping my hand down to a wooden club I kept handy under the counter. I looked at the guy and got a little scared. It wasn't hard to see he really meant what he said.

"I ain't kidding, you sharpie," he said, and started around the side of my stall. He shoved his hand in one pocket of his jacket and right away I thought of that switchblade he'd flashed.

I snatched the club out and held it up just high enough so he could see it. "Hold it!" I said, trying to sound as mean as he looked. "Don't start no trouble in here if you know what's good for you. There's cops all over this place. And all I gotta do is yell 'Hey, Rube' and there'll be fifty guys down on you before you know what's happening!"

He stopped cold and looked straight at me, his face contorting in anger. One of his pals came over quick and grabbed him by the arm. "Better not, Frankie," he warned. "We can't afford no trouble now! Don't forget, man, we're still on probation for that gang fight."

When I heard that, my mind went back to a few weeks ago when I'd read about a big teenage gang war where one kid was killed and another one lost an eye. I wondered if these were three of the guys that were in it. They sure looked the parts, all right. Not that it made any difference right then, anyway. The guy called Frankie was still watching me, still keeping one hand in his pocket, still looking like he wanted to cut me up into one-inch squares.

"Maybe you're right," he said reluctantly to his friend. But he shook the guy's hand off his arm and straightened up real tall. Then he took out the knife and very slowly and deliberately flicked it open for me to see. He stuck one arm out in front of him and shined the blade up and down his jacket sleeve.

"I'll give you one more chance to give me one of them little radios," he said. "What about it?"

I glanced over my shoulder and saw two cops walking idly toward my layout. Then I looked back to the punk and said boldly, "Nothing doing, brother!"

Frankie's eyes narrowed. He closed the knife and put it back in his pocket. He had seen the cops, too, but his face didn't soften any. No fear at all showed in his eyes.

"Okay," he said softly. "I'll be seeing you later."

He turned and walked away, followed quickly by his two pals. I watched them move off into the stretch of midway, until they were lost in the crowd, and then I put the club back under the counter. The two cops went by and

I bobbed my head at them and they waved back. For a couple of minutes I just stood there watching the people, not even trying to snag a customer, and then I sat down and had a smoke.

I didn't have too many players after the three punks left, so I started getting my few personal things together. I'd sold my stock of prizes to one of the other hustlers who was going down south with a carnival. I started packing a few of the things for him.

A little after eleven, Corinne came over. She was one of the change girls at the Fascination layout; a brunette, stacked up nice, but kind of tough-looking like she'd been around—which she probably had.

"Hi, Sam," she greeted me.

"Hiya, doll. How's tricks?"

She shrugged her shoulders and came on behind the counter. "So-so," she said, sitting down on one of my camp stools. "What are you doing after we close tonight?"

"I dunno. Why?"

"Some of the gals are throwing a little party over at Rollo's. Wanna come?"

Rollo's Tap was a little place just outside the park. A lot of the last night crowd would be in there. I kept thinking about those three guys and how mean that Frankie looked.

"I don't think so, doll," I said. "I'm gonna be driving south early in the morning and I wanna get some sleep."

I had cleared nine grand that season and I was planning to take it easy for a few months down in Miami Beach. And the more I thought about those three guys, the more I was tempted to hit the highway right after I closed.

"Thanks anyway, Corry," I said. "I'll see you next season."

After she left, I shut off my banner lights and got the rest of the prizes packed. Along about midnight, all the big lights started to go out and pretty soon the midway was just about dark. The last of the people drifted toward the front gate. For some reason, I kept looking around me every couple of minutes, like I was expecting something to reach out and grab me. Those three guys were really under my skin.

The guy I sold my stuff to came over. He had his station wagon by his stall, but couldn't get it over to mine because the maintenance men were already dismantling the ferris wheel and it was laying across the drive. I helped him carry the boxes over to his place. We had to make five trips, but finally it was all packed in his wagon. He paid me and we said our good-byes and I started back to my stall to lock up for the last time.

The midway was dark and deserted all over now. I kept glancing around with every step, keeping away from the shadows and empty stalls. I wasn't exactly scared, but I was sure uncomfortable. Frankie had really got to me with his "I'll be seeing you later" bit.

I hurried on to my stall and picked up my little canvas bag and closed the place up. Just to be on the safe side, I decided to leave by the side gate. I was halfway there when I saw a shadow looming up ahead of me, coming slowly toward me. I froze in my tracks, too startled to even run. The shadow came closer, closer, until it was right up in my face.

Then a flashlight went on and I let out a long breath and smiled. I looked down into a wizened, weather-beaten face. Old Fritz, the night watchman.

"Whatya say, Sam," he greeted me. "Calling it a season, huh?"

"Yeah, Fritzie," I said, "guess so." I pulled out a handkerchief and wiped my face. "How about you?"

"Same," he said. "Front gate's closed already. Looks like you're the last one to leave."

"Yeah, next to you."

"Well, one more time around the midway for me and then out the side gate and she's closed up for the winter."

I slapped him on the shoulder and said, "Take it easy, Fritz," and walked away. When I got close to the side gate,

I looked back and saw his flashlight bobbing in the blackness far down the midway.

I pulled open the big iron gate and stepped out to the public sidewalk. The little side-street looked deserted, was dimly lit. Just as I was about to close the gate, I heard the snarling voice.

"Hello there, sharpie."

I swung around and faced Frankie. He was standing about six feet away from me, smiling coldly.

I started to step back through the gate, but two arms suddenly went around me from behind. Then I heard Frankie's laugh, low and mean, a cruel, sadistic laugh. He moved toward me slowly.

I wasn't scared now. I was terrified. These punks meant business! I realized I was going to have to fight for my life!

I don't know what made me do it—instinct, maybe, the law of survival—but all at once I was fighting like a wild man. As soon as Frankie was close enough to me, I hit him solidly in the stomach. Then I shoved backward as hard as I could and slammed the guy behind me into the iron gate. I heard his head hit the gate and felt his arms drop away from me. For a second then, I just stood there, feeling pretty damn brave over what I'd just done. Then something crashed into the side of my face and I saw stars. The third guy, I thought dumbly as I fell to the sidewalk, dropping my canvas bag, hitting the concrete solidly—I had forgotten about the third guy.

I just lay there, trying to focus my eyes and my mind, when I got caught by a hard kick in my side. I groaned, began to crawl away quickly, scrambling as best I could to my feet.

Then two of them were rushing toward me. One of them was Frankie, and he was holding the open switchblade in his hand. The guy with him was the one who had hit me from the side; light glinted off the brass knuckles on both his fists.

Desperately, I sized up the situation. I was to one side

of the exit gate now and they were beyond the other. The gate still stood partway open. I sucked in a mouthful of air and ran like hell for it.

I made it about six inches ahead of the guy with the brass knuckles. Leaping through the gate, I swung it behind me furiously, hoping frantically that it would catch and lock them out. Instead, it hit the guy square in the face and knocked him down. Then the gate swung wide open again.

I paused long enough to see Frankie stop and drag the guy to his feet. By this time, the third guy was up again too. All three of them started through the gate. I turned and ran like hell again, down the darkened midway, and behind me I heard three pairs of feet coming after me.

I ran until my lungs were bursting and my tongue hanging out. Then I had to stop or else fall on my face. I moved into the shadows and leaned heavily against one of the stalls. My hand touched crepe paper and I looked up suddenly. It was my own stall. Or was it? I looked around quickly. The Spook House was right behind me. Yeah, it was my stall, all right.

I turned back to the Spook House. It looked funny to me. The moonlight made it look odd, but that wasn't it. It was something else. I looked closer, squinting my eyes. Then I realized what it was. The doors—that's what looked funny. During the season they were red and white and yellow, bright carnival colors. Now they were a dull gray. All of the windows were too.

Then I remembered. They were metal storm doors, put on for the winter. The windows had matching metal shutters. Sure. I had watched one of the maintenance men put them on the back windows before I opened my stall that day. They fitted the windows and doors snugly and clamped in place with snap-locks. They could be opened from the outside but not the inside, and they—

The outside but not the inside—

A sudden crazy plan began to beat in my mind. I dropped to my knees and peered around the side of the stall. I listened intently. I couldn't see Frankie and his pals, but I could hear their footsteps. They had stopped running and were moving around quickly from one place to another, looking for me. I guessed they were about a hundred feet away.

I might make it, I thought wildly, if I hurry—

I turned and crept on my hands and knees toward the Spook House. The cement was hard on my knees. I kept going. I moved quickly, as quickly and as quietly as I could.

At last I made the front of the Spook House. I stopped for a second and listened again. The footsteps were getting louder. I started crawling as fast as I could go.

I went past the front door and down to the corner of the building and around the side. At the first window I came to, I stood up, staying close to the wall. I reached up and withdrew the latch slowly and opened the metal shutters, then reached past them and pulled gently at the window. Silently, I prayed. Then the window opened. I sighed heavily.

I left them both open and began to crawl back around to the front of the building. My luck was running perfect so far. Now if only the front door was unlocked. No reason why it shouldn't be, I thought hopefully. If the window was open, then the door should be open too. What would be the sense in locking the doors and leaving the windows open? What was the sense in locking anything at all, when the park had a ten-foot fence around it with electric current at the top to stop anybody who tried to climb it? I knew in my heart the front door would be unlocked. But still I trembled at the thought it might not.

I got back around to the front and back to the door, and again I stopped and listened. The footsteps of Frankie and his pals were so loud now, I thought they were right on top of me.

I stood up quickly and threw open the four snap-locks

that held the metal door in place. I didn't bother to be quiet anymore; it didn't make any difference now. They were so close to me, I knew I'd never be able to get away if they saw me. Not unless the inner door was unlocked. I slid the metal door roughly across the concrete. It made a loud, scraping sound in the stillness. I listened for an instant and heard the footsteps stop momentarily; then they began running toward me. I turned and tried the inner door.

The door flew open. I started breathing again.

I ran in quickly and began feeling my way along the wall in the pitch darkness. I had been in the Spook House a couple of times and I tried to remember the layout. I knew I was in the first room, the one with all the scary pictures that light up all over the place. The window I had opened should be the first one along the next wall, the side wall.

I kept going, inch by inch, foot by foot, until I got to the corner. Then I heard them at the front door.

I froze. I could barely make out their figures in the open doorway. They were standing very still. I knew they were listening for me, waiting for me to make a move, a noise. The window was only a few feet away from me. I tried to take another step sideways, but the wooden floor began to creak and I stopped the movement of my foot at once.

I began to sweat. Maybe, I thought frantically, maybe I've trapped myself!

One of the figures in the doorway moved into the room and disappeared into the darkness. I could hear him as he felt around, his hands hitting the wall, his footsteps loud in the empty room.

My heart pounded wildly. I turned my head in the direction of the open window and tried to judge how far away it was, wondering if I could make it in two or three quick steps. I looked back toward the doorway, squinting my eyes, trying to figure how much closer I was to the window than they were to me. Then I heard the guy inside the room make another noise. He sounded dangerously close to me. I expected any minute to feel his hands reach out and grab me by the throat. Suddenly, I wanted desperately to run for that window, to dive right through it. But deep down inside me I knew I would never make it. The guy in the room would take off after me as soon as I took the first step. The few seconds it would take me to scramble through the window would be all he needed to get to me. My feet probably wouldn't even touch the ground. If only they would look on the other side of the room, go the other way—

Then I got a brainstorm. Quickly, I unbuckled my belt and slipped it off my trousers. I wrapped it around my trembling hand, then took it off and pulled it into a tight ball. I fingered it anxiously, hoping it would be heavy enough.

Holding my breath, I raised the belt above my head and tossed it lightly across the room. It seemed like twenty minutes before it landed. Then it hit and hit perfectly. It sounded exactly like a clumsy footstep. I braced myself and got ready to move.

The two figures disappeared from the doorway and moved across the room, away from me. I heard the guy that was already in the room run toward the noise.

Then *I* moved. I hurried along the side wall, not caring about the noise I made, knowing the sound of my footsteps would be silenced by the noise of their own.

I groped ahead of myself in the blackness until my hand found the empty space of the window. I threw a leg over the ledge and got out fast.

I paused for a split second outside the window, listening to the movements inside. Then, leaving the window open, I slammed the steel shutters closed and quickly shoved the latch in place. I pulled at them twice to make sure they were shut good and tight, then turned and started for the front door.

All the panic and tension and fear began to take hold of me then. I was panting for breath, shaking all over; my side burned like fire, where I had been kicked, and my cheek was numb with pain where the brass knuckles had smashed against my jaw; my mouth was dry, my tongue swollen, and my eyes blurred with sudden tears. I ran like a drunk man, tripping twice, falling to my sore knees once, groping along the side of the building blindly. And all the time a single thought in my mind, screaming at me: The door—the door—run—run—run—

I made the corner of the building and hurried along the front. I stumbled again and almost fell a second time, clutched at the wall to keep my balance. I cursed. I sobbed. But I kept moving. And I made it to the door.

From inside I could hear a mutter of voices. I dragged the heavy metal door forward. It came toward me noisily in jerky, broken motions that matched my rising and falling strength.

In an instant of silence, from inside again, I heard loud, echoing footsteps running toward me. I heard Frankie curse. The sounds grew louder, nearer. I dragged the door closer, then stepped behind it and braced my body against it. I got a last burst of strength from somewhere and pushed for all I was worth.

The door would have closed all the way with the last push, but just before it slammed shut, an arm shot through the opening and stopped it. The heavy steel edge smashed into the arm and I heard a sharp, sickening crack. From within, echoing loudly but muffled by the almost closed door, came an agonizing scream. I leaned my weight against the door and, in the dim moonlight, I watched the protruding fist writhe and twist. And then the fingers opened and stiffened, and then went limp, and as they did, I heard something fall to the concrete at my feet. It was the switchblade knife. I stared at it dumbly. The hand obviously belonged to Frankie.

I let up the pressure against the door just a little, and the arm fell back inside. I slammed the door fully closed then and braced myself against it heavily as I groped with the snap-locks. Heavy fists pounded and heavy feet kicked at the door from the inside. But it did no good. The fourth snap-lock fell in place and the big door was tight.

I heard them yelling as I walked slowly away, down past my old stall, on down the darkened midway. Before I had gone far, I stopped to rest, to listen. I couldn't hear them anymore. It's them doors, I thought. Them heavy metal doors. They keep all the noise inside.

I went on back to the side gate. From there I could see the bobbing white spot of old Fritz's flashlight as he came down the side-street of the midway. It was two-and-a-half miles around the park and Fritz looked like he was still a quarter of a mile away. I didn't wait for him, but picked up my bag where it had dropped and walked on out of the park.

At the corner I stepped into a phone booth. Digging a dime from my pocket, I dropped it in the slot and dialed the operator. She answered right away.

"Give—give me the police," I said softly.

I could hear her making the connection. My face was throbbing in pain. I reached up and touched it gently with one finger. It was tender, swollen, crusted with dried blood. I felt my side then, where I had been kicked. When my hand touched one spot, I had to moan in agony. My ribs, I thought, must be broken.

I was hurt, trembling, crying again—and mad. They were dirty hoodlums. Rotten, good-for-nothing, punk hoodlums.

So what now? The cops come and get them and lock them up for a few days and then some judge has to turn them loose again because they're under age? Just kids, is that it? Teenagers? A little wild, somebody will say, but not really bad kids. And then they'd be back on the streets again.

I shook my head slowly. No, not this time. Not these three. Not if I could help it.

I hung up the phone, got my dime back and stepped out of the booth. As I walked slowly down the street, I thought: It's going to be a long cold winter in that Spook House, boys.

"I," SAID THE FLY

Robert Edmond Alter

This evocative, richly colloquial novelette about a Disneyland-type carnival in Florida—a place called Neverland that features a Swamp Ride, a Dracula's Castle, a Tarzan House, a Treasure Island, and a murderer on the loose—originally appeared in Argosy *in 1965 and was the basis for Alter's 1966 paperback original,* Carny Kill. *Alter did not live to see publication of the novel; he died tragically of cancer early that same year, at the age of forty. During his less than ten years as a professional writer, he published more than two hundred short stories, fourteen juvenile novels, and two other adult novels of suspense. Had he lived, and as "'I,' Said the Fly" conclusively proves, Robert Edmond Alter would have become a major voice in contemporary suspense and adventure fiction.*

"Who saw him die?"
"I," said the fly,
"With my little eye.
I saw him die."

IT WAS one of those tourist traps that have turned the coast of Florida into a glittering façade. It was on the outskirts, on the tidelands, where acreage is cheap—a take-off on Disneyland.

It was owned and operated by an old carny man named Robert Cochrane. Disney had the Swiss Family Robinson Tree; Cochrane had the Tarzan House. Disney had a Jungle Ride; Cochrane had a Swamp Ride at Neverland. That was the name of the trap. Neverland.

They had a regular old-fashioned carnival attraction tucked behind a monstrosity called Dracula's Castle, where all kinds of wired spooks sprang at you with ear-splitting screams and where your girl's skirt was blown up around her ears. I made for it like a homing pigeon.

They had the illusion show and the shooting gallery and the fat lady and the tattooed man and the strip show. But it was all a joke, a part of the façade. The carny attraction was only there for atmosphere. So Ma could turn to Pa and say, "Why it's just like a regular sideshow, ain't it, Elmo?" Just good wholesome fun. Something else Robert Cochrane had learned from Mr. Disney.

At the shooting gallery, a soldier was making a sap of himself by missing all the little white rabbits as they glided by on their pivots.

"Where do I find The Man?" I asked the operator, a predatory shooting-gallery type.

"Something wrong?" he asked me quietly.

"Need a job," I told him.

"Carny?"

"Yeah." I named a couple of outfits.

"Spiel?"

"Um. And sleight of hand. The usual," I told him.

He called out to a girl who was passing through the outer crowd. "Billie! 'Mere, huh?"

This girl looked as sharp as a New York City model. She had candy-floss hair that made you hungry. She stopped and looked toward us inquiringly, then walked our way.

You meet a girl like this, and you can feel your lousy fifty-two-dollar suit grow wrinkles, and you wish you had shaved later in the day instead of the first thing in the morning.

"He wants to see Rob. A job. Take him, huh?"

Billie looked at me again and said, "Sure."

We walked off together.

The barker on the illusion show bally platform was an adenoidal looking man who used his adenoma voice as part of his stock in trade. He was spieling to a group of marks about the spider lady.

"She scrabbles, she climbs, she spins a web."

Then I looked at him again. He was staring over his marks at me. I didn't say anything or make a sign. I kept on walking with Billie. But she had noticed.

"Something?" she asked incuriously.

"Uh-uh." There was no sense in telling her that Bill Duff and I had once worked in a carny together. That Bill Duff used to hang around my wife like a bee around honey. That Bill Duff lost an eyetooth one night when I lost my patience.

"What do you do around here, Billie?" I asked.

"I'm one of the nautch girls. I do a specialty dance. Only it's more the Twist than anything Far East."

"I'll bet you're good. I'll come see you in action sometime."

"Not if Rob gives you a job, you won't." She was firm about that.

They had a tavern which really wasn't a tavern, and they called it the Klondike. It was right out of the 1898 gold rush: lots of Yukon atmosphere. They had a floor show where the girls in the big feathered hats whirled around and threw up their skirts and saluted the audience with their bottoms. A sort of cancan. They only served soft drinks. It was pretty cute.

Billie took me around to the back. "You'll find Rob upstairs," she said.

"All right," I said. "Now I know where to find Rob. Where do I find you, Billie?"

"I told you where I work."

She smiled and it was a very pretty thing and I wanted to reach out and take hold of her.

"If you get the job, I'll know where to find you. Word gets around." Then she said, "Oh. You didn't mention your name."

"I never do if I can help it. So I go by the first half of my last. Thax."

"Thaxton?"

"Uh-huh."

"I'm Billie Peeler."

I looked at her. It was too much of a coincidence to be true.

She laughed. "My agent gave it to me. I hope you get the job."

"It doesn't really matter, does it?"

Her green-gold eyes gave me a look of mild speculation. "That's entirely up to you—Thax."

I wasn't sure I got that. Then I looked at her eyes again and I was sure. And it did matter whether I got that job or not.

This Robert Cochrane reminded me of a character out of "The Informer." As Irish as Paddy's potato. Built like one, too. Big, round and pretty rough. About sixty.

"C'mon in and grab a seat. Carny man, huh?" He grinned at me.

"Word gets around." I sat in a chair on the other side of his desk.

"Gabby gave me a buzz," he explained. "The shooting-gallery op. What have you done?"

I named a few outfits I had worked for. "My wife used to have an act. I spieled for her."

"What's your name?"

"L. M. Thaxton. Thax is good enough."

"Barkers are a dime a dozen. What about this sleight of hand you mentioned. You good at it?"

I hunched forward and put both my elbows on his desk, picked up a number four pyramid-shaped sinker he used as a paperweight and held it up to him in my left hand. Then I made a flicker of motion with my right forefinger and the split instant his eyes trembled, I ducked my left hand at the wrist and showed him my open palm.

The big trick in legerdemain is in directing the attention of your audience at the instant you substitute one thing for another. I had directed Cochrane's attention to my right hand when I shot the sinker down my left sleeve.

Cochrane was beaming like a kid. As old as he was and as long as he'd been around illusionists, he still got a kick out of that sort of thing.

"It's up your left sleeve, huh?"

"Sure. It was." I shot my left arm straight out at him and turned over my fist and opened it and it was still empty. He smiled and looked in my right hand and took back his paperweight.

"You've got the knack," he admitted. He thought about it. "Here's a thought. You good at the shell game?"

I said I was and he said, all right, he would put me in the carnival attraction with a stand and the shell game, to add to the atmosphere.

"This ain't the old carny you and I knew," he warned me. "We don't pick the marks up by the heels and shake

'em till they're dry. You'll notice we got mostly high-school
and college kids working here. Nice, clean kids that keep
the atmosphere homey. I want it to stay that way, Thax."
He meant it.

For a moment, I felt an old familiar unease. I wondered
if he had heard about me. There were some outfits up north
that wouldn't touch me with an elephant gaff.

"Sure," I said. "I won't give you any grief." I meant
it. I liked him.

Then he named a price and I didn't think much of it
and I gave one with a better name, which he countered,
and I countered it, and we settled somewhere in between.
Then he gave me a card that said I was employed by the
Cochrane Enterprises.

"Got a place to sack?" he asked. "There's a bunkhouse
around behind the Watusi Village. Some of the boys
use it."

"I'll make out," I told him.

It was dusk when I came out and Neverland was full
of clamor. Cochrane's got a good play.

The place was laid out like a wagon wheel with a big
garden in the hub. It had a fountain with colored lights
and liquid music coming out of the water and that sort of
thing. The coke and popcorn and ice-cream venders
wheeled their barrows up and down the flowered lanes.

The luck boys were there, too. It's easy to spot them
when you know what to look for. There was one—a big
curlyhaired, rose-cheeked man who might have passed for
a prosperous lawyer—who was holding up his hand to attract the attention of a big group of marks.

"The management has requested me to warn you that
there's been a report of a pickpocket in here this evening.
Please, ladies and gentlemen, watch out for your wallets
and purses."

It was an old dodge. I grinned at the luck boy and
held up my five-dollar bill and put it back in my pocket.

I decided to grab a bite before I scouted up a flop for

the night, and I went up a path to a quaint little restaurant called the Queen Anne Cottage.

I was jostled on the steps by some people coming out and I told one of them to watch it, buster. He asked me how I'd like a bent nose. Then his wife or his secretary or whatever she was broke it up.

When I put my hand in my pocket my five was gone. Those luck boys were thorough.

I was standing on the porch muttering to myself when a college kid wearing a red-and-white guide uniform stepped up to me and asked was I Mr. Thaxton, sir?

"Mrs. Cochrane wants to see you, sir." He was really a very polite boy. One of Cochrane's nice, clean kids. "The owner's wife."

"Where do I find her?"

"She has a suite of rooms above this restaurant, sir." That "sir" business made me feel my thirty-two years.

I went around back and up a maroon-carpeted stairway. I opened the door at the top and stepped into a blaze of light. It was like stepping into an interrogation room. Some kind of baby spot hit me all over with a brilliant pink light.

I had a quick, vague impression of Swedish modern. Then something went *ssst* right by my head and *thhook* in the paneled wall.

I was already on the floor. I turned a little and glanced up at the knife jutting out from the wall. It was no longer than a butcher knife and it had a mother-of-pearl handle and no hilt guard.

I knew that kind of knife. My wife used to throw them back when we were in carny together.

A throaty laugh came out of the darkness.

The lights went on and I saw my ex-wife reclining on some kind of cushy sofa made of satin pillows. She was wearing one of those gold-glittery outfits with the toreador jacket and skintight pants. And gold sandals.

She had changed her hair. It used to be platinum. Now she was flameheaded. But her face hadn't changed in five years: the same sensual, calculating look.

I got up and pulled the knife loose. It had perfect balance. No matter how you tossed it, the harpoon-sharp blade always led the way to the target. The mother-of-pearl handles had been her trademark. She had always been a great one for a classy show. Now she was Mrs. Robert Cochrane.

I wagged the blade at her. "Fun and games, huh, May?"

"I could have put your eye out if I'd wanted to," she said sweetly. "I've kept my hand in."

May had come out of San Berdo, California. I was a husky young carny kid with a good spiel. When she outgrew me, she dumped me.

But what really amazed me was the Irishman—Robert Cochrane. He had known who I was and he had known about the jam I got into when May and I were working together for the Brody outfit.

"You tell Cochrane about you and me?" I asked her.

"Sure," she said. "When I first came to him."

"You have anything to do with hiring me?" I said.

"I didn't even know you were on the lot, darling, till Bill Duff told me."

"Cozy for you and Bill, huh? This set-up."

"Duff showed up just like you did," she said in a stainless-steel voice. "Broke and whimpering for a job. Rob gave him the job because Rob can't turn down a carny buddy with a empty grouch bag. I would have told Duff to go take a flying leap straight at the spider lady."

"May, times have been so-so with me." I fluctuated one hand palm-down in midair to illustrate. "I need the job. Are you going to queer it?"

She reached a very pale, gold-tipped hand out to me. "Rob does all the hiring and firing, sweetie. I wouldn't dream of saying a word. Kiss me."

Five years is a long time. I sank into the satin pillows.

II

The big luck boy with the lawyerlike aspect was hovering near the front of the Queen Anne Cottage, like a shark finning around a ship to pick up its garbage. He was looking for another likely group of marks.

I went over and buttonholed him. "You and I need a talk back in the alley."

He started to grin and to reach into his pocket at the same time. "Hell, man," he said, "I didn't know you belonged. Should have guessed though, the way you were in the know. By the way, I'm Jerry." He fished out my five and passed it over without hard feelings. "You were asking for it, you know."

"That's right, I was," I admitted. "Was it the big guy that I bollixed with on the steps?"

"No. That was just another mark. Eddy was in the group and got him at the same time." The luck boy chuckled. "I couldn't help myself. I just had to put Eddy on you, once you'd challenged me."

"That Eddy must be good," I said as I handed the luck boy back his wallet.

He stared at the slab of leather. When he put it in his pocket, I gave him back his watch.

"A pro of the first water," he whispered. "Look, Thaxton, you're in the wrong racket. You don't want to play house with walnut shells with a natural talent like that! Rob Cochrane practically gives us old-timers a free hand. Within reason, that is."

"My name, racket and everything," I said. "You know it all already."

"Yeah," he said absently. "Word gets around. But look—"

"Uh-uh," I said. "It ain't in my line. But thanks for the offer."

I went into the Queen Anne and had a steak and showed the employment card to the cashier and she knocked the bill down to half. She was another one of those nice, clean student employees who helped the homey atmosphere.

I wandered about for a couple of hours just to get the lay of the lot. Along about eleven-thirty, some hairy-lunged college boy climbed up to the lookout tower in the Viking Camp and blew a horn that was ten feet long and suspended by rawhide thongs.

Hooo! the horn said in a fat, dismal voice. *Hooo!*

That meant the marks should start to clear out. Which suited me. I had to find a spot to grab some shut-eye.

In my wandering, I had seriously eyed Tarzan's Tree House. It was summer and the breeze blowing off the sea was mild, and this replica of Tarzan's movie home was free. I had even showed my open-sesame card and gone up in the bamboo-ribbed elevator to look the tree house over. I had noted a zebra-skin bed with elephant tusks for posts, where Me Tarzan and You Jane had supposedly enjoyed their connubial bliss.

The Tarzan House overlooked the Swamp Ride. They had about nine nice clean kids who ran the boats through the circular swamp. One of them came by me with a polite smile and a face full of freckles.

"All closed up for the night, sir."

I told him my name was Thax and showed him my magic, wonderful Neverland card.

"I haven't seen you around here, sir. Are you new?"

I admitted I was. I shooed him off, and when the coast was clear, I went up the plank steps that curved around a phony tree like a snake, and wobbled over the swaying bamboo footbridge to Tarzan's house.

I could see my way to my bed. There was a second smaller one against the other wall. That was Cheeta's bed.

I was whipped. I dropped off immediately. At one point in the night, I thought I heard Cheeta swing in through his window and drop into his bed. But I thought it was a dream.

I don't know how long the noise had been going on before it woke me up, but all I could think of was a thunderstorm.

That's what a gator's bellow sounds like. When he plants all four stumpy legs in the mud and really lets go, his voice has a sort of *barrr-ooom* to it like distant thunder.

It was morning. I looked at my wrist watch. Eight.

"Help! Somebody! C'mere!"

The voice was thin and urgent and some distance off. I went out on the porch and looked down at the Swamp Ride. It was laid out in a huge figure eight but I couldn't see all the waterways because the jungly growth was too dense. One of the little powered swamp boats was scooting back to the dock. The yelling seemed to be coming from there.

When I got down there, the powerboat was just pulling in and my friend Freckles was at the wheel. His freckles looked like measles against the ashen color of his face.

"It's awful! He's dead!" he gasped when he saw me.

I jumped into the boat with him. "Who? Who's dead? Where is he?"

"He's in the water, and those gators—"

I wasn't getting anywhere, and if I'd had any sense, I would have gotten out of there, because it wasn't any of my business. But who has any sense these days?

"Okay. Okay. Show me." I gave him a shake. "Show me where."

I could feel him shrinking right in my hands.

"I never saw a dead man before." His voice was hoarse now.

"Get out." I didn't need a hysteric on my hands. "Where is it?"

Freckles pointed across the bow at a jungle-arched waterway. Then he scrambled up on the dock. More and more people were gathering.

Freckles had left the power on. I gave the boat a healthy goose and went ripping down the waterway at about half a knot.

There was very little about the Swamp Ride that was phony. All the palmettos and sweet gums and tupelos and the intricate network of prehensile vines were real. There's no great trick to cultivating a swamp in Florida.

Even the gators were real. They came from a nearby gator farm. They were harmless old daddies who were used to being around people. All they wanted to do was sleep in the sun and wait for some kind man to bring them a little food.

I suppose that's why they were all riled now. They didn't know what to make of this outrageous man-size bundle of meat that had been dumped in their sheltered swamp.

I idled the boat toward them and they lumbered off into the water in a tail-spanking huff. I had to get out of the boat and into the water up to my knees to get the body.

It was face down and it was a large man, and when I rolled it over, it was Robert Cochrane. A long knife was standing up in the Irishman's chest.

It had a mother-of-pearl handle.

A fair crowd of Neverland employes and some uniformed lot guards had ganged around the dock when I got back with the boat and the body.

"You know who shived him?" one of the guards asked me.

I shook my head and said, "Who killed Cock Robin?"

They looked at me.

"Robert Cochrane, Cochrane Robert, Cock Robin. See?"

A broad, bluff-faced man in a two-hundred-dollar suit pushed through the crowd and started yelling at the guards.

"Who is it? Simpson! Who's been hurt?"

The guard named Simpson got up and told him it was the boss and that he was dead.

The man tucked in his mouth, and his eyes snapped at Simpson and at Cochrane's body and at me.

"Who the hell are you?"

"Thaxton."

"I don't know you."

"Makes us even. Who are you?"

He gave me a look that should have stuck four inches

out my back. "I'm Franks," he said. "Mr. Cochrane's business manager."

"I'm Thaxton," I said. "Mr. Cochrane's prestidigitator. He hired me yesterday."

He brushed by me.

Neverland didn't open until ten in the morning and it was now about eight-forty. I looked at the faces around me. I knew one of them. Billie. She was staring into the boat.

The law would arrive shortly. I went over and got Billie by the elbow and said, "Let's take a walk."

I felt a little like Alice in Wonderland. That's the way Neverland struck me when there weren't any people around.

"How did you happen to be there?" Billie asked.

"I spent the night in Tarzan's hut," I explained to her. "I even think Cheeta showed up."

I glanced back at the looming, joined trees. There was something monkey- or apelike away up there in the mid-branches. It stood out against the sky like a fly caught in a web.

"Am I seeing things?"

She looked up over her shoulder and smiled. "It's Terry Orme. He's Cheeta. A midget. Rob Cochrane hired him to dress up in an ape suit and make like Cheeta."

I looked back at the tree again. The little ape man was still hanging there in the sky, staring down at the boat that contained his dead boss.

We strolled down to a man-made lake complete with ducks and gliding swans. An island with real pine trees was out in the middle of it and an old-fashioned high-pooped schooner was moored alongside the island. A big sign over the dock on the mainland said: TREASURE ISLAND. The ticket-seller's stand was a window set in the side of a small old English structure that looked like a seaman's tavern. The warped signboard over the door said: ADMIRAL BEN-BOW TEAROOM.

My interest perked up. "Does that ship happen to be called the *Hispaniola*?"

"Yes. How did you know?"

"I'm a nut on *Treasure Island.*"

A school of rowboats was tied to the dock and I handed Billie into one of them and shoved off and shipped the oars.

"Every one of us is a nut some way or another," I said defensively. "So I read books."

"But you're a very special kind of nut, Thax. Because you don't fit in."

"Sure I do. Well enough to get by."

Billie looked at the green duck-dirtied water overboard. "Do you know what I was willing to do to get my first job in a carny? The owner was a Greek. A very fat, greasy Greek of fifty." She looked at me. "I wanted the job—a start—bad."

"All right," I said. "You've told me all about you and the Greek. Are you happy now?"

"No."

"Well, it doesn't really matter, does it?" I said.

She sighed. "That's my whole point. That's what you said yesterday when I hoped you'd get this job. But it *does* matter."

"How?" I wanted to know. "A hundred years from now, who's going to care?"

"I don't care about a hundred years from now or ten thousand years!" she said urgently. "We're here now. It's our turn. And they're never going to give us a second shot at it."

I said nothing. I rowed the boat.

"We've got to make the most of it. They start our kind out with nothing and if we slob around saying it doesn't really matter, then that's what we end up with. Nothing."

I beached the boat on Treasure Island and got out and gave her a hand. I started to pull her in to me.

"No, Thax," she said.

"Why not?"

"Because I'm not sure yet. I've got to be sure."

I drew her in and I kissed her and let her go.

She didn't say anything for a moment. Then: "We'd better get back."

III

The luck boy who had sicked Eddy the pickpocket on me last night was strolling by the Admiral Benbow when we arrived at the dock.

"How are things law-wise, Jerry?" I asked him.

"Booming. They've set up a police station in the Okefenokee Arcade. I get it they'd like for you to show up for a minute or two."

"Thanks, Jerry," Billie said. "Should I go with you, Thax?"

"Uh-uh. Why get involved? Go get ready for your show." I turned back to Jerry. "The law is going to let us open, isn't it?"

"Sure. Everything but the Swamp Ride. Lieutenant Ferris, the dick in charge, was set to hold us closed. But Madame C. changed his mind for him."

He meant May.

"I'll see you later, Thax," Billie said.

I liked the way she looked at me when she said it.

I said, "Sure. See you."

I liked this Lieutenant Ferris right off. He was an old-time dick. I don't mean he was a daddy graybeard. I mean he looked like those violent men who came out of prohibition and the depression—the ones with the iron-eyed faces that might have belonged on either side of the law but couldn't possibly belong to any other stratum of society. He was about fifty. A tired fifty.

"Sit anywhere," he told me.

There wasn't anywhere to sit, which didn't bother him because he was a stroller. He kept his hands in his pockets and his eyes on the floor and he walked up and down. I pushed some cheap souvenir doodads to one side and parked myself on a counter.

"Name?"

"Thaxton."

He glanced at me. "Well, are you going to add to that or just let it sit there?"

"Leslie Thaxton."

"How come you got into the act this morning?"

I told him about the tree house and about Freckles—Jerry—yelling down the roof.

"So you decided to haul the stiff all over the Swamp Ride."

"I didn't know but what those gators were eating somebody alive."

"The big shot, Lloyd Franks, tells me those gators are as safe as house pets."

"I didn't know that," I said. "I only walked on the lot yesterday."

Ferris strolled away from me. "What was the kid doing out there at that time of morning?"

"Part of his job, I suppose."

"The kid says it was his turn to show up early and try out the boats. Seems they do it every morning. That's one of the things that has me puzzled."

"What?"

"Dumping Cochrane in there. I can't see any reason for it. He was killed by the shiv about two A.M. He wouldn't be in there taking the Swamp Ride at that time of night. It follows he was killed somewhere else. So why haul the body in there? The gators wouldn't touch it, and the whole place ain't deep enough to hide a dead rat."

"You mean the murderer must have known the body would be found right away in the Swamp Ride, so why not leave it where it was?"

"Yeah. And here's another thing. How did he get it in there? You can't handle any of those swamp boats without power. And if the murderer had used one of them, somebody around here would have heard the motor." He looked at me. "You, for instance. You were sleeping right over the boats."

"Never heard a thing," I told him. "Slept like a baby."

Except for that time I dreamed Cheeta came home. What had Orme been up to?

A tough-faced harness bull clomped into the arcade and handed Ferris a shoe box. After a few grumbled words he left. Ferris opened the shoe box and took out a knife that could only be the murder weapon. He studied it for a minute and then showed it to me.

"Recognize the kind of knife it is?"

"Knife-thrower's. Perfect balance."

"Know who owns this particular one?" he asked.

"Might be anybody."

"Whoever he was, he wore gloves. No prints. Unless *you* wiped 'em off before you brought the body back to the dock."

"Try again," I suggested. "I'm not trying to cover up for anybody."

He waggled the blade absently, wearing a bemused expression. "Is there a knife-throwing act on this lot?"

"Not that I know of. But then, I just—"

"Yeah, I know. You just started here. You picked a hell of a swell time, didn't you?" he commented.

Gabby had a stand set up for me. It was next door to Bill Duff's bally platform. A shelf had been rigged behind my stand and it contained a vivid white orchid display.

"We let the marks win an orchid," Gabby told me. "You're just here for the atmosphere. These are what they call saprophytic orchids. Don't have much value except for botanical purposes. Big old swamp a couple miles from here and the things grow wild in there by the million. They're a dime a dozen."

"Just like barkers," I said.

"How's that?"

"Something Cochrane said to me last night," I told him.

A dull look came into Gabby's morose face. "I'm going to miss that old Irish bastard."

"A pretty good guy, wasn't he?"

"The best."

"Evidently somebody around here didn't think so," I said. "Who do you think had it in for him?"

Gabby gave me a challenging look. I looked over at Bill Duff. He was up on his bally spieling.

"Duff's big mouth has been going, huh? You know about me and May."

"She was a knife-thrower when she first came to this lot. Before she put the hooks in Rob and became Mrs. Big."

"You don't like May much, huh?"

"Name me somebody here that does."

"Cochrane must have."

"Rob was easy. He liked everyone. He was a pushover for her."

"So May killed him, huh?"

Gabby made a noise in his throat. "She's a natural."

I arranged the three walnut shells and the little ivory pea just so and made a couple of practice passes to see if my hand was still in. The shell game has long been abandoned in favor of more ingenious and less discreditable methods of robbery, but it still holds a certain degree of fascination for today's so-called sophisticated marks. I started drumming up trade.

"Here we are, ladies and gentlemen! Carnival croquet, the preacher's pastime. Who'll risk a quarter to win an orchid? A bee-utiful laelia flower shipped from the Brazilian jungles at great expense to the management."

I grinned at the marks to show them I was just kidding.

"Step up and take a trip on the rolling ivory. It's a healthy sport, a clean game, it's good for young and old! A child can understand it."

The marks were starting to gather.

"Gimme a quarter, hon," a cute little thing said to her boy friend.

I smiled at the cute little thing and made a slow pass—left over right and middle under left and finished a figure eight. Sightless Sam could have followed the pass. The cute little thing unerringly chose an empty. I had to thumb my spare pea into it to help her win.

"The little lady wins," I announced and handed her an orchid. "Now then, we're off on another journey. Who'll ride with me this time?"

I always let them win, sooner or later. Every so often, a smart boy would give me some lip service and I'd hit him for six bits before I'd donate an orchid to his girl. Working a shell game for fun can get to be a drag after a while, but it was good practice. And what the hell, it was a job.

Cheeta swung into Tarzan's tree house that night, through the window and into his bed. It was Terry Orme, the ape man.

I struck a match and we looked at each other. I had been sitting there in the dark waiting to see if he would show up.

"I'm your roomy," I told him. "My name is Thax."

He didn't say anything. He studied me until the match went out.

"There's a Coleman under that bed."

I rummaged under the zebra-clad bed and found the lantern and struck another match and ignited the two suspended bags in the lamp. A Coleman is brighter than the average light bulb but it can throw some weird shadows. Terry Orme wasn't but about forty inches high.

"You always come in through windows?" I asked him.

"You mind?" Tough little cuss.

"Uh-uh. I'm really working around to ask how come you're out climbing trees at this time of night?"

"How long have you had nose trouble?" he shot back.

I got up and walked over to him and put out my hand. "If we're going to be roomies, Orme, why not be friends?"

"Well—" Then he shook.

I smiled and went back and sat on my bed and gave

myself a smoke. He scowled at the floor and sent me a couple of covert glances.

"The marks watch me scramble around in that ape suit and they think I'm a real monkey," he said. "But as far as I'm concerned, I'm making a monkey out of them."

I nodded. I figured he would look at it that way. It gave him a slice of superiority. He needed it.

"I wouldn't have this job if I didn't like it." He was getting defiant now. "I like climbing around. You see and hear things. Things you'd never dream of."

"Is that what you were doing tonight?" I wondered.

He said yeah. Then he seemed to shrink inside himself again. He went back to his little bed and climbed up on it like a child.

"You getting soft on Billie Peeler?" he asked me suddenly.

I wondered if Terry had a crush on Billie. "Uh-huh."

He looked at his little hands. "She's a good kid. We worked together in K.C. a couple years back. She—"

There was a small knock of noise from somewhere outside the tree house, but close by. I glanced at Terry. He gave me a start. His delicately small face was frozen in terror.

I didn't say anything. I got up and walked over to the open doorway and stepped onto the porch and looked around. I didn't see any sign of movement.

"Just a noise in the night, I guess."

I didn't see anyone when I turned back into Tarzan's hut, either. Terry Orme had vanished.

I took a rowboat back to Treasure Island the next morning before the lot opened. I beached the boat a few yards astern of the *Hispaniola* and got out to look at the little island.

They had done a very nice job with the layout. They had humped up three scrubby little dirt hills and each one had a skull-and-crossbones sign planted at its base: Mizzenmast Hill, Spyglass Hill and Foremast Hill. Then they had

Flint's Stockade, where Jim Hawkins and Captain Smollett, Doctor Livesey and Squire Trelawney had held off Silver's cutthroats.

A sign reading To FLINT'S TREASURE PIT pointed down a woody path and I followed it into a sunny glen. The Treasure Pit was at the foot of a hardwood ridge. It was a shallow hole in the ground with a spade and a broken pick stuck in the dirt, and a tangle of blocks and tackle and an old half-buried sea chest with the name *Walrus* on it.

A wild man leaped right through a palmetto screen and landed like an animal smack in front of me. He had a tangled mop of gray hair and a beard to match and he was dressed in old bits of sailcloth and skins which were held together by brass buttons and rawhide thongs.

He hunched and hunkered and giggled and scratched himself and made erratic gestures with his hands.

"I'm poor Ben Gunn, I am!" he screeched. "And I haven't spoke with a Christian these three years."

Of course, they would have a Ben Gunn on the island. They probably had a one-legged character for Long John Silver, too. I started to laugh.

"Man," I said, shaking my head. "You really scared me."

The actor chuckled and straightened out of character. He was wiry and agile. "It gets 'em all," he said delightedly. "You're Thaxton, aren't you? The new chap with an interest in Billie?"

I looked at him. He slapped me on the back. "Just clowning, boy. Don't get sore. Billie's a good kid."

"That's just what Terry Orme told me," I said.

"You know Terry?" He looked mildly surprised.

"We're roomies up in the tree house. He lives there because he doesn't like people around. I'm there because I'm tap city," I explained.

"No kidding," he said. "I never knew Terry bunked up there." He smiled and shrugged. "Well, he's not the only screwball around here. I bunk aboard the *Hispaniola* myself. By the by, my name's Mike Ransome. C'mon. I want you to see my schooner."

He told me about Neverland's Treasure Island as we walked.

"It was all my idea. Old Cochrane went for it like a ton of bricks. Let me design the whole layout to suit myself. We take the marks aboard the *Hispaniola* over at the dock, see? Give 'em a sail around the island and then we land 'em and divide 'em into groups and give each group a treasure map. You know—that treasure hunt game kids play at parties? It works like that. Of course the actual treasure they finally find is only souvenirs— costume jewelry, junk like that—but it makes the marks happy."

He was as effusive as a kid about it. He trotted up the *Hispaniola*'s gangplank. "C'mon, Thax. I want you to see my cabin."

He pulled off his wig and beard and I could see that under the grease paint he was only about twenty-five. He lived in the schooner's aft cabin. He had a table set into the butt of the mizzenmast, and benches, and a bunk bed over some lockers, and the windows gave a nice light. He had bookshelves in the starboard wall.

"How about some music?"

He had a hi-fi in there and he put on a record. It was a heavy-bodied instrumental and it throbbed mood through the cabin. I haven't much ear for music. I couldn't get too excited over it.

Mike heated a pot of coffee on a hot plate and we sat down at the table to talk and smoke. He drank his java black, cup after cup. He seemed to grow more effusive all the time. After a while, he got on my nerves.

"Well," I said, "this has been nice, but the marks are about due to arrive. I've got to get to my stand. Thanks for the jo."

Mike saw me to the door. Halfway across the lake, I looked up from rowing and saw him. He had climbed the schooner's main shrouds and he was waving his wig and beard at me.

IV

The luck boy, Jerry, fell in with me when I reached Pioneer Town.

"The law has blundered upon what is known in the jargon as a clue. They figure they've found X marks the spot where Cochrane got it."

"Where?"

"They found a splotch of blood on the floor of the Admiral Benbow and it matches Cochrane's type. Nobody noticed it till last night because a tea table had been set over it. One of the rummies swamping out the joint found it after the lot closed at midnight."

I had no sooner got my stand set up and started my spiel than a handsome young plainclothes dick came at me. "Mr. Thaxton? Please come with me. Lieutenant Ferris wants to see you."

Ferris was sitting on one side of a table in the bunkhouse. He looked at me and his eyes were as opaque as two paving stones.

"You liar," he said.

I stared back at him.

"We've done a little inquiring on the wire since I last talked to you. Why'd you hold back on me about you and Mrs. Cochrane?"

"A sin of omission isn't a lie," I said. "You didn't ask me about my past marital mistakes."

"Look, Thaxton. If you had admitted to me that she used to be your wife, you could just as well have told me that she also used to be a professional knife thrower. And you could have told me that the shiv we found in Cochrane was one of hers!"

I said nothing. I dug out a cigarette and rolled it between my fingers. Ferris thumbnailed a match and then he held it out to me.

"You aren't as simple-minded as you make out, Thaxton," he said. "What's the first thing a man looks for in a murder case?"

"Motive?"

"Bet your sweet life. And here's another toughy for you. What one outstanding person has a motive in this particular case?"

"If you mean that May inherits the gold, say so. I don't know. I haven't been shown Cochrane's will."

"Your ex-wife picks up the full packet. Got any idea what it's worth?"

"Should be a fair-sized bundle."

"Yeah. This place grossed thirty million last year."

Now it was my turn to gape.

"You like the motive?"

"Money has a nice smell. But that doesn't prove she killed him."

"My boys found a jade earring on the mudbank where Cochrane's body was. Guess who owns the matching earring?"

"My ex-wife?"

"Your ex-wife. She was here on the lot the night he was murdered. She claims she was up in her suite asleep, but she has no witnesses."

It looked bad for May. The thing was, it was starting to look a little *too* bad. And I got the feeling that maybe Ferris was thinking the same thing. He didn't really look as pleased with his case as he should have.

"It's too neat," I said.

"All right," he admitted. "So it has the smell of a frame."

"The blow that killed Cochrane was a downward thrust. A knife-thrower strikes from a distance. He or she doesn't stab."

Ferris lit a cigarette. He said nothing.

"Aside from the fact that there's no valid reason why the body should have been moved from the Admiral Benbow to the Swamp Ride, how would a woman haul a big heavy body like that? Even if she had used one of those boats, how did she get the stiff from the tearoom to the Swamp Ride dock? And why would she leave that shiv in him when it practically stands up and shouts, 'This murder weapon belongs to May Cochrane!' "

Ferris studied the ashy tip on his cigarette. "Maybe she had help with moving the body." He looked at me. "Funny when you think about the timing. You show up, Cochrane gives you a job, you go see his wife—yeah, I know about your little visit with your ex-wife—and a few hours later, Cochrane gets killed and your ex-wife ends up with the gold."

"If you'd checked back far enough," I said, "you'd have found out that May divorced me because she hated my guts. It was coincidence that I ended up at her present husband's lot. It wasn't planned that way."

He mashed out his cigarette.

I got out of there. When I looked back through the screen door he was standing still and staring at the floor.

One of those cute little high-school things in the red-and-white guide outfit came up to me with a nice, clean, polite smile.

"Pardon me, sir, but aren't you Mr. Thaxton?"

I admitted I was.

"Mr. Franks has been looking everywhere for you, sir. He wants to see you right away."

"Where?"

"His office is upstairs over the storerooms, sir."

Billie was coming down the stairs and she stopped and smiled and said, "Thax."

"What's between you and Franks?" I wondered aloud.

"I just gave Franks my two weeks' notice," she said. "I'm quitting. Wait for me behind the nautch show tonight. I'll tell you then."

In the business manager's office, Franks was just closing his safe. He stood up in his two-hundred-dollar suit and came around his driftwood Rez desk to offer me his hand.

"Sit down, Thax, sit down," he urged in a falsely hearty voice.

I sat down in a chair.

"May?" Franks said into the telephone. "Thaxton's here now. Can you come over?"

Then he parked the phone back in its cradle. "You're a part of this show, Thaxton," he said. "And you were once Mrs. Cochrane's husband. I hope you are willing to see us through this trying time."

"As long as this 'trying time' doesn't pin a rose on me."

He frowned.

"Ferris is now toying around with two ideas," I told him. "One—I helped May knock over Cochrane, for money. Two—I did the deed on my own, for revenge."

The inner door opened without a preliminary knock. May stood framed there a moment, very dramatic in a silver skin-tight outfit. Like a red-headed shark.

"All right, May," I said. "Close the door and finish your entrance."

She closed the door and approached me with a little-girlish look of appeal. "Darling," she said in a soft, trilling voice. "I need your help."

"Sit down, will you, May?" I said. "You make me feel like a rabbit in a cornfield—with a hawk hovering overhead."

She was too nervous to sit. She started to pace Franks' office. I took out a cigarette and rolled it between my fingers.

"Darling," May said, "everybody thinks that I murdered Rob. It's all over the lot."

"You can't blame them, May. You're a natural for it. Look at the motive: money money money."

She started pacing again. "But I *didn't do it!* Why should I? Rob gave me everything."

"Uh-huh, but maybe you wanted everything except a sixty-year-old Irish husband. Maybe you wanted to marry some husky young buck who didn't have a dime and Cochrane said no divorce."

May came back to my chair with little red glints in

her eyes. "Can't you understand? I'm being framed for murder! *My* knife, *my* earring, *my* husband. I'm as good as convicted!" She looked at me calculatingly. "Sweetness, I only want you to do one little thing for me."

I looked at her.

"I want you to help me by not telling the law all about our private life. I'm in deep enough, darling, without having all the gory details thrown in."

"Ferris already knows we were once married, May."

She shook her head impatiently. "I don't mean that. I mean that little incident in Decatur."

That little incident in Decatur had almost cost me my life. That was the night I caught Bill Duff and May in Duff's trailer. That night, Duff had lost his eyetooth. Later, May had pitched a knife at me.

Franks cleared his throat. "Mrs. Cochrane would of course be very appreciative. I understand you arrived here somewhat strapped for money?"

May looked at me. "Will you take some and keep your mouth shut?"

"This may come as a jolt to you, sweetie," I said to her, "but the only money I'm going to take from you is what I earn on the lot. I won't tell Ferris you once tried to use me as a bull's-eye." I winked at Franks. "See you two very nice people later."

V

A fog-mist rolled in from the sea that night. It was damp, but not cold. It felt good on your skin, tingly and clean. It looked nice on the young girls' hair and on their outthrust sweaters. It put a spectacular halo around the high arc lights and made them a blue-white. It was ghostly. It seemed to make the voices of the children more shrill. People moved through it like stalking specters desperately trying to seek entertainment, excitement, escape.

The Viking horn went *hooo* like a dismal foghorn and

I gave away my last three orchids to three sad, spinster-looking females who had librarian or schoolteacher stamped on their tragically plain faces. They were very embarrassed and delighted and childlike about it.

I closed up my stand and went over to have a smoke with Gabby. He said, "Hop in and have a drink."

I climbed over the counter and helped him close up. A single, naked two-hundred-watt bulb hung in the place. The little white rabbits at the far end appeared to be frozen in their tracks with terror.

Gabby drew a pint from under the counter and passed it to me. It was scotch and it was good.

He took a good one and wiped his mouth and looked at me. "Got any ideas? About Rob Cochrane?"

"Why should I have ideas about that?" I asked.

"Because I understand The Man has started to switch his sights from Mrs. Big to you."

I looked at him. "Where'd you hear that?" I wanted to know.

"Bill Duff. Said it was from the horse's mouth."

"I just might decide to send Bill to the dentist again," I said.

"Somebody did that a couple of months ago."

"Yeah? Who?"

"Mike Ransome. They were over at the gambling room and Duff was on the sauce and he started to tell the boys an off-color story about him and May Cochrane. Nobody wanted to hear it because they all liked Rob, but Duff wouldn't knock it off. So Ransome put a fist in his big mouth."

"Ransome doesn't look like he could whip a Girl Scout."

"You ain't seen him in action. He's fast. Duff has the muscle and meanness, but he had no chance of landing one on Mike."

"Where is the gambling den? I'd like to look in some night."

"In the basement of Dracula's Castle. But they won't

let you within ten feet of a card table. Not with your educated mitts."

"I know it. I just like to watch." I got up. "Well," I said. "Thanks for the scotch. I gotta get."

I went around to the rear of the nautch show. Billie was waiting.

"Where'll we go?" I asked her.

"I don't care. I want to talk to you. Come on."

The last of the marks were filing out of the lot. Their voices sounded thin and lonely as they trudged off into the drifting mist. Everything was closing up. Lights were going out.

Billie led me across the smoky drawbridge to Dracula's Castle, and to a side door. She took my hand and we went up an inky corkscrew staircase. Around and around in blackness.

Billie opened a door. We stepped into a dark little room and it was like stepping into a page of *Ivanhoe*. The floor was flagstone. There was a large Gothic-like, archer-cross window in the outer wall and there was a canopy bed with high bedboards in one corner.

"Mr. Cochrane planned to make some kind of vampire roost out of this room," Billie said in a subdued voice. "The public isn't allowed up here yet. There aren't any lights."

She led me over to the canopy bed and we sat down in the dark. It squeaked.

"Talk about what?"

"Thax, how would you like to get away from all this?"

I leaned toward her. "How?"

"Let's run," she said softly. "Let's run away and not stop till we find a place so remote, so divorced from worldly problems that we'll think we're in Wonderland."

"The Wonderland Ride has a steep price tag."

"I've got the price of admission, Thax. Enough for both of us."

"You? How?"

"Savings. I'm a thrifty girl, and I know how to invest. I'm not as young as I may look. I've been coining the dollars for years. You'd be surprised. Besides, two smart people can always make out. We could go to the Mediterranean. I've always wanted to see the Mediterranean."

"Billie. Let's talk about it later."

"Thax." Her voice was a whisper, breathy, warm. . . . I walked Billie out to the parking lot. There were still about forty-odd cars scattered around. Billie's car was a white sixty-one MG. Cute little toy. I opened the door for her and she got in showing a lot of leg, which is what a girl has to do when she gets in or out of an MG.

"I'll see you tomorrow," I told Billie.

She gave me a bright searching smile. "Two weeks, Thax. Then the Mediterranean."

"Sure. Night-night."

Billie drove off across the lot in the topless MG toward town and the Regency Apartments, where she stayed.

Right inside the entrance was a big glassed-in map of Neverland. It was a bird's-eye view and it was very colorful and carefully detailed. It showed me something I hadn't realized before. One portion of the Swamp Ride backed up to the man-made lake. According to the map, there was only a rib of land separating the large body of water from the southern loop of the Swamp Ride's figure-eight pattern.

It planted the seed of an idea.

I scouted around till I ran down one of the night watchmen. I showed him my magical card and asked him if he had a spare flashlight he could lend me. He gave me his.

Neverland seemed lonely and haunted, like a long-lost Aztec city brooding in jungle mist. The one big light burned blue-white over the Swamp Ride's deserted dock. The little boats were all snug in their berths for the night. I climbed over the rail and went along the dock to the far shadowy end and jumped down to a weedy bank.

The fog was creeping over the dark water and coiling around the black roots, and the whole slimy place seemed to be writhing around me. Once I was in there—what with the fog and the dark and the unearthly silence—it was actually like being in a real swamp. I don't mean a little five-acre morass, but the Everglades or the Okefenokee. I wanted to find that little setback where I'd fished Cochrane out of the shallows.

The setback reared itself out of the swampy shadows. I played the flash over the water and the bank, but there really wasn't anything there I wanted to see. It was that finger of high ground behind the setback that interested me. I started walking over it.

There were a lot of tropical ferns and flowers and saw palmettos, and in about ten or twelve seconds, I came out on the opposite bank and found myself standing on the edge of the man-made lake. The distance between the lake and the waterway was about one hundred feet.

That made one thing quite clear—the way the murderer had moved the body from the tearoom into the Swamp Ride without too much strain and without being observed.

He—if it was a he—had hauled the body from the tearoom to the Admiral Benbow dock, put it into one of the rowboats, rowed it across the lake in the dark and landed about where I was now standing. Then he or she or they lugged the body over the rib of land and dumped it into the setback. Neat.

I retraced my path with the flash, looking for footprints in the earth. I didn't find anything except some of my own prints.

I stopped. The silence was eerie. I spun around and the flash sliced through the tropical growth. It made a white splotch on Bill Duff's face. He was about twelve feet away and half concealed in the palmettos.

"Peekaboo at you, too, Bill," I said.

He put up a spread hand to block the light. "Turn that thing off, will you? You want to blind me?"

"Let's take a look at your other hand first, Bill. I'd hate to find out in the dark that you had one of May's knives."

"That's real funny," Bill said. "About as funny as what

you told Ferris about me." He showed me his other hand. Empty.

I cut the light. "Don't be nasty, Bill. It just makes us even. You've been hustling around telling everyone that Ferris wants to tab me with the murder. What are you doing out here yourself, Bill? Returning to the scene of the crime perchance?"

"I saw a light out here when I was passing the Swamp Ride dock. I got curious."

It was a good answer, but it was a lie. He hadn't seen any light. Not from the dock. Not in that fog with two acres of jungle in between. He had either followed me in there or he had already been there when I showed up.

"You on a treasure hunt?" he asked me, sneering.

"Clues. I've turned P.I. It's a hell of a lot of fun."

"Tell me, so I can chuckle, too."

"I had an idea that maybe the law overlooked. Ferris was getting all sweaty because he couldn't figure how somebody—maybe you—got the stiff all the way in here without using one of those swamp boats and without being seen by anyone."

"And you've doped it all out for him," he said.

"I think so. Correct me if I'm wrong. You put it in one of the rowboats and scampered it across the lake and carted it over this hunk of land to the Swamp Ride."

He was quiet for a moment. Then he said, "You really are cute, Thax. Now do tell us why I did all this?"

"Well, somewhere along the line, May dumped you just like she dumped me. Then a couple of years ago, when you're down and out, you read in *Variety* or one of the trade papers that May had become Mrs. Cochrane Enterprises. So you hustle down here and get a job off her old man. But May won't give you a second tumble. You knife the old gent and proceed to hang a frame on May."

Duff snorted. "Crazy." He started to slouch off to the right. "It just doesn't wash, Thax."

His left came out of the dark and went off in my face

like a cherry bomb. I never saw it coming and I wasn't
set for it. I went right on over backwards and cradled my
head in a palmetto.

When I stumbled to my feet, Bill was gone. I found
the flashlight and followed the lake shore around to the
Admiral Benbow Tearoom.

Neverland was three-fourths nightblinded now and I
didn't see a soul. Across the inky lake, the rakish *Hispaniola*
was snuggled against the black mass of Treasure Island.
The stern lights were blazing festively on the schooner and
I could hear the faint throb of music coming across the
water.

I climbed into one of the rowboats and shoved off.

The fog was dissipating and the moon was climbing
the black back fence of the night like a great cat goddess.
Its image was in the water and it was cracked into a million
pieces and tossed about carelessly by my oar blades, its light
all loosened and rippling wild.

Mike Ransome had another semi-long-hair piece going
on his hi-fi and it pulsed a moody sensation through the
moony night.

"Hey, Thax!" Mike cried when I came in. "It's good
to see you! You can help me pass the long night. I'm the
king of the insomniacs, you know, now that Dashiell Ham-
mett is dead."

I didn't doubt it, with his nerves and the way he slurped
up black coffee. I noticed the pot was perking on the hotplate again. "Haven't you got anything to drink but that?"

Mike looked at me brightly. "You want gin?"

"I could stand it. I just lost a decision to your old spar-
ring partner." I tapped my mouth.

Mike looked at me with an expectant smile. "Who's
that, Thax?"

"Bill Duff. He landed one in the dark when I wasn't
looking. My own fault. I should have known better."

"Duff!" He grinned delightedly. "No kidding? Thax,
you could take three like him."

"Not in the dark," I said. "How about that drink?" He brought it out and I fed myself a shot of gin. It went down like a jackhammer. The trouble with gin is that it tastes like cheap perfume. I had another. It helped anesthetize my mouth.

"So what happened between you and Bill Duff?" Mike asked.

"It's an old beef. We used to work in carny years ago. Just a hangover grudge."

He grinned and got up and said, "Well, it's your business. Listen, I've got to run ashore. Late date."

I glanced at my wrist watch. It was after two A.M.

"Barmaid, I take it," I said.

He was busy putting himself into a bright, severely cut sports jacket. He winked at me.

"I like 'em at this time of night. Right?"

I said, "Umm."

"Make yourself at home, mate," Mike told me. "Finish the gin, and flop, if you want to."

"Thanks."

"I hate to run off like this." He seemed quite sincere. "But she won't keep. You know what I mean?"

"Go ahead, Mike. I know the rules."

He flashed another grin at me and made for the door. "Next time, Thax, we'll have a real talk. That's a promise." He slammed the door behind him, and was gone.

I finished off the gin and got up and staggered out on deck. The fog was completely gone and the moon waited in the rigging, fat and proud.

I reeled down the gangplank and across the beach and bumbled into the boat. How I got those oars shipped and managed to row myself across the lake will always remain a mystery.

The next thing I knew, Jerry had me under the armpits and he was saying, "Thax! You all right, Thax?"

"I'm sick."

"Where shall I take you?"

"Tree house," I told him. "Live in tree house with Cheeta, away away up in the rockyby blue."

He reeled me into Tarzan's hut and aimed me at the bed with a good push. I collapsed like a bag of nails. Everything was going around like a fiery catherine wheel and my stomach wanted to send up a rocket.

Little mice were playing on my shoulder blades. It was still dark. I didn't like the mice. I wanted them to go away. I squirmed and muttered *uh-uh* at them. But they wouldn't go away. They kept scrabbling at me. Then I suddenly realized they were talking to me.

"Thax. Hey, Thax. Wake up, will you? I gotta talk to you. Listen to me, can't you? I got trouble."

They weren't little mice. They were little hands. I pushed my face deeper into the leopard-skin pillow and said *uh-uh* again. I felt bad. I wanted to die. I didn't want to talk to anybody.

But I wish I had. Maybe I could have helped the little guy. Maybe he wouldn't have had to die that night.

VI

The scream belonged to Dracula's Castle. It definitely did not belong in Tarzan's tree house because it wasn't a fun scream. It was pure terror.

It seemed to go off right under me. Then it stopped.

I sat up. A mutter of voices rolled up under me. A gang of people were milling around on the ground. Most of them were standing over something just to the left of the base of the tree. About five of them had flashlights and were chopping up the night with cold white light.

By the time I reached the ground, Ferris was standing in front of me.

"What about that over there?" Ferris said, pointing toward the base of the tree.

I turned and looked. A couple of people stepped out of the way and I saw a little dark shape lying crumpled on the ground.

It was a very still little shape and it had small, pointed features and its eyes were open and sparking with reflected light and they seemed to be staring straight at me.

He wasn't wearing his ape suit, but Cheeta was dead just the same.

I was sitting at the table in the bunkhouse with Ferris who was feeding me black coffee.

"You sober enough to talk now? You want to tell papa about it?"

"I didn't push him."

"Did I say you did?"

"You're working up to it."

He walked away. He didn't look happy. "Let's take first things first so we'll know where we stand. I can turn in one of two reports and there will be no kickback. Suicide or accident." He looked at me. "What don't you like about the first one?"

I gave it a little thought. "Well, I don't know the statistics on what percentage of midgets commit suicide, but I'll bet a buck it's mighty low."

"Old wives' talk," Ferris said. "Come on. Why didn't he kill himself?"

"Because he was afraid," I said. "It was a physical fear for his life. I've seen guys like him in Korea. They're usually the ones who break and run. And a scared man who is running for his life doesn't stop to take it himself."

"And Terry Orme was scared?"

"Yeah. I had a talk with him a couple of nights back. He didn't say it, but he was scared. Don't ask me what of. I don't know. Then early this morning, he came into the tree house and tried to wake me. Said he had to talk to me. Said he had trouble. It doesn't add up to suicide within the same hour."

"Too bad you were so drunk you couldn't help him."

I took out a cigarette and rolled it between my fingers. He strolled over and thumbnailed a match for me.

"What don't you like about the second one?" he asked.

"Accident."

"That's the easy way out for you," I said. "Nobody would ever question it because it seems so logical. He was always climbing trees, and everybody knows that if you climb trees long enough, the odds are you'll finally fall."

"So what's wrong with it?"

"One thing. The little bastard was good at it. He could climb like a monkey, and I've never heard of a monkey having an accident."

"If it hadn't been for Cochrane's murder, I'd never give Orme's death a second thought," Ferris admitted. "But . . ."

"But Cochrane's murder looks like a frame for his wife," I broke in. "And I used to be married to his wife and Terry Orme and I were roomies up in the tree house and I've admitted we were both up there alone just before he took the big leap. Right?"

He looked at me. "Funny how handy you are whenever a body turns up."

I smiled. "You're trying to put the cart before the horse. I'm never found standing by my lone over the body. Somebody else always spots bingo before I arrive. There must have been twenty ghouls gawking over Orme's body before I made my grand entrance. Who was it, by the way, who drew the lucky ticket this morning?"

"An old friend of yours, Thaxton. William H. Duff."

The initial haunted me, but I couldn't think why just then. "Bill? What was he doing around here in those wee hours?"

"Said he was looking for you. Wondering what you were up to. Said he'd found you out in the middle of the Swamp Ride a few hours earlier, snooping around with a flashlight." Ferris' voice turned casual. "Any special little thing you were looking for, Thaxton?"

"Just working out an idea I had." I told him about my rowboat and lake theory.

He grunted but I could see it appealed to him. He went to the door and told one of his storm troopers to scout him up a map of the place.

"You were talking about how somebody else always finds the bodies before you do," he said to me. "Funny thing—that Jimmy Bentley, the freckle-faced kid who found Cochrane's body? He's not around any more."

"No? What happened to him?"

"Dunno. I wanted to check with him on some little point last night. So when I send a cop to go find him, he comes back and says they say Bentley up and quit yesterday. No notice, nothing. Just plain gone."

Ferris hadn't decided to lead me by the ear to the nearest jail, so I was still a free agent. I went over to the payroll office and asked for Freckles' home address. They didn't want to give it to me at first, but after a bit of con, I convinced them that I was a friend of his and owed him a sawbuck and wanted to be certain he got it before he took off.

The address they forked over was back in the pine woods near some swamp or other. Not far from Neverland.

I went around to the rear of the nautch show and knocked on the door. Billie was wearing a kimono.

I told her I wanted to borrow her MG for a couple of hours. "I want to look up one of the Swamp Ride ops who quit yesterday. Just an idea I'm playing around with."

"You mean about the murders, Thax?" she said.

"The law hasn't said it's plural yet, Billie. Terry might have had an accident, you know."

"Sure, I know. But the word is already around that it wasn't an accident. That he was pushed."

"Who's spreading the word? Bill Duff?" I was feeling mean.

Billie gave me an odd look. "Thax—what's wrong, honey? You act funny."

I shrugged. "At first, it was pretty obvious that someone was out to make a patsy out of May. But lately, I've got the feeling that *I'm* being slowly pushed into a blind corner."

"Wait for me," Billie said. "I'll put on some clothes. I'm going with you."

"What about your job?"

"What about it? I'm quitting, aren't I? To hell with 'em."

I had a smoke while I waited for her. She came out in an expensive blue suit and we left the lot.

Billie knew where to go. I drove the MG. She sat deep in the red-leather bucket seat, with her head back on the folded tonneau, and watched the sky. The wind made persistent little snatches at her candy-floss hair. It was just like expensive platinum in the bright lemon sun.

We followed the curve of the shore for a few miles. The narrow strip of pale white beach was off on our left and it looked lonely and end-of-the-worldish, with its continuous line of surf quietly foaming like milk. Now and then, we would come to a stand of royal palms and we would see a straggly clutter of meager huts nestled among the smooth boles. Fisherman shanties. Maybe some artists.

Finally, we drove into a remote little settlement which was a bend in a country road by land and the flowing of one swamp lake into another by water.

There was a turpentine still and a general store and a huddle of shanties which crouched back under the cabbage palms and the pawpaw trees. Old Negresses had brought baskets of fruit, vegetables, tortoise eggs, and black beans to sell under the shade of a *tupelo*. They closed up market in the afternoon by simply packing their merchandise on their heads.

I asked the owner of the general store where the Bentleys lived. He was a beak-faced man in a wrinkled shirt and he gave me a sour look.

"You sound like a Northern fella. Bentleys is over there."

What he meant was a place just across a gallberry flat. It was a farmhouse and it had a simple grace of line, low and rambling and one-storied, and it had gone gray and cracked for want of paint. There was a tin roof and it was mostly rust, and the porch barely left you enough room to pass in front of the broken-backed wicker chairs.

It was Freckles' brawny brother-in-law who came to the door, and he was about as co-operative as a wounded grizzly.

"Naw, you cain't see Jimmy. He don't want to see nobody."

"I'm a friend of his," I said. "Just tell him it's Thaxton from Neverland. The guy who lives in the tree house."

"He don't want a see nobody from Neverland," the brawny one informed me. "Is that plain, or do I got to show you?"

I had an idea he *could* show me. He looked like a mighty burly boy.

Freckles suddenly appeared in the doorway. He had the same scared look Terry Orme had had. "That's okay, Flem. Hi, Thax."

He and I and Billie sat down on the porch. I looked at Freckles.

"How come you up and quit, Jim?"

"Well, gosh, Mr. Thaxton. I just felt like it is all."

"Come on. Something's bugging you. It's just as plain as those freckles on your map."

"All right. You want the truth? I was scared," he said.

"Of what?"

"That's the whole trouble. I don't know exactly. I guess finding Mr. Cochrane like I did really upset me. And those darn cops on me all the time with questions. I mean, like every time I turned around. That Lieutenant Ferris always sending for me, and—well—yesterday."

"What about yesterday?"

"That Cheeta midget—Terry Orme? He gave me the high sign from back in the jungle when I was taking a load of customers through the Swamp Ride. So when I had a break, I went back in there to see what he wanted."

"And?"

"Well, I don't know. That's the whole trouble. He was real vague and edgy about it. Wouldn't really come out and say what he wanted. Kept beating around the bush."

"What *did* he say—vague or otherwise?" I insisted.

"He kept trying to find out if anybody had been around asking me questions about him."

"Did he mean the cops?"

"No. He meant anybody else. Somebody who worked at Neverland."

"But he didn't mention any name."

"No. And I tried to ask him who he meant exactly, but he kept hedging." The kid looked at me with a look of appeal in his orange-peppered face. "And he was scared, Mr. Thaxton. I don't know what of, but he was real scared. He nearly had the shakes. I guess that's what finally bugged me into quitting. I don't know anything about that murder and I don't want to know. I just want to be left alone."

"You mean you got scared because you thought there might be somebody on the lot who figured you *did* know something about the murder? Something that wasn't safe for you to know?"

He nodded. "I guess so."

"Have the police been out here to see you?" I asked.

"Yeah, this morning. A squad car showed up early. But I didn't want any more of that business. I skipped out the back and hid in the palmettos. Flem told 'em I'd gone north. Which is just what I think I'll do," he added grimly.

I was sure he would, once he heard that Terry Orme was dead. I gave Billie a warning look. The kid would find out soon enough, and he was already too scared to eat his dinner. Why spook him ahead of time?

"Then you didn't find out what it was the law wanted?"

"No, sir."

I thought about it for a while. "That morning you found

Cochrane. Is it the usual custom to take the boats around the whole Swamp Ride every morning before opening time?"

"No, that was just a freak thing. Usually, all we have to do is see if they'll start up and then line 'em up in position for the customers. But that one boat didn't seem to have any poop that morning, so I decided to give it a spin around the ride to see if I could work out the kinks."

"Do most of the employes know that? I mean that you usually warm up the boats right there at the dock?"

"Well yeah—I guess so."

"Did anyone ever ask you about it? I mean before you found Cochrane?"

"No. Nobody ever asked me for the time of day—until *after* I found him. Now that's all I get from everybody. Questions!"

I gave him a benevolent smile. "Well, that's what makes the world go round. Questions and answers. Thanks for answering mine. Let's go, Billie."

VII

I gave Billie a phony excuse for not meeting her that night after closing time. What I wanted to do was look up Jerry. I went over to Dracula's Castle and got directions from one of the sweep-up men and then I scouted up a back door.

The stairs inside went down. I went to a private door. It was locked. The barker who spieled for the nautch show opened to my knock.

"Just sight-seeing, Phil," I told him.

Jerry was in there but he was hanging around watching a poker game. I decided to stick around and watch a few hands myself.

Dracula's basement was used nightly for a gambling hall. The membership was strictly exclusive. Neverland employes only. They had about four tables going. Gabby was at one of them with Bill Duff and Mike Ransome˙ and a college kid named Smitty. They were playing draw.

Mike saw me and waved.

Bill Duff gave me a look. To Mike, he said, "One."

Mike dealt the cards around.

"Grab yourself a drink, Thax," Gabby said.

"Just a beer," I said. I went around behind Mike and drew up a chair.

"I sure hate to give a lamb a fleecing," Mike said, "but the lamb is baaing for it. Right, Bill?"

Duff scowled at him but said nothing. I got the impression that Mike had been riding him.

Mike opened for a five, Gabby bumped five, and Mike stayed out. When the hand was finished, Mike laid down his cards face up, showing two jacks for openers. He opened the next hand and dropped out again, and when the hand was completed, he faced his cards up, exposing two small pairs.

"You should have drawn to that, Mike," I said. "You might have gotten a full."

He just grinned.

He passed four hands in a row and then drew three ladies. He opened, drew but didn't better it, and got out. Duff won on two pair and Mike showed his openers. Gabby stared at him.

"Don't you like to win, Mike? You had Duff's doubles beat."

Mike chuckled. "Wasn't good enough for my money. I want a big one when I catch old Bill's purse."

He let another two or three hands go by, then he saw a ten-dollar bet and raised it the same amount. Gabby and Smitty called and Duff raised a ten. Mike raised twenty. Gabby folded and Smitty saw. Duff tipped it another twenty. It seemed to be what Mike was waiting for.

"Ha!" He shoved in two twenties.

Smitty backed out and Duff studied Mike with glacial eyes. Mike grinned at him. I started to hold my breath.

"No," Duff said grimly and tossed in his cards. "I ain't getting suckered into that."

Mike spread his cards up. The best he had was a ten high. The expression on Duff's face was a thing to behold, and it didn't help his disposition much when Mike started to laugh.

I thought I knew what Mike was up to. There are three ways to play poker. Play your hand for just what it's worth. Play hunches. Play against the man who wants most to win. Mike was trying the third method.

The man who is desperate to win will usually overplay his hands. The need to win shuts out his luck. And if you can get him mad, he's dead.

Mike lost a few small hands and let a couple of fat ones go by. Duff was steady winner, and he started to perk up. He didn't think Mike would try another bluff.

Duff opened with a casual five. Gabby stayed, Smitty doubled it and Mike raised Smitty. Duff called. They drew and again Duff teased them along for a five. Gabby must have smelled a mouse and got out. Smitty hung in there apprehensively, and Mike raised a ten. Duff smiled and pushed in two twenties. Smitty traded his hand for a drink.

Mike could hardly sit still in his chair. He turned to me with a happy grin and showed me his hand and I looked at it poker-faced. Then he counted out four twenties and happily tossed them in the middle of the table.

Nobody said anything. Duff stared at Mike. "Are you bluffing again, you bastard?"

Mike grinned, drumming his fingers on the table top.

"No," Duff said. "You wouldn't try that twice." He flipped in his hand.

Mike yelled and spread out his own, face up. Nobody could believe it except me, and I'd already seen it. A pair of treys. A very feeble pair of treys.

"What the hell kind of poker is this?" Duff growled.

Mike laughed delightedly and scooped up the bills. "How about a change of pace, Billy Boy?" he said to Duff. "Let's try a calm game of stud, five-card."

He made the rounds with the cards. He had the spade six showing. He didn't look at his hole card. Gabby opened on a black ace. Everybody stayed. Mike went around. He got the spade two. Duff had a pair of eights showing.

"Ten," Duff said. They all went along with it.

Mike's next card was the spade three. Duff drew a jack. The pair eight was still high. He made it ten again. Mike still hadn't peeked at his hole card.

He got the spade five on the next trip. Duff reached for a cigarette. He now had three eights and a little boy showing. He pretended not to notice Mike's possible.

"Time to separate the men from the boys," Duff said. He gave the pot a sixty-dollar tilt. I knew him. He played a hand for just what it was worth. He either had another eight or another jack in the cellar. Gabby and Smitty went home in a hurry.

Mike gave me a wink. "I think we should give old Bill a run for his money, Thax."

I didn't say anything. The thing that bugged me was that Mike still hadn't looked at his hole card. He's stacked it, I thought.

I think maybe the same thought crossed Duff's mind. Mike started counting out his stack of tens and twenties and said, "I believe we agreed on table stakes, gentlemen?"

I looked at his up cards again. Two, three, five, six of spades. Was the spade four in the cellar or wasn't it?

"See the sixty, Billy baby," Mike said, "and bump a bill."

Duff wet his lips, studying Mike's cards.

All Duff had was eights over jacks, or he wouldn't stall. He decided to bull his way through. He threw in five twenties and followed that with two twenties and a ten and said, "Bump again."

Mike chuckled and started to count his bills.

Duff was about as taut as a fiddle string. "C'mon. What are you gonna do? See or fold?"

Mike looked at him in mock surprise. "See or fold? I thought this was poker? Let's see here—"

He lifted one corner of his hole card with his thumbnail. I couldn't see it. Then he went back to counting his bills. "I have ten-twenty-forty-sixty-eighty-ninety-one yard. And twenty-forty-sixty-seventy-eighty-two bills!" He grinned at Duff.

Duff's eyes bored auger holes into Mike's four show cards. "I haven't got that much."

"I'm not an unreasonable man, McDuff. Tomorrow's pay day. I'll trust you until then."

Duff didn't like it at all, none of it. He was beat. He folded up his hand. "Take it," he said.

Mike tipped back his head and let out a laugh. It was a high trill of pure delight. Then he got up and picked up his winnings and stuffed them any old way in his pockets, like the Scarecrow of Oz, and handed me his hole card.

"Give it to Bill at Christmas, Thax," he said. "I've got a late date on."

He walked away and I looked at the card while all the other guys in that room looked at me.

"Well!" Duff demanded.

I handed him the card. It was very red and it had two faces. It didn't go with a low spade straight flush at all.

I drew Jerry out into the hall. He was still all ga-ga over that last hand. "Have you ever seen anything like it?" he wanted to know. "I tell you, that Ransome is wild! That was the bluff of the century."

Maybe. But I'd known Bill Duff a long time. He was the kind of cheap flashboy who begged for a cleaning. Anyhow, I had something else entirely on my mind.

"Listen, Jerry. How are you in the Jimmy Valentine scene? Can you bust a box, if you have to?"

He drew back from me as if appalled by the question. "No. I don't have the touch. But Eddy does, if it's a simple box. What's the pitch?"

"I'm looking for information, not for loot. So I don't think what we take will be missed. Nobody should call copper because of it."

"That's good. Eddy isn't looking for law problems. He'll do it."

This Eddy reminded me of the mousy little beak-nosed character who used to play in all the gangster movies twenty-five years back. Nervous, stuttery, with the predatory look of a voracious moray eel.

"What—what kind a box is it?" he wanted to know.

The three of us were standing in the inky shadows of the alleyway between the storehouse and the bunkhouse. Lloyd Franks' office was right above us. Eddy's busy little bird eyes batted here, there, anywhere except on the face of the person he was talking to. He made me jumpy.

"I don't know," I answered him. "I'm no box man."

"Yeah, but is it a wall—a wall job or an upright, or—or a combo or what? Know what I mean? What—what is it?" he asked.

"It's not in a wall and it's a combination box," I told him.

"Well, all—all right, then." He rubbed the fingertips of his right hand against his pants leg. "I—I just want to know, see? What kind—what kind it is, see?"

"C'mon," Jerry said. "Let's get going before one of the security guards comes staggering by."

Truth to tell, I had my sincere doubts about this Eddy; he was so nervous and jittery. But I dropped all doubt as soon as he took on the first locked door with his little pick tool. He had that thing open quicker than I could have turned the knob.

We went up the stairs with a fountain-pen flash to guide us. Eddy kept mumbling to himself and rubbing his fingertips on his pants.

The thing I liked about Jerry is that he never once asked me why I wanted to break into Franks' office and crack his safe. It gave me a good feeling. A man who will trust you on face value is a rare find today.

The door to Franks' office gave Eddy about as much trouble as I would expect to find in opening a cracker box. We stepped into the large room and I flashed the light at the distant safe. Eddy approached the box on a right oblique, sizing it up as he went.

"Yeah," he muttered. "It'll—it'll take—take a couple a minutes. Know what I mean? Couple a minutes."

I nodded sagely in the dark. He was the real article as far as I was concerned. He could do no wrong. I held the light for him as he gave the dial the first practice spin.

"Turn it—turn it off, huh?" he whispered. "It distracts—distracts my concentration. Know what I mean? My concentration."

Jerry was sitting in Franks' chair nonchalantly going through Franks' desk, drawer by drawer, using the moon through the window behind him to see by.

Eddy had his left ear against the combination dial, listening to the tumblers. He sandpapered his fingertips a couple of times on the rug and tried again.

"Seven—seventeen right," he mumbled to himself, "four left."

He had it open. I hunkered down with the pocket flash and started through the papers. I was looking for an envelope and I turned it up in less than a minute. Jerry had left the desk and he and Eddy were both watching me expectantly.

I didn't say anything. I slipped the envelope in my pocket and stood up and nudged the safe door closed with my knee. Eddy knelt down and wiped the dial with a handkerchief.

"What brand of hooch do you like, Eddy?" I asked him. "I owe you about a gallon of it."

His eyes blinked from right to left and back again. "No—no thanks. I never—never touch it, see? It makes—makes you nervous. Know what I mean? Makes you too nervous."

VIII

The next two days were sleigh rides. Nobody was murdered and I didn't stumble over any bodies and Ferris left me alone. I worked at my stand with my little shells and that went well, too. No beefs.

I was working my stand the second night and getting a good Saturday night play, and my mind was as innocently blank as a two-year-old's. Then I looked around and saw a couple of bad-news birds coming my way.

I swept up my walnut shells and said, "That's all for now, folks. The hawks are about."

The two hard characters waited till my marks drifted off and then one of them stepped up and drew his wallet and flashed a badge at me.

"Mr. Thaxton? Lieutenant Ferris wants to see you."

"Only two of you this time?" I said.

They were somewhat on the newbreed pattern, but not quite. The one who had flashed the buzzer was of medium height, spare-built—a thin-faced, dark man giving the impression of a steel hardness not wholly physical. I classified him as a tough baby.

The other one was maybe twenty-three. He had fair, wavy hair like a halo over a youthful, almost girlish face. There was something a little wrong with his baby-blue eyes and with the tense way he grinned at me.

I shrugged at Gabby and the three of us walked out of the sideshow.

I started to turn south once we reached the hub of the central garden, thinking we would go on over to the bunkhouse. But the thin-faced man took me by the elbow and said, "No. We're going to headquarters." We headed for the parking lot.

I'm not simple—just slow. I started to lag my pace.

"Maybe I better have another peek at your buzzer," I suggested to the thin-faced man.

He took me by the arm. "Let's not have any trouble, Mr. Thaxton."

Pansy-face spoke for the first time. "Naw. He don't want no trouble, Chad," he said a-grinning.

Chad stopped short. We were standing by a dark new sedan. It wasn't a police car.

A third man was sitting behind the wheel. He looked out the window at me with bright little piggy eyes.

"Okay?"

"Okay," Chad said.

I pivoted like a soldier doing an about-face and planted my right in Pansy-face's breadbasket, and at the same time Chad gave me a chop behind the neck with the edge of his hand. Pansy-face and I leaned together like a couple of far gone drunks trying to hold each other up.

Then Pansy-face gutted me and I swung to the left with a windy grunt and doubled over. I felt the hard, positive business end of a pistol barrel in the small of my back.

"He tagged me, Chad!" Pansy-face cried. I think he was on something. I didn't smell any booze, so it was probably a needle.

"Get in the car."

Pansy-face got me under both armpits and gave me a heave from behind. He followed me into the car and then he slammed the door after himself.

"Okay," I said in a strained voice. "Okay, I've had enough."

It was important to me that he believed he had me cowed. I didn't want him reaching for his shoulder holster with the intention of subduing me further with his gun. If he reached, he would discover that the holster was empty.

I had palmed his forty-five while we were hugging each other and I slipped it under my belt when I swung away and doubled up.

I let it rest where it was. The driver was holding a snub-nosed revolver on me while Chad went around the back of the car and got in up front on the passenger side.

Chad pulled his gun and rested it on top of his seat, aiming in my direction.

"Go," he said to the driver.

We turned out onto the highway. I could just make out the gray strip of beach with its pale line of foam running along on the left side of us.

"How serious is it?" I asked him. "Do I just get a working over from the hophead here, or are you going whole hog?"

"I wouldn't worry about it, Mr. Thaxton," Chad said. "One way or another, you've got to face it."

"Sure," I agreed. "But you don't have any objection about telling me *why* I've got to face it, do you?"

"I wouldn't know, Mr. Thaxton."

I had figured that. He was a sharp big-city hood and he did nasty little jobs like this on consignment.

"But you know who hired you, don't you?" I said.

"I know that somebody pays me. Beyond that point, I don't sweat it," he said calmly.

We turned off the main drag and went down a lightless back road at a casual forty. It wasn't paved. I could hear the pebbles banging off the bottom of the frame and a lot of sand or dirt was hissing inside the fenders.

Chad watched me very closely. He said, "We close?"

"Uh-huh," the driver said. "Any place along here. Nearest farmhouse is five miles."

I glanced out the window. A continuous murky scar on the dark earth was running along our right side. A drainage ditch, I supposed. Some kind of coulee.

"This will do."

The driver applied the brakes. The car stopped. The twin beams of light converged and showed us fifty yards of drab dirt road rolling flatly on into the dark night.

"A little accident is going to be arranged, huh?"

"A hit-and-run accident," he said. "Too bad about this, Mr. Thaxton, but business is business."

Pansy-face leaned on the door handle. It opened about an inch.

I said, "Any of you know what became of the hophead's gun?"

They did what I thought they would. Pansy-face slapped a hand to his left armpit and Chad's eyes leaped right after Pansy-face's surprised gesture.

I had the forty-five out and I pulled the trigger at Chad's chest but it kicked and he caught the slug in the Adam's apple.

I lunged against Pansy-face and the door shot open. We went sprawling through it and hit the road together. I started rolling like a log as the driver's snubnose chattered out the window after me.

I got behind the car and came up in a crouch.

I started crawling about it, working parallel to the road and going in the same direction as the headlights. The driver was yelling at Pansy-face.

"Take the right side. I'll take the left. He must a jumped in one ditch."

"He's mine! You hear me? Wait'll I get Chad's gun."

I kept on crawling along the ditch. Then I snaked up to the edge and looked back down the road.

The car's headlights glowered at me like jack-o'-lantern eyes. Pansy-face's silhouette cut across them. He was holding Chad's pistol at hip level. I eased myself out of the ditch and sat down in the road facing the car and rested my gun arm on my right knee.

I called, "Down here."

Pansy-face spun around with the front of the car at his back and gave me a beautiful full-front silhouette. I squeezed off but it went high and nabbed him in the left shoulder, throwing him back against the nose of the hood. His knees buckled and he went down in the road like a dropped shirt.

The driver piled back into the car. I snapped one at him. The motor was idling.

He forgot about Pansy-face.

"Bob, watch—"

The car lurched forward and went *thlump*. A shriek ripped the fabric of the night.

The driver was already rattled, and the realization that he had just mashed Pansy-face unglued him completely. The big, rumbling, crystal-eyed sedan came hurtling down the road at me. I started jerking off shots at the windshield, and it swerved out of control to the left and turned over.

I climbed out of the ditch. I wiped off the automatic and pitched it in the field by the wreck.

It cost me an hour to reach the highway and another half-hour to find an all-night coffee stand. I phoned for a taxi from there and it was twelve forty-five when I paid off the hack in front of Billie's apartment.

Billie was getting ready for bed and she was in one of those skimpy nylon nighties. She looked at me as if I'd just dropped out of the moon.

"Why, Thax!"

I stepped into her room and closed the door. "I had a little trouble."

She gave me a half-wondering, half-critical look. "You look like you've been rolling in it. What happened?"

I told her it was a car accident.

"Well, whose car? Was anybody hurt?" she asked.

"Nobody was hurt. Just three guys were killed. Okay I use your bathroom? I feel as grimy as a Union Pacific engineer."

I told her about it after I got out of the shower. "It was an anachronism. An old-fashioned ride. Like something out of the gangster days."

"But why, Thax? Who would want to do such a thing to you?"

"Someone who figures I'm getting too smart," I said.

"You mean the same person who killed Rob Cochrane and Terry Orme?"

I shook my head and asked her if she had a drink around

there. After-reaction was setting in and I suddenly needed a drink very badly. She had bourbon.

"No," I told her. "It wasn't the same person. The person who fixed Cochrane and Orme does his own dirty work. This is someone else's style."

Billie looked annoyed. "I don't understand. Just how many people at Neverland have homicidal tendencies?"

I grinned at her. "One too many. That's what's had me going in circles so long. I didn't figure it that way."

We drove to Neverland around noon. We had decided I should find myself a room somewhere. There were no doors I could lock in Tarzan's hut and it was no longer a very safe place for me to sleep.

"I've got a couple of clean shirts and what-not tucked under Tarzan's bed," I told her. "I'll pick 'em up after we close tonight and meet you at the main gate."

"Thax," Billie said, "be careful. Don't trust anyone."

"Don't worry," I said. "I'll take care of myself. See you tonight."

I was never more wrong in my life. I wasn't going to see her that night at all and someone else was going to take care of me.

It was a hot, almost sultry day with no help from the sea, and we had a good crowd. I worked my stand for a few hours, but my mind wasn't on it. I kept waiting for something to happen, and when nothing did, I began to wonder if I'd been wrong.

The way I figured it, a crack had to appear in the egg-shell soon so that the chick could show its beak. When it didn't, I started to get nervous.

I stayed at my stand until about four and then I went over to Gabby's gallery.

"Smoke break," I said.

He was agreeable. "Want a snort?"

"No. But let's step around back a minute. Okay no?"

We went around to the little tented area and lit up.

There was a small locked shack back there and I knew he kept his twenty-twos and live ammo inside.

I said, "Look, Gabby, I need a gun."

The corners of Gabby's mouth dipped into points. "Why don't you use your head, Thax, and cut and run?"

"I'm in too deep. I've got to go along with it."

"You mean you *want* to go along with it," Gabby said.

"Can you help me or not?"

Gabby scowled at the ground. "I've got a handgun. But you're a fool if you try to use it."

He unlocked the shack door and went inside and came out again with an automatic in his hand. He didn't look one bit happy about it when he passed over the weapon.

It was another forty-five, a Colt. I thumbed the clip latch and extracted the magazine. It was loaded. I palmed it home and pulled the slide and made sure the safety was on. Then I shoved it under my belt and buttoned my jacket over it and nodded at Gabby.

"Maybe I won't have to use it," I said. "Maybe somebody will figure out another way for me."

The funny thing was that somebody already had.

Nothing happened. Six o'clock ticked around and I knocked off and went over to the Queen Anne Cottage and had a New York cut.

I went back to my stand and still nothing happened. Bill Duff had been giving me peculiar stares for about an hour, and finally around eight or so, he strolled over and said hello.

I showed him the little pea and covered it and made a right-over-left pass and he tapped the right shell with his finger. I didn't palm it because there was no profit in it. Anyhow, he had something on his mind and I didn't want to derail his train of thought.

"You want your orchid giftwrapped?" I asked him.

"Keep it," he told me. "I've been thinking, Thax, that you and I are a couple of saps."

"I'll go along with about half of that," I said.

"I'm serious. We've been at loggerheads when, if we had any brains, we'd be a team. I mean we should start putting our heads together."

"What is it that you want to share with me?"

"C'mon," he snapped. "You know as well as I do what the score is. There's a fortune in it."

"Um. I said that to a man last night and nearly got my head blown off." I started to rotate the walnut shells. "The trouble with you, Bill, is you want to go fishing with my bait. You're seeing about a yard beyond Ferris' view—while I'm looking at the whole vista. No deal."

The Viking horn moaned and the marks started their noisy, confused, semi-happy evacuation. There would probably be much misbehaving in the cars in the parking lot that night.

I went up to the tree house to dig out my spare shirts and shorts and socks. The truth was, I felt a little sad about leaving Tarzan's hut. Maybe I was too much like those who wouldn't let youth slip by, like Peter Pan or Mike Ransome. Maybe I was doomed to bumble through life without ever realizing total maturity.

I pulled out the coke-bottle carton where I kept my spare shirts and underwear and stared at it in the brilliant light of Terry Orme's Coleman lantern. And with an odd sense of unreality, I felt the world turn back twenty-some years—back to the first time I read *Treasure Island* and came to the part where Blind Pew put the piece of paper in Billy Bones' rum-palsied hand.

A little round piece of paper was pinned to my top shirt. It was black on one side and white on the other, and two words had been printed on the white side:

One o'clock.

IX

But what is the black spot, Captain? Jim Hawkins had asked.

That's a summons, Mate, Billy Bones had answered.

And that's what this black spot was—a summons for me.

I left the tree house and went down to the Admiral Benbow. The *Hispaniola* was moored for the night against Treasure Island. The stern windows were open and a blocky shaft of light made an orange puddle on the shallow water under the schooner's counter. Soft music throbbed over the dark, man-made lake.

I got in a boat and rowed to the island.

The cabin door flew open and Mike Ransome stood in the flood of light grinning at me.

"Thax! I've been expecting you."

I held out the black spot to him. He took it and chuckled, making a gesture inviting me in. Then he took a quick look behind me before he closed the door.

"Come alone, Thax? I rather thought you would."

"Sure."

I took a casual turn around the cabin. The hi-fi was still purring soft mood music. There was a triangular wardrobe in the angle between the forward bulkhead and the starboard wall. It was faced with two louvered doors and I got the impression that the right hand door stirred slightly as I walked by. I went to the stern and parked on one of the open window frames, folded my arms and smiled at Mike.

"Care for a drink?" he asked me.

"No, thanks. That last one I had out here was murder. I mean that in the literal sense."

Mike chuckled and went over to the hi-fi and killed the music.

"You put something in that gin, didn't you?" I said.

He was enjoying himself immensely. He nearly danced over to the hotplate. "I'm going to have some coffee. You? No? Well now, Thax, why would I want to put anything in your drink?"

"Because I bunked with Terry Orme, and because you

wanted me blotto when you paid our tree house a little visit that night."

Mike's eyes watched me brightly over the rim of his coffee cup. "You can tell a story better than that, surely. You mustn't start in the middle."

I was agreeable. "All right, I'll back up to the beginning. You fell for May. Or maybe I should extend that and say you fell for May and her husband's money. But the husband was in the way. To eliminate him was no great problem. The rub was that as soon as he turned up murdered, everybody would immediately point the finger at May—because of the money motive. So, in your ingenious way, you worked out a neat little scheme.

"You would murder Cochrane and you would frame it to fit May. But the frame would be so obvious that even a blind man would be able to recognize it when it started to smell. The law would play with it for a while and then they would set her aside and start looking around for another suspect with a motive. May would be a nice, innocent, rich widow—all for you.

"I don't think you had set an actual date for Cochrane's murder. You were probably still trying to iron out the various wrinkles in your bent little brain—until the day I showed up. You knew my past history and I must have looked like a natural to you. The jealous ex-husband, dead broke and with a vengeful heart. Good. You decided to hit Cochrane that same night."

I took out a cigarette and rolled it between my fingers. "I think you made a date with old man Cochrane for after closing time. Probably you told him you had a brand-new scheme for Treasure Island and you wanted him to meet you and kick it around. He agreed. He'd come out to the *Hispaniola* late that night. But you didn't want to do him in that close to your home base. So when he came down to the Admiral Benbow dock, you were already waiting for him in the tearoom."

Mike watched me, beaming.

"The lights would be out, of course. You would call

him over to the tearoom on some pretext or other. When he stepped through the door into pitch darkness, you were there waiting with the knife. Bingo."

"Fascinating."

"Isn't it? And it gets better." I fished out a match and lit up. "Then you tote him into one of the rowboats and you row across the lake in the dark and you cart him over the little stretch of land and dump him in the Swamp Ride. With May's knife still in him, of course. And you remember to plant May's jade earring on the mud bank where any stumble-bum cop will find it. Then back to the *Hispaniola* and the black coffee and insomnia."

I grinned at him. "You know, I couldn't quite pin you at first."

"How's that, Thax?"

"I mean all the high-strung energy. It's obvious that you're on something, but I never put you down as a needle nut. It's bennys, huh? Or dexamyl or dexedrine? That's the reason for all the black coffee. It keeps activating the pep pills."

"Let me ask you this. Why didn't I just leave the body in the tea room?"

"That's one of the things that started me thinking about you as a possible suspect. Look what happened in *Treasure Island*. Everyone figured the treasure should be in Flint's cache because all the facts pointed to that conclusion. But when they got there, they drew a blank, because foxy old Ben Gunn had already picked up the loot and moved it somewhere else. Dandy joke.

"That's your style, Mike. You love a good laugh at other people's expense. That business of leaping out at me like Ben Gunn, and of boasting about jumping out on all the little girls. You like to shock people, Mike. You like to hit 'em with a startling surprise and then stand back and laugh. And you love a risk. You're the kind of nut who actually enjoys living on the edge of disaster. Like that gamble you took with Bill Duff in the poker game. That was pure brinksmanship."

Mike laughed delightedly. "Will you ever forget the look on Bill's face? Good old Bill! But go on, Thax. I'm enjoying this."

"There was no reason on earth to move that body," I said. "You did it for pure shock value. If you'd left it in the tearoom, the first waitress who opened up in the morning would walk in and see it and go *gaa!* Not much fun in that. Just one person. But if you dumped it in the Swamp Ride, you could really raise the roof. A whole boatload of happy marks *ohing* and *ahing* along the waterway. Then they turn the bend and what do they see floating in the water?"

Mike laughed and slapped his hands. "Beautiful! And I'm still sick it didn't work."

"Yes," I said dryly. "What a shame that freckle-faced kid squelched all the fun." I pitched my cigarette butt through the stern window and said, "So now we come to Terry Orme.

"Just when you figured you'd pulled a perfect crime, blackmail walked in and put the screws on you. So you knew there had been a witness, but you didn't know who. Then I accidentally gave you the tip when I told you Orme bunked in the tree house. Sure, you figured. Orme is always climbing around in the dark, peeking in on other people's business. Orme had to be the witness."

"And you walked in here and asked for a drink."

"And you doped it and I passed out and then you laid for Orme in the tree house."

"And then?" Mike prompted me.

"There isn't much more," I said. "Right after Terry took the big drop is when I put on my thinking cap, and my thoughts slowly turned me in your direction. So I had to be eliminated next."

Mike was smiling at me. He said nothing.

"But that was the big slip-up," I said. "Because *you* didn't handle it. If you had, I'd probably be one day dead right now."

"Go ahead," Mike said. "Tell us why I didn't handle it."

"Because I figure you didn't even know about it, Mike. And the person who did was already too panicky to have a third murder turn up on the lot. So she hired some big-city bad boys to do the deed in some far-out remote spot."

I looked at the louvered wardrobe across the cabin. "Is that right, May?"

There was a pause and then both louvered doors swung noiselessly open and May stood there as gorgeous as a picture, in a bright, tight, red outfit that accentuated her flame hair. She was holding one of her pearl-handled knives.

"You're so smart, darling," May said to me in her stainless-steel voice. "It's simply breathtaking to listen to you."

"Maybe I can get a job with Ferris," I said.

"I don't see how, darling," May said. "I really don't. Because I don't think you're going to be for hire much longer. Hasn't your brilliant mind figured out why we lured you out here tonight?"

"I think I can make a guess as to how both of you thought I'd react once I saw Mike's summons. You figured I'd rush out here and tell you all I know—which I have just done—and then I'd make a play at holding you up for blackmail. Which isn't a part of my plan."

Mike raised his brows at me. "Is this a rib, Thax? You honestly never intended to make a stab at blackmail?"

"I honestly never did, Mike. So, sure, I'd like a big chunk of May's dough for keeping my mouth shut, but it won't work. The deal has already gone sour. There's too many angles to it. Too many people have tried to climb onto the bandwagon."

I watched May's hand—the one with the knife.

"Let's face it," I said. "You baited the trap with blackmail when you drew me out here tonight. But we all know you have something more practical in mind."

"Then why did you come out here, Thax?" Mike asked.

"Because he's a fool!" May said sharply. "He's always

been a fool. He thinks he can talk his way out of anything."

I leaned forward as if to stand up. In the next instant, I had May covered with the automatic.

"Drop the knife, May."

Mike lowered his coffee cup to the table. "You wouldn't really kill us, would you, Thax?"

May started to raise the knife. I pulled the trigger.

The hammer said *click*. I was all tensed for the expectant blast and the stupid thing said *click!*

Mike grinned at me. "Wet powder, Master 'Awkins?" he asked in an Israel Hands' voice.

I looked at May. She was smiling as she cocked the knife over her shoulder.

"Catch, May!" I flipped the automatic to her underhand.

The knife went *thhook* in the stern post by my head as I went out the window—right on over in a backward somersault, crashing feet-first into the black shallows.

The muck underfoot was mushy. I came up thrashing and spitting and stood up with the lake to my waist. I looked up at the *Hispaniola*'s counter.

Mike Ransome was standing at the center window, wrenching the knife free of the sternpost. Then he darted back into the cabin.

He was going to cut me off from the rowboat. I wasn't much as a swimmer and that was out, anyhow, because he could quickly overhaul me in the boat. I slogged ashore and headed for the underbrush.

A scud of clouds passed over the moon's face. It suited me. If I couldn't see Mike, he couldn't see me. I crawled a little way up Mizzenmast Hill, sticking close to the brush.

I couldn't hear him, or anything. The island, the lake, all of Neverland and the whole world beyond seemed to be one immense silence. That suited me, too—but Mizzenmast Hill did not. It was too open. I needed the black shelter of tall trees.

I crawled again, working around the base of the man-made hill and heading inland. I figured I would slip out of my clothes and chance swimming for it once I reached the far side of the island.

The ground flattened out and the trees loomed. I stood. The ground was velvety and springy under my feet, carpeted with dead pine needles and leaves and mold. I started walking.

Clawing branches and soft lacy things kept brushing at my face and body. I started groping along with my right hand stretched out. It came up against something soft, covered by cloth. I felt a button.

There was a sharp intake of breath. I heard or sensed a sudden slash of motion in the dark as I sprang back and crouched for another spring, anywhere, tense and expectant.

Nothing happened. A minute dragged by. I knew Mike was crouching and waiting without sound or movement only a few feet away.

The stillness came apart with a sudden whir of wings as a preying owl made his shrill-laugh cry. I jumped and shifted to the right. Mike leaped forward with a whisk of leaves and then I whirled in another direction and crouched again.

We waited. Nothing happened. I hunkered down and felt the ground with my right hand. It would be too much to ask to find a stick or a rock for a weapon so I carefully scooped up a handful of dirt.

I straightened up. There was no sound at all.

Without warning, a bright flare of light snapped open like the burst of a bomb, and I saw Mike standing six feet away. He had a match in his left hand and May's knife in his right. The blade shone with the thin, red light from the match dancing along the edge.

Mike was grinning at me and his thin face looked satanic in the yellowy light.

"Jim"—he was playing Israel Hands again—"I reckon we're fouled, you and me, and we'll have to sign articles."

He made a quick, snatching motion with his left hand to whip out the match and I chucked my handful of dirt at his face as he pounced toward me. I dropped to the ground and felt his shins collide with my shoulder. Then I was up and going while Mike was still in the underbrush.

I broke through an opening between two huge-trunked trees and started to run. I could hear Mike scrambling right behind me. Just then, I ran smack into a tree with both arms outflung. All I could do was hug it dazedly.

I felt Mike brush past me in a rush. There was a thud and a rattle of dry branches and a gasp and a sense of something running into nothing and falling through it. Finally a clatter of stones ended in a throaty cry like *uuuah!* Then nothing.

I stepped away from the tree. A black patch of mystery fell away in the darkness below me. I was standing on the lip of a ridge. The black patch down at the base was some kind of pit.

I climbed down the slope and realized I was standing in Flint's Treasure Pit. Mike Ransome was there, too, but he wasn't standing.

I rolled him over and fished out a match and struck it. The light sparked in his eyes. He was staring up at me.

He had put his hands in front of his chest to break his fall. But he had completely forgotten that May's knife was in his right hand.

X

May was pacing up and down through a grayish garland of cigarette smoke when I opened the cabin door. She came to a full, abrupt stop and looked at me.

"Thax."

I said, "He's dead, May. He fell on your knife."

She kept staring at me and her black pupils glowed with a dull, red light. Then she sat down, and it was a good thing the table bench was right behind her or I think she would have gone out on the deck. She seemed to have forgotten the cigarette that was smoking itself between her pale, tapered fingers. She looked blankly at the floor.

"I loved him."

I think she was telling herself, and I think she meant it. I picked up Gabby's automatic and shoved it under my belt.

"What are you going to do?"

"Tell Ferris. I want out of this thing with a clean slate."

"Should I run, Thax?"

I shook my head. "It's too late to run, May. You couldn't get far enough fast enough. Besides, it doesn't really matter now, does it?"

"No," she said. "I guess it doesn't."

In the bunkhouse, I called Ferris on the phone.

He didn't get very excited about the news. "You were just about one giant step ahead of me."

"You mean you had already figured them for it? Mike Ransome in with May Cochrane?"

"Well, I was just rounding that bend," Ferris said. "We got a healthy line on them last night. Seems for the past two-three months, they've been renting a room here in town under the name of Mr. and Mrs. Millard Rankin, whenever old man Cochrane's back was turned. That sort of put the whole deal in a new light."

There was a pause on his end, and then he said, "So Ransome accidentally fell on his own knife, huh? And your ex-wife accidentally killed herself?"

"She didn't. She's still out there. I left her on the island."

"You just walked off and left her there?" he asked.

"It's all right," I said. "I took both rowboats and she doesn't know how to swim. She'll keep." I hung up.

I looked up Billie's number in the directory. There was no answer. I figured she was dead asleep and I let it ring a dozen times, but there was still no answer. I walked slowly out of the bunkhouse.

It was four by the time I reached the basement in

Dracula's Castle. I asked the lookout on the door if Gabby was still in the game and when he said yes, I said tell him I wanted to see him out in the hall a minute.

Gabby was wearing insomnia like smudges under his eyes when he stepped outside and closed the door after him. He looked at me with a tired, incurious expression and I handed him his automatic.

"Thanks for the loan," I said. "But you better replace the firing pin. It works better when all the parts are intact. You know."

Gabby looked at the gun in his hand and wet his lips. "Forgive me, Thax."

"Why did you do it? We were friends, weren't we?"

"Are they dead?" he asked. "Did you kill 'em?"

"Who? Mike and May? Mike is, and the johns are coming for May."

"They had me in a bind, Thax, and I didn't have enough guts to get up off the ground. About four years back, me and May worked for the same outfit up north. There was a beef one night on the lot and a mark got killed. I sapped too hard. A few of the carnys knew who did it, but they figured the rube had it coming so they clammed up. May was one of 'em.

"I should have known better. I came here a couple of years back and got a job with Cochrane. I didn't know that May was his wife or that she was even on the lot. Then one day she walks by my gallery and looks at me. That's all, just looks. No sign, no word. But I knew then she was going to make me pay somehow, sometime. Every day for two years, I've waited for the axe to fall. And it finally did, three days back.

"Mike Ransome came to see me. He gave me this toy. He knew that you and me had become buddy-buddy and he had an idea that before very long you'd be looking around for a gun. He figured you'd come to me. I was to give you this Roscoe. Said it was all part of a joke he was going to pull on you, and that I'd better help with my end of it unless I wanted the law to take another healthy look at that four-year-old murder."

He raised his head. "At least I tried to head you off. I told you not to take it—to cut and run instead."

"That's right, Gabby," I said, nodding. "You tried."

I remembered the unused room up in Dracula's Castle. I went up there and closed the door and threw myself on the bed. The last thing I heard was the wailing police sirens coming from a long, long way off.

Someone was pulling my shoulder. I opened my eyes. Billie was standing over me. Her eyes were very wide and dark and her face looked pallid. She was wearing a V of worry between her plucked brows.

"Thax, I've been looking everywhere for you! And so have the police. How long have you been up here?" she wanted to know.

I said to her, "Where were you last night, or early this morning? I tried to phone you."

"I was right here. I never went home. When you didn't meet me at the gate, I went over to the tree house to see what had happened to you. I saw your shirts and things on the floor so I stayed there to wait for you. Then I guess I fell asleep. Some policeman woke me up over an hour ago. He was looking for you." She sat down on the edge of the bed. "Thax—they're saying that Mike Ransome was killed last night. Is it true?"

"That's right. He had an accident and fell on one of May's knives," I informed her.

"What happened to her?"

I looked at her. "Nothing that I know of. The last I saw of her, she was sitting in the *Hispaniola* in a daze waiting for the law to come cart her away."

Billie made a little impatient shake with her head. "I don't understand."

"Mike and May killed old man Cochrane," I said. "Mike did the dirty work. But when blackmail reared its ugly head, they discovered there had been a witness. And that's when things started to get messy."

"Blackmail?" Billie said. "Who? Bill Duff?"

"Duff had an idea what it was all about, and he had blackmail on the brain. But he couldn't get it off the ground because he lacked a vital part. He didn't have a witness."

"A witness? The blackmailer had a witness to Rob Cochrane's murder?" Billie sounded amazed.

I turned and looked at her. "That's right, Billie. You did have one for a while, didn't you?"

She sat rigidly composed. Her eyes were still very wide, very dark. Without moving a muscle, except for her mouth, she said, "That really isn't very funny, Thax."

"No," I agreed, "it isn't. I stopped laughing some time back."

I reached in my pocket and drew out the envelope I had taken from Lloyd Franks' safe. I handed it to Billie.

She looked at the envelope, at the words written across the face of it: TO BE OPENED ONLY IN THE EVENT OF MY DEATH, BILLIE PEELER. It had been sealed originally, but I had opened it after I lifted it. Billie knew that I knew that the page of paper inside was blank. She put the envelope in her purse and looked at me.

"Terry Orme," I said, "was a bitter, lonely little guy who hated normal people. I think in his bent little way he thought he was getting even with them by spying on their personal lives. It gave him a superior feeling. I'm just guessing about this, but I figure he knew all about May and Mike, and the night he saw Mike dump Cochrane in the Swamp Ride, he was clever enough to put two and two together.

"It meant money to him, big money. May could afford it. But the rub was that he was afraid to approach them personally. Can you picture a gutless midget walking up to a tall murderer and saying, 'I'm going to blackmail you, buster?' So he needed a go-between. Someone who had the courage and intelligence to tackle blackmail and get away with it."

I put my hands in my pockets and dug down deep.

"You were one of the very few people the sad little bastard liked. You used to work together in Kansas City and he probably knew you were a shrewd cookie who would stop at nothing to grab a bundle. So he told you about Mike and May—dumped the whole package in your lap and probably asked for fifty-fifty. Or did you cut him down?"

Billie said absolutely nothing. She just watched me.

"Probably the only stipulation Terry made was that you wouldn't tell Mike or May that he was the witness. Which was the way you would have played it anyhow because you *are* a shrewd cookie. So you wrote down just what Terry had seen and told you and sealed it in a not-to-be-opened-unless envelope to turn over to some lawyer. That would be your safeguard against Mike and May. They'd be afraid to touch you with that hanging over their heads.

"Nearly every blackmailer thinks of that angle. Each warns his mark that he's done it, even when probably he hasn't. And you knew that Mike was the kind of nut who just might gamble that you *hadn't* put anything on paper, and go ahead and risk eliminating you. So you put a curve on your pitch. You made out the envelope and sealed a blank piece of paper in it and turned it over to Lloyd Franks. Remember, I met you coming from his office the next day?"

Billie watched me.

"Then you told May what you had done and said she and Mike could check with Franks if they didn't believe you. The reason you didn't put anything on paper is because you weren't certain just how far you could trust Franks.

"Terry wasn't absolutely certain he could trust you, either. That's why he got so jumpy. He was scared that you might cross him and tell Mike that he was your witness, and then Mike would kill him. Mike did find out and he did take care of the little guy.

"Mike was a good chess player. The most damaging hold you had over him was that eyewitness. Once he had removed that player from the board, all you had against him was hearsay evidence. However, you were still a threat

to him because you could tell the law all you knew, even
if you couldn't prove any of it. So I figure they agreed to
go ahead and pay you off in one lump sum for your nuisance
value. That's how it went, didn't it?"

I looked at her.

"I take it that May told you you'd have to wait a couple
of weeks until she could find a valid excuse to dig into
her husband's estate for the ante. How much was it, by
the way?"

"One hundred thousand," Billie said promptly and
calmly.

"You ever see any of it?"

"One fourth. May had twenty-five thousand in cash of
her own." Billie dug in her purse for a cigarette. She found
her own match. Then she blew smoke toward me.

"We can leave any time," she said. "Just as we planned."

I stared at her. I said, "You're kidding. Billie. My dear
ex-wife didn't know I was onto her and her boy friend until
someone told her I was getting warm. And you, dear heart,
were the only person who knew it. You really can't expect
me to be crazy about the idea, my love. . . .

Billie stared at me through the smoke swirl.

"Thax, I wanted that money so badly. You only get a
chance like this once in a lifetime. I couldn't let anything
happen to that money. That's why I went to May, to
warn her."

"So she could hire some hoods to eliminate me!" I said.

"I never dreamed she'd do anything like that. I thought
she'd try to buy you off. I thought you'd be reasonable."
Her voice trailed off.

I looked out the window down at Neverland. Three
or four of Ferris' storm troopers were hurrying about. Everything looked bright and peaceful, like a great, enchanted
land where once, long ago, men had toiled and built and
dreamed and then gone away.

"Billie, I think you'd better take your twenty-five grand
and run with it just as fast and as far as you can. And if

you're lucky, maybe you'll even reach the Mediterranean."

Her eyes reminded me of May's eyes. That same dull red gleam back in the pupils. "You won't come with me?" she asked pleadingly.

"No. Because I could never trust you, Billie."

"You stupid fool!" Then she stopped.

I listened to her heels click down the steps until they were only an echo. Then I roused myself and went downstairs and into the clean, bright strength of the new day.

After all, it didn't really matter very much, did it?